Alma Mater

An Historical Novel
by
Pamela Borden Heckert

Pamela Borden Heckert

ALMA MATER

Pamela Borden Heckert

Illustrations by Sasha Williams

Book layout/design by Alyssa Ohnmacht

Kindle Direct Publishing 2019

ISBN 97-81090341778

Library of Congress Control Number: 2019937431

Cover photo: the class of 1863, St Mary's Hall, Burlington,
New Jersey, with permission of Doane Academy

Welland Canal map, page 5, courtesy of Geographicus Rare Antique
Maps, Wikimedia Commons, from the Map of Canada West or Upper
Canada, J. H. Colton (1800-1893), *Colton's Atlas of the World*, Vol. 1,
New York, 1855 (First Edition – G.W. Colton).

Light of the Moon, Inc. - Publishing Division
Book Design/Production/Consulting
Carbondale, Colorado • www.lightofthemooninc.com

Alma Mater

THAT OUR DAUGHTERS MAY BE AS
THE POLISHED CORNERS OF THE TEMPLE

To the friends I made at St Mary's Hall and still have fifty years later, and to all those who, for over 180 years, attended St Mary's Hall, Burlington College, and Doane Academy. In our own ways we have lived in service to God, family, community, and country, becoming as "the Polished Corners of the Temple"

Right Onward!

In Memory
of my paternal grandmother
Edna Beatrice Thickson Borden
(4 September 1903 – 20 November 1983)
who, as a girl of 11, bravely left her Canadian home
on 14 July 1915, crossed at Niagara Falls
with younger siblings Hilda and Jack,
and embarked on a new life in the
United States of America

Contents

DISCLAIMER

This book is a work of historical fiction based on real people whose genealogy and census records are available to the public. Although most individuals portrayed in this book existed, the conversations and situations herein are imagined. Characterizations of personalities are likewise fabricated. Any resemblance to living persons is completely coincidental or fictionalized. Any errors or omissions, especially genealogical assumptions, rest solely with the author with the exception of census data which may have been mistranscribed. Canadian and American spelling of the nineteenth century has been used wherever possible for authenticity.

Preface

My first inkling of this book came while volunteering in the archives of Doane Academy with former volunteer Director of Archives Alice (Lollie) Berger Rogers, once a St Mary's Hall pupil herself. Descendants of graduates frequently asked the school to confirm the attendance of their relatives, necessitating our thumbing through old registration books. Lollie and I decided to create a searchable spreadsheet so we could look for these names more easily.

On the first day of our project, Lollie was reading from the earliest St Mary's Hall Register in our collection, dated 1855 – 64. As she turned the brittle yellow pages with her white-gloved hands, I typed in the girls' arrival dates, names, addresses and parents' names. Among the 169 winter term pupils were four girls, two pairs of sisters, from St Catharines and Thorold C.W., places I did not know existed. The initials C.W. turned out to be the designation at the time for Canada West before it became the modern province of Ontario in 1867. Farther down the list was a girl from Toronto and farther still, one from Port Robinson C.W., near Thorold. There were also four girls from Lockport, NY whom I began to research, but something personal made me focus on the Canadian girls instead.

In 1912 Anne Beatrice Wilkes Thickson, the mother of my paternal grandmother, suffered an embolism and died eleven days after giving birth to her sixth child. She was twenty-nine. We do not know how her husband first coped with four children and no wife. However, the Great War broke out in 1914 and the Canadian Army beckoned. John Thickson responded. His youngest child, George, was adopted by John's sister and her husband. At the tender age of eleven, my grandmother was sent from her home in Bowmanville, Ontario with her two other younger siblings to live in the United States with relatives. All we know about their journey is from an immigration record showing they arrived by steamship at Niagara Falls, NY on 14 July 1915. John Thickson joined the army in June 1916 at thirty-seven.

Upon seeing the group of Canadian pupils in the school register and knowing my grandmother's experience, I was immediately intrigued and wondered how and why they had traveled to the United States in 1855 and how old they were at the time. I joined *Ancestry.com* and traced their families as much as I could. The results of my research there led to more inquiries online about many facets of the 1850s on both sides of the Niagara River: education; transportation; telegraphy; clothing; Episcopal and Presbyterian church history; farm life; the Fugitive Slave Act; as well as Canadian history and geography. I also learned about life in the nineteenth century through on-site visits to American and Canadian museums and historical societies, and through countless online sources.

I tried to visualize and recreate the St Mary's Hall campus of 1855, but the numerous physical changes and lack of primary source documentation made it a challenge. I omitted clear mention of the first Christmas Mystery, the school's traditional presentation of the Nativity story, because I found no primary source to confirm the year of its first performance. Mrs Fearnley's history of the school reports undated costumed tableaux, but not specifically the Christmas story. Neither was there a letter from Emma or Anna Shannon (pupils 1857–1859) confirming the performance as we know it today. I chose to include the reading of fortunes for Shrove Tuesday pancakes, a tradition practised when I was a student in the 1960s; its year of origination is also unknown, but the holiday served a purpose in my narrative. *Mea culpa!*

Most of the demographic details of the girls and their families were found in census data and other resources available on *Ancestry.com*. The more I searched, the more I learned, and the more often I had to go back and edit what I had written earlier to incorporate the new information. I was surprised to discover one of the girls, Harriet, is my distant cousin through a common seventeenth century ancestor, Francis Borden, who settled in Shrewsbury, Monmouth County, New Jersey. Her grandmother, Esther Borden Lippincott, was the daughter of a Tory/Loyalist who escaped death at the hands of Rebel Patriots during the American Revolution. In the end I realized the girls' families had origins in the former British colonies: Pennsylvania (Burns and Mittlebergers), Connecticut (Fullers), New York (McFarlands) and New Jersey (Taylors).

Through my research I found so many connections among the girls' families before and after they went to St Mary's Hall that I began to develop a story that would weave their lives together. I hope my audience will enjoy reading about these girls as much as I did while searching for them and dreaming up this tale.

Pamela Borden Heckert
Redstone, Colorado
January 2019

The Families

Thomas Burns, attorney. Son of a Presbyterian minister and teacher, a Scottish immigrant who came to Canada from Pennsylvania
Henrietta, née Mittleberger, his wife, granddaughter of Huguenots who emigrated from Baden-Wurttemberg, Germany to Pennsylvania before the American Revolutionary war, settling in Montréal
>   **Emma Helena Rykert,** 1839
>   **Julia Maria,** 1840
>   **Isabella Ann,** 1843
>   **Arthur Nelson,** 1846
>   **Henrietta Elizabeth (Libby),** 1850
>   **Llewellyn,** 1855
>   **Florence Britannia (Florrie),** 1858

❦ ❦ ❦

The Rev. Thomas (Tom) Fuller, Anglican (Episcopal) minister. Son of an Irish-born soldier
Cynthia, née Street, his wife, granddaughter of United Empire Loyalists from Connecticut
>   **Mary Margaret,** 1836
>   **Thomas Richard & Samuel Street,** 1838 (twins)
>   **Laura Abigail,** 1840
>   **Elizabeth Street (Lizzie),** 1843
>   **William B (Willy),** 1845
>   **Valancy England (Val),** 1850
>   **Shelton Brock,** 1853
>   **Henry Hobart,** 1856

❦ ❦ ❦

Duncan McFarland, entrepreneur. Son of a Scot, British Royal Navy boat-builder, originally based in New York State
Margaret, née Elliott, his wife, born in Albany, NY
>   **John Cameron,** 1828, a physician
>   **Duncan Elliott,** 1830, a miller
>   **Agnes, née Blake,** 1827, his wife from the town of Niagara
>   **Margaret Jane,** 1842

John Fennings Taylor, the Younger, Deputy Clerk of the
  Legislative Council, Canadian Provincial Parliament,
  emigrated from London to Canada in 1836
Mary Elizabeth, née Denison, his wife, daughter of Esther
  Borden Lippincott Denison, United Empire Loyalist
> **Harriet Esther,** 1839
> **Mary Sophia,** 1845
> **George,** 1849

Georgina, née Nanton, Fennings' second wife, granddaughter of
  Caribbean plantation owners

John Fennings Taylor, the Elder, Clerk of the Legislative
  Council. Emigrated from England to marry his cousin
Elizabeth Sophia, née Denison, his wife; "Aunt Betsy"
> **Maria,** their daughter, 1836-1933

ST MARY'S HALL

The Rt. Rev. George Washington Doane, second Episcopal
  bishop of New Jersey, born 1799
Eliza Greene Perkins Doane, his wife, a widow with three
  children when they married in 1828
> **George Hobart Doane,** their son, became a
> Roman Catholic priest, 1855
> **William Croswell Doane,** their son, became the
> first bishop of Albany, New York

Rev. Dr. D. Caldwell Millett, Principal, Chaplain and Head of
  the Family
Miss Nancy Stanley, Vice Principal, born in upstate New York
Mrs Lamotte, Irish-born matron of St Mary's Hall

5

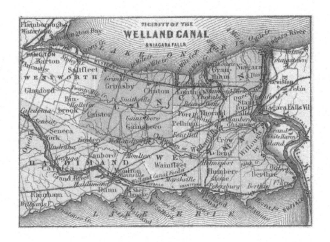

CHAPTER 1

Two Fathers

JUNE 1855, THOROLD, CANADA WEST

"Here's the information I promised you," said Tom Fuller, reaching into a roomy pocket of his long frockcoat. "This is a serious school for Margaret Jane. From what you say, she exhausts her teacher with her questions."

Duncan McFarland accepted the thick booklet from the younger man. "Aye, you're right there, Tom. Her teacher, John Leetze, has told me he can offer Margaret Jane no more. But she's twelve now, nigh on thirteen, and, y'know, old enough to leave off her studies at the Common School."

"But, my friend, if she's so interested in learning, doesn't she deserve to study all she can in a place like this, devoted to educating girls like her?" asked Tom. He tapped the latest St Mary's Hall catalogue in Duncan's hand. "She still wouldn't even be allowed to do the classics or mathematics at the grammar school down in St Catharines. But she'll be expected to study them at *this* school."

The June 1855 meeting of the Thorold Township Agricultural

7

Society had just ended at the Thorold House, a hotel in the village of the same name. Thorold lay atop the rugged three hundred-foot high Niagara Escarpment that residents called "the Mountain". The village had become a busy agricultural and commercial centre on the edge of the Welland Canal, an engineering marvel cut thirty years ago through the Niagara Peninsula to connect Lake Ontario with the higher but more shallow Lake Erie. Duncan McFarland, president of the society, had once again efficiently run the meeting of member farmers, and with the help of Tom Fuller, the vice president, the initial plan for the annual fair next autumn was decided. Local men would exhibit their finest livestock along with grains, vegetables, and fruit grown on the surrounding farmland, the area now commonly considered the Garden of Canada West. Messrs McFarland and Fuller had founded the group and had been friendly rivals for years, competing against each other in several categories every October.

After collecting their papers, the two men donned wide-brimmed hats to go out into the brisk evening air. It had been one of those clear, blue-sky days when one could look to the north and see the shimmering waters of Lake Ontario beyond the canal and the town of St Catharines. Even at this hour the early summer sun was still high over the fields that stretched the expanse of the fertile Niagara Peninsula. Farmers, as well as their families, profited from the additional daylight now after months of Canadian winter darkness.

"But, Tom, what still holds me back from enrolment is her mother—she will miss her so. My Margaret counts much on her help in the household nowadays, especially with the harvest and preserving now that she's older," said sandy-haired Duncan. He teared up at the thought of losing his youngest child to the Yanks in the United States of America.

Only forty years ago Britain had been at war with the young nation, and several deadly battles were fought in the Niagara area where Duncan had grown up. In fact, his father had died a few months after escaping a prisoner of war camp near Albany, New York. John McFarland returned to find his homestead looted and spared only because it was used as a hospital. His death left the twelve-year-old Duncan an orphan.

"See here, Duncan, Thomas Burns is sending his two eldest

girls back to New Jersey for their third winter term. They've been home for the summer as before. McClure, the head master down at St Thomas' School in St Catharines, has finished his medical studies, and he's going west to London to practise medicine. He won't be available to tutor them as he had agreed. Thomas is anxious for his daughters to continue their formal education. He looked again into the ladies' schools in the province, and they're still not at all challenging. They offer little more than languages and needlework. St Mary's Hall teaches mathematics, history, and sciences, as well as the expected female arts—music, painting, drawing. But, more importantly, 'tis a family-like school."

"That, Tom, is desirable, I am sure, but who's in charge of it?" Duncan furrowed his brow and squinted as he leafed through the detailed catalogue.

"The Episcopal bishop of New Jersey, the Right Reverend George Washington Doane. I met him two years ago at the General Convention in New York City. Very impressive man. There is also a principal called 'the head of the family'. Thomas told me that when Bishop Doane established St Mary's Hall in 1837, nearly twenty years ago now, he tried to manage it all himself, but it became too much. Now a board of trustees oversees the business end of it for him. We've been corresponding regularly since we met. He talks fondly about the girls as if they were his own daughters. He keeps an open house. The girls may visit him at will. 'Tis quite a comfortable home for them with his wife, Mrs Eliza Doane, along with many learned and accomplished faculty."

"But Tom, isn't it rather a long journey down to New Jersey to go to a school?"

"Of course, it is, Duncan, but 'tis the first thorough Episcopal Church school for young ladies in North America. There aren't similar good opportunities for educating our girls here in Canada, neither West nor East. I've already offered to take the Burns girls back to Burlington in late September—Mrs Burns will be confined at that time. So, you needn't worry that Margaret Jane will have to travel alone or that you must take time away from your businesses to escort her. I'm sure that our five girls will be thrilled to have a railway adventure. Then to spend a whole term together at such a stimulating place … Do you not see the advantages, my friend?"

"Aye, I do, Tom. I certainly do. But, she's still just twelve, and then there's the fact that we McFarlands *are* Presbyterians," said the stout, red-bearded gentleman.

Duncan was now more than a bit sceptical about sending Margaret Jane out of the country at such a tender age. And to American Episcopalians to boot. Despite his infant baptism into the Anglican church, then the only church in the town of Niagara, his large Scottish family was Presbyterian in belief and practise.

The Reverend Mr Thomas Brock Fuller straightened and chuckled at this remark. Compared to Duncan, he was tall, an imposing forty-five-year-old man dressed in a dark broadcloth suit and white cravat. His clothing and demeanour fit his status as the founding rector of St John the Evangelist, the magnificent new stone church being built on Mill Street in Thorold. Despite his many responsibilities in overseeing its construction and his two current parishes, old St Peter's in Thorold and St Paul's in Port Robinson, he was not without a sense of humour.

"I well understand that, Duncan, or you'd be sitting in the first pew of *my* congregation every Sunday, wouldn't you, man?" teased his friend with a wink. "Bishop Doane welcomes girls of all denominations, and he said there are some who arrive only aged eleven, even younger than Margaret Jane. There are twice daily services in the chapel and the necessary discipline to ensure study, but nothing that a girl as good-natured as Margaret Jane cannot abide for a few years of her life."

"A few years!" exclaimed Duncan. He paused at the thought of not seeing his daughter for so long. "Is Burlington big enough to have a Presbyterian church, Tom?"

"Oh, yes, indeed. I recall the bishop saying there's a large one in the High Street not far from the school buildings. Cortlandt Van Rensselaer established it the same year as the school. He and Bishop Doane are good friends. In fact, he said two of Van Rensselaer's female cousins were recently graduated from the Hall. It certainly won't do Margaret Jane ill if she's so keen on learning! My Lizzie's a bit younger than your daughter, but I imagine they'll both benefit greatly from the attention to academics. Right now, Lizzie's more interested in collecting flowers and climbing trees than doing her lessons."

"Aye, Tom, I know Margaret Jane wants to learn as much as

she can. She's very curious about our animals especially. I shall talk it over with Mrs McFarland to-night after we've read this. She was born over in Albany where those Van Rensselaers hail from. I well know the name. P'raps she'll warm to the idea of sending Margaret Jane down to New Jersey if she knows there are Presbyterians and New York people there. When does the term begin? When would she have to leave?"

"The winter term begins the first of November. It's recommended the pupils be there in advance, as that is All Saints' Day. The school is also open for the vacation month prior, so I plan to arrive in Burlington by the first of October. Then I can be back here in plenty of time for our fair. The fee for the vacation month is nominal, and 'twill give them time to adjust to the place. Thomas recommended an excellent hotel in Burlington where I shall stop with them the first night. He advised 'twill take only four days in the cars to travel to New Jersey, about five hundred miles. The route is much improved of late, and faster with Mr Roebling's new rail road suspension bridge."

Duncan's blue eyes lit up, for he appreciated this latest addition to modern transportation.

"Of course, it is! I heard there are thirty trains a day now crossing it. Imagine driving a carriage on the lower deck when a locomotive rumbles above and the Niagara River rushing two hundred fifty feet below!"

"Yes, apparently Mr Roebling insists that locomotives go only five miles per hour over his bridge, but beyond it, they can speed along at nearly twenty-five miles per hour now. It truly has changed how we travel."

"Indeed. How many rail lines will you have to take, Tom? It sounds like a long trip."

"'Twill be arduous, to be sure, but I've puzzled it out with Thomas and the station master in St Catharines. There are many more possible routes this year. New York is crisscrossed with railways, and more open every month, it seems. I've also consulted with the vice principal at St Mary's Hall, Miss Nancy Stanley. She hails from the Geneva area and has travelled the route by rail recently. Given all that, I've decided that we shall take the Great Western Railway first over to Tonawanda station, and at Canandaigua we drop down to Elmira to change lines. But first I'll stop with the girls for the night at the Jefferson House on the southern end of Seneca Lake. In the morning we continue on to the station town of Hancock, New York on the Upper Delaware River to spend the second night. Then let me see ... Jersey City, a port just across from New York City, the last overnight stop before Burlington. We shall spend it at a comfortable inn that Bishop Doane recommended. He's familiar with the area, as he served a few years at Trinity Church across the bay in Manhattan. The next morning, we must board a steamship ferry to go down the Arthur Kill to South Amboy, New Jersey. From there we reach our final destination on the Camden and Amboy line in only three hours. It's an excellent railway that passes directly through Burlington. We should arrive in time for tea if all goes to plan," explained Tom.

"That does sound like an exhausting journey." Duncan paused to think of another question. "And what kind of country is Burlington?"

"Burlington ... it's an old Quaker city, older than Philadelphia, both original parts of William Penn's colonial grant from the Crown. Now it's well populated with all manner of tradesmen and professionals, in particular shoemakers. It once required a sailing ferry trip down the Delaware River to Penn's town. Now it can be just an hour or so in the cars. The school often takes pupils to Philadelphia for diversion. The county surrounding Burlington is farmland all the way to the Atlantic Ocean, according to the bishop. And the school has a small farm, as well as a hothouse and greenhouse."

"So, there should be plenty of good, fresh food as we have right here in Niagara," said Duncan with a smile. "And how large a place is the school itself?"

"The several buildings are located on the Green Bank of Burlington beside the river. The bishop's own garden and grounds adjacent are open for the girls' enjoyment too. Near his house is Burlington College for boys and young men, the second of his educational institutions."

"A college for boys ... next door? Do the boys and girls have opportunity to meet?" sputtered Duncan, surprised by this revelation.

"Oh, my word, I'm told they meet once a year for their Independence Day celebration in July. Not even for Christmas do they mingle, Duncan. Do not worry! But I am sure only the most pious and upstanding families send their boys to Burlington College. Many are preparing for ministry."

"I guess we shall have to trust the bishop in that regard, won't we?" He remained silent as he considered the situation.

"And so, Duncan! I shall make the necessary arrangements for our party as soon as I have your assent. I've already posted a letter requesting registration for Laurie and Lizzie."

"Aye, Tom, thank you for the catalogue. I appreciate this opportunity for Margaret Jane. I only wish it weren't so far away. She's just twelve years old after all, and she's been so shy and quiet of late. We shan't see her again for months, eh? Her mother will miss her so." He paused again, then went on, "She is our only daughter now."

"There, there, Duncan. I understand your loss," said Tom, as he patted his friend on the shoulder. "I know how difficult it's been for you and Mrs McFarland to bury so many little girls. The cholera took its toll on the children."

"Aye, difficult, 'tis true. Our boys are robust, but our wee girls … lost too young."

"Yes, they certainly were, but you must agree all of our daughters will benefit from this sort of education. Alas, too soon they'll become wives, mothers, and leaders in their communities. They'll bring much knowledge and wisdom to their families over the course of their lives if they're given the chance to learn."

Duncan, a thrifty Scotsman, then thought of the inevitable expenses of sending a child away to school. His son John had gone up to Upper Canada College in Toronto years ago. "What are the fees there, Tom?"

"When you read in the catalogue, you will see that the letters, sciences, languages, as well as histories and music—all are offered—for the same fee, one hundred fifty dollars per term. I figure that's less than forty pounds. Quite reasonable for a programme such as this. Speak to your wife to-night, and send me a message when you've decided. 'Tis still three months before we have to depart. There's plenty of time to write the bishop to say Margaret Jane will be a pupil, or to ask questions."

The two men shook hands and parted. Duncan untied his horse and climbed into the dusty farm waggon laden with supplies for the drive south to his house in Port Robinson. Tom got into his shiny black buggy for the quick trip back to the Fullers' farmhouse near Ten Mile Creek in Thorold Township. Both men carried thoughts about their precious daughters and the lives ahead of them.

CHAPTER 2

The McFarland Family of Port Robinson

FRIDAY, 6 JULY 1855

"Margaret Jane, leave off what you're doing and come down at once! Mama's in the carriage with Agnes and your brothers! We're going to be late, lassie!" called Duncan McFarland.

His daughter held up her long skirt with one hand and dashed down the front stairs of the family's two-storey brick and frame house in South Street in the canal-side settlement of Port Robinson. "Coming, Father!" said Margaret Jane. Her red curls bounced and threatened at any moment to come undone from all the pins her mother had just used to arrange them. Clutching her parasol under one arm, she pulled the straw bonnet over her head and tried in vain to tie the two dark blue ribbons together as she ran down the gravel path.

At the end of the path, Duncan waited to help his daughter from the carriage stone up into the waiting vehicle. As she rose, her bonnet fell to the ground. Her father bent to pick it up.

Brushing it off, he said, "I wish you'd been ready at the appointed time, lass. The ceremony begins at four o'clock. I must be in place well before that. Now we shall have to drive a bit faster."

"I'm sorry, Father. I couldn't find my parasol for the longest time, but then I did ... downstairs on the hall tree. I should have looked there first."

"Indeed," said her father. He closed the gate after the carriage passed through and climbed up into it with some effort.

❦ ❦ ❦

To-day, in nearby Merrittsville, the cornerstone of the new Welland County Court House and Gaol was to be laid. The village, formerly called Aqueduct because of an aqueduct built to carry the canal through it, was the proud winner of the competition to host the most important civic building in the newly established Welland County. Merrittsville's future was bright.

The organisers had asked Duncan McFarland to be marshal of the procession because Duncan was an enterprising man who had lived in the Port Robinson area for twenty-five years. In his early twenties, he had established a general store and grist mill near Allanburgh to supply the farmers and residents of the area. Then he had become the first postmaster of Port Robinson and a customs officer as the village grew into an important canal port of entry. He was a colonel in the local militia called up to keep order during the 1837 Rebellion and later to intervene in disputes between factions of canallers. Duncan also served six years as District Councillor representing Thorold before he was elected for a term as a Reform Party member of the Third Parliament. Many, but certainly not all, of his neighbours admired him for his service as Commissioner of Queen's Bench, or magistrate. It could be said his career in public service began when he helped defend his besieged hometown of Niagara. He was a horse groom and powder monkey at the age of ten, making him one of the youngest veterans of the War of 1812.

Duncan's father John, a boat-builder for the Royal Navy, had petitioned for and received a large freehold of land in Niagara from the British Crown to compensate his loyal service during the American Revolutionary War. After their father died in 1815, Duncan's elder brother John Jr distributed the family holdings to the three brothers and arranged to provide for his unmarried sisters. He then doggedly sought and finally won compensation for their father's serious wartime losses in Niagara when the town was burned in 1813. Duncan's share allowed him to become a prime developer of property near the Welland Canal. He had been buying and selling land in the district for years now and was well known as a fair and honest businessman.

❦ ❦ ❦

The gentleman took his place on the front seat of the open carriage beside his twenty-four-year-old son Duncan Elliot McFarland. Called Dunc to distinguish him from his father, he sat in the middle of the bench, holding the reins. On Dunc's left side was the McFarlands' older son, John Cameron, bouncing one leg with impatience, and fuming at the delay. Margaret Jane arranged her billowing, ankle-length white frock round her as she sat on the black leather rear seat. It was a tight squeeze between her mother and Dunc's sweetheart, Agnes Blake, who were similarly encumbered by their own bonnets, voluminous skirts and parasols.

Dunc had recently bought land from his father and was establishing himself in business with his own grist mill. Now that he would have an income, he and Agnes, eighteen, had begun courting in earnest. The two had met each other as children in Niagara where Agnes, her widowed mother, and younger brother shared a home with the girl's Grandmother Rogers and uncle. The Rogers were well known in town; Uncle John Rogers was a merchant and the Town Clerk. The Rogers, Blakes, and the Niagara McFarlands were all members of St Andrew's Presbyterian Church and socialised together. The Port Robinson McFarlands often stopped with cousins at the historic brick homestead south of town where Dunc's father had grown up along the Niagara River.

Agnes had come to stay with the McFarlands for a fortnight to help with their large kitchen garden. Dunc planned to take her home this Sunday afternoon, accompanied by his father, who would use the opportunity again to visit his siblings and their families. It was a long drive on sometimes poor roads and always required spending the night; however, Dunc could afford to leave his fledgling business at this time of year, as it was between grain harvests.

The young man got the two chestnut draft horses moving with a click of his tongue and a snap of the reins. When they started, the sturdy animals strained with the heavy load of six people in the open carriage. As the horses walked along the canal, the family discussed the day's events. The women had been looking forward to the diversion and the chance to show off their new summer dresses and bonnets. Margaret Jane wondered aloud if anyone she knew would be there and silently what she would do to pass the time. The men would no doubt use the occasion to discuss local and parliamentary politics with their peers. The Toronto newspapers carried accounts of recent battles in the Crimean Peninsula in faraway Russia. World events were sure to come up as topics of conversation.

It would take about an hour to travel the four miles on the old clay road from Port Robinson southwest to the new county seat. After crossing the canal locks, Dunc trotted the horses down Front Street and dust rose from the wheels. The ladies complained, so Dunc slowed the team. His father began to fidget and fuss about being late and checked his pocket watch several times as they continued along the road toward Merrittsville.

At one point, Duncan nearly panicked at the thought of breaking an axle on the old road and missing the whole event. He reminded himself that the new Macadam turnpike would be much quicker and smoother. However, it was still in the planning stages, and the first section was only to be east of the canal between Thorold and Port Robinson, no help to him to-day. Duncan's innate Scottish thrift might have prevented his paying the combined tolls on six people, a carriage, and two horses anyway. He chuckled to himself as he recognised the irony. He was president of the Thorold and Port Robinson Macadamised Road Committee in charge of its design, funding, and setting of tolls.

❧ ❧ ❧

Crowds were gathering in the square when the McFarlands turned into Main Street. They were not late, however; in fact, there were fifteen minutes to spare, and Duncan was much re-lieved. The rays of brilliant July sun, still high in the sky at nearly four o'clock, beat down on the populace. All were glad to have hats, bonnets, and parasols to shield their faces, though they relished the warmth of summer.

John helped the ladies out, and Dunc turned over the rig to the livery boy. He joined his family and Agnes, taking her arm in his. Dr John Frazer, the current warden of Welland County, spotted the McFarlands right away and walked over to greet them. He showed the family where to assemble for the procession of spectators before leading his good friend Duncan away to await further instructions.

Other dignitaries arrived, tipped their hats to the ladies, and greeted Duncan with a handshake. Everyone was dressed in their Sunday finery for the special occasion. The Port Robinson Brass Band, in splendid uniform, finished tuning their instruments and struck up a lively air to entertain the crowd until the procession began. At precisely four o'clock, Dr Frazer signaled, and the diminutive Duncan McFarland, Esquire, squared his shoulders and stood as tall as he could, beaming with pride. The band played an energetic march tune as Duncan led the musicians from Barney's Inn to the new building across the street. A gaggle of spectators, magistrates, council members, and officers followed with Dr Frazer at the end. The whole company then ascended a temporary stairway to the floor that covered the basement. Dr Frazer and two workmen positioned the cornerstone into which a sealed vase had been placed. This vessel contained several recent local newspapers plus a letterpress perspective view and description of the building itself.

When all were quiet, the county clerk read aloud the message engraved on the plate covering the vase:

This cornerstone of the Welland County Court House and Gaol was laid by John Frazer, Esq., M.D., Member of Provincial Parliament, Warden of the County of Welland on Friday, the 6th day of July, A.D. 1855

The crowd of several hundred roared three cheers to Queen Victoria: "Hip, hip, hurrah! Hip, hip, hurrah! Hip, hip, hurrah!"

Three volleys of gunfire by the local amateur artillerymen rang out a Royal Salute over the trees beside the courthouse. Then the band played "Rule Britannia" with great joy; some voices sang the lyrics to Thomas Augustine Arne's popular tune. Dr Frazer spoke briefly of the satisfactory end to the long and bitter struggle to divide the original large Lincoln County that resulted in the creation of a separate Welland County. He appealed to the crowd to let bygones be bygones.

Though the edifice would not be completed for another six months, it was a beautiful design by Kevis Tully. The architect of the St Catharines Courthouse had again drawn his inspiration from classical buildings in Italy. The elegant façade gave onto the Welland Canal that promised continued prosperity for the citizens. The courthouse would be a fine addition to the village and would serve the county for years to come.

❦ ❦ ❦

When the applause died down after the final musical selection, the McFarlands and the other honoured guests repaired to the nearby picnic grove where a cold supper was ready for them. The breeze freshened, rustling the leaves of the trees over long tables covered with white tablecloths, glassware, and cutlery. Duncan and his family sat on benches at the head table with Dr Frazer and his. They sipped cold lemonade and raspberry vinegar beverages as the meal was served: roasted chicken, rolls, and pickles followed by a dessert of Victoria cakes and fresh strawberry ice cream kept cold on blocks of ice in the shade provided by tall elm trees.

When Duncan saw that his daughter had finished her meal, he stood and tapped her gently on the shoulder. "Please join me for a wee stroll, lassie."

"With pleasure, Father," said the girl, rising from her seat. She opened her parasol as Duncan offered his arm. She hooked hers through his as they bid the rest of the table goodbye.

Once away from the others, he led her down a path through the green expanse of lawn that overlooked the Welland River. A family of mallards was gliding past, and the late afternoon sun revealed the brilliant colours of the drake.

"Aren't they sweet?" said Margaret Jane, looking at the string of ducklings following their mother through the green water.

Duncan stopped and, adopting a serious air, turned toward Margaret Jane. "Your mother and I have decided to make a change for your education, lass." He paused. "Although you're old enough to leave school, you still seem eager to learn and have far exceeded the Common School programme in Port Robinson. I've looked into other places for you to go for study. Quite honestly, the schools here in this part of Canada still restrict education for clever girls like you. I've now heard of a place in the United States, and I've sent the registration fees for you to begin in October. I hope you'll be pleased with our choice."

He looked intently into her light blue eyes, trying to guess her reaction. "Have you any questions, lass?"

"Father, I'm astonished! I'd no idea that you were thinking of sending me away to school! That's wonderful! I was so bored with Mr Leetze this year. He makes me do the same thing over and over again. I doubt he knows very much more than I do, and he's seventeen!" Then she thought of the effect it would have on the family. "But, what will Mama do without me at home? Won't she be lonely? Won't she need me?"

"Well, of course she'll miss you, her dear daughter. You've been a great help to her since your school term ended, but I've persuaded her that this is important and the right thing to do for you. You'll be going to another family of sorts—a large one of over one hundred fifty girls. There'll be staff to care for you, as well as a minister, a man called George Washington Doane. His wife is a gracious and pleasant lady, I'm told. Together they treat the girls as if they were their own daughters."

"Oh, Father, I think I shall be too frightened to go to such a large school as that! I won't know a soul," fretted the twelve-year-old, now seeming to lose her initial enthusiasm.

"Well, lassie, you are wrong about that. You've heard that Laura and Elizabeth Fuller are going away to a place called St Mary's Hall?"

Margaret Jane nodded.

"That's where you are going as well, lass," said her father. "Mr Fuller has agreed to take you all the way to the state of New Jersey, with two other girls from St Catharines."

"Oh, my, Father! I'm glad that I shall at least know Laura and Elizabeth. I see them every year at the fair. But I shall miss you and Mama and Dunc and John so much! And whatever shall I do without Agnes too? She's almost a sister to me now. I've enjoyed her time with us very much."

"Well, I have a feeling that Agnes and Dunc will have some news very soon themselves. Mama may have some more help in the house after you leave."

"Father, do you think they will be betrothed soon?"

"I do, lassie. I certainly do," said Duncan with a grin.

CHAPTER 3

The Taylor Family of Toronto

WEDNESDAY, 15 AUGUST 1855

Harriet Esther Taylor crumpled the letter in disgust and threw it down on the thick patterned carpet that covered the floor of her bedroom. Her father Fennings had written from Québec City saying she would be going to school in the United States, to the state of New Jersey, near the old colonial capital of Philadelphia.

Why is he sending me out of Canada to school? Doesn't he love me anymore? New Jersey! It's so far away! wondered Harriet.

And although she had heard stories about relatives who'd come from there when it was a colony, her brave maternal grandmother Esther Borden Lippincott Denison for one, she knew absolutely no one in the United States!

Harriet had been looking forward to living again on the grounds of Bellevue, a Denison family estate in Toronto. Bellevue boasted three family houses in a park-like setting at the end of half-mile-long Denison Avenue. The original large house built in 1815 by Harriet's grandfather, George Taylor Denison, dominated the end of a winding, shaded lane and was surrounded by his farm and orchards. The Taylors lived in a house on one side of the lane, halfway to the main house; the third house was built closer to Denison Avenue. When the Taylors left Montréal in 1849, Fennings accepted his father-in-law's offer to live at Bellevue for the good of his young wife, Mary Elizabeth, and their three children. The estate, in the northwest quadrant of the city, was not ideally located for his own needs; it was a considerable carriage ride to reach his government office in King Street across from Parliament near the lake. Mary Elizabeth was happy being close to her family though.

When they removed to Toronto, Harriet was nearly ten. She enjoyed being part of the large Denison family, her mother's people, who were prominent in Toronto society. Many cousins, aunts, and uncles lived nearby, and the grounds were a beautiful place to play with woods, gardens, and a ravine leading to Russell Creek. The smoke and noise of the city were kept far away to the southeast by the prevailing winds. The family's idyllic life there had been short-lived though. After less than two years, her mother died. The beautiful house at Bellevue was closed up. Her father took Harriet and her siblings even farther down the St Lawrence River than Montréal. They returned to the old city of Québec, site of the next Parliament session.

Harriet would not have much longer to enjoy her lovely, cosy bedroom in the house that reminded her of her mother. It seemed as if she had just finished unpacking and putting away her belongings after the steamship voyage along the north shore of Lake Ontario. Now she would have to pack again to go somewhere else. She did not understand.

❦ ❦ ❦

Since the disastrous 1849 riots and fires that burned the Parliament buildings in Montréal, the seat of provincial government had "perambulated" between Toronto and Québec. Government employees like Mr Taylor had to relocate with Parliament, taking his family and household staff with him—a costly, disruptive, and time-consuming proposition. After three years living in a cramped rented house in Québec, the capital city of Canada East, the Taylor family had recently transferred five hundred miles west again, assured that it would soon be Toronto's turn to host the Canadian Provincial Parliament.

Harriet knew the current Parliament was still arguing about where the permanent site of government should be. There was a deadlock on the issue. Sessions were set and then postponed over and over again. According to the latest agreement, the next one was supposed to begin on the fifteenth of September, but in Québec City, not Toronto, and this new school was to start on the first of November. So how in the world was Harriet to get to New Jersey if her father was needed in Québec?

No, Harriet just couldn't understand her father's decision. Why did she have to leave the family now that she was back at home in English-speaking Toronto near the Denisons? She was nearly sixteen and could be the lady of the Taylor house if she left off her studies, and, at her age, she was permitted to do so. She loved the thought of hosting elegant dinners for her father, but without a wife, he hadn't entertained at all in Québec.

Fennings Taylor had become a widower four years ago. His three children had been young; Harriet was eleven, Mary Elizabeth Sophia was six, and little George not even two. It was a terrible shock to all three to lose their mother so suddenly. Since Mr Taylor was Deputy Clerk of the Legislative Council, the upper house of the Parliament, they were well enough off to employ plenty of household help. They already had Mrs Dowling, their capable housekeeper, and Miss Adelaide Fellows, the children's governess who knew the family well, had accompanied them from Québec. Now they also employed Maeve Armstrong, a new housemaid; Mrs Palmer the cook; Terence the manservant for the house; and lastly Eamon, who was in charge of the horses and carriage and everything else out of doors at Bellevue. But all the help in the world could not replace the loving embrace of their young mother. Harriet longed for that feeling again.

Harriet missed her father terribly when he could not kiss her goodnight or wink at her from the other end of the mahogany dinner table. His hectic schedule during late-night sessions also meant she often had to eat supper with Mary, Georgie, and Miss Fellows. She was clearly too old to do that but was given no choice in the matter if he were working late. Now that he was down in Québec for the summer waiting on Parliament, she did not know when she would see him again.

❦ ❦ ❦

When she attended the Ursulines' school in Québec as a day student, Harriet had little interest in ciphering or science. However, the one academic area that did interest her was geography. The idea of exotic places intrigued her. Recently she liked reading the ladies' magazines Maeve lent her, especially *Godey's Lady's Book* from Philadelphia, to see the newest fashions. The engravings, stories, and poetry were wonderful too! Her father also had in his extensive library a now well-thumbed book with interesting lithographs of far-off places. When she was left on her own, Harriet loved to page through the large format volume covered in red leather. As she gazed at the pictures, she dreamt of travelling abroad someday, perhaps on a honeymoon, or to Australia to see the kangaroos!

Harriet had a fairly good idea of where New York, New Jersey, and Pennsylvania were because she had spent long hours studying her beautiful Newton's terrestrial floor globe. It was accorded a place of honour in their well-appointed, wood-paneled library. Recognising her fascination with geography, her parents had given it to her for her tenth birth-day. The globe was one of the few pieces her father had had packed with special care and shipped back and forth from Québec, at her insistence, and at great expense. She enjoyed sitting by it, spinning, and searching for the faraway places she had read about. She loved the idea of travelling to Paris or Rome or London, but New Jersey? That sounded very dull indeed.

❦ ❦ ❦

These days in Québec City, John Fennings Taylor, II was a terribly busy man. Called Fennings by his colleagues, so as not to be confused with his Uncle John, Clerk of the Legislative Council, the younger Taylor was deputy for his namesake. They both worked long days when the government was in session. Fennings' duties included keeping all of the Parliament business moving along, and, in consequence, he had met the men from all over Upper and Lower Canada who were involved at many levels of county and district government. He was personable, enjoyed his work and was quite accomplished after nearly twenty years in the position. He had taken the post soon after he arrived in Toronto from England in 1836.

Fennings knew his older daughter suffered from the lack of a mother, but his legislative responsibilities were time-consuming. He had little opportunity to look for a new wife to take the place of Mary Elizabeth Denison, who had died shortly after the birth of a baby boy. Tragically, the baby had not survived either. It had been a crushing blow to his young family but not an unknown one to his peers. Many men experienced widowhood and quickly sought to remarry. Fennings just had not had time to catch his breath. He missed Mary Elizabeth terribly, and he knew Harriet did too. The younger children doted on their governess, but Harriet was too old to need a governess. Miss Fellows, as good as she was, had limited energy and used it all up caring for little Mary and Georgie. She went to bed when they did, leaving Harriet to pursue her own activities in the evenings.

The father naturally worried about Harriet's future. Before her mother died, a series of women had tutored her at home with some of her Denison cousins. After that she had been one of the few Protestant day pupils at the venerable Ursulines' school in Québec City. She was not a natural student though, being more inclined to the arts. Last spring, she had enjoyed a few months with a drawing master who came to the house in the afternoons, but the man moved on to a more stable post at a ladies' school in Montréal. Harriet had lately become close to their housemaid, and Fennings had to admit he didn't like the result. Maeve, just twenty, was a recent immigrant from poor Ireland, a good household worker, but not well educated. He noticed Harriet was more interested in ladies' magazines than continuing any studies. Fennings had at first planned to leave her with the Ursulines but reconsidered when he learnt of the monastic existence required of resident pupils. Betsy, his Uncle John's wife, suggested that they find another school for Harriet once both families were back in Toronto.

Something had to change. Harriet was almost sixteen now. How would she ever find a decent husband if all she could talk about was the latest dress designs? She was an attractive young girl, medium height, with wavy light brown hair and blue eyes.

More importantly, she was kind and loving toward her siblings and the staff. But a prospective husband would appreciate a mate with an ability to carry on an intelligent conversation both at home and in society.

One Sunday in July after returning to Québec City, he attended services at their parish church, the Cathedral of the Holy Trinity, with the elder Taylors. Aunt Betsy picked up a catalogue and prospectus there for an Episcopal school for young ladies in the United States and gave it to Fennings as he left the church. He read it cover to cover and was particularly taken by the owner's description of the girls in his charge becoming as the "Polished Corners of the Temple". His pupils were educated to become wives and mothers who would in turn guide whole families, nurturing boys and girls of good character and intelligence. Their children and grandchildren would be expected to find many ways to improve the world in which they lived.

The decision was soon taken, the fees paid, the steamship and train tickets secured. Fennings investigated overnight accommodations in St Catharines, Canada West, two station towns in New York, then Jersey City, New Jersey and finally Burlington, New Jersey where St Mary's Hall was. It would be a taxing trip, but it would afford them time together that they had never enjoyed before. He looked forward to it in fact. It might be the only such opportunity before Harriet married and had her own family. The last but perhaps most vexing problem was to schedule the trip to avoid the Parliament session. The winter term at St Mary's Hall was to begin on the first of November. There was also a month of vacation offered in October for the pupils who arrived early. He hoped the Parliament's calendar would work out so that he could get Harriet to Burlington sometime before the term began.

CHAPTER 4

The Burns Family of St Catharines

LATE SEPTEMBER 1855

Isabella Ann Burns' usually sweet, pale face flushed as she shook her head with fury. "But Mama, Emma and Julia are going back to school in New Jersey. Why can't I? I'm twelve, exactly the same age as that girl from Thorold, Elizabeth Fuller. She's going this year! Papa said so."

One of her fine blond braids now hung loose, unpinned from the back of her head from the sudden motion. She just didn't understand why her parents, whom she loved so much, would deny her the same experience as her two older sisters. It was so unfair!

All week long, Emma and Julia had been packing their chests again, putting things in, taking things out, trying to fit in favourite items that were allowed in the small private spaces available in the dormitory of St Mary's Hall. Isabella wondered why she could not be travelling to the States with all the other girls. Mr Fuller, the minister of St Peter's Church up on the Mountain in Thorold, was to take his two daughters and the Burns sisters all the way to New Jersey on the railway.

The railway with its locomotive: that noisy, black smoke-spewing Iron Horse monster. Would her sisters get to see the falls at Niagara again as they trundled in the cars across the newest bridge linking Canada with the United States? The International Rail Road Suspension Bridge had opened just a few months ago. In April, Emma, Julia, and Aunt Arabella had returned to Canada crossing it only a few weeks after it was tested. Aunt Arabella was always willing to try new things. The trio had all got to see and hear the great waterfall rushing down the Niagara Escarpment.

Everyone in St Catharines was talking about the bridge. Isabella wanted to see it herself! She so wanted to be part of the adventure.

Emma and Julia were not even eighteen months apart in age and truly close sister-friends. Isabella, fully four years younger than Emma, tried hard to be part of their conversations, but felt always on the outside looking in. Even though the three girls shared one bed, top and tail, this summer, whilst the older ones were back from St Mary's Hall, Isabella never felt their equal. She had been moved out of the nursery when Emma and Julia started to go away to school in the winters. At first, she enjoyed her own room away from the babies, but then she felt a bit lonely. She had happily welcomed her sisters back every spring; she wanted to be considered an older child and part of their seemingly sophisticated lives.

But once again, it looked as if she would be left home with her annoying little brother Norman, now a rambunctious nine-year-old, and four-year-old Henrietta Elizabeth. Little Libby always wanted her attention, and frankly, Isabella was tired of playing mother to her when Emma and Julia were away. And Mama was going to have another baby in a matter of weeks. She was so tired; she would lie on the chaise longue in her bedroom all day long to relieve her poor swollen feet.

It is just so unfair! thought Isabella.

Mama looked up at her daughter and tried to remain calm once again. "Isabella dear, your father and I have discussed it. You are yet too young. You are already a pupil of Miss Seaman at the St George's School. There are plenty of letters and arithmetic for you to learn *there* this year. Perhaps you can go to St Mary's Hall when you are thirteen. Let's see how Emma and Julia like it again this winter. Then we shall talk."

"But Mama, they *do* like—"

Julia burst through her mother's open bedroom door. "Mama, I can't find my plaid dress! Do you suppose it's out with the laundry?"

"Julia, you have interrupted your sister and me. Please wait till we have finished our conversation. Excuse yourself, daughter."

Mrs Burns could be a bit abrupt in dealing with her many children, and her pregnancy only increased this tendency.

Julia made a sloppy curtsy to her mother and said, "Excuse me, Mama, I wondered when Patrick will fetch the last ironing for Emma and me. We leave for New Jersey in just three days! When will it be done?"

"Ask Kitty to see about the dress, Julia, and anything else that might be needed for your journey. Be sure to take back all your thickest winter things. It may not be as cold in New Jersey as it is here in the winter or for nearly as long, but you still should have them. Remember the wind off that river is fierce when you are taken out of doors," said her mother, as she moved onto her side to relieve some discomfort.

Despite her advanced pregnancy, she had been thinking about the conditions her daughters would face in their home away from home. Her paternal grandfather, Johann Christoph Mittleberger, had come to Canada from near Lancaster, Pennsylvania, not far from New Jersey. She remembered his stories of the land, its rivers and winters in that part of America. The girls had experienced mild weather in Burlington the last two winters there, but Henrietta Burns knew they had to be prepared for worse.

Isabella was now sulking. Her time with Mama was limited by the needs of her four siblings, and Julia had cut their important conversation short. She had not succeeded in her quest to be allowed to go to St Mary's Hall this year. The work would have to continue while her sisters were away. It looked certain she would again be stuck at home with *three* little ones, but perhaps she could still convince Papa. She pondered how to do that.

"What's bothering you, Bella? You're making a face!" asked fifteen-year-old Julia.

"I'm not permitted to go to St Mary's Hall with you and Emma. I shall have to wait again. I *always* have to wait!" she said indignantly. Then she dissolved into tears and ran from the room.

Mama sighed. A frown came over her weary face. "I just do not know what else to say to her, Julia. You were thirteen when you went away for the first time. Papa and I want to see how Isabella grows this winter before we send her all the way to Burlington. She is still so young and shows so much temper. Perhaps you can console her. She misses you greatly."

"Of course, Mama. She's my little sunshine. I shall miss her too. We shan't see any of you again until April. Papa said we must also remain there for the April vacation if we want to do the summer term. Summer term. That's the only way that Emma will ever graduate. I understand—the trip is long and expensive, and someone would have to fetch us."

With that, Julia, trying to hold back the tears in her reddened eyes, embraced her mother and left the room. She followed Isabella to the girls' bedroom down the hall and round the corner.

❧ ❧ ❧

Emma was occupied, folding and packing with Catharine Kane, the Burns family's ladies' maid. Kitty was seventeen, a year older than Emma, and until she began working for the Burns family three years ago, had lived with her own parents and three younger brothers in a tiny, frame house in St Catharines. When her father, the sole breadwinner, was seriously injured in a mill accident, she had had to go into service with a family. Her mother took in sewing and laundry to make ends meet while her husband recovered. Kitty was placed with the Burns family, whom they knew from St George's Church of England. The girl was now as much another sister to Emma and Julia as young Isabella, with two notable exceptions: she took her meals with the other servants and lived on the third floor, sharing a room with little Mary Carroll, the recently hired housemaid from Ireland. Also living in the house were Mary Tracy, the cook, and Patrick Coffey, the coachman and handyman, who hailed from Ireland too. All contributed to the smooth running of the large Burns household.

Kitty was always a great help with practical considerations. She seemed to know when it was prudent to wear new clothes or not-so-new ones if the weather was going to turn nasty, in case the passing horses, carriages, and stagecoaches might throw mud at the girls' heavy woolen skirts after the winter snow started to melt away in the spring.

Emma sat on the bed, holding up a thick cotton petticoat in front of her. "Kitty, I cannot understand why we have to wear these. They are so heavy. And how in the world am I to fit it into the chest now?"

Kitty took it from Emma, rolled it length-wise and squeezed the garment in along the edge of the trunk wall.

"There, Emma, all done. Be glad it is not a birdcage hoop you are trying to fit into that trunk! They are the new style from Paris, I hear. I allow you are ready now to leave us again. Extra linen, seven pairs of drawers, your two new dresses, a pair of slippers for inside wear, your winter cloak, bonnet, and muff. Three pairs of kid gloves. Three pairs of wool ones. Your Bible and the likeness of you and Julia taken at the circus August last." She paused and took a small brown paper parcel from her apron pocket. "But here, I have a little gift for you."

"What is this, Kitty dear? You can't have done it! I have nought in return for you!"

"Open it, Emma, please. 'Tis of no great account, just something to remember me by," said Kitty. Her hazel eyes were moist now. She was trying hard to hold back tears.

Emma tore open the heavy paper and out dropped a smooth grey rock. On it were painted initials, CK and EB with the year 1855.

"I picked it up on one of my Sunday walks along the lake with Mummy and thought of you, Emma. You are my rock, like the Niagara Gorge you told me about. You've been my friend for these three years living away from my family, and you make my life brighter for it. I hope that you'll look at it every day at St Mary's Hall and think of me here in Canada, your friend in St Catharines."

Kitty wiped her eyes with the corner of her apron as Emma took her other hand in hers.

"Of course, I shall think of you every day, Kitty! How could I

33

ever forget you? Why, you are like another sister to me, an older one and wiser too. Thank you very much. I shall have to leave you something just as special so you don't forget me."

"Oh, Emma, there's no chance of that. I shall be here every day, surrounded by your family: Bella, little Norman and Libby, your parents, and the new babe. How I shall love to cuddle and coo at it! There are always so many details to be addressed with a new babe in the house—and always the worry about the mother."

"Please don't remind me, Kitty. The last time was so frightening. Mama nearly died when the doctor couldn't get here through the snowstorm. She was lucky to be so healthy then and finally recover. I am only sorry that the babe did not survive. He was just too little."

"Childbirth is both wonderful and dangerous. We must give thanks to God for bringing both mother and child through the ordeal every time," said the older girl.

Isabella ran into the room with Julia close behind her.

"Emma, I'm not to go after all! I was hoping Mama would change her mind, but she is steadfast, and Papa too apparently. I'm to stay at home with Norman and Libby for the whole winter again, and maybe more!" Isabella stood stiff before them and clenched her fists in frustration. Her oval face was bright red again. Both her braids were now unpinned and reached halfway down her back.

Emma turned from Kitty and wrapped the child in her arms, squeezing her tight. "Bella, do not wish your life away! Be patient, dear one. Julia and I always write you letters from school. You will know exactly what to expect when the time comes for you to go—"

Julia interrupted her sister. "We, on the other hand, Bella, only knew what was written in the catalogue when we first went. Would you like to read it? Here, have a look!" Julia dared her, pulling a blue paper booklet out of the tray of her trunk. "There's a list of all the courses we must study and the regulation of our life. See if you like it so much when you have all the information!"

"No, no, no! I don't want to read it! I just *don't* want to be left at home with the little ones," Bella sobbed and threw herself on the high bed. The distraught girl sank her face into the intricately patterned, quilted counterpane covering the featherbed. Kitty, who had just spent half an hour fluffing the featherbed after its daily airing, shook her head, smiled, and rolled her eyes to Heaven.

Julia clucked, "Bella, you're so dramatic. P'raps you *should* go to St Mary's Hall for a little discipline. I'm sure Bishop Doane wouldn't approve of your current behaviour."

"Julia is right, Bella. You don't have the facts, and you don't *want* the facts. You need to be patient and see then how it really is to go away from your family for so long. We have done it twice already. There is plenty of time for you to go away to school. After all, Julia was thirteen when she went. You are only twelve," reminded Emma.

"Yes, I am only twelve, but so is Elizabeth Fuller. Why does she get to go and I do not?" She rolled over and looked up at the other girls, her cheeks now tear-stained.

"Because yours is a different family, Bella," said Kitty. "Every family is different. Parents are different. People are different."

Bella sat up and looked at Kitty. "Kitty Kane, you're not even a member of this family!" shouted Bella, who immediately wished she had not said this and clapped her hand over her mouth.

Emma and Julia gasped. Kitty blanched and looked crestfallen.

"Bella, you are just showing how little you know! Of course Kitty is part of this family. What would we three do without her help? Apologise to her straightaway, or I shall go to Mama!" said Emma.

Bella looked sheepish and got off the bed. She walked over to Kitty, who was now ready to go out the door. "I'm sorry, Kitty. You are right. Mama and Papa *should* decide what is best for us all. It's just so hard to be left behind. And you *are* part of our family."

Kitty stopped and put her arms round the girl's slender shoulders.

"Dear Bella, we shall have such fun together again this winter. I shall make sure that you and Norman and Libby get out in the snow and make some angels. We can make some maple taffy on the snow like last year. You remember? Patrick will take us all on sleigh rides over the fields, and then when spring comes, 'twill be only a few weeks more till your sisters return. In the meantime, you will also have your own lessons at school with Miss Seaman. We shall study them together, you and I."

Bella sighed. "Thank you, Kitty. I dearly love you. I was a horrible beastly beast. I'm just so sad to be left behind."

Kitty squeezed her favourite charge. "I know, Bella. I know."

❦ ❦ ❦

That afternoon, Julia sat dreamy-eyed in a comfortable wickerwork chair on the verandah of the Burns' stately brick home. She was twisting her long dark curls about her fingers as she thought of William Adams Mittleberger, her favourite cousin and best friend. William was a year older than she, sixteen now, and they had grown up together, living on opposite corners of the fifteen-acre block of land that their fathers owned. The son of her mother Henrietta's eldest brother Henry, William was the middle child of five surviving children.

William and his younger brother Charles were lately trying to choose a profession. Up until recently there had only been a few acceptable professions for gentlemen: the law, the church, or the military. Charles was planning to read law with his uncle Thomas Burns. William might decide to apprentice with him too, but he was also interested in other modern options. In the middle of the nineteenth century, society was changing; there were now careers in industry, government, banking, and commerce to consider. William liked working with numbers; he could follow his father into banking, but he might instead ask to work for his uncle John F. Mittleberger, a successful businessman who owned several mills. The close family relationships in St Catharines led naturally to occupations a man could have for his entire life.

The Mittleberger family had German-American roots. Their Huguenot ancestors had immigrated from Baden-Württemberg to Pennsylvania and then fled to Montréal as Loyalists before the fighting began in 1775. After their father died, Henrietta joined her brother in St Catharines where he had been apprenticed to William Hamilton Merritt, visionary father of the Welland Canal.

Henrietta lived with Henry, his second wife Eliza Adams, and their children until she met and married Thomas Burns. Though Thomas was the son of a Scottish Presbyterian minister and schoolmaster in Niagara, he and Henrietta were wed in the Church of England and were raising their family as Episcopalians. The two brothers-in-law were very civic-minded. Both served on the vestry of St George's; Thomas was police magistrate and Henry was postmaster and founded the fire company.

❦ ❦ ❦

Beginning at Port Dalhousie on the lake, the Welland Canal snaked through the town of St Catharines and south to Lake Erie. Every day during shipping season, vessels plied its waters. Some laden with wheat from farms in other parts of Canada West would sail up to the town's grist mills. Steamers would take the flour back down the canal and cross thirty miles of the lake to Toronto or go west to Hamilton where the product would be sold to bakers and grocers. Everyone needed flour to bake bread; it was a staple food. There were also hundreds of other ships bringing raw materials from northern mines to foundries built on the northern edge of the canal. The Welland Canal had brought prosperity to the region, but the industries had also brought noise, odours, and smoke.

Although St Catharines was a growing canal and mill town, there were still large tracts of open land to the west and north along the shores of brilliant blue Lake Ontario. Farms and woodlands, interrupted by the occasional village, continued east all the way to the old capital town of Niagara. It had been an unusually hot summer on the Niagara Peninsula. The late season thunderstorms and rains had nearly ruined the spring wheat harvest. Both farmers and millers faced a reduced income this year as a result. Everyone was feeling a bit wilted from the heat and humidity that persisted into mid-September. Then the wind direction changed, and the cooler north winds coming off Lake Ontario brought renewed energy to the residents. The more seasonable dry weather was a welcome relief and marked the beginning of the annual striking colour changes of the maple, elm, and oak trees. The air seemed clearer and cleaner, pushing any smoke and unpleasant tannery odours out of the city. Fall was coming, and families were now engaged in storing up food for the long Canadian winter.

But first there would be a service of thanksgiving at St George's Church on Sunday to celebrate the harvest season, as difficult as it had been. Julia hoped to see her Mittleberger cousins together there once more before she left for St Mary's Hall. She had picked out the perfect dress and her new bonnet of brown *velours royale*, trimmed with the grosgrain rosette ribbon. She also needed to break in her new black boots with the shiny bone buttons so they wouldn't hurt her feet on the four-day trip to New Jersey. New footwear could be awfully painful if you didn't, even if they were custom-made by the bootmaker with your own last! An infected blister could make you seriously ill.

On Monday, Julia would be off to the States again. She would write to William every week and tell him all about her third term at St Mary's Hall. William would still be at home this year, a student at the District Grammar School in the classics programme reserved for boys. He and Julia would be studying some of the same subjects though, some that girls were not yet allowed to learn in any Canadian school. That was the main reason she and Emma had been sent to New Jersey two years ago, an opportunity for a better education. Maybe someday there would be changes for women's schooling in Canada, but certainly not yet.

If she were truthful, Julia would admit that she was not that keen to leave St Catharines this time. Of course, she wanted to keep busy, but she would miss William and his ready smile, shiny dark hair, clear blue eyes, and sympathetic ear during their walks through the orchard between their houses. They had spent a glorious summer together. Who would be her confidant while she was away in Burlington?

❦ ❦ ❦

On Monday morning, after Emma and Julia departed for the railway station with their father, Kitty entered the now quiet girls' bedroom. She gazed wistfully at the chest of drawers that stood emptied of the older girls' wardrobe. She was surprised to see that the framed ambrotype of Emma and Julia was still atop the chest. Beneath it was an envelope with her name on it. She opened it and took out a note.

> *Dear Kitty,*
> *   Please keep this likeness to remind you how much we are sisters at heart. Thank you for all that you have done for us. We shall miss you.*
> *   Fondly,*
> *   Emma and Julia*

CHAPTER 5

The Fuller Family of Thorold

LATE SEPTEMBER 1855

Cynthia Street Fuller called to her youngest daughter from the front porch of the rambling stone and frame farmhouse in Thorold Township, "Elizabeth, you must come inside straightaway to finish your packing. Bring your brothers too!"

Mrs Fuller was the eldest daughter of the late Samuel Street, Jr, born in 1775 to Nehemiah and Thankful Moody Street in Norwalk, Connecticut. The boy was named for his Uncle Samuel, Nehemiah's brother. As the American colonial rebellion worsened, the two Street brothers brought their families north out of Connecticut because, as Tories, they supported the British crown. After the Revolutionary War ended, Nehemiah was killed in a robbery in Buffalo, New York, and his widow, Thankful, returned to Connecticut with her five children. In 1796, when he was twenty-one, young Samuel joined his namesake in Canada to find his fortune. He became a prominent land developer in the Niagara Peninsula after the British crown awarded him six hundred acres as the son of a United Empire Loyalist.

Cynthia Fuller felt a great responsibility to raise her children to be worthy of their storied Loyalist heritage. As mother of eight children, she was not to be ignored as the undisputed head of the noisy Fuller household. Her husband, Tom, was usually too preoccupied with his many pastoral responsibilities at two congregations, let alone the needs of their large farm, to be concerned with the daily operation of the household or the children. His wife, on the other hand, was one to be reckoned with on issues of order and discipline.

Their youngest daughter Lizzie, as her father affectionately called her, could challenge any mother. She was already taller than her two sisters, gangly, and now lightly freckled from the sun because she had eschewed bonnets all summer. Lizzie was most often outside in fine weather, leading her three little brothers into all kinds of exploration of Beechlands, the Fullers' 135-acre farm, named for the towering beech trees growing round the house and in the nearby woods. She loved nothing more than to climb the apple trees in the two-acre orchard behind the house, or to lie on her belly, turning over a log or a rock, examining the beetles that resided there. Bonnets just got in the way, and then she got into trouble with her mother when they were soiled. She was the last to be concerned with cleanliness or punctuality too. An active twelve-year-old always looking for new experiences, Lizzie was not at all anxious to spend time sitting in the house, even in winter.

Lizzie was a leader now among her younger siblings. Ten-year-old Willy was ever eager for a new adventure with his favourite sister, and little Valancy adored her too. Not wanting to be left out the youngest boy, Shelton, almost three, toddled along behind them all, begging Lizzie to pick him up when his little limbs tired. Their twin brothers, Dick and Sam, had also doted on Lizzie because she was a willing learner. They taught her how to fish and climb trees at a young age, despite her skirts. Together they enjoyed exploring the twenty acres of mature woods on the edge of the crop fields. They pretended they were Indians and made their own bows and arrows. The twins taught her to ice skate on the big pond and to make snow forts for their snowball fights. They were seventeen now and away at university in Toronto. Lizzie missed her older brothers, but she was also proud to be able to teach the little ones what she knew about the natural world.

Upon hearing her mother's voice, Lizzie sighed. With great reluctance, she replaced the abandoned robin's nest she had spotted hidden well among the leaves of the once fragrant lilac bush that thrived in a corner of the front garden. From the verandah draped in hops vines, outside the dining room earlier in the summer, the children had enjoyed watching the parent birds spend barely an hour to build the nest and then take turns feeding their young. One by one the fledglings learnt to fly, to the delight of Lizzie and her brothers. The garden, surrounded by a white picket fence to keep the grazing cows and sheep out, was a haven of shrubs and rose bushes tended lovingly by Mrs Fuller in her precious spare time.

"Coming, Mother!" Lizzie called back, dejected, as she wiped her hands on her white apron. "Let's go, boys," she said as she took the hands of five-year-old Val and little Shelly. "Come on, Willy, you too."

❦ ❦ ❦

Elizabeth was not looking forward to finishing the task assigned to her. She had to fill her two valises with four days of plain clothes to wear during their train trip south. One did not want to ruin one's best dresses travelling in the cars, subjecting them to cinder burns, wood ash, and the general dirt and mud of railroad stations and unpaved streets. She had already packed a trunk with her new and better things. The school discouraged fancy wear and jewellery—that was not a problem for young Lizzie. Leaving behind her beloved natural science collections was, however. All last summer she had painstakingly collected and labelled boxes of small rocks, insects, and flowers. She was not pleased to part from them now for an indeterminate period of time. Could she trust Willy to keep them safe as she would? She could not take them with her. There would be no room for collections in the small amount of space allotted to each girl in the dormitory of that crowded school. *Oh, well,* she thought, *it's only till April, and it's beside a river. P'raps I shall learn to swim!*

She and her thirteen-year-old sister Laura were being sent to St Mary's Hall in New Jersey, an American state somewhere far south of the Canadian border. Lizzie had a vague idea of where that was, but her forte was not geography at the Common School she attended in Thorold Township. Last year, her older sister Mary Margaret was named head teacher of the little one-room school, and Lizzie loved being free to decide whether she did her lessons or not. She took advantage as much as possible of Mary Margaret's sweet disposition. The kind-hearted nineteen-year-old teacher understood her delightful little sister had considerable trouble sitting still for recitations. Lizzie had endless concentration when the lessons interested her, when she could see or touch things herself, but her mind wandered if she had to do long figures or memorise a poem. Natural science, specifically botany and entomology, were more interesting to her. Even mineralogy attracted Lizzie Fuller more than numbers and letters. Learning French and playing the piano-forte were even farther down on her list, but her father had already decided that she would be a pupil of both at her new school.

❦ ❦ ❦

Once inside, Lizzie found her mother upstairs in the second-floor bedroom the two girls shared. Mrs Fuller was placing Laura's freshly laundered shifts and petticoats into the drawers of the wood and iron-bound trunk. There were also linen handkerchiefs and both cotton and worsted hose, enough for the six months or more that they would be away. Mrs Fuller enjoyed doing intimate things like this for her children, although the family employed and housed seven servants on the grounds to keep the large household running. There were still six children at home with Mary Margaret yet unmarried.

I can't imagine the size of the laundry at that school with one hundred fifty girls! I know how much work it is just to do for our family of eight, thought Mrs Fuller.

Lizzie flung herself on the delicate rosewood lady chair beside the bureau where her mother was transferring clothing to the trunk.

"Elizabeth Street Fuller, will you please mind the furniture! And look at your frock! You are a young lady and should not be going about looking like a navvie!" she said, comparing her daughter to the men who dug the Welland Canal.

"I'm sorry, Mother. We were just out of doors having fun. We were examining the robin's nest. It's the one we've been watching all summer." She looked at the empty leather valises on the floor. "I am so tired of packing, packing, packing. When do we have to go?"

As she watched her mother work, Lizzie sat straighter on the burgundy velvet tufted cushion of the dainty spindle-back chair. She placed her hands on her lap in a vain effort to cover the dirty handprints on her apron.

"To-morrow is Sunday and we shall attend the Harvest Service over at St Peter's. On Monday we shall leave bright and early with Father for the railway in St Catharines. Father said Margaret Jane will meet us there at the station. They will probably overnight at the Welland House."

"Margaret Jane McFarland, from Port Robinson?"

"Yes, Colonel McFarland's daughter, dear, Father's friend. I thought you knew she was going along."

"No, I didn't. I don't know her well. I only spoke to her at the fair for a few minutes last year. Do you s'pose we shall all be in the same rooms at the school, Mother?" asked Lizzie.

"There are many rooms, dear, but for sleeping the matron strives to keep relatives and friends together. So, I'm not sure if you will be with both Laura and Margaret Jane. You will have to see."

"Oh, I don't like that idea, Mother. What if I can't get on with the other girls?" Lizzie stood, distressed.

Mrs Fuller looked straight into the eyes of her daughter and took her in her arms. She picked some spent lilac blooms out of her dishevelled brown hair. "Dear heart, you'll be in a new, even larger family, but 'twill be a Christian one based on love, just like ours. Every girl there will have the same worries you will about being far away from home. The teachers know this and will take it into account. You'll be fine, and Laura will be with you."

"But will she be studying with me?" asked Lizzie forlornly, burrowing her head into her mother's shoulder.

"Your father and Bishop Doane have decided on a course of study for each of you dependent on the results of an examination you will sit."

Lizzie jumped back. "An examination! Oh, Mother, what will

45

they ask me? I didn't do well last year at the examination when the inspectors came! Will they send me away if I fail?"

Lizzie now wished she had not been so keen on avoiding lessons at school.

"No, no, my darling. They will merely place you with other girls who need to learn the same things as you. Do not worry. I've read all the letters from Bishop Doane. There's a large School Room with modern desks to work on your lessons, and then there are other small rooms for recitations in French or Latin. For piano and singing, you'll go to one of their many music rooms," explained Mrs Fuller.

"French! Latin! Piano! Singing! Oh, no, you know I don't like singing, Mother. Shall I have to sing?" moaned Lizzie, who now had even stronger misgivings about going away to this school.

"Elizabeth, you sing hymns every week in church, do you not?"

"That's different, Mother, no one is listening to *me*!"

"Do not worry about singing, Elizabeth. It's a decision made by Bishop Doane, and choir singing is reserved for the older girls. Let's finish up your valises so that we can get on with dinner. Father is anxious to complete his packing too."

❦ ❦ ❦

Laura Abigail Fuller was in the music room, tucked in a corner of the older section of the house. Though small, it boasted two long windows, one on each wall that provided plenty of light for reading music. It was newly wallpapered with an Oriental design of her mother's choosing, and featured several tables covered with knickknacks in porcelain. In one corner was a plant stand holding a large fern. On the floor was a colourful carpet featuring the same yellow tones as the wallpaper.

Laura was lost in thought, playing Mrs Fuller's cherished piano-forte, a polished rosewood square model imported from the Chickering Company in Boston, Massachusetts. Cynthia Street had brought it to the marriage in 1835 as part of her dowry. Laura had benefitted from years of listening to her mother performing every evening for the family and had a gift for playing by ear herself. Although she had years ago learnt to read musical notes thanks to her teacher, Mrs McIntosh, she now could perform dozens of long pieces by heart. No one needed to nag Laura Fuller to practise her music, as she loved playing, whether alone or for others. Laura found solace in the instrument, and she exhibited unusual emotion for someone her age. While her younger sister Elizabeth avoided music at every opportunity, Laura was, like her mother, a natural musician.

The petite, dark-haired girl was ambivalent about her parents' decision to send Elizabeth and herself away to New Jersey for school. At nearly fourteen, Laura was already dreaming about attending the Toronto Normal School to become a teacher, since girls were permitted to study there too. She had to be sixteen though. Her sister Mary Margaret, the only teacher at the crowded schoolhouse near their home, allowed Laura to be a monitor to the younger boys and girls since Laura was no longer required by her age to study. Laura enjoyed listening to the children's recitations but disliked how easily Elizabeth could manipulate Mary Margaret. The two older sisters often disagreed about how to handle Elizabeth in the schoolroom. In one way, she would be glad to see Elizabeth held accountable at this new school. On the other hand, Laura loved being a teacher more than being a pupil. But perhaps she was just bored in Thorold. Maybe St Mary's Hall would ignite her interest in new subjects of study.

When she finished the piece, she heard her father applauding her performance. He had crept in and sat behind her on the chestnut brown mohair-covered settee.

"Papa, I didn't know you were there! Thank you!" She stood from the instrument and curtseyed to him demurely.

"My dear, you are a wonder. I love to listen to you play. What was it?"

"*Andante Favori* in F Major. It's by Beethoven. Mrs McIntosh has been helping me with it. I love it too," said Laura.

"Laurie, dear, I shall miss hearing you play when you're in New Jersey," admitted the doting father.

"Papa, I thought you and Mother *wanted* us to go to St Mary's Hall?"

"Well, of course we do. We want the best for you, but we both shall still miss you two girls. The little boys will too, especially Willy and Val."

"Why Willy and Val, Papa?"

"Because Lizzie and her brothers are thick as thieves, you know. They're always outside together engaged in a quest of some sort, while you are here delighting us with music."

"Oh, of course all of them will miss her. She's their leader and chief scientist, isn't she? Whatever will she do when she's at a school with only girls?"

"P'raps she will become a leader of girls there, unless she discovers the boys' school next door!"

"Papa, you don't worry she will break the rules, do you?" asked Laura, furrowing her brow.

"I hope not, Laurie. But Lizzie's not an easy girl to control, is she? She may strike out on her own if she sees an opportunity or a challenge. I hope you'll watch over her while you are away."

"Papa, from what I've read, there are strict rules against meeting the young men of Burlington College. I shall be sure to suggest that Elizabeth behave well, so as not to embarrass our family. Are you very concerned that she will?"

"I'm certain 'twould never be intentional, but you know she's rather headstrong and doesn't always think before she acts, my dear Laurie." Mr Fuller, the experienced father of eight very different children, knew Lizzie had always been the most adventurous of the three girls.

"All right, Papa. I understand your concern. I shall endeavour to influence her behaviour if I can," promised Laura solemnly, as she patted his hand.

"And I intend to remind Bishop Doane as well as to her high-spirited nature when I see him in Burlington," said her father with a smile.

CHAPTER 6

Journey to New Jersey

THURSDAY, 27 SEPTEMBER 1855, ST CATHARINES
At the Great Western Railway station on the western edge of town, carriages were dropping off passengers for the early morning train to New York State. The Fuller and Burns families were in place, tickets in hand, their trunks ready to be loaded into the baggage cars when they arrived from Jordan Station and points west. Emma, Julia, Laura, and Elizabeth were huddled together in the Ladies' Waiting Room, talking excitedly with Mrs Fuller. The two fathers, Thomas Burns and Tom Fuller, stood by the long windows over in the smoke-filled Men's Waiting Room, discussing the details of the impending journey. All three adults kept looking expectantly toward the station doors. Where was Margaret Jane?

At last the train chugged away from St Catharines after many tearful goodbyes. The four schoolgirls took seats on the platform side of the car and waved through the sooty windows until they could no longer see the parent they left behind. The more experienced passengers who boarded with them took seats that might provide the best views of the Niagara Gorge and the river rushing through it.

❦ ❦ ❦

Unfortunately, Laura and Elizabeth Fuller were disappointed. The famous Horseshoe Falls at Niagara, a natural wonder of the world, was not visible eastbound in the dense mist thrown up by the falls. As the locomotive slowly crossed Johann Augustus Roebling's marvellous suspension bridge, the girls promised each other they would be sure to see the falls upon their return. Perhaps they could even convince their fathers to take a ride under them on the famous *Maid of the Mist*!

❦ ❦ ❦

The cars rumbled along for an hour or so southward to the station at Tonawanda, now a busy railroad hub as well as the western terminus of New York's Erie Canal. There the party changed to the Canandaigua and Elmira Railway line. Halfway between Tonawanda and Batavia, New York, the passengers were annoyed when the brakes squealed, and there was an hour-long stop to wait on a siding for a westbound train to pass. The girls busied themselves with needlework, reading, or conversation to while away the time. Mr Fuller admired the gently rolling hills from his window seat when he tired from his own reading. Finally, the other train passed, and their engine started off again with a lurch and a puff of steam. When the cars arrived at the picturesque country town of Batavia, hungry travellers disembarked and headed down the dusty street to find their mid-day meal. The train would be stopped for about thirty minutes this time to load more passengers, as well as the water and wood to make the steam that powered the hulking locomotive.

Mr Fuller had brought a supply of food from home for his group of young ladies during the day-long trip to Watkins. Since there was no dining car, the Fuller party remained in their seats, where the girls cradled paper-wrapped treats on their full skirts, protected by the large white linen napkins their chaperone had provided. Stewards offered thirsty passengers glasses of water at all the stops. The girls were careful lest they spill when the engine shuddered as it sat on the tracks, breathing like a legendary dragon.

The meal finished and all passengers returned, the conductor called "all aboard" one last time before the train headed to the wide flat valley east toward Canandaigua. It was a quaint little settlement at the north end of the Finger Lake of the same name where the Canandaigua and Elmira Railroad tracks turned south. The four-year-old railroad snaked through the fertile countryside between Canandaigua Lake and Seneca Lake on its way to Watkins. The whole region was becoming prosperous as a result of its recent agricultural successes and the extensive system of railroads available to take produce to market in all directions. The new train routes had also spurred development of resort towns on the beautiful Finger Lakes. Summer vacationers from Buffalo, Rochester, and New York City ventured there to enjoy the change of scenery and cooler temperatures.

A couple of stops and two hours later, the train arrived at the tiny station at Penn Yan, creatively named for the Pennsylvanians and New England Yankees who'd settled it. The town sat at the top of a beautiful lake whose bright blue water glistened in the sun. The girls could not believe the colour was real. Early European settlers called it Crooked Lake, although the indigenous tribes used different names for it. The Iroquois named it Keuka or "canoe landing", and the Seneca language translated it as "lake with an elbow". Land surveyors later determined that it was indeed Y-shaped. On the west side of the lake, the passengers could see tidy farmhouses and outbuildings up on a bluff. Hardwood trees, still full of green leaves, and the occasional pine tree lined either side of the tracks, at times so close the girls thought they might reach out and touch them. Some enterprising farmers had planted grape vines in neat rows along the lakeshore, evidence of the fledgling winemaking industry in New York State.

The city of Elmira lay about four more hours south. It was a prosperous railroad junction of over ten thousand people and boasted numerous inns offering weary strangers a place to rest. However, on their first day of travel, the St Mary's Hall group intended to reach only Watkins, a village station at the head of Seneca Lake, another of the glacial Finger Lakes in western New York. Watkins had equally good accommodations and ended their travel at just the right time of day so the party could enjoy a decent supper and longer rest. It had already been a challenging experience for those who, like Lizzie Fuller, were not accustomed to sitting for prolonged periods. The girls and the gentleman accompanying them all looked forward to a hot bath and a good meal after a long day inhaling wood smoke and being jolted back and forth over the tracks.

❦ ❦ ❦

Laura and Elizabeth Fuller shared a small room on the third floor of the Jefferson House and, after their baths and an excellent meal, were preparing for bed. The girls unbuttoned each other's dinner dresses and hung them on the wall pegs to air overnight. In the morning they would roll them carefully and place them back in the valises to wear again the next evening. Once comfortable in their white flannel nightdresses, the sisters combed each other's long hair, then braided and tied it loosely with a ribbon for the night. They brushed their teeth at the washstand with the new bone and horsehair bristle brushes Mrs Fuller had purchased at the Hendershots' emporium in Thorold. At last, they put on knit nightcaps to keep their heads warm in the chilly room.

The Fuller girls were still thinking about Margaret Jane, who had not boarded the train in St Catharines. They wondered what had happened that no message was sent about a change in plans. The two sisters knelt side by side and recited the Lord's Prayer before they offered a silent prayer of thanks for their continued safe travel and for Margaret Jane, whatever her trouble might be. Glad to be able to recline at last, they climbed into the bed and pulled the heavy wool blankets up to their chins. The girls kissed each other goodnight on the cheek and said, as they did every night at home with a giggle, "Don't let the bedbugs bite!" The duo was soon sound asleep, exhausted from the excitement of the day and the promise of more adventure, for to-morrow they faced yet another long day of travel.

❦ ❦ ❦

The day dawned cloudy and cool in Watkins. *The weather may be turning poor after the last few beautiful early autumn days*, thought Mr Fuller, as he knocked on the door of his daughters' room. A few moments later, Laura opened the door and peeked out, rubbing her eyes in the dim light of the hallway.

"Good morning, Laurie. I trust you slept well?"

"Yes, Papa, of course we did. It was lovely and warm in the bed with Elizabeth. But it doesn't feel so warm now though! I shall wake her, and we shall be down to breakfast in two shakes of a lamb's tail," said Laura.

"I shall meet you in the dining room then, Laurie. Mind the train leaves at eight and a half," he said, checking the gift from his wife—a gold pocket watch whose chain drooped from his vest loop. "And now I shall wake Emma and Julia." He turned on his heel and walked down the hall to the next room, where he repeated his message, before descending to the first floor to take his morning cup of tea.

❦ ❦ ❦

The three passenger cars were full on the southbound morning train to Elmira, New York where the travellers would connect to the third line of their journey, the New York and Erie Railroad. To-day Emma and Julia Burns were sitting together in the fourth row near the back of the car, giggling about some cows they had observed through the smudged windows. Laura and Lizzie were deep in conversation while their father dozed, by now bored with the routine of travel. He was not unlike his daughter Lizzie, preferring to be engaged in activity or conversation. After two water stops and one for wood, the locomotive chugged into the Binghamton station. Once more the train emptied, but this time the five Canadians joined the crowd seeking nourishment in the station restaurant or at one of the nearby inns.

After the travellers returned from their hurried and less than satisfying mid-day dinner at the station restaurant, the engine creaked and snorted its way out of the town. Light rain began to fall. If cold southwesterly winds blew over Lake Erie, the air rising from its shallow, warmer water produced heavy snowfall north and east of the lake. They were already well south of the area of New York State prone to this phenomenon. Mr Fuller gave thanks it wasn't any colder to-day. In fact, it was warm enough in the car to remove one's wrap.

The conductor took all aspects of his job seriously, especially keeping his passengers comfortable. He stoked the two wood stoves throughout the day to keep an even temperature in each car he tended. It was impossible to read anything while bouncing along the tracks; his twenty passengers occupied themselves chatting and gazing out the windows. Soon they would be tracing the meandering course of the west branch of the Delaware River. The train would stop at stations on both sides of the same river that also flowed past St Mary's Hall.

❦ ❦ ❦

"Jersey City!" bellowed the conductor, as the train braked on its way into the little wooden station. Rain was coming down in sheets for the second day. The four girls did not look forward to leaving the warm, dry rail car, even though it meant the end of a shorter day of travel. To-morrow morning they were to take a new variety of transportation, a steamship ferry, no matter what the weather. They would have to travel south down Newark Bay into the Arthur Kill and then a short distance out into Raritan Bay. Their destination was the port of South Amboy, New Jersey, the northern terminus of the Camden and Amboy Rail Road. The last rail road connexion! To-morrow afternoon they would finally reach Burlington, New Jersey. It had already been a difficult and uncomfortable three days of smoky, noisy, bumpy railway travel, but the end was in sight.

During the journey, bit by bit, Emma and Julia described life at St Mary's Hall to the Fuller girls. Now Laura was anxious to experience the life of a pupil there herself. Elizabeth was still not so sure she would like it.

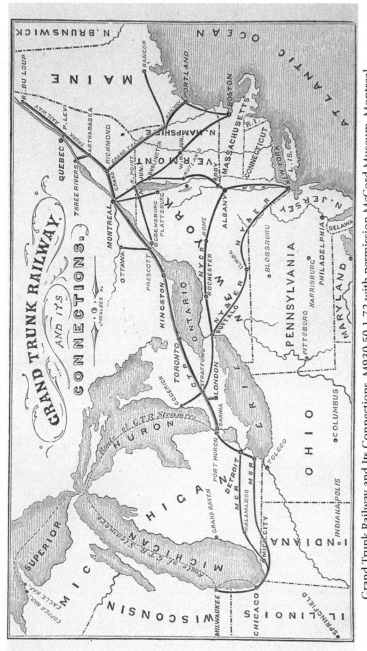

Grand Trunk Railway and Its Connections, M930.50.1.72 with permission McCord Museum, Montreal.

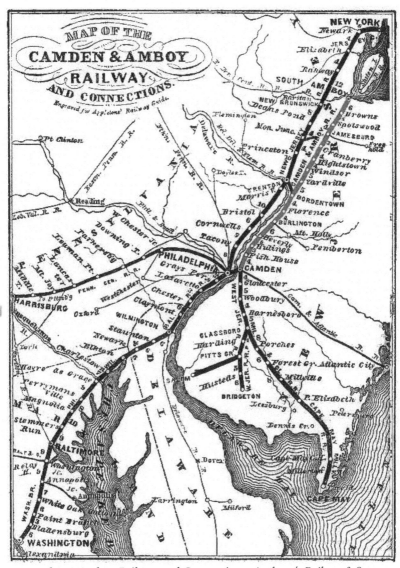

Camden & Amboy Railway and Connections: *Appleton's Railway & Steam Navigation Guide*, 1869. Wikimedia Commons. Courtesy of CPRR.org.

CHAPTER 7

Arrival at St Mary's Hall

SUNDAY, 30 SEPTEMBER 1855, BURLINGTON, NEW JERSEY

"Papa, when shall we get there?" asked Lizzie again, as she peered through the window of the car.

"I'm sure you'll see the steeple of St Mary's Church, daughter, even in this rain, before we reach the city. Remember how we came into Elmira and Binghamton? You could see the church spires before anything else. We're due in Burlington in half an hour. Keep watch, my dear."

At a quarter-mile away, through the hazy rain-filled sky, the soaring spire of St Mary's Episcopal Church appeared above the trees. It was indeed the first landmark visible as the locomotive slowed to enter the nearly two hundred-year-old city. Emma clutched Julia's hand, relieved that their latest journey was over. Emma, in particular, was excited to renew her friendships there and embark on a new round of studies. Julia was glad to be back with her friends at St Mary's too, but not as anxious to see what this term would bring academically.

When the train came to a stop with a long squeal and a blast of steam, Laura rose to collect her cloak from a vacant seat. Lizzie stood and then could not find her reticule. She bent to look for it on the floor under the seat. It must have slipped away sometime since their last stop just a few miles ago in Florence. She was sure she had had it in her lap then.

Lizzie was horrified to think she had lost the beautiful new silk and leather bag, a gift from her mother for the trip. So far, she had been able to keep track of it. There were only a few coins and a handkerchief in it, but she did not want to lose this, her very first grown-up accessory. What would she say to her mother if she lost it on the first go?

Laura would be sure to tell Mother if Lizzie did not.

Lizzie was about to get down on all fours to look for the reticule on the muddy floor when Emma playfully dangled it in front of her face with a quizzical look. "Are you missing something, Elizabeth?" asked Emma. The reticule had indeed slid behind her seat. Emma had recognised it as Lizzie's and picked it up by the drawstring as she passed by.

Lizzie sighed with relief and thanked Emma profusely as she took the dainty bag. She brushed it off as best she could. She was also glad that her mother had wisely chosen a medium shade of brown for her daughter's gloves. Lizzie thought, *In future I shall have to take better care of my new things.*

❦ ❦ ❦

The Camden and Amboy Rail Road was laid down the middle of Broad Street. There being no station house yet in Burlington, the train stopped at its intersection with High Street. When the engine's bell rang to indicate the cars' arrival, some passengers were still enjoying the comfort of a small waiting room in the nearby Beldin House. Outside, others ready to board pulled their woolen cloaks tighter round them as they left the protection of their closed carriages waiting in the street. Carriages, horses, and waggons streamed to the train from all directions: High Street from the city wharf on the north end, and the countryside to the south, plus both ends of Broad.

After so many days' travel, the Fuller party knew they did not have to dash out into the inclement weather. There were plenty of other passengers ready and willing to leave the warmth of the little wooden cars before they did. They were now the seasoned travellers!

Mr Fuller took out three large umbrellas made of oiled black silk stretched over slender whalebone ribs: one for the Burns girls, one for his daughters, and one for himself. The umbrellas had come in handy these last three days of bad weather, despite being cumbersome and heavy to carry when wet. Although the girls were eager to leave the train that had confined them, they waited patiently until all the other passengers exited. Mr Fuller left the car first and arranged for porters to take their valises to the inn. The trunks would be delivered to the school before nightfall.

The conductor helped the young ladies, clutching their long full skirts, descend the glistening wooden steps placed beside the car. They hoped not to slip down or snag their skirts. Mr Fuller gallantly opened each umbrella, and he and his charges made the short walk over to the Beldin House on the corner with two porters and a cart in tow.

❦ ❦ ❦

Mr Fuller hired a closed carriage with horses and driver from the livery next door to take them all to the Green Bank neighbourhood of Burlington. He also asked the driver to take the most interesting route to the school. With Emma and Julia as guides, the Fullers were anxious to see the city.

The streets, mud-filled from the previous days of torrential rains, were rutted. The driver had to negotiate them with care to avoid damaging the wheels and axles, or unduly jostling his passengers. When the storm finally moved out, northerly winds accompanying a new high-pressure system would bring crisp, cold Canadian air and brilliant sunshine to the area. The streets would soon be dry again.

Emma and Julia, who had already spent ten months in Burlington, pointed out important landmarks along the way as the horses clip-clopped down High Street toward the busy city wharf. First on the left, they passed the red brick Friends Meeting House. Shops of every kind lined both sides of the busy thoroughfare. At Union Street, two blocks before the river with its wharves,

Emma pointed out the historic site of the City Hall and Allinson Apothecary on the right. The carriage turned left into Union Street, and Laura remarked the neat brick houses, many of which were built when New Jersey was still a British colony. At the end of the block, the driver made a right turn down Wood Street. Emma explained this section was called Professors' Row because many of the married faculty lived in it. Shortly after, the carriage turned left into Pearl Street where there was just a handful of newer houses with fields, small orchards, and kitchen gardens separating them. Milch cows grazed in the fields, and chickens flew out of the path of the carriage. Another right turn brought them to Talbot Street, named for the first rector of St Mary's Episcopal Church. On the right at the end of the block, Emma showed them the home of the Presbyterian minister, the Rev. Mr Cortlandt Van Rensselaer, with its own river landing. Opposite was a stately brick Colonial style house built nearly one hundred years ago in 1756, the former summer home of Edward Shippen, a Philadelphia lawyer. Shippen was the father of Peggy, who married the notorious Revolutionary War traitor Benedict Arnold.

The carriage turned left into Delaware Street, a narrow lane that paralleled the river. A few hundred yards farther along the Green Bank, the carriage passed the several buildings of St Mary's Hall, including the little Chapel of the Holy Innocents. It drew up to the entrance of Riverside, the gracious home of Bishop and Mrs Doane. Designed by Scottish architect John Notman and completed in 1838, the three-storey Italianate house overlooking the river and the Pennsylvania shore was finished in buff-coloured stucco with brown trim. It was the grandest house in the city and one of the first of its design in the United States.

When the carriage stopped in the crushed oyster shell driveway, a young ginger-haired steward was waiting to greet them on the stone terrace of the house. Dressed for the wind and cool weather in a black woolen cloak and bowler hat, Michael Dunn helped Mr Fuller and the girls out of the carriage. With a lilting Irish brogue, he welcomed them to Riverside. He recognised both Emma and Julia and called them by name, "Miss Burns". Mr Fuller was delighted to hear Michael's accent, but did not admit to his own Irish heritage, not knowing whether it might cause discomfort for the man. English and Irish strife remained unresolved.

The girls gathered their skirts to walk up the three low granite steps leading to the terrace and a pair of arched front doors. Above this entrance to the house was a lovely balcony supported by two carved brackets, a perfect place for viewing the river in good weather. Michael opened the doors for them with a bow, and the guests entered the vestibule where Michael's wife Jane received their wraps.

Jane ushered them through a set of massive double doors into a spacious reception hall paved with terra cotta tiles. Laura heard footsteps clicking and echoing up an unseen stairwell. Then through an open doorway on her left, the girl spied the stairs in question. The stairway to the second floor featured an interesting cast iron balustrade topped by a mahogany handrail supported by a carved lotus-shaped newel post. The plain plaster walls of the stair hall were cream-coloured and contrasted sharply with the dark wood of the railing. The staircase itself was decorated with intricate carvings under each step. Laura thought it was unfortunate that such beautiful woodwork was hidden from view.

Mrs Doane, a tiny, serious-looking lady with dark eyes, her grey hair pulled straight back and arranged in a bun, stood in the middle of the reception hall. She wore a delicate white lace cap on her head and a similar shawl round her shoulders, tied loosely over her ample bosom. Charming pearl and gold earrings dangled from her ears. As she introduced herself, she extended her hand to each guest, adding in a soft voice that the bishop was in the library just to her right. Emma and Julia were a bit surprised that she did not seem to remember them. However, they had been away for nearly six months again, and they only saw Mrs Doane on special occasions. The lady would have to memorise the names of over 150 girls, perhaps too much to ask of someone over sixty-five!

The elegant wood-paneled library featured three walls of floor-to-ceiling bookshelves filled with beautiful leather volumes protected by glass doors. In the centre of the room was a refectory table surrounded by ten sturdy wooden chairs with red leather seats. A pleasant wood fire crackled in the arched fireplace, beginning to counter the autumn chill brought in by the north winds blowing off the river. Bishop George Washington Doane stood with his back to the full-length bay window that gave out on the Delaware. Bathed in the fading sunlight that streamed through it, the tall, bespectacled middle-aged gentleman in clerical garb had a fairly military bearing. His grey hair was worn long, and it curled down round his ears, although at age fifty-six, he was now balding on top. He had a long straight nose, firm jaw, and square chin. Bishop Doane was fully engaged in his role as host, eyes twinkling through his spectacles. He was animated as he chatted with the fourteen other new pupils who had arrived that day with their chaperones, and he laughed often.

The bishop looked over and saw Tom Fuller and the girls at the doorway. He excused himself from his conversation and strode over to greet his newest visitors with a wide smile and outstretched hand.

"Mr Fuller, I presume—from Canada West! I heard you'd arrived at the inn. How nice to see you again. It was what? Two years ago that we met at the convention? How was your journey? And please introduce me to the young ladies. I understand you've also escorted the Burns girls back to us to-day," said the bishop, as he shook hands with the Canadian clergyman.

"Bishop Doane, the pleasure is again mine. May I present my daughters, Laura and Elizabeth Fuller, and yes, Emma and Julia have returned once more from St Catharines," said Tom, standing aside so the girls could greet the bishop.

Each girl curtseyed and bowed her head slightly as Mr Fuller mentioned her name.

Lizzie murmured, "Pleased to meet you, sir."

Laura asked, "How do you do, Bishop?"

Bishop Doane smiled and nodded to his new pupils. "Young ladies, welcome to St Mary's Hall. I hope you'll be comfortable here with us, your new family."

❦ ❦ ❦

MONDAY, 1 OCTOBER 1855

After a delicious hot meal in the crowded hotel dining room and a good night's rest, the four girls from Canada enjoyed a final breakfast together at the Beldin House with Mr Fuller. The hotel maids were busy, and so they packed their own valises hastily. Mr Fuller requested a porter for his baggage. His train back to Jersey

City would depart at half-past twelve; he would have just enough time to deliver the girls to school and to take his leave.

At ten o'clock, the bishop's own carriage arrived to take the party back to the Green Bank. Bishop Doane had insisted on extending this courtesy to his Canadian colleague. The bishop remembered meeting Tom Fuller when he headed the Toronto delegation to the General Convention in New York City a few years back. They had discussed his daughters' becoming pupils at the school, but they were at that time too young. Since then, the two clergymen had kept up a correspondence that discussed not only church issues, but also the bishop's rather radical philosophy of educating girls.

The carriage footman helped each of the passengers step out of the conveyance and then off the long rectangular carriage stone in front of the Main House of St Mary's Hall. Mr Fuller stood back on the brick sidewalk to allow Emma and Julia to pass by first. The sisters started up the familiar path arm in arm, anxious to see what changes had been made to the place while they were home for the summer term.

Samuel Gummere had built the red brick building, or Main House of St Mary's Hall, in 1829 to be a Quaker school for young ladies. It boasted four stories with a fenced widow's walk on the roof ridge. From it the pupils could, in fine weather, take some fresh air and have a bird's eye view of the river and neighbourhood. There were small dormer windows on the fourth floor where staff slept. Pupils slept in two large rooms on the third floor. Full-length windows on all four sides of the two lower floors let in plenty of air and light for classrooms and public rooms.

As Lizzie started up the walk behind Emma and Julia, she looked to her right and clapped her hands with glee. She ran over to the tree to rub its smooth grey bark.

"Look, Papa, it's a lovely, tall beech tree, just like ours, and right next to the chapel! I shall be reminded of our home at Beechlands whenever I see it."

Mr Fuller winked at Lizzie, admiring her love and knowledge of nature, even at her tender age. He offered an arm to each of his daughters, and together they climbed the six wide granite steps to the stately front porch.

Mr Fuller rang the wrought iron doorbell mounted beside the towering white double doors. Michael Dunn, this time attired in a crisp, white tunic over black trousers, opened them, smiled, and bowed to the visitors. With a flourish, he indicated the direction they should go to find the parlour.

"Right this way, ladies and sir."

Mr Gummere had designed the interior of the house on a double plan. In case his school failed, it could have been easily remodelled into two dwellings with the simple addition of some partitions. The entry hall with its white plaster walls was enclosed by two louvered Venetian doors. The louvers closed to keep out the north wind in winter and if opened, allowed any breeze from the river to circulate in the hot summers. Inside those doors the hall was divided by a central brick partition, and beyond the partition, a double stairway led to the upper floors and down to the basement. On either side of the centre hall were two parlours that extended the depth of the house. The cheery fires in each of their fireplaces to-day augmented the recently installed gas heat that flowed through ornamental black iron registers embedded in the polished oak floors.

The girls and Mr Fuller entered the front east parlour. Lizzie looked warily at the only girl ahead of them and wondered if she were her age. Laura looked around the room and felt immediately at home. Colourful Persian rugs, similar to ones her mother favoured, covered most of the floor. Above the fireplace a pair of oil lamps sat at either end of the black marble mantelpiece. An oil painting of a seascape hung on the wall above it. Comfortable chairs flanked the fireplace and an embroidered fire screen stood to one side.

Miss Stanley, the vice principal, was seated at an escritoire in the middle of the room in front of the fireplace. She looked up and beckoned to the latest arrivals. When she recognised the Burns girls, she welcomed them back with a genuine smile. Mr Fuller approached Miss Stanley and introduced himself and his daughters. After she entered their names and addresses in the register, the woman gave each girl a card indicating the room where she would lodge, the name of the teacher in charge of the room, and that of the matron, Mrs La Motte. Miss Stanley was nothing if not organised! It had taken her several recent evenings to write them all out in her precise and elegant hand. Then, to make room for newcomers, the administrator asked those already registered to move into the rear parlour to visit with each other.

Emma and Julia, who had lived in the same dormitory room during their previous two terms, showed their cards to Laura and Lizzie. When Lizzie saw they were all in the same room, she cheered.

"Oh, hurrah, Laura! I *shall* be with you. I was so afraid that I wouldn't know a soul in the room. Now I shall be able to relax a little," said Lizzie with a sigh.

Laura hoped so too, and looking at Lizzie, she said, "Try not to worry so much. God is watching over us all. Nought bad is going to happen now. Our journey was absolutely smooth to get here and so much could have happened—train derailments, bridges collapsing, or steamboats sinking!"

Young Lizzie looked horrified at hearing all this from her normally calm and quiet sister.

"I'm sorry, Elizabeth! I didn't mean to frighten you, but it's true. I heard Bishop Doane tell Papa there was a terrible train accident here August last. We have been in God's hands all this time. Have faith in Him," counselled her sister.

"'Tis so, my dear Lizzie," said Mr Fuller, as he put his hand on her shoulder. "God is always watching over us. And with that thought, my daughters, I shall take my leave. You must get settled."

He embraced both his daughters warmly, kissing them each on the forehead. He bade good-bye to the four girls, satisfied that they were in competent, caring hands.

❧ ❧ ❧

After Mr Fuller left, the girls found the rear parlour also too warm, since they had not removed their outdoor clothing. The little room would be crowded with fourteen other new girls and the parents or guardians who accompanied them that day. Emma suggested they go up to their dormitory.

The sisters left the Main House through a rear door out to the *piazza*, a sort of hallway originally designed to be open in the Italian style. At some point in the school's short history, it was extended and enclosed to link smaller buildings added to house additional pupils. The present hallway stretched across the back of the Main House and connected the laboratory and gymnasium building, another small dormitory annex, the chapel, and the nursery building. Behind the nursery and adjacent to the walking Circle was a recent gift from a missionary in China, a young gingko tree whose fluttering fan-shaped leaves to-day were turning a beautiful golden colour. The little tree was already the subject of much attention by the girls of St Mary's Hall and sure to be beloved as it grew.

The *piazza* provided access to "the Circle" behind the house via a set of wooden steps. In the Circle mature trees shaded the pupils during their required hours of outdoor time, either sitting on benches fitted round the trees or taking exercise, such as engaging in games or walks along gravel paths through the bishop's well-tended flower gardens.

The girls passed through the hallway and stopped at the cloakroom where they hung their wraps on wooden pegs. Around the corner they entered the gymnasium, a long room that had two pillars down the middle of it. Lizzie loved the idea of being active indoors in bad weather, something she could not do very well at home in Canada. The room connected to it was smaller, and Emma called it the "la-bor'-a-to-ry". Lizzie had never been in such a place and couldn't wait to explore the mysterious collections that Julia said were stored in the cupboards on each wall. Perhaps she could have brought her own precious items after all. The teacher might have need of specimens from Canada. She would have to ask if Papa should send down her box. *Oh, but what if it were lost on the way! P'raps not a good idea after all,* she thought.

The group retraced their steps out to the hallway and took a set of stairs divided by a landing. At the top of the stairwell were two hallways. One went to the east annex dormitory, and the second led to their own on the second floor of the laboratory building. Laura wondered if she would ever find her way round this rabbit warren!

Miss Eliza Adams, the teacher-in-charge of the dormitory, was there to greet them. Emma made the introductions. Miss Adams informed the new girls about the basic rules of the room and the immediate schedule for the remainder of the day.

Eleven girls were expected to sleep in the dormitory. They had to wash and dress together in the limited space between the narrow beds that lined the walls. A storage chest for each girl was at the foot of her bed—in it a pupil could place books; keepsakes; small pieces of clothing like sashes and ribbons; and personal care items such as brushes, combs, and hairpins. Dresses with their full, gathered skirts were hung on pegs in wardrobes behind each bed. There were also shelves to store the hatboxes for their bonnets. Beside the bed, each girl had a washstand equipped with towel rack, ewer, and basin and under the bed, a chamber pot. The thin white linen towels issued to each girl dried quickly on the racks—if the room were warm.

In addition to the new gas heat system, a lone fireplace on the south wall heated the dormitory. Every morning in the colder months, porters brought in loads of wood from a common store kept in a far corner of the grounds. The female servants, most of them young women who had fled Ireland's serious potato famine in the 1840s, were tasked with keeping the fires going.

The entire structure featured glass windows of six-over-six panes to admit the maximum sunlight. Because the building was located in the shadow of the Main House on the north side and somewhat shaded by trees growing in the Circle on the south side, its three rooms were still dim. To augment the natural light, the dormitory and indeed the whole school now had gaslight wall sconces that were trimmed low at night. This was a great improvement over the old sperm whale oil lamps that required frequent cleaning. The teachers were the only ones allowed to keep emergency tallow candles in the event the gas failed, as fire was an ever-present threat.

❦ ❦ ❦

For the vacation month of October, only six girls occupied the large dormitory room since Margaret Jane had curiously not made the trip. In addition to the four Canadian girls were Anna Cooke from outside New York City and little Vicky Haight, Lizzie's age, from Westfield, New York, across Lake Erie from the Niagara Peninsula. The Burns and Fuller sisters did their best to make them feel part of the group in spite of their being outnumbered.

They were the sole American pupils in the room! So far everyone was getting along famously.

Lizzie remained a bit anxious about how things would go once the others moved in before term. She wondered if she would still be the youngest in the room after vacation ended. Miss Adams had not yet provided that information.

"Elizabeth," called Laura. "Have you a white button in your box? I lost one from my *basque* to-day. I can't wear it like this to-morrow."

"I'm sure I do, sister, but I put my button box and sewing kit down at the bottom of my storage chest. I didn't think I would need it. I'll look for you in a minute ... You know, I have been meaning to ask you something ever since Papa left. Would you mind terribly calling me Lizzie from now on? I much prefer it to Elizabeth. I always assume I have done something wrong if you call me that—as if I hear Mother calling me. I would like my new friends here to call me Lizzie too."

"Whatever do you mean?" asked the older girl.

"I mean, we're here in Burlington, among new friends, and I would like to be called Lizzie, like Papa does. It just seems more like who I am."

"I don't know if Mother will approve of that, Elizab ... I mean, Lizzie."

"She doesn't correct Papa, does she? It's *my* name, after all!"

"Of course, 'tis your name, but they gave it you! At your baptism."

"Oh, Laura, honestly! I call you Laurie sometimes, and so does Papa, so why does it bother you if I am called Lizzie?"

"I guess it shouldn't, but 'tis going to be difficult for me after twelve years calling you Elizabeth!"

CHAPTER 8

October Vacation

TUESDAY, 9 OCTOBER 1855

"Elizabeth, are you awake?" whispered Laurie.

"Mmmm … Laurie? What is it?"

"We have to go to Philadelphia to-day, but I don't really feel like travelling again so soon. I've been thinking about it all night. I didn't sleep very well."

"Why not?"

"I was thinking about those poor people who died in the railway accident."

"But, Laurie, you were the one who told me not to worry, that we were in God's hands all the time."

"Yes, I know, but now I wonder if it is safe to go."

"Well, that's what the telegraph is for, Laurie. Papa told me the conductor sends a message that the train is coming, and then the others have to wait for ours to pass."

"But that didn't work here last summer, did it? I think I would rather *sail* down to the city, would you not?"

"Sailing is slower, Laurie. It's fine if you aren't in a hurry. But you don't go unless there's wind, unless you are on a steamer, of course. The railway is much faster and more comfortable, and no one will get seasick!"

"I suppose you are right, Elizab—Lizzie." Laura was still getting used to calling her sister by her nickname.

Just then they heard the first peals of the chapel bell to wake the pupils. The six girls slipped out of bed to dress and make their beds. Then they fell onto their knees for the customary ten minutes of private devotions and Bible reading before they made their way downstairs to breakfast. Laura's prayers included one for their safety on the trip to Philadelphia.

❦ ❦ ❦

A line of eighteen girls, punctuated by two chaperones, walked two by two, linked arm in arm, down the Green Bank. They turned the corner into narrow Talbot Street between Stone Cottage, the Van Rensselaer house, and the Shippen House with its scandalous association with American traitors exiled to England. Lizzie and Vicky, the two youngest pupils, giggled as they shuffled the fallen leaves and acorns in front of them; the older girls moved sedately along, talking to their partners in hushed tones. Two hens fluttered out over the street as the girls walked toward them.

At the corner of Broad Street, the group turned east toward High Street and walked by New and Old St Mary's Church. Their train had not yet arrived, and the pupils enjoyed the free time to mingle and chat with one another.

A Quaker lady passed by the group, and after she was out of earshot, Emma said, "Laura, if you think you've seen enough Quaker ladies here, wait till you get to Philadelphia! It's an old Quaker city like Burlington. The English Quaker William Penn established it as a haven of religious tolerance."

"I've seen Quakers before, Emma. There's a Quaker meeting over in Pelham, you know. I've often seen the ladies shopping at Hendershot's too."

"Well, we have more than a few Quaker families in St Catharines. They've been quite involved with settling the fugitive American slaves. As you just saw, most of the Quaker ladies here wear the same plain colours with white shawls and, of course, their distinctive little bonnets. I hear them often speaking to each other, saying thee and thou. It's—"

Lizzie tapped Laura on the arm, interrupting Emma's lecture, much to Laura's relief. "I know we're going to have dinner at a restaurant, but what else are we to do all day?"

Emma turned and looked at Lizzie, annoyed at the impertinence of the younger girl. "Elizabeth, we were talking, your sister and I."

Lizzie was abashed and apologised to Emma forthwith. She was learning that the older girl could be a bit abrasive, but then continuing undeterred, Lizzie repeated her question.

"Well, what are we going to do?"

Emma scowled at Lizzie, sighed and said, "Mr Hewitt is conducting us to the Athenaeum first. It's another beautiful building designed by Mr John Notman. He was the architect of our chapel and Riverside, Elizabeth. It's quite a pleasant place to spend time. Then we shall dine and drive out to Laurel Hill Cemetery before taking our ferry back to New Jersey at three and a half. We should be back in Burlington for supper at six."

"What's the Athenaeum?" asked Laura.

"A museum," said Julia. "Wait till you see the ceilings! Over twenty feet high! Chock full of furniture and books. American, of course. They have lots of interesting old objects to see."

"Very well, but why are we going to a cemetery, Emma? What can you do there?" asked Lizzie.

"It's quite beautiful and known for its landscaping. Mr Notman designed it as well as our bishop's gardens. Mr Hewitt likes to do this trip every autumn for new pupils. It's my third visit. I think it's a lovely, peaceful place to take a walk in fine weather. You'll see," said Emma.

🐝 🐝 🐝

The train arrived safely in Camden an hour later, much to Laura's relief. The scholars disembarked and didn't have to wait long for the little steamship ferry to take them across to Dock Street on the west bank of the Delaware River. The crossing was uneventful, and the group didn't mind walking five blocks west to the Athenaeum at Washington Square in the cool, crisp

71

weather. The ten-year-old brownstone building was built in the Italian palazzo style that Notman was popularising in America. It had three storeys and featured a balcony over the front door supported by carved brackets, similar to Riverside's. The windows of each floor were of different dimensions though, with the longest ones being on the second storey where the library and reading rooms were. They provided ample sunlight for the patrons.

Laura was amazed by the tall Corinthian columns in the elegant library and Great Stairwell. After an hour exploring the collections in the magnificent building, the scholars and their guides were ready for dinner. The group walked north to Market Street and on the way, they passed Independence Hall in the oldest part of the colonial city where history was made in 1776.

Market Street was bustling at this time of day. There were people from all over the world. Sailors and passengers leaving sea-going ships docked at the old port were all looking for a meal or a place to rest. Catering to their needs, shops, hotels, taverns, restaurants and eating houses lined the thoroughfare. The girls heard people speaking European languages as well as the various accents of English from different parts of the British Empire. England, Scotland, Ireland, and the Caribbean islands were represented.

Mr Hewitt had made arrangements with the proprietors of his favourite restaurant in Market Street to have a hot meal ready for them at noon. They could afterward carry on with their visit to the cemetery and be back in time for the ferry and train to Burlington. Lizzie thought the best part of the meal was the ice cream—flavoured with bits of raspberries!

After their dinner at Mr Fulmer's restaurant, the St Mary's Hall group waited in Market Street for a horse-drawn omnibus to take them out to Laurel Hill, up Seventh Street and on to Ridge Avenue. The cemetery was much too far to walk, being north and west of the centre of town. These days the omnibuses had to compete with cars running along the street railway laid down the middle of Market Street. Pedestrians had to be alert and look both ways. When an unoccupied omnibus stopped, Mr Hewitt paid the fare and helped his charges board. As they passed by Franklin Square and Arch Street, he told them about the park named for Benjamin Franklin and the house where Betsy Ross, the seamstress who sewed the first American flag, purportedly had lived. Those two sites would have to wait for another visit to the city.

🐝 🐝 🐝

Lizzie was glad she had come to Laurel Hill after all. It was indeed beautiful with many different kinds of trees and plants overlooking the placid Schuylkill River. She began to count the trees and gave up after fifty-eight. She wandered among the sculpted memorials and tombstones, including one placed for a famous American named Thomas McKean, a signer of the Declaration of Independence and a former Pennsylvania governor.

The girl was imagining how much her little brothers would enjoy this place too, when she spied an inviting green hill leading down to the river. Suddenly she had a yen to lie down and just roll all the way down it. She looked round and saw no one who could object.

She sat, lay back across the hill, stretched out her limbs, crossed her arms and pushed herself off with one foot. Down she went, over and over, picking up speed. Then afraid she might not be able to stop, Lizzie grabbed at the grass as she rolled, pulling tufts out by the roots. At last, the slope of the hill decreased, and she slowed enough to catch her breath before she reached the river's edge.

"Elizabeth Fuller! What are you doing?"

Lizzie recognised Laura's angry voice immediately. She guessed she would be in trouble. She managed to stop herself and sat up. Her bonnet was knocked askew. Lizzie tried to straighten it on her head and retie the bow. She did not notice the grass stains on her yellow gingham frock.

Laura was, by this time, running toward her along the river bank.

"Elizabeth, it's time for us to go! Look at yourself! You're covered with bits of grass. I can't believe you did this. Mother would be horrified!"

"I'm all right, Laurie. I just needed to try it! We don't have a hill like this. It's so flat at home."

Laura shook her head and offered her hand to pull Lizzie to her feet.

"I don't know how you'll explain your appearance to Miss Adams and Mr Hewitt, Sister. We're ready to go back to the city now. I was sent to find you."

"What? I'm all right," said Lizzie, as she picked off some leaves clinging to her skirt.

"Elizabeth, Father worried that you would do something like this. I can't prevent you from acting like a little child. I can't be with you every minute. You should have stayed with your partner. Mary Badham might have been able to keep you out of trouble. Where is she?"

"Oh, she wanted to be with Ann Browne. Those Southern girls only want to sit on a bench under a tree. You can do that any day at St Mary's Hall," said Lizzie, giving a sniff.

Laura looked at Lizzie sternly. "I really don't know what to say, Sister."

"Then don't say anything, Sister!" Lizzie said, mocking Laura's tone. She turned on her heel and sprinted toward the path. Laura had to run as fast as she could to catch up with her.

In stony silence, the pair arrived back at the white columned main gatehouse to meet the rest of their party. Laura loved Elizabeth very much, but sometimes she didn't understand why she acted as she did. *She's still a child in so many ways,* she thought, *although only a year younger than I am. P'raps she just needs to grow out of acting like a young boy. P'raps it was Dick and Sam's fault for treating her like a brother.*

Laura had to write a letter home to-night. Pupils were expected to write letters three times a week during vacation, and required weekly letters to families took precedence over those to friends and neighbours. Mrs La Motte always checked on this as she collected them, unsealed, to post. Somehow, even with the full complement of 150 scholars, she was able to remember who had written to parents or not. She would then dutifully notify the curator of St Mary's Hall, Mr Charles M. Harker, of the number of stamps needed so he could deduct the sum from each girl's account.

Laura wondered if she should tell her parents about to-day's escapade.

Or would Elizabeth herself confess her misdeed?

❦ ❦ ❦

The sun fell lower in the sky, chilling the air, as the train left Camden. Once back at the school, the girls had only a few minutes to freshen up before the brass supper gong rang. They were tired from walking, grateful to be back safe from their sojourn, and would be happy to go to bed after a long day exploring the sights and sounds of Philadelphia.

❦ ❦ ❦

TUESDAY, 16 OCTOBER 1855

Miss Adams followed her six pupils out of the School Room after Dr Millett's morning service of prayers and Bible lessons ended. It was warmer already, and they carried their wraps over their arms. As they walked through the Circle behind the Main House, Mr Jacob was spreading what looked like a large canvas sail on the ground under the chestnut tree.

"Young ladies! I need yah help! Take a basket! Come and git these here chestnuts before the squirrels git 'em! But mind the spikes on them, missies!"

Lizzie dropped her shawl on the ground and began to skip toward the tree. Vicky did likewise and followed Lizzie to the sail. Anna Cooke, Emma, Julia, and Laura continued their more sedate pace. As they neared the tree, they saw the gathering baskets, and each took one. Other schoolmates were already there, most with baskets in hand, anxious to begin the contest. Anna Bull, in her new role as teacher-in-training, stood by to watch the fun.

Mr Jacob climbed up a ladder to the shed roof. Then, with a long stick, he beat the nearest branches to bring down the chestnuts. The prickly green shells dropped and rolled around on the sail. Those that were ripe enough yielded their smooth brown treat; the girls scrambled to gather them. Later Mr Jacob would have to put on his thickest leather gloves to pry any mature ones still peeking out of the cracked shells. Lizzie and Vicky shouted with glee, trying to outdo one another. By lifting the canvas sail Lizzie found she was able to scoop more into her basket without ever touching the offending spikes. She hoped no one else would notice her brilliant technique.

The man climbed down from the shed, moved the sail and put up the ladder to attack another section of the tree with his stick. Again, the girls squealed as they pushed each other away to collect the shiny nuts. More than once Julia felt the pain of a chestnut husk. She thought, *Mr Jacob should give us all leather gloves for this job!*

When that part of the tree was deprived of its fruit, Mr Jacob moved the ladder and sail yet again. After a half-hour of work, each girl counted her catch, and tiny Lucy Peck from Alabama was the winner. Everyone handed over their bounty to the cook, who was waiting at the kitchen entrance. She would roast some for supper to-day and store the rest for Thanksgiving turkey stuffing.

❦ ❦ ❦

THURSDAY, 25 OCTOBER 1855

"Young ladies," said Miss Adams, the novice teacher who shared and supervised their dormitory. "I have an announcement. Gather round."

It was half-past twelve and the girls had just come upstairs after a morning tending the late blooming asters in Bishop Doane's garden behind Riverside. They were chatting, washing their hands, combing their hair and otherwise getting ready for dinner. Vacation days were numbered, and the girls wanted to enjoy every minute of free time before the winter term routine began next week.

"What is it, Eliza, er ... Miss Adams?" asked Emma, quickly correcting herself.

Eliza Clarke Adams was a down-to-earth young woman from a small family in the country town of Lyons, New York. Her father was a merchant in Lyons near Seneca Falls and Geneva, the same area where Miss Stanley had grown up. Eliza had completed her programme and graduated from St Mary's Hall in the class of March 1854. She was such a talented pupil that Miss Stanley invited her to stay on to teach. Eliza, now all of twenty years old, had been a senior girl in the same dormitory with Emma and Julia during their first term at St Mary's. She and Emma had become close that first year; Eliza was sympathetic to the Burns sisters' initial homesickness. Emma admired Eliza and was now considering following in her path to become a teacher herself. She wished they could still be friends, but young Miss Adams was trying hard to maintain her position of authority with the pupils under her care. It was difficult because some of them had become friends, despite their age difference.

"Dr Millett has given permission for us all to remain downstairs to-night for a special event."

"What special event?" asked Julia.

"We shall be using a telescope to view the total lunar eclipse!" said Miss Adams.

"A telescope!" exclaimed Emma.

"The total lunar eclipse! What is that?" asked Lizzie.

"I could tell you, but I want you to wait for *Herr Doktor* Schmidt's lecture about it this afternoon in the School Room."

"Oh, please, please, please, Miss Adams! Don't keep us in the dark! What is it?" pleaded Lizzie.

Miss Adams relented. "Well, then, who has studied Latin?" she asked.

"I know that *luna* means moon in Latin," said Laura. "It's *la lune* in French. Like the old song, *Au Clair de la Lune.*"

"*Exactement*, Laura," replied the teacher in French.

"And eclipse means to cover up," added Julia.

"Right again," said Miss Adams. "So, what is covering what?"

"I don't know," murmured Lizzie. She prided herself in her knowledge of the natural world and was embarrassed at her ignorance of this subject. Astronomy was not something she had studied at the Common School of Thorold, though her father had many times pointed out major bodies in the night sky: Jupiter, Venus, Orion's Belt, the Milky Way, the Dippers, and the North Star. Mary Margaret and Laura had been sticklers on spelling and arithmetic at school, and they only cared about reciting, not studying the sky or the earth, it seemed.

"That's all I am going to tell you at this moment! I don't want to spoil *Herr* Dr Schmidt's lecture for you. Now finish up your *toilette*, and let's go down to dinner, scholars."

❦ ❦ ❦

At four o'clock the teaching staff and all the girls were seated in the separate School Room building where *Herr* Dr Schmidt had set up his shiny brass telescope. Behind him on the blackboard he had drawn a diagram of the path of the lunar eclipse. The short, bandy-legged German was an amateur astronomer along with being a teacher of Latin and his mother tongue. *Herr* Dr Schmidt had left his hometown of Soldau, Germany about six years ago. There were many rumours circulating about him. One was that he had been married there, but his young wife died, accounting for his often sad demeanour. Other stories were that he was a revolutionary university student who had fled for his life after the 1848 republican upheavals in Berlin. No one dared ask him, of course. It was too personal. Besides, the stories were probably more exciting than the truth!

Some of the older girls made sport of him, mocking his thick accent behind his back, but he was a shy, kindly thirty-six-year-old man, and they would not truly have wanted to hurt his feelings. He was alone and had no family in his new country except for fellow teachers and his pupils at St Mary's Hall and Burlington College. He took rooms at the college as did other single male faculty members. He experienced a genuine joy talking to anyone who would listen about what interested him. As he spoke, he stroked the end of his beard, a mass of thick red curls, and he often chewed his bottom lip as he considered answers to perplexing questions.

"Und now, young ladies, I vant you to look at dis model on de table. Dere are t'ree orbs. De yellow one, of course, is de sun. De blue is our Eart'. De small vite one is, of course, our moon. If you can imagine now de Eart' moving und turning betveen de two odders. Its shadow casts upon de little moon. Slowly, slowly it advahnces across de moon und ven complete, de moon vill turn a leetle bit red. Den as ve continue, de moon begins to reappear," explained the learned man.

"*Verstehen Sie?*" he asked. On the first day of lessons all of his pupils learnt that this meant "do you understand?" in German.

"How long will it take, *Herr Doktor*?" asked Mrs La Motte, who spoke with the vestiges of an Irish accent.

"Ach, I vould say about four to five hours."

"And when will it begin?" asked Miss Stanley.

"At about eleven o'clock to-night," asserted *Herr* Dr Schmidt.

Emma Crow, who had arrived that afternoon from North Carolina, raised her hand. "Must we watch the entire eclipse, sir? I am so tired out from my journey."

Herr Dr Schmidt replied, "Vy, of course not, but if you vish, you may."

Mrs La Motte then commanded the attention of the twenty girls with a rap of her pointer on the windowsill.

"Young ladies, the rector has decided that you will not be required to wake at the usual time to-morrow morning. We shall have a sort of holiday. We shall break-fast at nine o'clock, have no luncheon, but dinner will be at one, the usual time this month. You are dismissed now until supper. Cook tells me it will be milktoast this evening. P'raps you should take a bit of rest now," said the matron.

❧ ❧ ❧

After prayers, the girls had been sent to bed at the usual vacation bedtime of eight o'clock, but most were so excited that they had not slept more than a few minutes. Miss Adams' little brass bell awakened the darkened room at precisely eleven.

Lizzie popped out of bed and dressed as quickly as she could. She nudged Laura, who was still sound asleep. The girls poured cold water into their bowls and splashed their eyes to wake themselves up. When all were ready, Miss Adams led her charges downstairs to the cloakroom single file to find their wraps. Out on the chilly Green Bank, Miss Stanley and Dr Millett were waiting, equipped with several large tin-ware barn lanterns. The candles inside them flickered. *Herr* Dr Schmidt was there with his telescope already set up and pointed toward the moon.

The penumbra was in progress, and without a telescope the girls could see the moon going into shadow.

Most of the pupils had never experienced such a celestial show in their young lives. They listened as *Herr* Dr Schmidt explained how the ancients had regarded such phenomena as omens for future misfortune. He talked about the passing of Halley's Comet in 1066 when King Harold of England lost the battle of Hastings to William the Conqueror, and in London, the total solar eclipse of 1135 that foreshadowed the death of King Henry the first. The spectators took turns looking through the long lens as they tried to make out the features of the moon's surface before they disappeared from view. The girls were in awe as the moon gradually vanished before their very eyes.

Some of the girls gathered in the damp night air were not thrilled in the least with this evening's activity; having to wait their turn to use the instrument made them even less willing to participate. There was nowhere to sit and nothing to do but listen to the waves lapping quietly at the sea wall.

Suddenly there was a clamour to the west, and a loud cheer went up from the direction of Burlington College: "Hip, hip, hooray! Hip, hip, hooray! Hip, hip, hooray for St Mary's Hall!"

The girls giggled. The young gentlemen next door were also outside at this hour, studying more than the heavens with their own teacher Dr Jacob Zehner.

CHAPTER 9

A New Pupil

TUESDAY, 30 OCTOBER 1855

It was late afternoon and Harriet and her father were seated in the rear of the Camden and Amboy Rail Road car, finishing up a final hand of piquet. Fennings Taylor had come to love the French card game during his five-year residence in Montréal. Just as the train came to a stop in Burlington, he failed to contain his enthusiasm.

"There—I've finally beaten you, my dear! It took three days, but I've done it!"

"Oh, Father. I let you win, and you know it," laughed his daughter, her light blue eyes dancing under long eyelashes.

"No, now that's not true. I've taught you too well perhaps! Let's get our things together. It's drizzling a bit. Let me get my cloak and I'll help you on with your wrap."

As the dapper gentleman prepared to exit the car, he picked up his exotic new umbrella, made of alpaca fabric stretched over slender steel ribs. It had a beautifully carved mahogany handle and was light-weight compared to the old-fashioned silk or cotton umbrellas. A fortnight ago it had arrived in Toronto from the haberdasher James Smith and Sons, Ltd., London, England, in time for the planned journey south. The device had been quite an object of curiosity yesterday in Jersey City. Although he had lived in Canada for nearly twenty years, he still enjoyed the finer products imported from his homeland.

Fennings Taylor was born and raised in Hackney, a borough in northeast London. Shortly after he arrived in Toronto in 1836, he met and married Mary Elizabeth Denison, a second cousin on his father's side. Born in Upper Canada, Mary Elizabeth was the daughter of Colonel George Taylor Denison and his first wife, the late Esther Borden Lippincott. Esther's father, Richard Lippincott, was a United Empire Loyalist born in Shrewsbury, Monmouth County, New Jersey, near the Atlantic coast. He escaped to Nova Scotia with his family and his life during the American Revolution.

At first, young Fennings was reluctant to be employed in government service. He was afraid his colleagues would assume he was hired because of his uncle's influence. However, he performed his duties well and was now respected and satisfied with his career. Unfortunately, after his beloved Mary Elizabeth's death, he became a lonely widower, and the care and worry about the children and the household weighed on his mind, even with plenty of servants to help. Ensuring Harriet got a superior education was the priority of his overall plan for the family. Finding a new wife was second to that. Perhaps now that Parliament would be sitting in Toronto again for the next few years, he would have some time to socialise with more English-speakers.

The uprooting of the motherless children to Québec City for the last three years had been hardest on Harriet. She was old enough to understand the circumstances of her mother's death, and she missed her extended Denison family in Toronto.

"Harriet dear, we shall stop at the best hotel in the High Street for these two nights. 'Tis the sole appropriate one in town for us. I understand the others are either on the waterfront or above a noisy tavern. I plan to hire a carriage and driver for the time we're here as well. We might be able to take a pleasant ride round the city to-morrow if the weather clears. Someone from the school must fetch your trunk to-day. I trust you need nought from it," said Fennings to his daughter as he helped her on with her cloak.

"No, Father, I'm sure I have everything I need for a few more days," replied Harriet.

Fennings led her through the narrow aisle to the door in the middle of the car where the portable wooden steps were being put in place next to it. He exited first and then offered his hand to help her down to the new city she would call home.

Little did they know they were treading the same soil as her Loyalist great-grandfather Richard Lippincott when he escaped from the old Burlington gaol in 1776.

❦ ❦ ❦

THURSDAY, 1 NOVEMBER 1855

While pupils from as far away as Vermont, Alabama, or Florida often stayed for the vacation months, many girls who lived in nearby states like New York, Pennsylvania, and New Jersey arrived just a day or two before the start of winter term. On this day, All Saints' Day in the church calendar, St Mary's Hall welcomed ninety-six more girls, including Harriet Taylor. She became the newest resident of the dormitory occupied by Emma, Julia, Laura, and Lizzie as well as six other girls from New York State.

Mrs La Motte led the way up the stairs to the second floor, followed by Harriet. They found Miss Adams waiting on the landing, and the matron made the introductions. She then bade the girl farewell and disappeared back down the stairs, her little lace cap fluttering in her wake. Harriet entered the Spartan dormitory, followed by Miss Adams.

The girl paled and swallowed hard. This plain rectangular room was to be her home for the coming five months, and she had to share it with ten other girls and a teacher!

As the eldest child of her family, she hadn't shared a room since she left the nursery at age nine when little George was born. After that she enjoyed a room all to herself with an elegant, scrolled mahogany bed imported from England and a matching side table topped with rose marble quarried in Carrara, Italy. Her soft, creamy white English wool blanket, a wedding gift to her mother, had kept her very warm indeed on winter nights whether she was in Toronto or Québec. There was also a French walnut armoire with three looking glass panels to hold her many stylish dresses and shoes. Inside those doors were several drawers for her collection of stockings, handkerchiefs, and underclothes. The heavy window draperies in her bedroom at Bellevue were of sumptuous dark green velvet trimmed with gold tassels, her beloved mother's selection.

Harriet wanted for nothing—except a mother's love. Her most precious possession, one of the few pieces they had shipped back and forth from Québec, was her mother's "bonheur du jour", a dainty, ladies' writing desk. It was made in London, with a little gallery on top and a drawer to store her writing implements. Harriet liked to place it in front of the window overlooking the gardens of Bellevue. She would miss that desk the most while she was at school. She remembered her mother sitting at it every morning to write letters to her numerous family members.

How shall I ever survive here? she wondered.

During term, the pupils of St Mary's Hall were permitted to be in the dormitory room only before dinner began at half-past two. Miss Adams' scholars were washing their hands and combing their hair, talking in hushed voices. Before the teacher had a chance to introduce Harriet, Emma saw her enter the room. She noticed Harriet's sudden pallor.

Concerned, Emma walked briskly over to the girl and asked, "Miss, are you quite all right? You look as if you've seen a phantom!"

"Oh, it's nought, really. I … I … didn't realise I'd be sharing a room with so many other girls."

"Is that all? We think it's lovely," chimed in Julia, as she too approached Harriet. "We don't have to share a bed like we did at home this summer! It's Heaven!"

"You will get used to it here," said Emma. "The conversations we have before lights out! We talk about all sorts of things, my sister, Julia, and I. Indeed, I wonder what our little sister Isabella is doing at home now that she has the bed all to herself again? That will be an adjustment for her too, won't it, Julia?"

"Yes, I expect so," said Julia. "But we sleep far better here!" she laughed.

"You both had to share a bed with your sister?" asked Harriet.

"Oh, yes, we do when we go home for the summers. The nice part is that we're always warm enough and never need a heavy counterpane. The bad part was that Isabella seems to run in her sleep and kicks us unmercifully. We made her sleep on the outside edge and took turns in the middle!" explained Emma.

"My brother and sister are younger than I. They still occupy the nursery with their nurse. I can't imagine sleeping in a bed with another body! Oh, where are my manners? I'm Harriet Taylor from Toronto, Canada."

"Toronto! We're from St Catharines! My name is Emma Burns, and this is Julia."

"Oh, Emma, St Catharines?! I know it! Papa and I took the train from there. We stayed at the Welland House the night before we left."

"Did you cross the lake the same day then?" asked Julia.

"Why, yes, we took the steamer over to Port Dalhousie. Luckily, it was a perfect day, totally calm waters ... I'm so happy to meet you and to know that there are two other Canadians here with me."

"Harriet, we're not even the first Canadian pupils to come to St Mary's Hall. Five girls from Yarmouth in Nova Scotia graduated some years past," said Emma.

"But we're not the only Canadians here now either. Over there are two more," added Julia, nodding toward the opposite corner of the room where Laura was engaged tidying Lizzie's hair. "Laura and Lizzie Fuller —from Thorold Township up on the Mountain above St Catharines. We all travelled here together with their father a month ago."

"You jest! I can't believe it. Five of us? What luck!" Harriet was elated that she would perhaps have a ready-made group of friends from her country. She thought of how she already missed her older cousin and best friend Maria in Toronto.

"Well, there should have been a sixth if Margaret Jane had come, but her mother wouldn't let her leave her side," said Julia.

"Hush, Julia! We don't even know what happened that day," scolded Emma.

"Oh, but that's wonderful!" countered Harriet. "She's so lucky to have her mother love her like that. My mother died having a baby when I was eleven ... I still miss her so." Harriet's expression changed to one of profound sadness, and her eyes welled with tears.

"I am sorry to know that, Harriet," said Julia. "Our mother just had a baby boy a fortnight ago. Papa wrote to tell us. We pray every day that she continues to do well. The babe is big and healthy. He's been named Llewellyn, but I think that's a horrible name, don't you? I plan to call him Lewie!"

"That is lovely news, Julia. I'm very happy for your family," said Harriet quietly. A fleeting smile crossed her face.

At that moment Miss Adams rang her bell to end conversations and to line up to go down to dinner. There was no time to orientate Harriet to the routines of St Mary's Hall. The schoolmates put away their brushes and combs. They left the dormitory single file, a custom that discouraged any chatter. The dinner gong sounded in the hallway below as they took to the stairs.

❧ ❧ ❧

The entire student body of St Mary's Hall descended the steep steps at once to the eating room in the basement of the Main House. The girls held on to the smooth mahogany bannisters with one hand and their skirts with the other. The sound of three hundred feet echoed in the cavernous room that extended the entire depth of the house but only half its width. The busy school kitchen occupied the other side. Daylight entered the space through six sixteen-light windows above ground level, and gaslights flickering on the wall further illuminated both rooms.

The scholars sat on either side of eight horseshoe-shaped tables covered with plain white linen tablecloths. A teacher at each end of the curve served the food family-style to her dormitory pupils. To accommodate ample skirts and ease of movement, everyone sat on individual stools rather than benches. Now that the full complement of 150 pupils was present, the girls were elbow to elbow at table. One school officer was seated at the curve of the table to ensure that the young ladies were well-behaved during meals. Any infractions would result in demerits, affecting weekly comportment grades.

Emma took a clean white linen napkin from the stack on the sideboard and gave it to Harriet. They sat down beside each other at Miss Adams' table to await the meal. The new girl realised straightaway that no one was permitted to talk during dinner, a detail that her new friends had neglected to mention upstairs. Everyone was too hungry to talk anyway. After spreading the large napkin on her lap, Harriet clasped her hands, bowed her head and joined in reciting a familiar Episcopal grace

The meal was abundant, with roast beef, potatoes, and plenty of bread and fresh butter. The latter was made from the milk of the cows that grazed in the field between the bishop's house and the college buildings. There were also late season tomatoes from the kitchen garden and pickles made from last summer's cucumbers. To-day there was a pudding, apple dumplings, with a sauce the girls made themselves at the table from butter and sugar.

The meal ended, and each girl placed her napkin in her napkin ring and left it at her place. Harriet's ring was still in her trunk and, of course, she had not had time to retrieve it. It was a silver round with her first name engraved on it, a gift from her Aunt Betsy when she was born. She rolled her napkin as tight as she could and placed it next to her plate, hoping no one would notice. She did not want to make extra laundry for the staff.

The girls said another prayer of thanksgiving in unison to end the meal, and they filed out in three lines, one for each staircase of the house. After dinner on a normal school day, the scholars were expected to rest for two hours before it was time to study their lessons from the morning. To-day, the first day of term, there had not been any lessons yet, but examinations were held for those new girls who had arrived the day before.

Harriet was glad to have some quiet time. She hadn't been at any school since last June. She was somewhat unnerved by all of the rules, supervision, and the crowds of girls. She had been a day student at her previous school in Québec City and was not used to living with so many people at home. It had been a tranquil house in Toronto when she left, despite the occasional antics of her little brother and sister. All in all, she deemed it an extremely trying day, and to-morrow she would be examined for placement. The thought made her cringe.

CHAPTER 10

Winter Term Begins

FRIDAY, 2 NOVEMBER 1855

All St Mary's Hall pupils soon learnt that the course of their day was measured by the tolling of a bell, and Harriet was no exception. On her first morning, promptly at six o'clock, the night watchman, Mr Hall, rang the rising bell. Perched atop the south end of the chapel roof, this early alarm signalled the beginning of one hour for the pupils to wash and dress in silence. Then the girls knelt at their bedsides for ten minutes of private devotions and Bible reading. The bell tolled gently and continuously during this private prayer time.

With devotions ended, the breakfast bell rang at a quarter past seven and the girls filed silently from all directions downstairs to break their fast with tea, bread, and a piece of beef from last night's dinner. The passageways and eating room were filled with the aroma of yeast, for to-day was a hot bread morning. Harriet rejoiced. She loved the smell of bread baking in the house; she loved its chewiness and the taste of fresh melted butter on it even more. The pupils took their places at tables set with matching china plates and tea cups. Emma invited Harriet again to sit beside her where Harriet found her napkin tucked under her plate. Upon each plate was a single flower. She was surprised and puzzled by this but could not ask anyone about it during the meal. Harriet wondered, *Who was responsible for this sweet gesture, and where could so many flowers come from at this hour?*

After the meal, the weather was unseasonably warm, and it seemed the whole school went outdoors. The younger pupils were in the Circle engaging in games of Hide and Seek or Tag. Some of the little girls sang and danced to *All Around the Mulberry Bush* or *London Bridge*. Laura and Lizzie played Graces, tossing and catching beribboned rings in the air. The oldest pupils, including Emma, Julia, and Harriet, strolled sedately a few times round the Circle before the service of Morning Prayer began at nine o'clock.

To-day, as usual, the principal and chaplain Dr Millett was conducting the service in the little stone chapel. Built of uncoursed sandstone blocks, it was designed by Scottish architect John Notman in the Gothic Revival style and consecrated in 1847. This morning, when the chapel bell rang for Morning Prayer, Miss Adams' girls entered directly from the Circle, reaching the south porch entrance by a set of wide wooden steps. Inside, as she walked up the centre aisle laid with red Minton tiles, Harriet looked up at the nave ceiling with its arched, open-frame timbers. In the low light of Evening Prayer last night, she had not noticed them. She thought the ceiling resembled the hull of a ship. The altar at the north end stood under a colourful stained glass window modelled on one Bishop Doane had admired during his 1841 visit to the church of Stanton St John in Oxfordshire, England. The words "Behold the handmaid of the Lord. Be it unto me according to Thy word" were writ large on unfurling scrolls on either side of a cross of glory emerging from a swirling dark mass of clouds. Above the cross two windows depicted a cluster of grapes and a wheatsheaf representing Christ in the wine and bread of the Eucharist, and another above them showed a dove, representing the Holy Spirit. Echoing the shape of the altar window was a plaster casting painted with the words: "Blessed be the King who cometh in the name of the Lord. Hosanna in the Highest".

A carved and polished communion rail and a pair of stone

steps extending the width of the chancel marked its boundary. To the left of the altar was the Bishop's Throne, and a lectern from which the lessons were read stood on the right. Cross stitch and needlepoint samplers of the Apostle's Creed and the Lord's Prayer, gifts of the Mission School in Athens, Greece, hung on the wall, flanking the altar. Bishop Doane was a strong supporter of the Church Missionary Society.

Likewise the congregation and the choir spaces were divided by an aisle. On the west side of it was the organ in its alcove and on the east, a pair of arched doors painted dark brown opened into the hallway of the chapel annex. A baptismal font of Caen stone was installed on a pedestal just inside these doors. Echoing this division, the chancel and choir space featured single lancet stained glass windows, whilst the congregation windows were double-width. Harriet thought it was a beautiful little place to worship, not on the order or same style as the Cathedral of the Holy Trinity in Québec, but lovely in its own way.

For the first brisk days of fall, the staff and girls had to wear their cloaks to worship in the chapel, but on the coldest days of winter, the chapel was abandoned for the one-storey School Room building that was quicker and easier to heat. Of course, that also required going out of doors, but the girls became used to scurrying between the buildings in all kinds of weather.

After Morning Prayer, the pupils had more free time to socialise or prepare lessons before the school day began. Every girl spent portions of the day in the School Room, studying at her own desk seated in alphabetical order. Located behind the Main House, the white clapboard structure was built by the previous owner of the property, Mr Gummere, for his own school for girls. Near the doorway of the School Room was a wooden dais on which Miss Charlotte Cronyn, the Teacher-in-Charge, sat high at a desk to better monitor her pupils' behaviour. One wall had a long slate blackboard on which pupils would work out arithmetic or algebra problems. The girls studied there between recitations with instructors in the various classrooms of the Main House.

Six classrooms were on the second floor of the Main House. Two large ones faced the Circle with its tall shade trees; two other equally spacious classrooms and two smaller ones gave out onto the river. More than one pupil of St Mary's Hall found it more fascinating to stare out those river-view windows to watch the fishing boats, sloops, steamship ferries, and barges pass by than to attend to recitations. No wonder wise teachers arranged desks to face inside walls!

Sometimes the north wind blew so fiercely off the river that the window frames rattled and whistled. On those days, the girls clutched their thickest wool blanket shawls round them. The staff's best efforts to keep fires burning in the brick fireplaces were often no match for the wind. New pupils quickly learnt that, in winter, fingerless gloves were essential in the classroom. Who could manage a chalk and slate when her hands were frozen?

❦ ❦ ❦

On this the first full day of term, Harriet had to sit an examination for placement into the proper department, either Middle or Senior. The examiner was Miss Lovina Chamberlain, the principal teacher, a formidable person with a perpetually pained expression on her face, as if she were hurting somewhere.

She couldn't be that old, but perhaps she's afflicted with some unknown ailment, Harriet mused, when she first was introduced to her.

Now as she entered the little classroom on the second floor of the east annex of the Main House, pen case in hand, Harriet checked her harsh assessment of the woman. She decided to see how the hour went before she judged her further.

Miss Chamberlain greeted Harriet and bade her set her things on a desk. The pupil was expected to stand for the first part, the oral examination comprised of ten general knowledge questions. Some were about geography and world history that the girl answered correctly, pointing with confidence to places on Miss Chamberlain's floor globe. Others related to the United States and its own short history, which she knew less well: the first president George Washington, the year 1776, and the Declaration of Independence beginning the war. The meaning and purpose of the American Constitution escaped her. Since she had studied with French nuns for the last three years, her knowledge of French history was considerably better than English, in spite of her having an English-born father. There weren't any questions about any of the French revolutions though, and she feared she got the one wrong about King Charles I and Cromwell. Harriet sighed with relief when the questioning ended, and Miss Chamberlain, with a hint of a smile, congratulated her on doing well so far.

Next, the teacher asked Harriet to write and parse four sentences on the blackboard. Harriet had learnt how to do this from a tutor she had in Toronto, but that was years ago, before her mother died. She had not done any parsing in English at all in Québec with the Ursulines. If only someone had warned her! She would have tried to revise how to do them last night. She took up the chalk and began to draw the ovals and lines indicating the parts of speech. It was coming back to her how to do it, but she couldn't remember the English words for the parts of speech. She didn't even know them in French. In spite of the cool temperature in the room, Harriet felt beads of perspiration on her forehead. She had butterflies in her stomach. She was getting nowhere with the task.

"I'm very sorry, Miss Chamberlain. I've been at school in Québec and we didn't do these."

"That's all right, Miss Taylor. We shall continue." The woman made some notes in a ledger on her desk. At last the teacher stood and went to the blackboard herself. Referring to the ledger, she wrote several arithmetic and higher mathematics problems on the board.

Harriet easily came up with the correct answers to four fraction problems. Then she winced, hesitated, and obviously struggled. She stared at the rest of the numbers and symbols. Harriet thought she could feel the woman's eyes on her back. *Why is she watching me so closely?*

She became more and more nervous. She took out the linen handkerchief from her sleeve and wiped the perspiration away. *Not very ladylike,* she thought.

Finally, she put the chalk down and said, "Miss Chamberlain, is this geometry and algebra? I have no idea what to do with these." She paused and confessed, "I never have done well with numbers." She refused to cry, although she felt she might.

Miss Chamberlain gave the pupil a sympathetic look, and then wrote a few more words in her ledger.

"Miss Taylor, I have so noted that your studies ended with

93

arithmetic. We shall move on now to your composition. Please sit down. For the remaining time, you are to write an essay of one page on the subject of the most pleasant way to spend an afternoon," she said as she laid two pieces of paper and an ink bottle on the desk.

Harriet was nearly exhausted after her failures at parsing and mathematics. She sat at the desk, closed her eyes and tried to clear her mind. As she listened to Miss Chamberlain's writing prompt, she felt relief. She decided straightaway that she would write about spending an afternoon with her family at her uncle Robert's home, the original house built at Bellevue. He was her favourite of the three Denison uncles. Bellevue had been her grandfather's estate in Toronto and her mother's childhood home. Since his father's death, Uncle Robert and his family lived there with his stepmother Maria Coates Denison. It was a beautiful farm with an orchard and a ravine on the north side. The house, located in thick woods, was built at the end of the War of 1812, and was where Harriet's mother was born. Harriet loved to visit the old place, sit in her mother's childhood bedroom and imagine how it would have been to grow up there with an older sister and three brothers. She loved to talk to Uncle Robert and old Mrs Denison about her mother.

She dipped her pen in the ink bottle and got to work.

At last the hour was over, and Miss Chamberlain collected Harriet's essay. Skimming it, she said, "I am sure Miss Stanley will be pleased to read this, Miss Taylor." She would report her findings to Miss Stanley, and based on the results, she suspected that the vice principal would choose to place Harriet in a lower division of the Senior Class, since she had not studied advanced mathematics.

❦ ❦ ❦

Meals and more worship services punctuated the daily schedule. The growing girls took a mid-morning lunch of a few crackers or ginger cakes to tide them over until the main meal was cooked and served in the afternoon. After the first hour of lessons, the chapel bell rang at noon, inviting both pupils and faculty to a brief, voluntary service of prayer. For some, it was a welcome respite from the stress of recitations; for others, it was a reason to ask the Lord's help to get them through the rest of the day without being called upon. Younger pupils, or those who did not wish to attend the service, were permitted free time, outside again if pleasant weather, until lessons resumed.

When the first afternoon lesson was over, the whole student body gathered in the School Room to sing the Doxology. After freshening up in their dormitories, they went downstairs to eat their hearty dinner, now taken later than during vacation. Half-hour long music lessons began after dinner. With twenty-four pianos being played all over the school, the din was enough to hinder any coherent thought or conversations. Harriet could not bear the competing notes coming from all directions. As Harriet had not been "classed" yet for piano, she had no lesson to take. She entered the chapel to seek some solitude in prayer.

When the bell tolled again, Harriet closed the chapel door and joined the other pupils streaming out to the School Room to memorise the daily collect and morning lessons.

❦ ❦ ❦

Miss Cronyn interrupted the pupils' study in the quiet School Room. "Miss Taylor," said she, folding the note just handed to her by Ellen, the young Irish woman tasked with delivering messages throughout the school. "Come to me, please."

Harriet looked up from her prayer book and the collect she was trying to memorise. She had a premonition that this would be bad news. She put her book away in the desk and approached the dais.

"Please see Miss Stanley in her room, Miss. She has the results of your placement examination."

"Yes, Miss Cronyn," said Harriet. She felt a lump in her throat as she followed Ellen down the aisle of desks. Girls looked at her as she passed by.

Julia winked and whispered, "You'll be fine!"

They stopped in the foyer so that Harriet could put on her cloak and bonnet. Then Ellen led her over to the Main House and to Miss Stanley's small classroom on the first floor of the east annex. Harriet was grateful that Ellen was there to guide her since she had so far only travelled in a group of pupils and, after only one day in residence, didn't know her way round the place.

Miss Stanley's room was one of the ones with the big drafty windows that faced north. A loden green blanket shawl draped over her shoulders, the vice principal sat at her desk, marking a paper. The room was still cool as the furnaces were not yet "up", having only been activated the day before. Mr Harker, the curator, adhered religiously to the heating schedule, firing up the system on the first of November and shutting it down on March 31 whether it was cold outside or not. The residents and staff knew they should always be prepared to don or doff a garment.

"Miss Stanley, Miss Harriet Taylor," said Ellen, before taking her leave with a curtsy.

Ellen had not said more than two words to Harriet on the way through the Circle and up the back steps. Harriet thought perhaps the staff was not allowed to speak to the pupils. She had been an inmate of the school for just a few hours and hadn't yet figured out how Americans treat servants. She had a comfortable relationship with Maeve at home, although her father did not approve of it. He preferred a formal household on the English model he grew up with in London. Harriet would have to observe how the American girls behaved with staff and act accordingly.

"Good afternoon, Miss Stanley." Harriet curtseyed.

"Good afternoon, my dear. Please do sit down."

Harriet took a seat at one of the desks in front of Miss Stanley's. She shivered and remembered she had left her shawl in the dormitory.

"Miss Chamberlain has reported to me the results of your examination, and we have considered your situation carefully. Your knowledge of geography is commendable. She was quite impressed by your use of the globe. Your command of spoken English is excellent, in spite of a few mispronunciations. I imagine they are the result of your previous studies done in French. A few misspellings in English, but your composition is very well written, despite the problems you had with parsing this morning. I consulted with the bishop, and he has decided that you should be admitted to the Elocution class and English poetry analysis, which includes advanced work on composition with the bishop himself." She waited for Harriet to ask a question, but none came.

Harriet accepted the praise with a smile, but she dreaded the inevitable criticism about her mathematics skill.

"'Tis unfortunate that you have not begun geometry by now. That's a deciding factor in a pupil's placement for the term. You shall have to work on your mathematics. For this reason, you will be with the Middle Class A scholars this term, the highest group in the division. If you make good progress, 'tis very possible that you'll be advanced next term to Senior D, but for now it seems this is the best placement we can advise."

Harriet looked down at her lap, crestfallen. She did not know what to say. She was sixteen years old! The eldest girls in Middle A were perhaps fourteen. She was embarrassed that she had not done better to-day in the examination. But she doubted there was any recourse or appeal.

Miss Stanley continued, "You're permitted to study some courses of your choice, Miss Taylor. Do you prefer conchology or botany?"

Harriet thought for a few seconds before answering. "I suppose conchology would be interesting. That's shells, isn't it, Miss Stanley?"

"Correct. Miss Mary Rodney is the teacher, one of our recent graduates. She's devoted to the subject. She comes from Lewes, Delaware on the Atlantic Ocean where she's collected hundreds of specimens. You will learn much from her." She paused to see if Harriet spoke.

Harriet was silent. At this point, as disappointed as she was, Harriet had no preference. She liked flowers and admired the gardens at Bellevue, but knew nothing about shells, having been raised in cities.

"And do you wish to continue in French with *Monsieur* Baquet or begin a new language? *Signor* Paladini teaches Italian and Spanish. It will be *Herr* Dr Schmidt for German."

"Oh, I should like to continue French here, Miss Stanley. I adore it."

"Have you a preference for Latin or Greek?"

"Latin, please." She had studied the classical language with the Ursulines.

"Very well. Would you like to do Drawing and Painting as well?"

"Yes, Miss Stanley. I had a drawing master in Québec. I enjoyed it very much and missed it when he left the city."

"I see." Miss Stanley made some more notes on her paper. "You will also be trained to sing Sacred Music, and you'll study the History of England this term with the Middle A girls. We shall make sure you know what happened betwixt King Charles I and Oliver Cromwell. Your father will be pleased," she said with a wink. "You may return to the School Room now, my dear."

"Yes, Miss Stanley. Thank you," said Harriet as she stood from the desk to fetch her cloak and bonnet off the wall peg. Then remembering her manners, she turned around and made a quick curtsy to the woman, holding back her tears.

"Everything will be all right, Harriet. Don't worry. Good afternoon, dear," said the teacher as she took up her pen and went back to her previous work.

❧ ❧ ❧

Her eyes stung with tears of shame. Harriet hurried down the stairs and out the back door of the Main House to the Circle, clutching her cloak round her. She couldn't believe the bad luck she had with numbers. She would have some work to do on that score. And then to forget the English words for parsing sentences? It seems her studies in French were now a detriment rather than an asset. Well, the parsing shouldn't be too hard to revise if she could make some friends in the dormitory. They would help her, wouldn't they?

❧ ❧ ❧

Harriet re-entered the School Room after she composed herself. She stood tall and walked serenely to her seat. She looked over at Julia who mouthed, "Is everything all right?"

Harriet shook her head and got back to her memorisation before the bell rang for supper in the Main House. She was thankful that she couldn't talk to anyone about her experience with the examination while she was walking single file through the Circle.

She didn't know what the other girls would think of her, and she didn't know how to ask for help from these strangers.

The bell rang for supper at six. The light, final meal of the day was followed by Mrs La Motte's distributing the mail. Harriet had none, but the Burns sisters each had a stack from home that they tore open immediately. There were a few more minutes of free time until the final hour of study began in the School Room at seven. Some girls read their mail or practised their dancing in the young ladies' saloon. This evening it seemed most of the student body chose "the Walk". The girls trod the gravel in the Circle until it was time to go back to the School Room. Harriet successfully avoided her dormitory mates, preferring to walk by herself.

When the bell rang to end the study period, the entire school community went over to the chapel for Evening Prayer. After the brief, tranquil service, each girl shook hands with Bishop Doane and Mrs La Motte, who bade them good night at the east chapel door. The weary pupils trudged upstairs to get ready for bed. They welcomed the rest after long, regimented days. The teachers assigned to each dormitory ensured that the gas lights were dimmed well before the chapel bell sounded for the last time at nine.

❦ ❦ ❦

The next morning, before the rising bell, Julia poked Harriet.

"What?" whispered Harriet.

"I wondered how you were. You didn't speak to me all evening."

"I am classed in Middle A, Julia."

"Are you? Well, that's not so bad. I'm only in Senior D. We're still probably in some of the same lessons."

"I don't know. Poetry Analysis maybe. Elocution and Grammar."

"Hurray, yes! We shall tackle them together, Harriet."

"I'm happy for that! I chose French and Latin, two things I know I can do. I'm going to need help in geometry, Julia. Are you good at that?"

"Well, you'll be with Laura then. But I took it last term—I should remember something! Emma's better at it though. She's really quite smart with numbers. Doing trigonometry this term Frankly, I don't see it useful ... What else?"

"Conchology with Miss Rodney and English History."

"Oh, I did them both last year. You'll be with Laura for them too. Prepare to memorise!"

CHAPTER 11

An Uncomfortable Triangle

WEDNESDAY, 14 NOVEMBER 1855

In the middle of the line of eleven girls, all heads covered by bonnets, Emma and Julia pulled their thick wool shawls closer round them as they negotiated the drafty piazza between their dormitory building and the chapel. Miss Adams' pupils were in danger of being late for Morning Prayer to-day because, even given an hour, they had not finished their *toilette* on time. It seems many of the girls had trouble finding their shoes after antics the night before.

Harriet was ahead of Anna Cooke to-day, last in the line in front of Miss Adams. Emma was glad, for she wanted a few minutes alone with her sister before the service began. It was difficult to find opportunities for private conversations at St Mary's Hall; so much time was spent in communal activities. Perhaps in better weather they could have snatched a few minutes to talk while walking in the garden, but lately it had been so rainy and windy that no one, not even Lizzie Fuller, wanted to venture out of doors. Their umbrellas would have broken in the winds.

Emma took Julia by the elbow as they passed the infirmary hallway and pushed her out of the line.

"What are you doing, Emma?" asked Julia, shaking her arm away.

"Sister, I need to speak to you about Harriet," Emma whispered.

"Now? Hattie? What about Hattie?" asked Julia, using the nickname she had given her new friend.

Emma steered the younger girl left into the little hall that led to the Young Ladies' Parlour as the line of pupils continued into the chapel.

"I shall be direct. You spend all of your free moments with her, Julia. I think she is having an unbecoming effect on you."

Julia opened her eyes wide in disbelief. "Unbecoming effect on me? Whatever do you mean by that, Emma?"

"I mean to say that she is different to us, Julia. She is from the city, and you act differently round her—as if you are trying to be someone else."

"I can't believe you are saying that, Emma! I am trying to be a friend to her. She didn't know any of us when she arrived. Besides, I thought you liked her. You sat beside her at dinner on her very first day. And now you think ill of her?" countered Julia.

"I don't think ill of her. She apparently is used to having beautiful things, and there is nought wrong with that, but I see you are changing because of her. I doubt Papa and Mama will be happy if you become like Harriet."

"Emma, you ought to get to know Hattie yourself. She's a lonely girl. You know her mother died. She talks about her all the time. I suppose her father gives her whatever she wants because he wants her to be happy. I don't care what you say about her. I am going to be a good friend to Hattie. She's told me all about Toronto and Montréal. She lived in Québec City for three years and actually speaks French because she went to a convent school there. She has been helping me with my French lessons, you know."

"Her French! Julia, her accent is *Québecois*. It is rough. When *Monsieur* Baquet hears her speak, he must assign her demerits on the spot!" scoffed Emma.

"But, he *has* spoken with her. I allow he is quite taken with her abilities. And yes, I know she has some odd pronunciations, but *I* think it is charming."

"Charming? You would be better served listening to *Herr* Dr Schmidt speak French rather than Harriet Taylor."

"Well, Emma, I shall continue to practise with her, no matter. In return, I've been helping her with her parsing and the geometry. She feels ashamed being put down in the Middle Class instead of with us in the Senior, but I told her it doesn't depend on age. It's because she didn't have the same kind of schooling in Québec. She much prefers drawing and geography. She knows a lot about places all over the world. Just ask her!"

"Julia, you prove my point. You are so taken with Harriet Taylor, that you believe everything she says. Has she even been abroad?" snapped Emma. "Now let's go, or we shall be marked late."

And with that, the chapel bell began to peal, and the girls darted into the corridor and through the doorway, just ahead of Dr Millett.

❦ ❦ ❦

As the tolling ended, Emma and Julia, both looking perturbed, slid across the smooth tiles into their dormitory's second pew. Miss Adams, seated on the aisle, gave them a quizzical glance as they squeezed through the narrow space to sit in their normal places beside her. The two were not officially late because the organ prelude had not started, but the teacher wondered how they had got so far behind her. There would be no consequences for their *tête à tête* unless Miss Stanley questioned their independent arrival. Miss Stanley knew that Emma and Julia were usually well-behaved.

During Morning Prayer, Emma found it difficult to concentrate on the lesson Dr Millett was reading. Her mind wandered. She wondered if she were being too hard on her sister. To be truthful, she was jealous of the time Julia was now spending with Harriet, as little as that might be. She realised they were new friends, but that now left *her* out. She was used to having Julia's ear. Maybe that was how little Isabella felt, always on the outside looking in. Perhaps she should write to her about Julia and Harriet. Yes, that is what she would do –but letters could only be written on Saturdays during term.

❦ ❦ ❦

Saturday, 17 November 1855
Burlington, New Jersey

Dear Sister Isabella,
    I hope you, Mama and Papa and the little ones are doing well. It has been cold and windy here of late. The hallway stoves and basement furnaces have been trying hard to keep the buildings warm. I am bundled in my thick shawl just now to write you from the School Room during my free time to-day. This building stays warm because it is so small. Julia and I have been studying hours and hours since we got back. We do not see much of each other during the daytime because we are most often in different classes. For example, she is studying algebra this term, and I am in the trigonometry class. We are together for French, Sacred Music, singing, and our drawing and painting class with Mr Engstrom. We have several new girls in our dormitory from the state of New York, and they are mostly nice. Julia has made a new friend of Harriet Taylor from Toronto. Julia is spending a lot of nights whispering to her, as their beds are next to each other. She says Harriet is lonely and Julia wants to be her friend. Harriet and I are the same age, and I don't know why she doesn't want to be my friend too. I was very nice to her at first, but it seems she likes Julia better. I don't know what I have done wrong. I miss my dear friends Leonora and Mary. They graduated last year, and both went back home to Hartford, Connecticut. I have got two letters from Leonora but none from Mary. Please greet Kitty and the family, dear little sister, and give baby Llewellyn a lovely squeeze from me. I imagine he is getting big and looking around at everything now. I dearly hope to see you all in April when this term is over, and we can come home again for the summer.

Your loving sister,
Emma

CHAPTER 12

News from Canada

THURSDAY, 22 NOVEMBER 1855

Miss Stanley climbed the single flight of stairs to the second floor dormitory where she found Emma and Julia together. After returning from a Thanksgiving service at the Presbyterian church, the roommates were getting ready for the annual festive Thanksgiving dinner, a holiday set aside to give special thanks to God. The woman had been delaying this task so as to gather her thoughts since her urgent meeting this morning with Bishop Doane. She hated to ruin the occasion for the Burns sisters, but she needed to give them time to adjust to the turn of events. She crossed the room and stopped at the end of Emma's bed. Both girls instinctively turned from their looking glasses when they sensed her gaze.

"Good afternoon, Miss Stanley," said Julia cheerfully, as she curtseyed.

"Good afternoon, Julia," replied the vice principal. Her demeanour belied her automatic reply though. Her jaw was tense, and her small dark eyes looked intent instead of having their normal gentle gaze.

"Miss Stanley, what is it?" asked Emma. She knew that this visit to a dormitory was unusual for the administrator.

"Oh, young ladies!" she sighed, wringing her hands together. "I have some rather bad news from your home. Please sit down." The girls obeyed and sat side by side on the crisp white bedspread covering Emma's bed.

"Your mother has taken ill and the baby needs care until she is well. We received this news to-day in a telegraph from your father. He wishes Emma to come home straightaway to help with the household. Julia will remain. The bishop has asked me to accompany you part way home, Emma. Your Aunt Arabella will meet us at the Canandaigua station the day after to-morrow. We shall leave on the morning train." After this rapid-fire delivery, Miss Stanley realised that she might have been too severe and added, "I am so sorry to tell you this, girls."

Emma and Julia looked at each other, shocked. Seeing Emma tear up, Julia took her hand in hers and gave it a firm squeeze. Miss Stanley leaned over and opened her arms to embrace them both. Emma tried in vain to stop the tears from flowing. Miss Stanley released them and pulled out her white linen handkerchief. She gently dried the girl's tears.

"I'm so sorry, Emma," she repeated. "This is quite a bit to take in, I know. Wash your face, and come down to dinner now, my dear." The woman turned and left the dormitory.

The roommates crowded round the Burns sisters. Everyone had heard what Miss Stanley said. Lizzie dared to pat Emma on her shoulder. Harriet stood by to support her friend Julia.

Julia blurted out, "Emma, I can't believe it. I don't want you to leave! I know you were looking forward to studying this term. You love it here more than I do now."

"Yes, you're right. I don't want to leave, Julia, but Papa has decided. I have no choice. Mama must be in a bad way. Remember how her ankles were so swollen? P'raps she can't even walk now!" Emma began to sniffle again.

"There, there, dear sister, don't let's worry about that now. We don't really know what is wrong with poor Mama," comforted her sister. "Let's do what Miss Stanley says—go down to dinner. We can talk more after."

❧ ❧ ❧

The aroma of roasting meats and spiced pies baking had wafted all over the school that morning. The several ovens had been going for hours to roast enough turkeys, geese, and chickens. It was a pity that Emma and Julia had no appetite for the sumptuous feast the cooks had prepared for the St Mary's Hall family. That afternoon the diners also tucked into New Jersey cranberries, celery dishes, Irish potatoes, mashed turnips, and pumpkin pie for dessert. Harriet and the Fuller girls were not at all timid about partaking, even though their friends from St Catharines were just picking at their food.

The holiday allowed the girls to talk at table to-day; the din was ear-splitting with so many voices at once, even if each girl tried to keep the volume low. In between bites, Emma and Julia told their friends on either side of the table the sad reason for Emma's imminent departure.

After dinner the pupils did not go outdoors, as it was bitter cold and windy. Instead they dispersed to every corner of the buildings, some to the saloon to pursue their fancywork projects, some to the parlours to dance and play games, others to practise their piano lessons. Laura was playing a rather sombre piece on the saloon instrument when Emma and Julia entered the room together and sat on a favourite upholstered settee. Emma became tearful again, thinking of how she would have to pack up her belongings that evening for the arduous trip home to Canada. She took out a fine linen handkerchief on which she had embroidered a design of blue and yellow pansies in one corner and blew her nose.

"Oh, Laura, please, won't you play something cheerful? It's bad enough that Emma has to leave without making her feel worse with that sad music you are playing. What is it?" begged Julia.

"Emma, I am sorry! It's Chopin, a ballad I am learning with Miss Hewitt. I didn't realise it was upsetting you. Here, I shall leave off, and you can be alone," said Laura.

"No, no," said Emma. "I shall be all right. I love your playing, but choose something happy, please!"

"How about this one?" suggested the accomplished pianist.

"It's one of his *mazurkas*." She began a tune that made Julia want to dance. She pulled Emma to her feet, and they swayed and whirled to the rhythm of the lively piece.

After Laura finished playing, she turned from the piano-forte and asked, "Emma, what time is the train to-morrow?"

"I'm not sure. Miss Stanley just said early in the morning. P'raps the first train of the day. I shall have to get a good night's sleep, but I fear I might not. I have been thinking about Mama all day. I—"

"Oh, Emma, I do wish I could go home in your stead," Julia interrupted her sister.

Emma looked at Julia. "I wish so too, Julia. I know you'd rather be there, but Papa has decided. It is my duty to obey him. I'm the eldest child."

❦ ❦ ❦

At Evening Prayer, Bishop Doane included the name of Henrietta Burns in the prayers of intercession and for the safe travel of Emma and Miss Stanley to New York State. Emma and Julia were both emotional throughout the service, praying about their mother. As the girls filed out in their dormitory groups, the bishop and Mrs La Motte took longer to shake hands with Emma and wished her well on her journey home.

Emma's schoolmates in the dormitory were sympathetic to her plight. Before bedtime they helped her pack her things into the trunk that Mr Jacob brought up from storage. When it came time for prayers, both Emma and Julia again asked God to watch over their mother and baby Llewellyn. Julia fervently wished her father had decided to bring her home instead. She was only a few months younger than Emma. Surely, she could do what needed to be done at home—and then she could see William regularly again too. However, Papa had decided, and there was no way at this point to dispute that Emma should come home straightaway. The rector and Miss Stanley would uphold his order.

❦ ❦ ❦

Whereas Mr Fuller had arranged a rather leisurely paced trip from Canada in September, Miss Stanley had to plan a more rigorous one to conduct Emma homeward in the quickest manner. The duo would take a morning train to South Amboy, followed by the noon steamship ferry to Jersey City and then an afternoon train all the way to Hancock, New York. After a night's rest at the inn there, they would take another early train to Canandaigua by way of Binghamton and Elmira. Some of the trip would no doubt be done in twilight at this time of year, something Miss Stanley disliked. Avoiding hazards on the tracks required caution and slower speeds. The journey would be rather trying compared to Emma's most recent southbound experience.

Emma, searching for something positive in the situation, was at least looking forward to getting to know Miss Stanley better on this trip. The vice principal was a rather tall, middle-aged woman who wore her dark hair pulled back on either side of a centre part in the fashion of the day. She, like the other women faculty, tended to wear subdued colours, plain dress designs and little jewellery, commonly only a brooch on her *basque*.

Nancy McCullough Stanley was born and raised in a large family that lived in a farming area near Geneva in western New York. Geneva was at the north end of Seneca Lake, one of the Finger Lakes. The area around it was known for flower nurseries that thrived in its fertile soil. When Miss Stanley was twenty, her father Erastus died, and she went out to work as a teacher in a school for girls in Geneva. After three years there, she left to take a teaching position at the new Rutgers Female Institute in New York City. For seven years she taught pupils of the First Department in a building just a few blocks from the East River.

One Sunday after the service at her Episcopal parish, All Saints Free Church in Henry Street, Miss Stanley heard of the opening for a vice principal at St Mary's Hall, an Episcopal school for girls. With the arrival of thousands of Irish fleeing poverty and famine, the neighbourhood of Henry Street was changing. After so many years living in New York City, she was ready for a new challenge and not unhappy to return to a small town. She applied and was employed based on her long and appreciated service at Rutgers. She immediately liked Burlington, its countryside, and the intimate atmosphere of St Mary's Hall. The school reminded her of the fellowship she enjoyed with her own large family. Soon after she arrived in 1846, she asked the rector if her younger cousin Jane, an orphan, could be hired to teach music, and he agreed.

Miss Stanley had often made this same trip north to spend holiday months with her four older sisters who still lived in the farmhouse at Stanley Corners. Thus, she knew well the ins and outs of the route in 1855. Emma was pleasantly surprised to find that she was an excellent travelling companion and an interesting conversationalist. The woman's years spent in New York City afforded her an abundance of stories to tell, with lessons of history and morality included.

❧ ❧ ❧

When Emma boarded the train in Burlington, she carried a parcel wrapped in heavy brown paper tied with a slender hemp cord, a last-minute gift that Miss Adams had pressed into her hands at the front door of the Main House. A few minutes after the train left Bordentown, Emma opened the package and found a beautifully bound book. On the spine was printed *Uncle Tom's Cabin*, by Harriet Beecher Stowe, Illustrated Edition, and two images in gilt, a cabin and a little girl. The cover of the handsome red volume was embossed with a depiction of Christ standing over a prostrate man being menaced by two others. Miss Stanley watched as Emma opened it; the woman leaned over and patted the title page proclaiming its 1853 publication in Boston. "Emma, this book is an important one. 'Twas very generous of Miss Adams to give it you. I'm certain 'tis the same volume she received as a Christmas gift from her parents when she was herself a pupil. 'Tis famous now, and there've been many thousands of copies sold. Do you know it?"

"No, Miss Stanley, I don't, but I remember when she received it. It was the first year I was at St Mary's. Have you read it? Who is Uncle Tom?"

"He's the hero of the book, but more significantly, the book is about the value of human life and the horrible scourge of slavery still being practised in parts of the United States," said Miss Stanley.

"Well, there's no slavery in Canada anymore, Miss Stanley. Great Britain abolished it years ago. In fact, my town has wel-

110

comed American fugitive slaves for years. I've met many of them, including a lady they call Moses, a Miss Harriet Tubman. She herself has brought over many courageous people from the southern states. Indeed, she lives in my town of St Catharines."

"I had no idea. Tell me more, Emma," urged the woman.

"Indeed. She is well known in our town. Miss Tubman is a tiny but brave little lady. She was born into slavery in Maryland and injured at a young age by an overseer who threw something heavy at her. I was told it hit her squarely in the head, and she gets spells from it. Even so, she somehow managed to escape to freedom in the North and then dared to go back and forth to bring her own family and many other people all the way up to Canada. In clear weather, she followed the North Star at night through the fields and woods and small rivers to guide her charges to safe houses along the way. They stayed in homes of Quaker Friends where they would rest and eat during the day. Our Uncle Merritt provided some land in St Catharines for her people to build a church. He introduced my father and me to Miss Tubman last summer."

"That's fascinating, Emma." Miss Stanley took the book and began to thumb the pages herself. "I read this about a year ago, and it made me weep, my dear. My country has a lot of heartache ahead, I fear. This book enriched my understanding of slavery and its terrible effects. Although New Jersey abolished the practise years ago, there are still many people affected by it. If they were born before 1804, according to the law that was passed, they could be required to serve their old masters here as permanent indentured servants. In fact, some of those born after 1804 still are made to serve apprenticeships before they can be considered free. Perhaps as a Canadian you have no need to read this book, but it is still a moving experience."

"Oh, I intend to read it, Miss Stanley," said Emma. "I would like to understand why Americans in the South yet believe in enslaving their fellow man."

"Yes, I'm sure this book would upset many of your Southern schoolmates, Emma. After living with us in the North where all people are now born free, I hope those young ladies will return home with different attitudes."

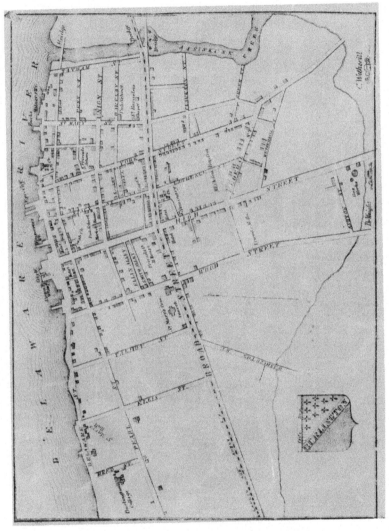

New Map of Burlington County, 1859
Library of Congress, Geography and Map Division,
public domain map published before 1924

CHAPTER 13

Another New Pupil Arrives

SATURDAY, 8 DECEMBER 1855

After a morning spent tidying their spaces in the dormitory, forty-four girls were rewarded with an excursion to High Street in Burlington City. The young ladies were excited to leave the Green Bank after a long week of study. Each dormitory group was chaperoned by their assistant teacher: Miss Adams, Miss Rodney, Miss Theodora Gilmore, and Miss Eliza Cowman. The girls planned to buy things permitted with funds doled out from their individual accounts. Their lists included pencils, ink, stationery, and scent, perhaps some destined for secret Christmas gifts to their friends and dormitory mates. The bishop discouraged the practise of gift-giving among the girls, but the staff, many former pupils themselves, conveniently looked the other way when they saw friends showing love and kindness to each other.

Sadly, they had to return to the school grounds in time for dinner, so the trip had to be quick, with purchases limited to those places providing the products most needed and fastest service. No time for window-shopping! Upon completion of their transactions at the stationer's in High Street, the pupils reunited with their partners in front of Allinson's Pharmacy to go back to school. Arms laden with bundles, the chattering pairs of girls started off down the brick walks toward the river. The weather was brisk, and the sun shone down brightly through the leafless trees along High Street. A shiny black livery carriage pulled by two shaggy horses slowly passed them at the corner of High and Union Streets. The scholars, bundled in their grey winter cloaks and bonnets, were too intent on their own conversations to notice a petite young girl with red curls and ice blue eyes looking out of the carriage window at the spectacle of so many school girls walking down the block.

❦ ❦ ❦

Laura and Lizzie, hungry, tired, and cold from their outing, had trudged upstairs and were washing up for dinner when Mrs La Motte and Margaret Jane appeared into the dormitory doorway together.

"Young ladies of Canada, I've brought someone you might know," said the good-natured matron with a wink, as she neared the beds assigned to Laura and Lizzie.

Lizzie turned in the direction of the woman's voice and recognised Margaret Jane at once. She was wearing a green and blue plaid taffeta skirt, a band of blue velvet encircling its hem. A matching plaid sash crossed her chest and the dark blue waist she wore. The whole outfit set off her light red hair to good effect. She looked very much the proud Scottish lass with white hose and black morocco slippers showing out from under her skirt. She held her green velvet bonnet in one hand and a leather valise in the other.

"Margaret Jane! You *have* come! Papa's letter said you should be here this month. What a good day to arrive. It's Saturday! We don't have lessons all day long!" said Lizzie.

Then she saw Mrs La Motte raise her eyebrows and purse her lips together. Perhaps she shouldn't have said the last bit, Lizzie thought, but it was true in any case.

Harriet and Julia, returning from their morning composition class with Bishop Doane in his library at Riverside, joined the trio and crowded round the newcomer. Laura was quick to introduce Harriet and Julia, who had also heard about Margaret Jane's plight via Mr Fuller's letters to his daughters.

"I'm so relieved to be here! I'm so tired of travelling. It was such a long trip with Father, you know. Four days in the cars, rocking to and fro, and the noise and the smoke and all the stops. We nearly hit a cow on the tracks this morning leaving Yardville! Thank the Lord it was smart enough to move off in time."

Mrs La Motte cut short the girl's remarks. "Margaret Jane, you'll use this bed next to Julia's. It was her sister's. Emma had to leave when their mother took ill. You may put your clothes on the pegs and in the cupboard. There's also a shelf over the bed for your hatbox. Mr Jacob will bring up your trunk straightaway so that you can fill the chest there at the foot of the bed. Keep all of your small things in it. Your chambermaid is Lucinda. She'll bring you water in the morning and change your bed weekly when your laundry is done. Your friends will tell you which day that is. Other mornings you're expected to make your own bed before devotions. It's all very easy. Now wash your face and hands and comb your hair if need be, dearie. Yes, need be!" She winked at Margaret Jane. "The bell will ring for dinner any minute. Girls, I expect you to tell Margaret Jane all she needs to know about our dinner."

"Oh, yes, Mrs La Motte, we shall," replied Julia.

"I know you will, dearie," said the matron with a smile as she turned to leave the room.

❦ ❦ ❦

The four Canadian pupils crowded round Margaret Jane.

"Margaret Jane, what happened?" asked Lizzie, after Mrs La Motte had disappeared downstairs. "No one knew you weren't coming on the train that day."

"Oh, Lizzie, I was so anxious to come down here with you all! Father had told me all about St Mary's Hall. Mama was fine with it for weeks and then, that day in the morning, she decided she couldn't bear to be alone in the house with only the men! My father. My brothers. They're not married yet. She thought she would be lonely without me and have all the work of the household too. It didn't help later that she heard about the awful accident here with the train and the waggon last summer. Then she didn't want me to travel in the cars at all."

"Yes, we heard about that after we got here too. It happened only a couple of weeks before we arrived. The town was still abuzz about it when we got here. The man in the waggon was a doctor, out with his family, and the train backed up," said Laura.

"Then what changed her mind, Margaret Jane?" asked Julia.

"Well, since I wasn't going to school anymore I had a lot of time to talk to her alone. It happened to be my thirteenth birthday, September fourth, so I shall always remember the day that we had our first serious talk together. We were picking peaches that morning, and she told me about my sisters and how they were taken ill and died and how other women's babies suffered. And the women grieving the losses and having so many babies until they are old and tired. We had a lot of good talks about important subjects after that. I never knew she had so much heartache inside."

"It's true, Margaret Jane. My mother died having a baby too, and she was young. I miss her still. It's been four years," interjected Harriet.

"Oh, my, Margaret Jane, this is Harriet Taylor, by the way. She's from Toronto."

"Pleased to meet you, Harriet." The two girls' eyes met.

"But still, why did she reconsider?" asked Julia.

"Well, my brother John is a physician, and, as I said, he lives in our house. We all watch him fret about his sick patients. He's called to their bedsides day and night. Hearing him talk about them and their problems, I decided that I wanted to be a physician too. And I told Mama that I needed to go back to school to do that. I want to help women and children live good long lives. I don't want to be just a wife and mother myself. I want to make a difference," said the determined young girl.

"A physician! Can a girl be a physician?" challenged Laura.

"Well, I don't see why not. John is often overworked tending to women having trouble giving birth and then their ailing babes. The second summer, he says, they're always getting sick, and many die after they wean. He would welcome some help I should think. There are local women helping others have babies all the time, you know—every town has midwives. How difficult can it be? Mother says 'twould be very hard for a woman to become a physician, though. But she finally let me come down here because she realised I was serious. And I was so bored at home."

"Oh, well, you won't be bored here," said Lizzie. "We're up at dawn and doing something every minute till we fall into bed at night."

"You exaggerate, Lizzie," corrected Julia. "We have to have a lie-down before we study, and they make us go outside unless it's pouring. You'll see, Margaret Jane! Anyhow, I am glad to meet you. Let's go down to dinner, and then we shall all help you put away your things."

CHAPTER 14

Winter at the Hall

CHRISTMAS EVE, MONDAY, 24 DECEMBER 1855
All of the resident pupils understood that, while they were at
St Mary's Hall, they would not be spending Christmas with their
own families. Bishop Doane took pains to emphasise in the
school catalogue that while at St Mary's Hall, the school was their
family away from home. Only Christmas Day would be a holiday
from lessons, and additional time away from their studies was
strictly forbidden. Of course, Burlington or Mount Holly girls
could celebrate the birth of Jesus with family and friends on December twenty-fifth. Most would end the day with a festive, satisfying meal after attending church services, but they also had to
return to their lessons at St Mary's Hall the very next day.

To-day, after the last morning lesson, Lizzie waved good-bye
to her new friend Susan Harker as she rode off in the carriage
with her father to join her family in Mount Holly. Harriet, Laura,
and Julia were among the remaining pupils who attended the optional noon chapel service. Margaret Jane, being Presbyterian, did
not go to these as a rule. She thought twice-daily services and private devotions were more than enough worship time for her. She

preferred to be outside enjoying the fresh air rather than be confined in the chapel. To-day Lizzie joined her. The anticipation of Christmas was just too much for Lizzie! And given a choice, she would never sit still inside if she could be out of doors.

After the service ended, the seniors stayed behind to attend to their traditional task of decorating the chapel with fresh evergreen boughs, wreaths, and holly branches that the porters had cut from trees on the grounds and delivered to the little porch at the top of the chapel steps. It was always a thrill for the younger girls to walk in and see the gas-lit chapel decorated for Christmas. The powerful pine aroma was intoxicating. The red and green colours of the holly branches were a cheery contrast to the cream-coloured walls. Junior and Middle pupils, practising their most elegant Gothic script, had spent the last few days copying and decorating Christmas verses from the prophets and the Gospels. The seniors posted them on the walls along with intricate Christmas emblems cut from paper. Younger pupils were kept busy that afternoon placing greenery in every possible corner of the house and their dormitories.

The completion of decorating meant the scholars could now spend a few minutes before dinner delivering or hiding the little gifts that they had made for their friends. While buying gifts for each other was strongly discouraged, handmade ones were tolerated by the staff with a wink and a good-natured smile. The girls had put much thought and time into creating the products destined for their cherished schoolmates, their sisters at St Mary's Hall. Some of the most pious girls gave copies of Bishop Doane's Advent sermons to their friends with mixed reception. The Christmas holiday also meant that extra food and treats were available at all times of the day. All through December, barrels and boxes were delivered from families and friends of the pupils and staff. In the saloon, hallways, and parlours there were bowls of raisins, nuts, and apples for the taking. Cakes, crackers, soda and wine biscuits, dried meats and sweetmeats were shared with the whole school family between and during meals.

After dinner, Laura and the most musically accomplished girls took turns playing the piano in the saloon so that the rest could listen, relax, or dance. Others caught up on their leisure reading or letter writing in the School Room.

❦ ❦ ❦

It had been mild weather of late, and the river was still open for navigation. There would be no snow for Christmas this year with temperatures like these, but this afternoon the sky was grey and cloudy. At four o'clock Lizzie felt the urge to escape outside again. She had taken a lovely red apple from the barrel sent by Miss Salter's family in Boston; Lizzie wanted to eat it before supper. She and Margaret Jane put on their cloaks and bonnets to join Harriet and Julia for an hour's walk round the Circle before darkness fell. Laura stayed in to practise Christmas music and set the tone for the holiday for anyone who would appreciate her effort.

The cook served some simple pancakes for supper that evening, and no one thought ill of it since the inmates knew tomorrow's Christmas dinner would be ample. Because there would be a Christmas eve service later that night, the pupils were allowed to visit all over the building until ten o'clock. The five Canadian girls, in due course, gathered in their dormitory to exchange gifts and open presents from home before they had to line up for chapel.

"Hattie, what's in that large package?" asked Julia, after they had finished their gift exchange.

"Something from Father. It came this morning," answered Harriet.

"Oh, do open it! It looks intriguing!" said Margaret Jane.

Harriet slipped off the braided hemp string and opened the brown paper, revealing a parcel wrapped in crisp white tissue paper tied with a wide red satin ribbon. She untied the bow and took off the tissue paper. Inside was a flat box. When she opened the lid and pulled back the paper, she saw a soft, white woolen cape, embroidered with flowers in red, green, blue, and yellow yarn.

"Oh, my, Hattie. It's beautiful! Put it on for us!" exclaimed Julia.

"Yes, do," urged Lizzie.

With tears in her eyes, Harriet untied the white silk cords; she had recognised the cape immediately. As she unfolded it and shook it out, a calling card fell on the floor. Laura picked it up, saw that there was a message written on it and handed it to her friend.

"What is it, Hattie?" Julia noticed Harriet's tears, and she put her arm round the girl's shoulder.

"Read the card, Hattie," said Laura quietly.

"It was my mother's. I remember it." She read the card to herself. "Father wants me to have it now that I'm a young lady. He said I remind him of my mother." Harriet began to sniffle. Laura at once offered her handkerchief and Harriet dabbed at her eyes.

"Oh, Hattie, it is beautiful. Please put it on," repeated Julia.

"I can't! It was hers, and she's gone forever!"

"Hattie, she's not truly gone if she's in your heart," said Laura. "She has eternal life that way."

"Wouldn't you disappoint your father if you didn't accept his gift, Hattie?" asked Julia.

"Yes, you might put it on, for him, Hattie, and see," said Margaret Jane.

"Well, all right," said Harriet as she stood and draped the precious object round her shoulders. Julia gently pushed her friend's hair out of the way and tied the cords in a bow for her. The others stood back to admire the gift.

"Oh, it is stunning, Hattie! Look in your glass!" said Laura.

Harriet turned and peeked at herself in the looking glass. She could only see her face and the shoulders of the cape, even on tiptoe. Then she had a flash of memory of her mother from five years ago when she was expecting her baby. Mary Elizabeth Taylor had received the cape from her husband for Christmas and had worn it in the house to keep warm that winter until her confinement in April.

She dissolved into sobs, "Oh, Mama! I miss you so!"

Harriet's schoolmates surrounded her and embraced her one after the other. Julia was crying with her when Miss Stanley came into the dormitory to wish them all a happy Christmas. She saw the commotion on the other side of the room and approached the group.

"Is anything wrong, girls?" said the vice principal.

Lizzie answered first. "Hattie received a beautiful cape from her father, but it was her mother's, and it's made her sad."

Miss Stanley took Harriet's hand and consoled her, "Ah, there, there, Harriet. It's Christmas Eve and a time to be joyous, not sad! Let us remember that your mother is with our Lord. She wants you to be happy here on Earth."

"I'm trying hard to believe that, Miss Stanley, but I miss her so much. My friends here all still have their mothers."

"I agree that we cannot all understand your loss, Harriet. I was lucky enough to have my mother into adulthood, but now that she is gone, I miss her too, especially when I return home. Remember that your father has given you this gift in her memory. I'm sure he wants you to be warm and to wear it in good health. Honour his gift with that in mind. I imagine 'twas difficult for him to part with it," said the woman.

"Thank you, Miss Stanley, I shall try to remember that." Harriet turned back to the glass on the wall to conceal her renewed tears.

Miss Adams came out from behind her velvet curtain, little brass bell in hand, to check the clock on the mantelpiece. She greeted the vice principal with a curtsy and Miss Stanley wished them all a happy Christmas and a good night before she left to attend to her own eleven senior scholars.

❧ ❧ ❧

At half-past ten, Mrs La Motte opened the transept doors, and all of the girls filed silently into the chapel from the narrow hallway linked to the Main House. Candles were ablaze, and the gaslights were turned low. Miss Hewitt was playing the prelude, "Wonderful Night", on the little organ as they entered. There was much oohing and aahing as the younger girls admired the verdant decorations applied by the seniors. The scent of pine boughs was pervasive as the worshippers sang joyous Christmas carols and recited prayers led by Dr Millett. The service ended with the German carol, "Stille Nacht", and the Christmas benediction.

Back in the dormitory at nearly midnight, the girls got into their nightdresses and brushed out their hair. For a Christmas gift, Julia was dampening and tying up Harriet's long wavy hair with six strips of cloth to make thick ringlets round her head. The pupils were at last climbing into bed when they heard voices below their windows. Oblivious to the cold night air, Lizzie threw open the window and shutters to better hear the beloved carols rising from Ellis Street. The young ladies of St Mary's Hall clutched their quilts round them as they listened. The Carols of the Waits was a new tradition introduced two seasons ago in Burlington. After the last notes faded away in the darkness, the folk moved on to the Main House to intone yet another set of Christmas hymns. The occupants of each dormitory fell back to their beds with the sweet music still echoing in their heads.

❦ ❦ ❦

After breakfast and Morning Prayer in the festive, albeit cold, chapel, the drowsy members of the Senior A class bundled up to go outdoors. They hurried through a fine drizzle along the path to Riverside on a mission to deliver the traditional senior Christmas gift to Bishop Doane. It was a cross fashioned of ivy leaves cut from those clinging to the chapel walls, interwoven and varnished to preserve its shape. In his study, the bishop feigned surprise, for this was an annual occurrence; he thanked them before placing the ornament in a prominent location therein.

When it was time to leave for St Mary's Church, he insisted that Michael drive Mrs Doane, prone to illness, in their carriage to avoid the damp. Clad in his black woolen cloak and hat, he huddled under a large umbrella to accompany the seniors, girls he considered daughters, on their last Christmas Day walk to the parish church. Normally such weather required the service of Holy Communion be celebrated in the chapel, but it was Christmas Day, and the whole school made the trek through the back streets to Broad Street. It was a parade of almost two hundred faculty, staff, and pupils, not to mention those from Burlington College.

Two hours later, when Miss Adams' pupils returned, cold and damp from the rain, they stopped first in the cloakroom to remove their overshoes and store their umbrellas, bonnets, and wraps. The various fireplaces and modern stoves were keeping the temperature up in the hallways; in some areas of the school it was even too warm as the girls made their way down to the eating room.

The kitchen staff stood ready to serve the sumptuous Christmas dinner. There was plentiful roast turkey again, plus chicken, mashed potatoes, sweet potatoes, mashed turnips and pickles, followed by a traditional flaming plum pudding for each table. The senior tables were served first, followed by the junior, middle and primary departments. Faculty allowed hushed talk among the pupils, but because of the sheer number in the room and the joy of the occasion, it was impossible to maintain the usual quiet. The meal lasted longer than the normal thirty minutes allotted, and after the customary closing grace, the girls filed out in their dormitory groups.

The afternoon was free of any scheduled events, and by turns the pupils used the time to visit, read, do needlework, or finish letters. The highlight of that evening's supper was the annual cup of coffee allotted the pupils. For Lizzie and Margaret Jane, it was their first taste of the bitter brew. They looked at each other, confused, until Julia giggled and added teaspoons of sugar and some cream to make it palatable.

The school family braved the relentless rain again to cross the Circle to the School Room where they watched the seniors present tableaux depicting exotic places, poems, historical and biblical events such as the Nativity. The girls had been working on them since Thanksgiving Day, and they wore elaborate costumes created from items begged from everyone's wardrobe.

🦌 🦌 🦌

Just before dinner on Saturday afternoon, January fifth, the wind changed, and with it came snow. It fell heavily all afternoon and night. On Sunday morning, Laura awoke first, opened the interior shutters and looked out the window plastered with snow. She shook Lizzie who, upon seeing the whiteness, shrieked with joy.

"Look at the snow! Hurrah! Look, Margaret Jane! Julia! Hattie!"

Harriet opened one eye and reached out of her nice warm bed to the floor. She felt around and picked up one of her slippers, aimed it in the general direction of Lizzie, and lobbed it toward the younger girl.

It missed its mark, but Lizzie picked up the missile and threw it back toward Hattie, whereupon Julia picked up both of her slippers and tossed one Margaret Jane's way and the other back at her friend Hattie.

Harriet sat up. "It's Epiphany Day, and it's Sunday! We shall be in church half the day! Let me sleep now!"

"Grumpy girl!" said Lizzie. "Can't you see it's snowed? It's all against the window." She wiped the windowpane and tried to peer outside through a layer of ice crystals. "I can't tell how much there is, but it's beautiful."

"I don't really care, Lizzie. I *have* seen snow before in Canada, you know!" She rolled over and closed her eyes again. "And give me back my slipper, please!"

That morning the girls missed the chapel bell ringing for *toilette*. Where was Mr Jacob? When Miss Adams realised there would be no bell tolling, she rang her own for the girls to start their hour-long routine in the accustomed silence. The water taken from the hot side stopcocks to fill the girls' ewers was so cold that many of them decided not to wash their faces at all. They cringed when they brushed their teeth with the icy water and dressed quickly, putting on extra flannel petticoats. It was going to be an unusual day if there was no one to ring the bell! Miss Adams looked at the mantel clock at seven and sounded her own little bell once to begin and end the ten minutes of devotions. She led her pupils downstairs where they found others in the eating room. There was a sense of adventure among the inmates! The departure from normal operations was exciting!

The girls were satisfied with the normal breakfast of tea, toast, and cold meat from yesterday's dinner. Mrs La Motte and Miss Stanley had cobbled it together from the cold storage area with the help of chambermaids Lucinda, Ellen, and Mary Ann. Cook had not made it in from her house only a few blocks away!

By ten o'clock, the sun shone brightly, but the air was frigid, below zero degrees Fahrenheit. The girls were relieved to hear it was too cold and snowy to make the usual Sunday trek to St Mary's Church. Instead, Dr Millett would lead a service in the School Room after he got fires going in its two fireplaces. The scholars wondered about the afternoon's long-awaited event though, the dinner that had long ago been dubbed the Bishop's Feast. Would it go on as planned?

❦ ❦ ❦

Michael Dunn and Mr Jacob spent the morning clearing a narrow path through the twenty-four inches of snow that lay on the ground between the house and Riverside. At two o'clock, pairs of girls and staff members carefully negotiated their way down the icy front steps spread with sawdust and ashes for traction. They hurried single file through the hundred foot passageway created between towering walls of snow. The episcopal mansion was already decorated, warmed, and lighted to greet the merry company. Bishop and Mrs Doane were determined to host their annual celebratory dinner for the staff and pupils of St Mary's Hall whom they considered family. They wouldn't have disappointed their "daughters" for the world!

Holly sprigs decked the doorways and mantelpieces and held back the long white muslin curtains at the leaded glass windows. The seniors' cross of ivy was prominently displayed on the long refectory table in the library. In each room a fire crackled in the fireplace. Laura and other talented girls took turns entertaining the company on the piano-forte in the cosy west drawing room before dinner was served.

❦ ❦ ❦

In the wake of the January blizzard was a prolonged period of brilliant cold days and freezing nights. Steamboat travel to and from Philadelphia annually came to a standstill until a not uncommon January thaw occurred, often late in the month. That was not to happen in 1856. The shallow Delaware River was frozen solid even where the busy ferry route between Bristol, Pennsylvania, and Burlington could, in other years, break up the fragile ice that formed overnight. Travellers and townspeople desperate to get to the other side bundled up and took sleighs or tried to walk across the river. Through the front windows of the Main House, the St Mary's girls watched contests between young men sailing elaborate iceboats they had designed and built. Others skated on the bumpy ice for exercise and amusement. Lizzie Fuller yearned to be outside with them, but she had left her skates at home.

❦ ❦ ❦

St Catharines, Canada
22 January 1856

Dearest Julia,

I just received your letter in the afternoon post, and it took twelve days to arrive! I loved reading about the blizzard and the Christmas tableaux and the wonderful party at the bishop's house. The Bishop's Feast must have been delicious, especially the venison and turkey. You know how I love turkey! Mama told me what oysters were and I don't think I would like them. She said she would get some in a tin for me to try. She used to eat them (huîtres) a lot when she lived in Montréal. We have also been sleighing round town since the last big snow. Uncle Henry gave us a new buffalo robe for the sleigh and it is very heavy and warm. We four can all be covered with room for more! Papa loves driving the sleigh.

Did Papa tell you in his letter that we had a Christmas tree this year for Mama? We put it on a table in the parlour and Emma and I helped Norman and Libby make decorations for it. We all put them on except for the little candles that Papa had to light. Mama was so happy with it. She said it reminded her of trees at Grandpa Mittleberger's house. She said it was a German tradition and it is just more popular now because Queen Victoria's husband is from Germany. I think Mama is feeling much stronger and happier since Emma came home. Baby Lewie is finally growing and doesn't cry so much. Mama was so sad before. She would lie curled up in her bed all day long and barely eat. Even Papa could not get her to dress to come downstairs. He had to get the baby a nurse but Mama is fairly back to her old self now. She was smiling on Christmas Day.

Your loving sister,
Bella

❦ ❦ ❦

SHROVE TUESDAY, 5 FEBRUARY 1856

When the rising bell awakened the girls in Miss Adams' dormitory, the windowpanes were again covered with delicate patterns of ice crystals. Outside a fine dusting of new snow lay on top of the old; the sky was bleak and grey.

Lizzie awoke, remembering that to-day was special in the church calendar. Shrove Tuesday was a day for confession and repentance during hours spent on one's knees in prayer. Lent, a season of self-examination and penitence, would begin to-morrow on Ash Wednesday. As the daughter of a clergyman, she knew very well that the Lenten season meant fasting and solemnity in preparation for Easter, the most joyous day of the church year. Bishop Doane expected his St Mary's Hall family to observe Lent strictly until Easter Day came this year on March 23. There would be no dancing permitted in the school for the coming weeks, and the daily serving of meat would be reduced and absent on Fridays altogether. The bishop had moderated some of his High Church practises over the last three years in response to the presentments he had suffered at the hands of some Low Church critics. He had examined them even more since September last when his elder son George converted to Roman Catholicism. The father continued to suffer greatly from this very personal desertion, and it caused him to reconsider some of his long-held Catholic aspirations for the Episcopal Church.

After dinner, the girls returned to the dormitory to rest until it was time for afternoon study. Lizzie had been rather down in the mouth all day because her birth-day was in a fortnight, during Lent again this year, as it often was. She wondered if Laurie remembered. She hadn't said a word about it. Did her friends even know when her birthday was?

She lay down on the white counterpane covering her bed and closed her eyes. She heard the other girls still moving about the room and whispering. She wondered why they too hadn't settled down by now.

"Surprise!" Margaret Jane yelled, as she pounced on her friend's stomach.

Lizzie's brown eyes flew open as she pushed her friend away. "What're you doing?!" she shrieked.

"Shh!" said Julia. "Miss Adams is on the stairs talking to Miss Cronyn."

"Here, look what we've brought you, Lizzie!" exclaimed Harriet, handing the younger girl a bundle tied with a piece of red satin ribbon saved from Christmas.

Lizzie pulled off the ribbon. The paper came undone, and the girl squealed with happiness. "Ooooh, dough balls!"

"Shh! We weren't supposed to go to Mitchell's, you know, but Margaret Jane and I sneaked away from the group last Saturday to buy them while Miss Adams was in the stationer's," said Harriet.

"Oh, my, this is wonderful! You know how I love dough balls. And I thought you would forget my birth-day this year."

"Now, Lizzie, how could I forget your birth-day? I know how it vexes you to have it so often fall during Lent," said her sister.

"Thank you, everyone! 'Tis a great surprise. Here, take a piece, all of you!"

"Oh no, thank you," said Julia. "I don't really care for them. You enjoy them for me, please."

"Don't mind if I do," said Margaret Jane, holding out her hand to Lizzie.

❦ ❦ ❦

That evening the cook used up a great quantity of eggs, milk, and sugar to make over three hundred pancakes for Shrove Tuesday supper. Each girl was served a stack of two, and four lucky pupils found slipped between their cakes either a button, a coin, a key, or a ring. Miss Stanley stood and read a short poem for each token, predicting the future for the winning girls in an amusing rhyme. The girls clapped for them all and gobbled up the sweet cakes, knowing this was the last such treat they would have until Easter.

❦ ❦ ❦

ASH WEDNESDAY, 6 FEBRUARY 1856

If it had been a regular, freezing day, the morning service would have been held in the School Room, but it was Ash Wednesday. The chapel was barely warm when the seniors settled themselves in the choir pews. The younger pupils walked single file in their dormitory groups, padding softly across the tiles in their black morocco slippers. They sat together in the nave pews with their teachers. From the chancel Dr Millett conducted the service of the Holy Eucharist with the Litany, reading from the large Book of Common Prayer. The whole congregation repeated the responses in unison. Margaret Jane tried to follow along as best she could as a Presbyterian unfamiliar with the Litany office. The service was longer than usual Morning Prayer, and the floor was cold and hard on the girl's bony knees. She tried to make a kneeling cushion by folding up the bottom of her cloak as she saw Julia and Lizzie doing the same on either side of her.

Margaret Jane saw someone's head drop in the row in front of her. Then the girl slumped over and leaned heavily against Miss Adams' shoulder. Miss Adams looked around hoping to see Miss McIntire, but the nurse was a Roman Catholic and could not attend services at the school. Hearing the unusual whispers among the girls, Miss Stanley left her pew to see if she could help.

"Who is it, Miss Adams?" she asked.

"Laura."

Miss Stanley motioned for Miss Adams to move aside and let her into the pew.

Miss Stanley whispered Laura's name, hoping to rouse her. After a couple of tries, Laura, groggy, raised her head.

"What happened?"

"You must have swooned, Laura. Let's make room for you to lie down on the pew seat," Miss Stanley whispered.

The pew seat was hard and narrow. The other girls had to squeeze together to allow Laura room to lie down. Dr Millett continued in the chancel uninterrupted. Miss Stanley returned to her seat, and Miss Adams patted Laura on the head as she tried to focus again on the Litany.

When the service ended, she helped Laura to her feet and guided her up the aisle to the east doors. Miss Stanley took over there and escorted Laura upstairs to the Nursery.

Lizzie wanted to go with her sister, but Miss Adams stopped her.

"You needn't worry, Elizabeth. Miss Stanley has Laura well in hand. Miss McIntire will see that she gets some food."

"But what's wrong?"

"'Tis probably nought. Girls swoon all the time, especially during the Litany. Just too long kneeling, I suppose."

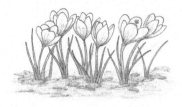

CHAPTER 15

Margaret Jane to the Rescue

FRIDAY, 7 MARCH 1856

March had come in like a lamb, and there was hope that the long, cold winter would soon be over as the first crocuses poked their colourful heads up out of the snow melting in the gardens and lawns of St Mary's Hall. Margaret Jane was lying in her bed, snug and warm under her quilts. It was early morning, before the first bell. She did not know why she was so wide-awake, but in the quiet dormitory, she was at peace, thinking about herself and her life.

The girl had not had time to be sad, lonely, or homesick since she arrived in Burlington. She had been working conscientiously at her studies and had been rewarded with stellar marks from her teachers. She excelled at Latin, algebra, and chemistry, receiving the mark of nine on each one for the last six weeks. She was not quite as natural a botanist as Lizzie Fuller was, but that was because her best friend had spent hours at home observing and collecting plants and insects. Margaret Jane was doing well at the histories too, making eights, but they did not interest her as much as science.

133

When she was a little girl, she had been certain of her future: husband, family, and children. She would be like her mother and the other women she knew in Port Robinson. There was just no question. What else was there for a girl to do in rural Canada West? But she often wondered now what her brother John would say if she asked him about her idea to learn medicine. Before Margaret Jane was born, he had watched their parents suffer. They lost three children under age five to illnesses that neither Dr King nor Dr Jukes had been able to cure. John was inspired to study medicine because of the anguish his family and the townspeople experienced due to cholera outbreaks and the frequent injuries suffered by the canal and mill workers.

Margaret Jane was herself a bit afraid of having children because of the inevitable losses a woman would encounter during her lifetime. Surely if a woman knew more about her body and common illnesses, she could have a healthier family and life.

As Margaret Jane gazed up at the plaster ceiling, her thoughts turned to the approaching April vacation month. Her parents had agreed to let her come home. Allowing for the eight-day round-trip train journey, it would only be a three-week visit. They must really miss her if they were willing to pay for another train trip! Her Scottish father did not like spending money unnecessarily. More likely, her mother just missed her. Margaret Jane decided to talk to John as soon as she got home about how she could become a physician. The girls in her chemistry class said there was a medical college for women in Philadelphia. She wondered if there were such a place in Canada.

Margaret Jane heard a commotion in the corner of the room. She rolled out of bed to see what the matter was, a thick counterpane clutched round her against the chilly air. "What's wrong? What happened?" she called into the semi-darkness.

"It's Laurie. She must have swooned again. She's on the floor. Come quick!" called Lizzie to the other girls in the dormitory room.

Margaret Jane ran to where Laurie lay on the floor and threw her counterpane over the stricken girl. Margaret Jane turned to Lizzie and said, "Go and fetch Mrs La Motte. Miss Adams must be already downstairs or she would have come out of her sanctum to see what was going on."

Lizzie sped down the hall, through the east annex, and over to the matron's room in the Main House, disturbing the rest of the second floor in her haste.

"Laurie, wake up!" said Margaret Jane. She tore the comforters off Laurie's bed and stuffed them under her friend's limbs. Then she began tapping the girl's hand. "Laurie, Laurie! It's me, Margaret Jane! Please wake up!"

In what seemed like hours but was really only a couple of minutes, Laurie was taking long, deep, noisy breaths and looking sleepily around her.

"What happened?" she asked the other girls as Mrs La Motte arrived, Lizzie leading the matron through the passageway.

"You must have swooned again, dearie. Elizabeth found you, and Margaret Jane and the others stayed with you till you woke. Margaret Jane, isn't this your counterpane? Well done, dearie. It kept her warm. Let's get you off this cold floor and into the bed. I shall send for the doctor and move you over to the infirmary straightaway. Are you hungry? Julia, ask Lucinda to fetch her something from the kitchen. Perhaps you didn't eat enough at supper, Laura?"

"I don't know, Mrs La Motte. I did eat everything on my plate, and I felt all right at bedtime. I got up to use the chamber pot just now and didn't get too far."

"I understand, dearie. Go ahead then, but be careful lest you fall out again. Thank you, girls. 'Tis almost time for the first bell. No time to get back to sleep. 'Twill just be an early day for us all. Well done, Margaret Jane. I shall tell the bishop about the kind and excellent care you gave your friend."

🐝 🐝 🐝

Laura was brought to the Nursery, two large rooms on the second floor of the long wooden building connected to the chapel annex. The walls of each room were lined with iron bedsteads interspersed with comfortable chairs and sofas. One room was for those inmates deemed contagious and the other for those with less serious ailments. Laura was not permitted visitors until Dr Charles Ellis had examined her and pronounced her not contagious. He thought the young girl might be suffering from chlorosis, a lack of iron in the blood that caused her skin to have a green tinge. Because this was the second incident, the doctor wrote her parents a letter to explain his diagnosis. He prescribed her iron tablets, a daily serving of liver, and a week of rest in the Nursery watched over dutifully by the school nurse, Miss Margaret McIntire.

When Lizzie was allowed to visit her sister, she was happy to see her feeling better, although still rather weak and pale. Miss McIntire ensured that Laura ate more frequent meals and that her patient was not out of bed except when absolutely essential. Lizzie was worried about her and prayed that she would soon be well enough to enjoy the upcoming holiday month. They had been invited to stay at the McHenry girls' family farm in nearby Mount Holly to have a change of scenery. Now what would happen to that glorious plan?

CHAPTER 16

Margaret Jane Seeks Advice

APRIL 1856, PORT ROBINSON

After the exhausting journey north from the United States and being away from home for four months, Margaret Jane was delighted to be back in her own featherbed. She had slept well, but awakened with her head full of questions to ask her twenty-seven-year-old brother Dr John McFarland.

Could I learn to be a physician? Where would I go to learn? What must I study? How long would it take?

She poured some cold water from the flowered porcelain ewer into the matching basin and gently washed her face with the softened piece of sea sponge. *It still smells of salt*, she thought, after months of sitting unused in the dish. She patted her face dry with the linen towel embroidered with her mother's initials MEM, for Margaret Elliot McFarland. She doffed her nightcap and pulled her nightdress over her head, revealing a white cotton chemise. Then she put on a fresh pair of white cotton stockings, rolling the garters over them to hold them in place, a pair of clean drawers, followed by one flannel petticoat. Opening her cupboard, she paused a minute and chose the blue cotton gingham dress rather than the green challis plaid. She stared at her hair critically in the small glass over the chest of drawers, shook her head and gave her curls a few strokes of the boar bristle brush. Ugh, tangles! She would let her mother fuss with it. She slipped on her soft indoor shoes to go downstairs. Before she closed the door to her room, she plucked her thick grey wool blanket shawl off the peg behind the door and wrapped it round her narrow shoulders for the morning dash outside.

When Margaret Jane returned from the backhouse, she changed out of her mother's curious new gaiters, rubber shoes made in the American state of Connecticut, and left them in the mudroom. They were wet on the outside from the trek out to the garden, but her stockings were dry, although her feet were cold. What an invention! She should ask to take some back to New Jersey for those rainy days crossing the Circle to the School Room.

Mrs McFarland was seated at the breakfast table in the morning room, sipping her tea. The early spring sun streamed through the large east window, lighting but barely warming the space. Margaret Jane leaned over and gave her mother a peck on the cheek.

"Good morning, Mama! I'm so happy to be home! I missed you and Father so much! Where is he this morning? I thought he would be here for breakfast."

"Good morning to you too, dear heart! You know we missed you too! Your father took the stage down to St Catharines to do some business. We thought we would let you sleep late. He'll be back for supper. Here, love, have some tea and bread. Do you want some oatmeal?"

Mrs McFarland served the tea from the English porcelain teapot into a matching cup and saucer decorated with roses, generous gifts from her brother Robert Elliott, a Port Robinson merchant. Then she called for Maria to fetch some oatmeal from the pot on the stove.

Margaret Jane drizzled warm maple syrup from the pitcher onto her hot cereal, and between swallows, she described in detail all of the reasons why she intended to be a doctor to women. Mrs McFarland listened carefully and wiped a tear from her face as the girl described how she wanted to make childbirth and infancy safer for women and children. So many of her friends at St

Mary's Hall had lost their mothers, either during childbirth or soon after, and nearly all had lost sisters and brothers to some kind of illness at a young age. It had also deeply impressed Margaret Jane that her own family had mourned daughters before her, and her mother had lost siblings in their infancy. More importantly, she had learnt from conversations with her friends at school that most women, not only Canadians, were worn out by near continuous pregnancies. Having a child every two years took a toll on their health.

"Margaret Jane, I'm very proud of you and your plans, but 'twill be a difficult pursuit. Medicine is a man's world. You must talk to John."

"Mama, that's exactly why I wanted to come home, to talk to him about being a physician. And to see you and Father, of course! P'raps I can even spend some time with him visiting patients while I am here, to see what it's like," said Margaret Jane as she stood to take her dishes out to the kitchen. "There he is now—coming down the stairs. I'm going to ask him straightaway!" The side door closed with a bang behind the young doctor who went sprinting to the barn.

❦ ❦ ❦

John was opening the barn doors to get his horse and buggy out when Margaret Jane caught up to him, running pell-mell out the back door of the house in her mother's gaiters, clutching her shawl round her.

"John, I'm glad I caught you! I want to talk to you about something important!"

"Not right now, Maggie. I'm off to see Mrs Feener's baby. She's in a bad way at the moment. I've just had a message."

"The tailor's wife? Can I help you there? I want to be a physician, John, like you!"

"A physician! My word, Maggie. You're still a child. Go in now to Mama. What has that school put in your head?" growled her brother as he pulled the horse in front of the buggy to hitch it.

"Oh, fine, John. Go on alone. I only travelled four days home to ask your advice, and this is how you treat me," said Margaret Jane, choking back the tears of hurt and surprise. She had always idolised her older brother, and this rebuff upon seeing him for the first time in months stung her.

"You would have learnt as much had you written me, Maggie, and saved yourself the trouble of a long journey. You are not warmly dressed, and I have work to do. Now go back inside!" ordered John, his face reddening. He cracked the buggy whip over the horse's back and drove out of the barn, leaving Margaret Jane alone and speechless.

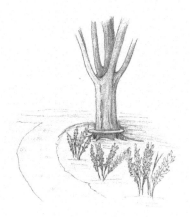

CHAPTER 17

Isabella Burns

LATE APRIL 1856, ST CATHARINES

At the end of March, Thomas Burns had travelled to Burlington himself to escort Julia, Margaret Jane, and the Fuller sisters back to Canada. His wife had asked to see Julia, and so he had changed his mind about Julia's staying at school. The visit had gone well for the first week while the weather was pleasant. Henrietta could go outside with her children to enjoy the sunshine, but when the clouds and rain returned, she showed signs of relapse, and baby Lewie—six months, teething and fussing day and night—added to her distress. The mother's behaviour then affected the older children, resulting in many tearful scenes.

After much soul-searching, Mr Burns finally decided it was better that two of his four daughters were out of the house while Henrietta was still recovering. Most days the baby and his nurse were as much as his poor exhausted wife could manage. Henrietta's mood had lightened when Emma came home in November when her obedient eldest child took over many mundane daily tasks. And although Thomas realised Emma was a more serious student than Julia, receiving excellent marks for the two terms

141

she had spent at St Mary's Hall, Julia and Bella would have to be the ones to continue their education in New Jersey. Even with Kitty's loving attention, Bella could be a challenge for both parents. At thirteen, Bella was now even more eager to be away from home.

Thomas sent a telegram requesting places for Isabella and Julia at St Mary's Hall for the summer term that began on the first of May. He would send the payment of three hundred dollars with Duncan McFarland, who would escort the three girls.

❦ ❦ ❦

Julia was reluctantly packing her trunk and valises to go back to New Jersey. She was rather lukewarm about studying anything more than needlework now after her most challenging winter term yet as a Senior D. She had gladly come home to see Mama and baby Llewellyn; she got to watch spring unfold in Niagara. She would have been quite happy to stay in St Catharines to help her family and quit her studies altogether. And, of course, she would have also been able to see William regularly if she remained in Canada.

Julia thought surely Emma would have welcomed her help with the household duties thrust upon her. Emma remained responsible for supervising the care of Norman and Libby, in addition to planning meals, ordering groceries, ensuring that the staff cleaned the house correctly and checking that the laundry was done to her mother's satisfaction. It was a lot for a seventeen-year-old to handle. Emma was lucky to have Kitty's able assistance with these tasks, and she valued their friendship immensely.

When it was time for her sisters to go to the station, Emma tearfully embraced Julia and Bella before they got into the carriage. Feeling the weight of the world on her young shoulders, Emma went back into the house alone. She found Kitty waiting in the foyer. Kitty was silent, but Emma knew that her friend understood her perfectly.

❦ ❦ ❦

BURLINGTON

Harriet had stayed at school for the April vacation at her father's insistence. She was disappointed because, after being out of the country for five months, she had looked forward to seeing him and her siblings. Obviously, he was busy with the Parliament session and couldn't take time out to fetch her. She had suggested she could go as far as St Catharines with the other girls, spend the night with the Burns family, and then take the steamer across the lake on her own, but there had not been enough time to arrange everything by post.

Harriet was lonely in the dormitory without her favourite St Mary's sisters, though she was getting to know the Lockport girls better, Julia and Ellie Tredway, along with Alice Van Valkenburg and Helen Mack. Mackie was amusing, noisily crunching apples, and making faces in the School Room during study hour, causing the girls to laugh out loud! Miss Cronyn could never seem to identify the source of the commotion. And no one would tell her!

The five of them had been to Philadelphia again last week with Mr Engstrom, Mr Hewitt, and his daughter. In the beautiful spring weather, they visited Franklin Park, tiny colonial Elfreth's Alley, and the Arch Street house that once belonged to flag maker Betsy Ross. After dinner they passed an hour at the Pennsylvania Academy of Fine Arts. Mr Engstrom had an exhibit of his oil paintings opening there for the summer, and he proudly explained his work to the group. Harriet adored the Academy and wished she could have spent more time there, or even to become a student there one day. They wandered through beautiful Rittenhouse Square before taking the ferry back to Camden.

🐿 🐿 🐿

SATURDAY, 3 MAY 1856

The Niagara travellers, Lizzie, Margaret Jane, and Julia, as well as Bella Burns, arrived back at St Mary's Hall on the third day of the summer term, along with nearly one hundred others, many of them new to the school. Late arrivals were not altogether acceptable in the eyes of the school administration, since it interrupted the smooth routine already established for the pupils. It also delayed the classing of any new scholars, such as Bella. However, there had been no other choice, as Mr McFarland was unable to leave his farm and business dealings sooner than the last week of April. He volunteered to escort the group this time as the other two fathers had done before him. Mr McFarland had planned a more intense trip with three long days in the cars, partly out of the urgent timing and partly because of the fourteen hours of daylight.

Bella, on her first train trip ever, had tried her best to glimpse the legendary falls that morning as they crossed the Niagara Gorge, but was disappointed. From the angle the bridge took going east, she could only see a tall curtain of mist and water in front of the them. She would have to wait until she returned to Canada to have another chance. Once in New York State, Bella enjoyed watching the lush spring green countryside go by, but then was shocked by noisy, dirty Jersey City. At last she welcomed the familiar look of the New Jersey farmland and the bustling little city of Burlington.

For three days Bella had quite enjoyed talking to Lizzie Fuller. In fact, they discovered they were close in age, born only nine days apart during two February snowstorms in 1843. In the cars Lizzie had regaled her with stories about school life and the amusing habits of the teachers at St Mary's. Bella hoped she would have a life-long friend in Lizzie; she seemed to have a light-hearted approach to school and the world in general.

❦ ❦ ❦

When the four weary travellers rushed into the dormitory, they found Harriet sitting on an upturned slop bucket, a beautiful pine lap desk balanced on her knees. She was writing a letter to her father to thank him for the new desk. She laid it on her bed and ran over to greet them all.

Julia was first to embrace Harriet, followed by Lizzie and Margaret Jane. "Hattie! I'm so glad to see you! I'm just exhausted!" said Julia.

"And this must be Bella! Julia wrote me you were coming. Welcome to our home away from home."

"Good afternoon, Hattie. I'm very pleased to meet you. Where's everyone else?" asked Bella.

"Miss Adams is downstairs right now with Ellie and Julia Tredway, but they'll be back soon, and then we must get ready for supper."

Harriet was glad to have her friends back to fill the room again. The dormitory atmosphere always changed with the comings and goings of different girls. After Emma left just three weeks into the winter term last year, Julia and Harriet became even better friends. Laura and Lizzie, as new girls, had remained close, but when Margaret Jane arrived in December, she and Lizzie developed a friendship that left Laura out. Apparently neither Margaret Jane nor Lizzie liked to sing Sacred Music on Friday evenings, and Laura, of course, did. Laura tried hard to befriend the Lockport girls that winter, but they proved to be rather insular. Not surprisingly, Laura Fuller, though recovered from her fainting spells, decided to stay in Thorold; her mother was expecting another baby in July. Lizzie was rather annoyed to have been called home with Laura since they had to cancel their vacation with the McHenrys.

Moods and alliances would no doubt be different during the coming months as well. It was Julia's first summer term; she had always gone home to Canada for the season, so she did not know what to expect. Anna Bull, considerably older than most of the girls, was skipping this term; she planned to come back from Dansville in November for her second term as a teacher candidate. Then little Fanny Wagner, so miserable being far away from her tight-knit family in Olean, NY, was not returning to St Mary's at all after just one term.

Bella was surprised by her new surroundings—so many narrow beds in such a large room. She always thought she would like being a pupil at St Mary's Hall when she read the letters from Emma and Julia. Bella was happy to be able to spend more time with Julia at school. Emma and Julia had always been close, and now it was her turn to develop a bond with the older sister she admired, and without competition from Emma. She was a bit confused by what Emma had told her about Julia's new friend, Harriet Taylor. Harriet seemed genuinely approachable, in spite of being from a different part of the country and having lived in cities like Toronto, Montréal, and Québec. Julia seemed to like her a lot. Bella hoped they could be friends too, despite their age difference.

Bella felt at home in Burlington right away. She thought the town was similar to St Catharines in many ways, most obviously its waterside location. However, living now at St Mary's Hall next to the Delaware River, Bella could watch the sloops, ferries, and barges go by as she and her schoolmates walked along the Green Bank. In odd moments during recitations in the Main House, she would dare to peek out the classroom windows facing the river. Bella's favourite place to watch the river traffic was the widow's walk high on its roof ridge, a special treat for the young ladies in fine weather. One had to climb a steep set of steps in the cockloft to a trap door. Mr Jacob and Mrs La Motte supervised the activity closely. Girls with a fear of heights did not ask to do this more than once.

❦ ❦ ❦

One warm June evening after supper when Mrs La Motte was distributing the post in the School Room, Bella, Julia and Harriet each received letters from home. Bella tore hers open and started to read at her desk. Julia and Harriet took their letters out to the Circle where they sat on a bench fitted round the trunk of a shady oak tree. They arranged their skirts and kicked off their shoes. At first they read silently, and then took turns reading parts aloud to each other. Bella then followed them outside, saw them giggling together and yearned to know the joke between them. Realising they weren't paying any attention to her, she turned and stalked off alone to the bishop's garden, where she continued to read the letter from her mother. She read the three-page missive with difficulty, as Mama's spelling was not too good, and her handwriting was cramped. She related how the family, especially little Norman and Libby, missed her now. Bella was happy that her mother was well enough to write to her. It was the first letter from her since she had arrived in Burlington six weeks ago. Thoughtful Emma and her father had both sent letters that included notes from Norman and drawings from little Libby.

When Bella finished reading, she picked up her skirts and skipped happily back down the path to the Circle. A gust of wind blew the pages from her hand. She stopped and gathered them up as they fluttered ahead of her. After she collected them all, she walked sedately over to her sister and Harriet. "Julia, little Lewie is sitting by himself now! And he has two more teeth."

"Bella, can't you see I'm talking to Hattie?"

"Julia, don't be so harsh to her!" defended Harriet.

"Well, she shouldn't interrupt. At home she's always interrupting people."

"I'm sorry, Julia. I was just so excited to tell you about Lewie. Did you know?"

"No, my letter to-day was from William, Bella. Mama wrote me last week and said nought about Lewie, only about how much she misses us. I'm glad he's coming along," said Julia. "Now I'd like to hear the rest of Hattie's letter from her father, Bella. Go away, please."

"No, Bella can listen. Let her stay," said Harriet, who genuinely liked Bella. She reminded her of her equally blonde and impetuous little sister Mary.

"Oh, very well, Bella. Come sit down," Julia said, swatting a mosquito away with a sigh. She opened her fan and began to wave it back and forth to keep the persistent insect away.

Harriet began again to read the letter aloud:

Bellevue
25 May 1856

My Dear Harriet,
    I write to-day to describe yesterday's events upon the occasion of our Queen's 37th birth-day. I trust there was no such celebration in Burlington! The day began before dawn in Beverley Street as I was staying with Uncle John and Aunt Betsy. Crowds of singing men roamed up and down it all night long. Apparently, it was a good excuse for the male citizens to drink ale, whisky, and wine in excess. There were many shouts of: "God Save the Queen!" After a rather sleepless night and late breakfast, Uncle and I decided to forgo watching the sailing regatta on Lake Ontario with our colleagues. Instead we drove out early to Dover Court for the usual picnic with Uncle Richard and his family. Mary and Georgie had already been delivered there yesterday with Miss Fellows. We picnicked under the leafy shade trees sur-

rounding the house, daffodils and tulips blooming in the garden. Your uncles, George and Robert, arrived and we four went to the afternoon horse races at the Upper Canada Turf Club. It was a wonderful time in the warm sun. Your aunts stayed back at the house with the children. The older cousins played games together in the woods and orchards while the small ones stayed close to the house running from one end of the verandah to the other, chasing kittens and puppies. The evening's highlight was a spectacular fireworks show conducted by a company of men we hired. Neighbours came from all around to watch it. The little ones did not much like the loud noises, clapping hands over their ears, but they loved the flashing colours against the night sky. The holiday ended with a torchlight procession of guests departing down the lane in their carriages. We all went to bed late and slept until well after sunrise. No one wanted to go to church, but Aunt Betsy insisted, and after a rushed breakfast, the whole of us trooped into St George-the-Martyr just in the nick of time for the eleven o'clock service. Many prayers of thanksgiving were said for the health and happiness of Her Majesty on the occasion of her birth-day.

I hope this letter finds you well, my dear daughter, and I look for yours in return.

Your loving father,
Fennings Taylor

Harriet was disappointed there hadn't been any such celebration in Burlington that day, but she understood well that the Americans had fought a long war to be rid of royalty!

CHAPTER 18

Summer in Burlington

FRIDAY, 4 JULY 1856

It had been such an awful, hot night! The air was heavy and humid. Barely a breeze moved through the dormitory despite all the windows being fully opened top and bottom. Lizzie had tossed and turned, awakening several times, and now at last she woke to see the early morning light. She could not believe how terrible she felt. It was as if the dormitory room had closed round her. She could hardly breathe. Her cotton nightdress was damp as she lay on the straw mattress, considering what to do about her discomfort. The only thing that could have been worse would be bedbugs biting!

To-day was Independence Day, the American national holiday established to celebrate the country's break from Britain nearly eighty years ago. There was to be a party that afternoon at River-side, and the boys and young men of Burlington College were to attend, along with the young ladies of St Mary's Hall. But Lizzie had hardly slept in the heat! Could she stay awake long enough to-day to take part in this once-a-year chance to speak to the scholars next door? The young ladies of St Mary's Hall only

glimpsed them at play outside, or perhaps when they were bring
ing in some errant cows from the field. Sometimes the girls saw
the young men leaving services at St Mary's Church, but they
never had opportunities to meet otherwise, let alone speak to
them. At thirteen, Lizzie was beginning to wonder about how
boys could be more than playmates. She pushed those thoughts
from her head as she wiped the perspiration from her brow with
the back of her hand.

But she had an idea. It was still early and the sun was not yet
up. She could hear no one else about. The rising bell had not
rung. She crept out of her bed, hoping that the old floorboards
would not creak and give her away. Then she stole out of the dormitory room and tiptoed down the stairs and round the corner
to the hallway. Along the covered porch through the open back
door into the sleeping Main House, she passed through the Venetian doors in the centre hallway and made sure they closed behind her without a sound. The panelled double front doors of
the brick house had also been left open to permit any possible
breeze from the river to enter the building overnight. She prayed
that the night watchman would be elsewhere on his rounds! Out
the open doorway and down the cool stone steps skipped bare-
foot Elizabeth Street Fuller, in her nightdress, free of camisoles
and petticoats, breathing in the slightly fresher air as she scampered across the clay lane toward the river. She was finally going
to be cool again! And when had she last been permitted to run?
Ah, yes, at Laurel Hill! Well, perhaps not exactly permitted, but
run she had.

The grass was cool and dew-laden under her feet. Close to the
stone sea wall were two majestic willow trees. Their long branches
trailed gracefully toward the lawn. It was almost high tide, and
the green river water lapped midway up the seawall.

Oh, she couldn't help herself! She grabbed a generous bunch
of soft willow branches with two hands, swung her body over the
wall and dropped into the cool water, landing on her feet.

Lizzie cringed with pain! She had forgot that the river bottom
was covered with rocks! Ouch! The sharp ones hurt her feet terribly. The smooth ones were slippery. She picked her way deeper
into the water, wincing with each step. Her nightdress was soaked
and had floated up to her waist, but she was cool! But now, turn-

ing toward the school buildings, she wondered how she was going to get back inside without being noticed. Not only would she have to climb out over the wall, but she would also be dripping wet, and she had brought nothing else to wear! On top of that, her pantalettes made it hard to move through the water with the fabric dragging on her limbs.

What to do?

At that moment she glimpsed a tall form dressed all in black walking westward down the lane toward the school. The sun was shining behind the pedestrian and it quickly became clear to Lizzie that this silhouette was none other than Bishop Doane.

Oh, horrors! Of all people to find her in this state! He hadn't seen her yet though. In panic, she ducked underwater as far down as she could. She had never done this except in her bath when she was a tiny child! She opened her eyes, but there was nothing to see in the murky Delaware. She held her breath for as long as she possibly could, and then for a few seconds longer, before she shot up out of the water with a splash and a gasp.

It was indeed Bishop Doane! He had already passed her by, but upon hearing a noise, that of her blasting out of the water, he changed direction and charged toward the water's edge. He first dropped his gold-topped cane on the grass. Then he pulled off his linen frock coat and tossed it away, anticipating the need to jump in the river himself to save the poor child from drowning.

He stopped at the wall upon seeing she was, indeed, unharmed and standing. "My dear, what are you doing in the river?" asked the astonished cleric.

"Oh, my goodness, Bishop! It was just so hot all night in the dormitory. I barely slept. I had to do something!"

Bishop Doane laughed and squinted at her. "Is it Elizabeth Fuller I see in the river, or the last run of shad?"

"Yes, Bishop. It is I, Elizabeth Fuller," she said sheepishly, looking down at her sodden self, twisting her long dark braid to squeeze out the water. "Will you send me home now, Bishop?"

He laughed again. "No, my dear, of course not! I can see you've done no harm to yourself, but now what are we to do about getting you out of the river and into the house? Have you brought no other clothes to the waterside, Elizabeth?" He looked round the bank and saw none.

"No, Bishop, I had a mind only of getting cool," said Lizzie as she tiptoed gingerly, making her way over the stony riverbed to the wall in front of him.

"And are you cool now, my daughter?"

"Oh, yes, Bishop, I am, quite, but I would like to stay cool a bit longer before going back inside. The river is lovely. I have never been bathing before, though we girls used to wade in our pond at the farm. Mother wouldn't allow us to bathe in it though on account of the ducks and geese. You know …"

The bishop laughed. Then he pointed out the nearby steps and offered her his hand as she reached the last one. She stood awkwardly in front of the bishop, her nightdress dripping on the grass. She grasped as much of the fabric as she dared and tried to wring it out.

The bishop picked up his frockcoat, pulled it round her shoulders, and adjusted the daisy in its buttonhole.

"Well then, I allow we could stay out here until the first bell rings, do you not agree? It's still early," he said, gauging the summer sun's angle in the eastern sky.

"But haven't you something to do now besides talk to me?" asked Lizzie, as she sat on the sea wall beside the bishop of New Jersey, her feet dangling in the water.

"Why, not this morning, Elizabeth. You remember 'tis our national holiday, and 'twill be a day of great rejoicing as our President John Adams once wished for us Americans. I've already written my speech. Dr Millett will take care of Morning Prayer as usual. I am sure you know that later Mrs Doane and I shall entertain at Riverside when the scholars from Burlington College parade over with their band to share dinner with us all. There will be several more patriotic speeches and then the town's fireworks display when darkness falls to-night. You'll be able to see them here from the Green Bank since they're shot over the river from the city wharf. It will be a full day of activity for all of us, Elizabeth."

"That sounds wonderful, Bishop, and I'm so looking forward to the party, but how am I to get back into the house?" Lizzie at last realised she was in a fix.

"Leave that to me, daughter. Leave that to me," replied the kindly father figure, as he rose and motioned toward the lane.

🦌 🦌 🦌

Once inside the dormitory, with the bell for private devotions ringing, Lizzie crept in behind her schoolmates who, all eyes closed, were kneeling dutifully beside their beds in prayer. She hoped no one had noticed her absence, but Julia, whose bed was next to hers, looked up as she felt the floorboards rise. The older girl said nothing but gave her a quizzical look and then stifled a giggle as she resumed her prayer.

When the bell stopped after the usual ten minutes, Julia and the other girls gathered round Lizzie.

"What happened to you? I thought you went to the back-house, but then you never returned. Where have you been?" demanded Julia.

"I was so hot last night. I tossed and turned. Then when I woke up so very early, I decided to cool off in the river. And here I am."

"What if Miss Adams sees you like that?" asked Bella. "Won't you be punished?"

"Matron already knows and Bishop Doane told her not to punish me because I was hot and I didn't hurt anyone," said Lizzie in her own defence.

"Well, aren't you lucky! I guess it's handy to be a minister's daughter, isn't it?" teased Julia.

"That's so unfair, Julia! The boys are allowed to bathe in the river all summer long. Why can't we?" Lizzie looked straight at Julia.

"For lack of a bathing costume, for one, Lizzie Fuller!"

"That doesn't stop the boys though, does it? They go romping in the water as God made them!" chimed in Bella.

Julia gasped, surprised that her little sister was so worldly.

"I have heard that some girls are wearing the new bloomers under a bathing dress. Wouldn't it be wonderful if we could get some and go bathing all of us together in the river? What a sight that would be for the watermen!" exclaimed Harriet.

🦌 🦌 🦌

153

After breakfast and Morning Prayer, the five Canadian friends went for their now customary walk in the Circle. They watched as the stewards and kitchen maids set up a large table at the foot of the back steps of the house. Great copper tanks of lemonade and raspberry vinegar beverage plus many loaves of pound cake were waiting for the hungry youngsters, only the beginning of a day-long celebration involving patriotism, food, music, and fellowship.

The girls of St Mary's Hall had already sampled the delicacies and sipped some lemonade when the chapel bell tolled at noon, signaling the march to Riverside by scholars of both St Mary's Hall and Burlington College. They soon heard music played by the approaching college band and hastened to form two lines with the matron leading the way from the Circle to the bishop's house.

Minutes later, there was a throng of people in front of Riverside: school-age boys and girls, college-age men, faculty, staff, guests, and members of the bishop's extended family. Mrs Doane, her daughter-in-law Kate, and her granddaughter Eliza, named for her grandmother, were watching from the balcony above the front door. Kate Doane, the former Sarah Katharine Condit, of Newark, NJ, had graduated from St Mary's Hall only four years ago herself. She was married to the Doanes' younger son William Croswell Doane, himself a graduate of Burlington College. Willy was now a deacon of the Episcopal Church and the rising star in the family. No one dared mention his older brother George, who had embraced the Church of Rome last year; it was an on-going embarrassment for the father and brother.

All the participants were waiting for the crowd to assemble and quiet down so that the programme could begin. Bishop Doane, wearing his heavy black academic robe despite the July heat, began his address. Twenty minutes later the audience applauded enthusiastically, and the band played "Yankee Doodle" and a new patriotic song they had recently learnt, the "Star Spangled Banner". It was written during the War of 1812 by Francis Scott Key at Fort McHenry in Baltimore harbour. A few in the crowd knew the lyrics well enough to sing with the music, but since they weren't yet widely known, many people just hummed along. Without delay, Dr Millett led three cheers for the Union before announcing the Bishop's Hour, the annual occasion for the boys and girls of Burlington College and St Mary's Hall to mingle in the bishop's beautiful fragrant garden before the picnic dinner was served.

❦ ❦ ❦

That Sunday, with the Independence Day celebration still fresh in their minds, the pupils of St Mary's Hall were enjoying the relaxed schedule of the holiday. To escape the heat and humidity of the house, Lizzie and Bella were out of doors in the Circle under the tall shade trees. Schoolmates were spending their free time after dinner visiting with each other before they had to walk back to church again. Sundays were packed full of prayers and scripture lessons, even in the summer.

"Look, Bella, I've made her a flower crown. What do you say?" asked Lizzie, holding the circlet of woven stems over her own head for effect.

"It's beautiful, Lizzie, but where did you get the flowers?"

"Oh, from the garden, of course. I asked the bishop, and he thought it was a grand idea for a gift. He said there were plenty to go around. The dahlias weren't open yet though. They would have been magnificent!" replied Lizzie.

"I am still amazed that you weren't in trouble with the matron for your antic the other day! How *ever* did you slip up to the dormitory that morning?"

"Oh, it was easy. The bishop told Mrs La Motte that we were having an important discussion outside, which was very true, and while the chapel bell was ringing, and everyone was at devotions, I just crept up the stairs! You saw me!"

"I certainly did! You were still dripping wet. I wish you had woken me to go out with you. I would have gone! We were all hot up here, even with the windows wide open. I was covered with mosquito bites too, once again. I hate them so!"

"Well, yes, I've been itching from them this week too. They get easily through the louvers. So, do you have something to give your sister to-day?"

Bella scrunched up her face and said, "I've put away some ink and paper for her that I bought in town last week. She said she was running low. I shall just tie it up with a ribbon in a handker chief, I guess."

"Of course, that's always practical. She does write a lot of letters to William, does she not?" asked Lizzie.

"Yes, they've been friends forever, those two. He's her favourite cousin. We have a lot of cousins, the Mittlebergers and the Burns side, in St Catharines. I've lost count. William's father is our mother's brother. We live in a house on the opposite side of the land Papa and Uncle Henry bought together years ago. And we all see each other often at church or at parties."

"Our family isn't so big as that. Our father was orphaned young, and he doesn't have brothers or sisters. Mother has a younger brother, Uncle Thomas, and two sisters, Aunt Julia and Aunt Caroline, but we don't see a lot of them. Uncle Thomas is busy with the Parliament, and my aunts live away with their husbands. But I have enough brothers and sisters to make up for it!" said Lizzie with a grin.

"So, when should we give Julia her birth-day gifts?" asked Bella.

"Well, I'd like her to have time to wear her crown of flowers before bedtime. P'raps right after supper? It's Sunday, so there won't be any post to read. I wonder if Harriet and Margaret Jane have finished their gifts? Harriet is so talented with her paints. Margaret Jane is another story though! She's always occupied with her studies. I bet she forgot all about our plan."

❦ ❦ ❦

Julia was thrilled and surprised by all of the little presents her friends and sister had gathered for her. She put on Bella's flower crown right away, although it was by then wilted in the summer heat. She spent some minutes admiring herself in the glass, dreaming of her wedding. Harriet had finished her watercolour of the bishop's garden for Julia with only minutes to spare. Unfortunately, a corner of the paper hadn't dried given the July humidity, and it smeared a bit. Harriet was, nevertheless, pleased with her effort. Mr Engstrom, the art teacher, had helped her capture the light in the garden beautifully; he was enormously talented, in Harriet's opinion.

Margaret Jane had, indeed, forgot about Julia's birth-day, and she gave her the two ginger cakes she had saved from the Independence Day picnic, along with an apology. They were a bit dry!

🦌 🦌 🦌

Thursday, the fourth of September dawned sultry and humid again in Burlington. There was still no relief from the heat of the summer season. The rising bell had not yet rung, and it was quiet in the second-floor dormitory. Only the soft breathing of the sleeping girls could be heard.

Lizzie was aware of the cooing mourning doves perched on the roof above her open window as she opened her eyes. She was still half-dreaming of home and her new baby brother, Henry, making those same sweet noises. Julia awoke almost simultaneously, and leaned on one elbow as the two girls looked at each other from across the room. Then Julia pointed to Hattie's bed next to Lizzie's. Lizzie got out of bed and gently tapped Hattie's shoulder. She groaned and rolled over, kicking off her sheet.

Lizzie tapped again more forcefully and whispered: "Time to get up, Hattie. It's Margaret Jane's birth-day, remember?" Hattie mumbled something slightly rude in French, *"Va t'en!"*, and buried her head into her moss pillow.

Lizzie persisted, "Hattie, it's celebration day. Wake up!"

With that, Harriet's eyes fluttered open, and she began to remember the occasion and all the plans. Her friends had surprised her only a week ago for her own birth-day with a sack of contraband dough balls from the Mitchell bakery on High Street and an hour of games outside after dinner. She had appreciated the recognition very much after a particularly frustrating week of lessons. Birth-days in the Taylor family were not regularly observed, but for the scholars of St Mary's Hall, all birth-days were worthy of celebration as a diversion from routine. The pupils enjoyed planning and executing surprises for each other. With over 150 girls, there could have been a birth-day every other day of the year! The staff could not rightly celebrate each girl's day, and rather chose to overlook these disruptions when they occurred.

Stretching and yawning, Harriet looked up at Lizzie's face and then popped to a sitting position with her limbs crossed tailor style inside her nightdress.

Meanwhile Julia reached over, nudged Bella in the next bed and delivered the same message. The four had been planning this day for a month. Even Miss Adams was in on the surprise this time. They were going to show their love and admiration for Margaret Jane before she had to leave St Mary's Hall.

The hard-working girl had been called back to Canada at the end of the summer term, just a few weeks hence. She assumed her father had decided either two terms of schooling in the States were enough for his daughter, or her mother needed her at home. Margaret Jane was devastated. It was bad enough that her brother had belittled her ambition to become a physician, but now it seemed both her parents were stifling her dreams as well. Since Miss Stanley gave her the news a week ago, the usually cheerful and studious girl had been despondent, just going through the motions of studying her lessons. Once a star pupil in her recitations, she had lost all interest in excelling. She had even got grades of seven in chemistry, a subject she loved. At this point in the term, most scholars of St Mary's Hall were spending more time on their studies because oral term examinations were looming in advance of the vacation month. How would Margaret Jane perform on them given her present state of mind? *Did it even matter?* she wondered.

The four co-conspirators pulled out the gifts for their friend from their hiding places. Lizzie had drawn a picture in charcoal of several interesting seashells from her conchology class with Miss Rodney. Using her best penmanship, Julia had written and illustrated a poem about their friendship in ink on expensive vellum paper she had bought in Philadelphia. Harriet had painted another charming watercolour of the bishop's garden in summer bloom like the one she had done for Julia, and Bella had spent hours embroidering a fine linen handkerchief with a trailing ivy motif, but it was still in the hoop. She had designed it herself, but the project was taking longer than expected to complete. Bella was reluctant to give it to her unfinished, then decided it was the thought that counted! She would promise to have it done before Margaret Jane left in three weeks.

When the friends were ready, they woke Miss Adams and the

other sound sleepers in the dormitory. Miss Adams rang her little brass bell as loud as she could, and Margaret Jane, apparently the soundest sleeper of them all, woke with a start. Everyone stood round her bed and joined in a hearty "Surprise! Happy Birth-day, Margaret Jane!"

One by one, her friends presented her with the precious hand-made gifts.

Margaret Jane sniffled, "I can't thank you enough! How can I leave you all? I shall miss you terribly. You're all like sisters to me!"

Miss Adams gave her an unexpected embrace and then said: "I've one more surprise for you, Margaret Jane!"

"Do tell!" said Margaret Jane.

Miss Adams said nothing but proceeded, despite her flimsy linen lawn nightdress, to turn a somersault right before her amazed eleven charges! Some of the girls tried to stifle a giggle; others laughed outright. A couple of them stood back, shocked at the acrobatics. Margaret Jane put Bella's embroidery hoop, needle still dangling, down on the bed and hesitated, then performed an identical move, feet pointed to the ceiling in a momentary handstand. As soon as she was finished, each of her friends tried to do the trick, followed by much clapping, whoops and hollering. This was not a feat the young ladies of St Mary's Hall learnt in calisthenics class, and if Mrs La Motte or Miss Stanley had heard the commotion, they would have put an immediate stop to the frivolity. Lizzie showed off her best cartwheel, perfected at home in the front garden with her brothers sworn to secrecy. One by one, the other girls tried to perform the move with varying degrees of success and giggles. Thankfully, their dormitory was in a separate wing off by itself, and no one else objected to the early morning cavorting.

It was only a matter of minutes before the rising bell began to toll, and the scholars of St Mary's Hall took up their normal silent routine. Margaret Jane would never forget her fourteenth birth-day celebration, thanks to her dear dormitory sisters and their teacher Miss Adams.

CHAPTER 19

A Near Cancellation

TUESDAY, 30 SEPTEMBER 1856, BURLINGTON

Harriet was packing the last items into her trunk for Mr Jacob to take away when Julia sat down on the bed beside her.

"Hattie, I'm going to miss you so much. I wish you weren't going home," she said, wiping away her tears.

"Oh, Julia, I wish it were otherwise too, but I'm not the scholar you others are, and I feel I'm wasting my time here trying to be. My marks have been terrible in maths and chemistry. Lizzie saved me in botany last month, and the only things I do well are drawing and painting," confided the girl. "Besides, I am seventeen now, and like Emma, I can be more helpful to my father at home. I'm going to teach Mary and Georgie all that I can, and at least in Toronto I shall be meeting people again. I feel so stifled here in Burlington. There is so little to do."

"Just the same, Hattie, I shall miss you. Will you write me every week?" asked Julia, disappointed that Hattie felt their friendship wasn't enough to keep her engaged here at the Hall. Hattie had begged her father to let her come home. She had made a convincing case and even arranged for her uncle to fetch her.

"I shall try, Julia. I shall be busy with my sister and brother, of course, and helping to run the household for Father. But I shall try," promised Hattie.

"I don't know what I shall do here without you. You've been such a good friend to me here since Emma left."

"You too, Julia. You're the only girl here I could talk to about important things. No one understands me like you do."

"We shall be sisters forever, shan't we?" said Julia, as she embraced Hattie fiercely.

"Yes, we shall. In just a few months, I've made a fast friend. I hope you can stop with us in Toronto sometime. P'raps after you've finished your studies here?"

"That would be wonderful, Hattie. I've never been across the lake. Toronto must be so interesting."

"Well, *I* believe it is, but p'raps you won't find it so. It's big and noisy and full of people. They're building all the time now Father says."

"It sounds absolutely intriguing. I imagine St Catharines is very small in comparison. I'd love to see Toronto. Is it as big as Philadelphia?"

"Oh, I don't know. I expect so. It isn't a terribly hard trip on the steamboat, you know. Thirty miles. Only a couple of hours. You can take the cars now all the way round the lake through Hamilton, but it takes much longer. I like the steamboat. It's so romantic out on the lake."

"Is that how you'll get back to Toronto this time?" asked Julia.

"Yes, I had a message that my uncle Robert arrived in Burlington yesterday. He'll conduct Margaret Jane and me home to Canada. We shall leave to-morrow on the first train to Amboy. We're taking the same route Father and I did to come down here last year. It seems like yesterday. This term has flown by, Julia. I have been so happy knowing you, even if my studies were frustrating."

"I feel the same too, Hattie. If you're finished packing, let's go for a walk in the bishop's garden before supper; the dahlias are still in bloom. Or we could see if the grapery has something to offer for your journey! What do you say?"

"Oh, that's a superb idea, dear friend."

❦ ❦ ❦

The next morning after prayers and breakfast, Captain Robert Brittain Denison, Hattie's favourite uncle and the youngest brother of her mother, arrived at the front doors of St Mary's Hall. Michael Dunn showed him into the east parlour, where he waited for Miss Stanley to be called from her room. Michael introduced the vice principal to the captain, who presented a letter of introduction from his brother-in-law Fennings Taylor and one from Duncan McFarland. These letters gave him permission to escort both Harriet and Margaret Jane back to Canada. Three other men arrived for the same reason, to escort their daughters, nieces, or sisters back to their families, either for the vacation month of October or because they had decided to end their studies.

Lizzie was also waiting with her valises in the west parlour with Susan Harker; the Harkers were hosting her for the month. Mr Harker was attending to some school business before he took the girls home to Mount Holly. He and Susan usually rode the little Mount Holly-Burlington rail road seven miles to and from their house on the outskirts of Mount Holly, but to-day he had brought the family carriage to accommodate Lizzie's baggage. Lizzie was anxious to explore the countryside there; it sounded much like her own home. Susan had told her many stories about her pets, including dogs, horses, and rabbits.

On the first day of the vacation month, the pupils who remained could choose their own activities after Morning Prayer in the chapel. Groups of girls lingered in the bishop's garden, the Circle or the School Room, writing letters. Margaret Jane and Harriet, already dressed in their travelling clothes, were passing by the ginkgo tree in the Circle with Julia and Bella when Ellen, the servant usually tasked with such errands, caught up to them with a message.

"Misses Harriet and Margaret Jane, you are to come with me at once. You have a gentleman caller," announced the woman in her Irish brogue.

"Oh, Hattie, Margaret Jane—I'm coming with you to say good-bye," said Julia.

"*Moi, aussi,*" added Bella, showing off her new knowledge of French to Hattie, who would most appreciate it.

Margaret Jane had been especially quiet this morning. She

surprised the girls beside her when she blurted out, "I don't want to go home! I shan't go home!" Her blue eyes flashed as she stamped one foot on the ground.

Harriet turned to the younger girl and took her hands in hers. "Dear Margaret Jane, we've talked about this day for weeks. Your parents want the best for you. Surely you're not going to question their judgement, are you?"

Margaret Jane sat on the wooden bench that encircled a tall oak tree. She spread her skirts round her with determination, as if she were rooted there. "I shall *not* go. I *refuse* to go."

Tiny Ellen McGloughlin stared at Margaret Jane, at a loss of what to do. She had no authority; she was only the messenger.

Harriet and Julia looked at each other and wondered how to proceed. Harriet's uncle was undoubtedly waiting in the parlour. There were a carriage, train tickets, and inns arranged, and other people who would be in Canada ready to collect Margaret Jane.

Julia took charge and pulled Harriet aside. She whispered, "Go with Ellen, and tell your uncle what's happened. Then find Miss Stanley. P'raps she can calm Margaret Jane and persuade her that she is being unreasonable."

Margaret Jane heard Julia's words. "I am *not* being unreasonable, Julia! I want to go to school, and I want to go to school *here*! I want to be a physician! Why don't they understand? I thought my mother understood. I thought she agreed. What changed?"

Harriet turned on her heel without comment, walked briskly through the Circle, and scampered up the back steps to the parlour where she found Miss Stanley with the gentlemen callers. Out of breath from her uncommon exertion, Harriet greeted her uncle, curtseyed, and extended her hand to him as she inquired as to his health and his journey thus far. She thanked him for coming all the way to Burlington to escort her, taking time away from his many responsibilities in Toronto: his wife, their four children, a small farm, and continuing his father's project of selling off portions of Bellevue, the family estate.

Then Harriet excused herself. She turned, curtseyed to Miss Stanley, and in a whisper asked for a word with her aside. "Miss Stanley, there's a problem in the Circle. Margaret Jane refuses to leave. I don't know what to do. My uncle Robert is charged with escorting her home."

"Refuses to go home? I know she has been feeling low and not attending to her studies, but refusing to go? To defy her parents? That doesn't sound like Margaret Jane. Michael, would you please go for the bishop? I think he needs to intervene."

❦ ❦ ❦

Michael found Bishop Doane in his study at Riverside, spectacles on, seated at his ornate walnut desk. After the steward explained the situation, the bishop left off his writing and began to sift through the piles of correspondence on his desk, looking for a particular letter. When he found it, he put on his frock coat and slipped the envelope into a pocket. He donned his hat and went out the back door of the big house, down the gravel paths, and over to the Circle to find Margaret Jane McFarland.

At the far end, poor Margaret Jane was sobbing now, eyes red and puffy, her face flushed, and her bonnet ribbons damp from the tears. Although Julia and Bella tried to comfort her with kind words, she was inconsolable. Some of the younger pupils, wondering what the problem was, had gathered near them.

As Bishop Doane approached the group, the other girls scattered so he could minister privately to the distraught pupil.

"There, there, Margaret Jane, what is the matter?" asked the cleric in his soothing, fatherly voice. He patted her hand gently.

"Good morning, Bishop," she said meekly, chastened, now aware that she had created a scene. She had been dreading this day, and it was her last chance to stay. She hadn't received any letters from her family since she wrote back protesting the order for her to leave St Mary's Hall. Why had no one written?

"Daughter, perhaps I may be of help. I see you are unhappy," said the father of two sons, but a veteran of nearly two decades as head of a girls' school.

Margaret Jane looked over at the bishop, who had taken a seat on the bench beside her. She began to sob again, covering her eyes with her gloved hands. "My parents demand that I go home to Canada. I fear I shan't be attending school there. That's why I came here—for learning—and I want to stay here with my school sisters," complained the girl between sniffles, gulps, and sobs.

"Oh, my dear, when your father wrote me to say you were now needed at home, perhaps I should have delivered the news myself. I did not understand that you were so against the plan. Your father wrote me this letter a fortnight ago, you see. I do apologise for not sharing it with you myself. There is some good news in it. Here, have a look, my dear." Bishop Doane passed the single sheet to her.

Margaret Jane read the letter in her father's familiar hand. "I knew my brother Dunc was married in June, but Agnes is to have a baby! Bishop Doane, sir, I am going to be an aunt! My brother is going to be a father! Oh, this changes everything! I *am* needed at home to help them." She paused, and then said, "But I still want to go to school. And I still want to go to school here with my St Mary's Hall sisters!"

She wanted to embrace Bishop Doane, but she didn't dare. He must have sensed this and patted her hand again and stood to leave. "My dear you must go home to your family," he said. "They need you."

Margaret Jane called to Julia and Bella. "I'm to be an aunt! I have to go home to help Mama with Agnes' baby next winter! I cannot stay. I must go home."

After embracing her friends one last time, Margaret Jane scurried into the Main House and found Harriet and Captain Denison waiting with Miss Stanley. The girl apologised profusely to them both and, after collecting her belongings, left the big brick house on the river for the last time. She gave a rueful look back at the willow trees, their branches swaying in the breeze. As the carriage horses clip-clopped down the Green Bank toward High Street, she thought how she would cherish her friends and memories of her time at St Mary's Hall.

The speedy intervention of Harriet, Miss Stanley, and the bishop allowed the travellers to make the ten o'clock train north to Amboy after all.

Now there were only three Canadian girls at St Mary's Hall.

CHAPTER 20

Autumn 1856

WEDNESDAY, 8 OCTOBER

The newest pupil at St Mary's Hall, Henrietta McHugh, had arrived from Delafield, Wisconsin a few days ago. Nettie, fifteen, conducted by her older brother the Rev. Stephen McHugh, had endured a long rail road trip from rural Wisconsin to Burlington. She had very much disliked the noise, the smoke, and the jostling over the tracks on her first long-distance rail road experience.

They made several overnight stops, the longest being when they spent three days in Chicago visiting the bishop of Illinois, the Right Reverend Henry John Whitehouse, and his family before continuing east.

All eight girls staying for the vacation month were assigned to Miss Adams' dormitory. Bella was the first to welcome Nettie to the room. The newcomer would take the bed next to Bella's until Lizzie returned from Susan Harker's. Then Nettie would move to her permanent dormitory group for the winter term. Mary Badham, Annie Parker, and Ella Hilliard, from North Carolina, and the two Page girls from New York City, occupied the other beds in the room for the month until their own dormitories

167

in the Main House were repainted. The visitors moved their things over with Julia and Bella's help.

Along with painting projects, the house was being cleaned from top to bottom. The pupils weren't permitted to help, and felt they were in the way of the hard-working staff moving furniture, washing windows and floors, polishing brass, and cleaning flues in preparation for the heating season. Without lessons to do, there were too many idle hours in the day. There was only so much needlework, fancy or not, that one could do. Walking in the Circle was tiresome, although the temperature was pleasant. The gardens were in need of less care now too in October. There was plenty of time in the evenings to practise the piano, or dance, but that too grew dull with such a small group of girls. The present inmates looked forward to weekly trips to Philadelphia this month to break the monotony. Nettie McHugh was grateful for a few days' rest before embarking on a new rail journey, however short the distance.

❦ ❦ ❦

During the ferry ride from Camden to the foot of Market Street, young Bella described to Nettie the neat grid of the city designed by its founder William Penn. She explained how the numbered streets were oriented east-west leading from the Delaware River and, in a short mnemonic rhyme she had made up to remember them, the order of the north-south streets of the oldest part of the city now named for trees: "Chestnut, Walnut, Locust, Spruce. Remember them, you silly goose."

The modern city of Philadelphia, its name derived from the Greek words meaning brotherly love, was a former capital of the young United States. It was much larger than either St Catharines or Burlington, let alone tiny Delafield, Wisconsin. Nettie, like Bella on her first trip to the city, was amazed at the number and variety of people she saw in the port, and compared it to her recent experience in Chicago, the growing port on Lake Michigan.

Each term school staff introduced the history of the area to new students from faraway states. The outing this week began with a stroll from the ferry wharf over to Chestnut Street to show Nettie the old Pennsylvania State House where the country's break from Britain was declared and the Constitution debated. The three-storey brick building was built in 1753 to house the colonial legislature. After the revolution, it became the Pennsylvania State House, until the city of Lancaster was named the state capital in 1799. In 1818, the city of Philadelphia bought the building to house the city council chambers on the second floor.

The highlight of their visit to the century-old edifice was to see the Liberty Bell on display in the Assembly Room. The room had recently been redesigned as a shrine to the founders with a marble statue of George Washington at one end and large and small portraits of other important men on the walls. The old cracked bell was mounted on a gaily decorated box, taller than a man. Curiously there was a stuffed bald eagle perched on top as if to guard it from the visitors. The six American girls looked up reverently at the relic that had tolled for the deaths of famous Americans and the Marquis de Lafayette. As loyal British subjects, Julia and Bella didn't share the same sentiments about the history, building, or the vaunted bell; however, after experiences like these in the city, they were able to relate more to their Mittleberger ancestors' roots in pre-Revolutionary Pennsylvania.

After touring the State House, the group of young ladies, led by Mr Hewitt, walked up to Tenth Street to the Academy of Fine Arts. Mr Benjamin Eakins was there to guide them through the galleries. Mr Eakins lived in Philadelphia and spent two days a week teaching calligraphy at St Mary's Hall and Burlington College. He was a brilliant tour guide, and always updated the staff on the latest news about culture in the city. There had been recent turmoil at the Academy. For years, women students had been welcomed at the Academy art school sculpture gallery every Monday, Wednesday, and Friday morning to copy the antique statuary; however, last April the Academy's board had not only abolished these ladies' days, but also directed that fig leaves be applied to the male statues to protect the modesty of any females who visited or studied there. Miss Ada Winans, a teacher of music at the Hall who had studied voice in Italy, was a chaperone to-day. She was effusive in her praise of the women's persistence under the new conditions; although, she remained infuriated by the puritanical new policy. On the other hand, Miss Lydia Germain, the shy daughter of the Rev. Reuben Germain, was relieved to see the coverings. She blushed even as she viewed the fig leaves. Miss Germain was assistant to Mr Engstrom, the art teacher; she was not an artist herself, but custodian of all supplies in the art room and responsible for its condition. As a timid and conservative soul, she did not share Miss Winans' enthusiasm for the natural human form. The girls from St Mary's Hall were still content to observe the talented women at work and talked with them at length about their painting and sculpture projects.

❦ ❦ ❦

As a matter of policy, Bishop Doane discouraged any spending of parents' money outside of necessities. Staff requested funds for special outings, which Mr Harker deducted from each pupil's account. On trips to Philadelphia, the scholars could shop for items of quality not usually available in Burlington. Approved purchases included bonnets, stockings, gloves, and various writing supplies. Chaperones always accompanied the girls into each shop to supervise spending.

Bella had lately developed a taste for dough balls, Lizzie's favourite contraband confection available at Mitchell's Bakery in Burlington. Bella thought they were divine too. Lizzie doled them out to her friends on Saturdays as a treat, but this month Lizzie was away in Mount Holly, and Bella had no source of the delicacy. Through careful questioning of Miss Winans last week, she learnt they were sold in a few confectioneries along Philadelphia's Market Street. To-day Bella remembered well where she might get them to replenish the dormitory's supply.

During term, it was not unusual for over fifty pupils to visit the city at once, but to-day the group touring was only the eight girls and four staff members. Everything was taking a lot less time; however, Miss Germain seemed to be hovering over Bella. The girl was afraid she wouldn't be able to make her special purchase. Bella calculated that Miss Winans might be willing to take Julia and herself to the confectioner, based on her previous conversations. She only had to figure out how to get into Miss Winans' group for the afternoon.

❦ ❦ ❦

Once back in Market Street, the party enjoyed their mid-day meal at Mr Fulmer's eating house. He had one long table ready, and assured Mr Hewitt quick service so that the girls could get on with their shopping.

"Miss Winans, I wonder if I might sit next to you to-day? I wanted to talk about this afternoon," said Bella.

"Why, certainly, Bella. Please do. Now, where would you like to go this afternoon?" said Miss Winans, as she tucked her escaping light brown curls under her bonnet.

Bella looked around to see who might be listening and then whispered, "I thought 'twould be nice to have some extra treats in our room to welcome back my friend Lizzie when she returns from Mount Holly. She adores dough balls, Miss Winans. You said they sell them at Mr Hagy's, the confectioner's. Could Julia and I slip up there with you after we finish the meal? It's only in the next block. Would you take us, please?"

Miss Winans, remembering Bella's previous line of questioning at school, smiled wryly at the conniving young girl. Bella reminded her of herself at the same age. A bit self-centred, but a person capable of the gifts of love and kindness at the end.

"Let me think, Bella. That one is too close. Ah! I have a better idea! We shall take a little more exercise and go back up to Mr Myer's at Tenth Street. Then there's a music shop on Sixth. I shall look for some new music for us to play. *Parfait!* We shall be away from the prying eyes," she whispered, winking one hazel eye playfully. She had noticed Miss Germain's watchful gaze too.

"Oh, thank you, Miss Winans! You're a saviour. Well, not really, but you know what I mean," bubbled Bella.

❦ ❦ ❦

When Bella arrived in May, she noticed a harp standing idle and covered in the corner of the young ladies' saloon on the first floor of the Nursery building. She had never thought much of playing an instrument at home; although, the family had an out of tune piano-forte in the parlour that Emma and Julia occasionally tried to play. Her family didn't promote musicianship, perhaps because of the number of children in the house capable of producing noise. Her father liked a quiet house so that he could read his law journals and newspapers. Their mother, a rather nervous sort, didn't welcome disruption in the household.

On a whim, Bella decided to ask Miss Stanley about harp lessons and learned that no one on the current staff was a harpist. Miss Winans, a teacher of voice, knew the basics of stringed instrument theory because she had studied guitar at St Mary's Hall. Miss Winans agreed to take her on as a pupil. She was not a trained harpist by any stretch of the imagination, but there was no one more enthusiastic than she and thus no better possible harp instructor at St Mary's Hall at the moment. The two determined a lesson schedule, and Bishop Doane approved it.

Bella had made such good progress during just five months of harp lessons that Miss Winans decided to put on a recital for the girls and staff at school during the October vacation. Bella wasn't confident yet when playing duets with Miss Winans' piano accompaniment. She would lose her place in the music and want to start over. She begged Miss Winans to limit it to a solo harp performance, and the teacher finally relented. Miss Winans invited voice and piano students to perform too. Julia preferred not to play the piano in front of others, but to-day she agreed since it was such a small, friendly audience.

After dinner, the bishop, along with other faculty and student spectators, gathered in the saloon. Chairs were brought in from all over the house and crowded the little room. Miss Winans introduced Bella playing the harp, and Maria Page, Julia, and Mary Badham, the piano-forte. Then she announced Nettie McHugh, Annie Parker, and Ella Hilliard who sang well-known songs. Bella played three short pieces by heart with only five mistakes, from which she, though tempted to repeat and correct, triumphantly recovered and continued to the end. Julia and Mary both played *études* by Chopin, and Maria played one of his lively *mazurkas*. Bella had heard Maria practising this music and wanted to dance to it in the worst way, but there was absolutely no room to do so in the little room. Under her skirts, she tapped her feet wildly in time with the notes. Perhaps she could persuade the girl to play it again after supper when dancing was permitted.

At the end of her performance, each girl stood and curtseyed, but in the awkward silence no one in the audience clapped.

Bishop Doane did not allow applause at St Mary's Hall. The only signs of approval were a nod, his appreciative smile, and his blue eyes sparkling behind silver-coloured spectacles.

❦ ❦ ❦

FRIDAY, 31 OCTOBER, ALL HALLOWS' EVE

Lizzie returned from the Harkers' home in Mount Holly full of tales of brisk autumn days spent exploring the fields, forests, and streams surrounding the town. Best of all, she brought back a gallon jug of cider and two bushel baskets of juicy red apples from the Harkers' trees to share with pupils and staff.

When Susan and Lizzie first walked to the shops in Mount Holly, Lizzie noticed how different it was from Burlington, the first county seat and the old provincial capital of West Jersey. For one thing, it was quieter. With its river and rail access, Burlington was a busy commercial centre with a large population and many businesses besides the usual tradesmen that every town had. Burlington had watermen, boatbuilders, and many house carpenters. Its predominant industry was shoemaking though. Horse-drawn carts and waggons carried products to and from the High Street wharf or market. Most shopkeepers lived above their businesses, conveniently located on both sides of the main street.

Mount Holly was a Quaker stronghold like Burlington and proud of its own colonial heritage. It succeeded Burlington as the county seat in 1796 because it was closer to the centre of the fast-growing county. Compared to Burlington, the streets of Mount Holly were full of well-dressed lawyers and clerks. All day long they hurried between their law offices and the courthouse to serve the legal needs of the civilian and criminal population. The prison was fittingly located in the centre of the town near the courthouse. A rail road ran the seven miles linking Mount Holly and Burlington, providing timely transportation of both goods and passengers, including day pupils like Susan Harker.

While a guest of the Harkers, Lizzie enjoyed daily rambles with Susan and her mother, identifying trees, birds, and animals along the way. Lizzie remarked that she had seen only bushy-tailed grey squirrels in New Jersey, black ones being more prevalent in Niagara. She missed feeding Albert, the black squirrel she named for Queen Victoria's consort. When Lizzie was home last spring, she had trained the squirrel to come to her for food. Lizzie wondered if Willy and Val were still feeding him in her absence. Little boys could be forgetful. She would have to ask them in her next letter.

❦ ❦ ❦

Mrs La Motte and Miss Cronyn stood on the dais in the School Room, preparing to distribute the post. The lucky girls rose from their seats as Miss Cronyn called their names.

"Elizabeth Fuller, you've some letters that arrived while you were away."

Lizzie jumped up and skipped to the dais, accepting the six fat envelopes. The top one was addressed to her in Laura's precise handwriting. There were also letters from Mary Margaret, her father and mother, and little Val. Even Shelly had scribbled a large S on the back of one envelope.

Back at her desk, she decided to read Laura's letter first as other girls passed by, skirts rustling. Lizzie tore open the seal and unfolded it.

Beechlands
9 October 1856

Dear Lizzie,

I trust you are enjoying your stay with Susan. I hope you remember your manners and act like a young lady so that Mother and Papa would be proud of you. I write to tell you all about Henry Hobart Fuller's baptism. Papa planned for our baby brother to be baptized at the first service ever at St John's on fifth October. He was thankfully an angel throughout the rite, at three months of age, even when Papa poured the water on his forehead. He just looked up surprised at Papa and then smiled at him! The church was full, of course. Mother and Henry were seated with us in the back of the nave near the font until the baptism. Uncle Thomas Street was a sponsor, as well as Mr Burns, Bella and Julia's father. Mother chose Mary Margaret to be his godmother because she did not want to choose betwixt Aunt Julia and Aunt Caroline. Mary Margaret held him so tenderly. It was very sweet to behold. At the end, Papa took Henry from her and paraded him up to the chancel and back again for all to see and admire. The church interior is beautiful. All the work was completed well before that Sunday. Mother chose fall flowers for the altar, and they complemented the hangings nicely. After the service, we had a delicious dinner together at the rectory with many uncles, aunts, and cousins. Poor Willy is getting ready to go away to the college in Toronto now. He is already homesick, and he hasn't yet left! Please write to him there as often as you can. You understand how important letters are from home.

Your loving sister,
Laura

CHAPTER 21

Margaret Jane at Home

NOVEMBER 1856, PORT ROBINSON

Margaret Jane had been at home for barely a month, and since her arrival, she had been busy with late season harvest tasks like many other females in the Niagara Peninsula. She helped her mother and Agnes bring in the remaining bounty from the kitchen garden and orchard. They collected mature seeds to be planted in the spring and snipped the herbs to dry in bunches hung in the attic. Dunc got up on the ladder and picked the last pears and apples from the orchard. Then the women wrapped the perfect apples in newspaper and placed them in the outside cellar built especially for keeping the fruit over the winter. They selected some damaged pears and apples to slice up and set them out to dry in a corner of the summer kitchen for mid-winter treats. Finally, Margaret Jane and her mother cut the last broccoli, cabbages, cauliflower, and brussels sprouts to store in the root cellar. Many an evening, Margaret Jane had fallen into bed tired to the bone as soon as it was dark.

Even when cool autumn temperatures arrived and the trees dropped their dried leaves, the work continued. Before the first hard frost of the season, they pulled the last root crops from the field beside the barn. They stored the vegetables, one after another, in separate sections of the large root cellar dug into the ground near the summer kitchen: carrots, potatoes, onions, parsnips, pumpkins, winter squash, rutabagas, and turnips.

One afternoon, the McFarland ladies and Maria, the cook, were slicing and grinding onions and peppers together to make a relish with vinegar. The kitchen reeked of onions, and their eyes were weeping freely. They very much disliked the job, but the end result was a favourite condiment to eat with McFarland roast beef.

With a gasp, Agnes dropped her knife to the floor and put both hands round her protruding abdomen.

"Agnes, what's the matter?" asked Mrs McFarland.

"I don't know! I've never felt this before. What could it be?"

"Let me see you!" said Maria, as she dropped a slippery handful of onion on the floor with a splat. Maria was only twenty-one, but fancied herself knowledgeable about nearly everything. Without asking permission, she reached out to feel Agnes' abdomen through her apron.

"Maria!" said Mrs McFarland. "What are you doing?"

"Begging your pardon, Mrs M," she said. "I was only wanting to help Mistress Agnes."

"I prefer that you tend to your task, Maria. We shall see to Agnes, Margaret Jane and I."

"Yes, Mrs M. Beg your pardon, Mistress Agnes," the girl said, as she curtseyed, chastened.

Margaret Jane said, "Agnes, what are you feeling?"

"It hurts. It's like a stomach cramp. A bad one. I need to lie down."

"Maria, you will have to finish up here. If you don't know what to do, come and find me," said Mrs McFarland.

Mrs McFarland and Margaret Jane each took one of Agnes' elbows and led the young woman out of the summer kitchen, through the garden, and up the steps into the house. Once inside, Agnes groaned and darted to the bench under the window in the mudroom.

"You can rest in John's consulting room, but his couch isn't very comfortable," said Mrs McFarland.

"In a minute, please. I just need to get my breath," said Agnes.

Margaret Jane and her mother looked at each other, concerned.

A few minutes later, her mother-in-law asked, "Is it better? May I touch you?"

"Yes, why?"

Margaret Jane stood in front of Agnes. "The baby is to come in the spring?"

"That's what Midwife said, yes. I ceased being unwell in July."

"Then it is much too soon for it to be coming now, Agnes," said Mrs McFarland, abandoning the idea of examining her son's wife. "We need to get you into bed. Can you climb the stairs?"

"P'raps I can … let me sit here a bit."

"May I feel your stomach?" asked Margaret Jane.

"Go ahead," said Agnes, tears beginning to fall. "I'm worried."

Margaret Jane put her palm lightly on Agnes' belly and waited. In a few minutes, she felt the abdominal muscles tighten, and Agnes began to utter another groan, her hand covering her mouth.

"We need to get her to lie down here, Margaret Jane, on the first floor. Into the consulting room. It's our only choice. She shouldn't climb the stairs. She shouldn't exert herself," said Mrs McFarland.

Margaret Jane guided Agnes through the hall and into John's room. She helped her up onto the couch. Her mother went upstairs to fetch a blanket and pillow.

"Margaret Jane, I'm afraid! What's happening to me?"

"Try not to worry, Agnes. Lie down, and try to relax. Maybe the pains will stop if you rest here. We've been working very hard lately. You might have overdone."

"Overdone? I was sitting at a table. I wasn't even standing."

"I know, but we have all been busy with the harvest. P'raps you should have rested more."

"Do you think the child will come now?"

"I don't know, Agnes. I'm not a physician. And John's out, of course! We could send for Mrs Drew," said Margaret Jane.

"Yes, the midwife. She was here a fortnight ago. She said everything was fine."

Mrs McFarland came back into the room with a pillow and blanket for Agnes.

"Mama, I think we should send Maria for the midwife. No one else is here."

"I shall send her. You stay here with Agnes, dear," said her mother.

❦ ❦ ❦

Unfortunately, before Maria could get back with Mrs Drew, Agnes' tiny baby was born. Margaret Jane and her mother tried as best they could to warm it, but Mrs McFarland knew the child was much too young to survive. The two were crying together with the shocked and grieving mother when Maria and Mrs Drew walked in the door.

❦ ❦ ❦

DECEMBER 1856

Agnes was recovering slowly from her child's premature delivery but gaining strength every day. John watched over her, making sure that she ate sufficient iron-rich foods to replenish her blood supply. At John's insistence, Maria made little steak and kidney pies for her. Dunc was solicitous of her, offering to help her climb the stairs. The two men uncharacteristically waited on her. Margaret Jane was touched and amused by this change in her brothers' usually gruff behaviour. She wondered if her father had behaved the same way when her mother gave birth or her sisters were ill.

❦ ❦ ❦

Preparations for Christmas were underway. There hadn't been any appreciable snow as yet, which was unusual for the Niagara Peninsula. Margaret Jane went outside to cut boughs of holly and evergreen to decorate the mantelpieces and the banisters throughout the house. She hoped the indoor decorations would lift Agnes' spirits. One day, she and Agnes and her mother even took the stagecoach up to Hendershots' in St Catharines to shop. They bought gifts and paper stuffs to make Christmas symbols to place around the house as Margaret Jane and her schoolmates had done last year at St Mary's Hall. The girl showed Agnes and Mrs McFarland how to make them, and as they worked, they sang Christmas carols that Margaret Jane had learnt at the school.

When the dark January cold set in, the girl missed her friends woefully, but even more so, her studies. Since Agnes' miscarriage in November, several times a week now she had been creeping into John's consulting room to read his medical books when he was out on a call. The heaviest and thickest one was about human anatomy, beautifully illustrated. She was curious about how the illustrations had been obtained. Amazed by the small print and number of pages in his various books, she wondered if she were smart enough to learn all that was in them. One text written in French was about obstetrics. Her French was not that good after only two terms at St Mary's, but the illustrations helped her understand the birth process and answered some questions she had about what had happened to Agnes. The little book by Pierre Cazeaux became her favourite reading in the moments stolen from her other household work that winter.

❦ ❦ ❦

SUNDAY, 8 MARCH 1857

It was a freezing night and Margaret Jane was awakened by insistent loud pounding on the front door below her bedroom window. The noise was followed by John's familiar footsteps going downstairs. Soon she could tell he was bounding up the steps again. Minutes later, she heard him trying to be quiet, descending once more. Then he must have paused to pull on his thick rubber boots, winter coat, hat and gloves before he closed the heavy oak door behind him, the iron knocker banging. After a time, she heard his horse whinny as it left the barn, pulling John and the messenger in the sleigh off to some emergency, probably a baby who had to be born in the depths of a Canadian winter or someone extremely ill. She wanted to go with him, despite the weather. She yearned to be part of the care and the cure for people.

When she awoke again later that morning, it was still semi-dark in her room. Snow covered the panes of her second-floor window. She cleared the cold glass with her hand but couldn't see through it. She wondered how much snow had fallen. In January there had been three feet in one storm! It had taken the men half a day to clear a path out to the back house. That was also the night that her mother's father, dear old Grandpa Elliott, died over at Uncle Andrew's house. Her mother had stayed with him for several days as his life ebbed away.

After dressing warmly, she went downstairs to find her mother and Agnes in the kitchen rather than the morning room. Dunc was coming in the back door with an armload of wood for the big iron cook stove. Maria should have been busy making breakfast, and Frances, the housemaid who ordinarily would have brought in wood for the kitchen, was also among the missing. And where was her father?

"Good morning, Mama, Agnes, Dunc." Margaret Jane gave them each a kiss on the cheek and then sat down in a straight back chair at the long trestle table. "What are we doing out here this morning?"

Agnes smiled and got up from the table to fetch a cup and saucer for Margaret Jane as Dunc loaded the cook stove with a few logs.

"Maria and Frances aren't here yet to-day. Because of the storm, I imagine. It's yet cold in the other rooms. We thought we would be cosier in here, dear, in front of the stove," said her mother.

Agnes poured tea for Margaret Jane and then passed her the sugar and milk.

Agnes started to giggle.

"What's funny?" asked Margaret Jane.

"We have some news, Dunc and I," said her sister-in-law.

"Oh? Well, what is it then? Tell me."

"Another child is coming—this summer."

Margaret Jane popped out of her chair and gave Agnes a long, tight squeeze round her shoulders. "That's wonderful news! I'm so happy for you both.

CHAPTER 22

Transitions

THURSDAY, 26 MARCH 1857, BURLINGTON

In the gardens of St Mary's Hall, early daffodils were blooming, and forsythia blossoms were opening, showing off their brilliant yellow colours in the pale light of early spring. Trees were
beginning to bud after the unseasonably mild weather following
record cold temperatures in January. All of the ice had melted in
the river, and water traffic was once again possible.

To-day, the pupils assembled in the School Room to witness
the annual graduation exercises. The twenty-three seniors,
flanked by Bishop Doane and the Rev. Dr Millett, sat on a platform decorated with potted azaleas from the conservatory at
Riverside. Nurse McIntire pinned the traditional three ivy leaves
on each senior's white muslin shirtwaist before the oral examinations and essays began. For the last week, the senior girls had
been practising their chosen work: essays on Greek, German, Italian, and French literature to be delivered in each language. Several presentations were about American history; others treated
European art or music.

The baccalaureate ceremony, the seniors' last as pupils of St

Mary's Hall, was held in the Chapel of the Holy Innocents. All the girls, departing or not, received Bishop Doane's Commencement address with much emotion. The young ladies were going out to begin their adult lives, some becoming wives, some teachers, others simply to rejoin their families in far-flung states.

Afterward, there was a celebratory meal before the girls who were leaving scattered to finish packing their belongings for "Breaking Up Day" to-morrow. The new graduates placed their beautifully engraved diplomas, rolled up and tied with a blue ribbon, in the top tray of their trunks where they wouldn't be crushed. By train or carriage, they left St Mary's Hall after many tearful embraces and promises to write.

As always, some pupils stayed on for the April vacation. This year, however, Lizzie, Julia, and Isabella were among those ending their studies at the school. They were going home permanently to Canada. The trio had been surprised when Mrs La Motte informed them of the simultaneous orders from their parents.

❦ ❦ ❦

The March 6 decision of the American Supreme Court in the case of the slave, Dred Scott, had disturbed the anti-slavery community in both countries. The Burns family disapproved of the decision and were wary of its possible consequences. St Catharines had become a terminus of the Underground Railroad since the Fugitive Slave Act passed in 1850. William Hamilton Merritt, a close Burns family friend and relative by marriage, was a loyal supporter of the fugitive slave community. He was a vocal critic of the court's opinion that slaves could not be American citizens and could not bring suit for their freedom, or anything else for that matter. The decision also opened up the question of slavery being legalised in states where it had already been banned, and of new American states allowing the practise. Thomas Burns was concerned the volatile situation would lead to war in the United States, and he persuaded Tom Fuller of the wisdom of bringing their three girls home to Canada before something exacerbated the conflict.

To make matters worse, on 12 March, Lizzie Fuller's uncle, Thomas Clark Street, Member of the Provincial Parliament, had narrowly escaped death in the tragic Desjardins Canal railway accident near Hamilton, Canada West, just breaking his collarbone. One of his associates, Samuel Zimmerman, a railway shareholder and businessman, lost his life in the disaster caused by a broken axle. The entire community of Niagara was shaken by the event. Although train travel was commonplace in 1857, it remained fraught with danger. The two families took this as the last straw and sent letters to Burlington forthwith, ending the girls' time there at the conclusion of the winter term.

Lizzie was dismayed. She had grown to enjoy school life during her three terms, especially her conchology lessons with Miss Rodney and their walks at low-tide on the stony beach of the Delaware. She realised she had few prospects in life beyond marriage and motherhood. If she learnt enough to teach her own children, her education in Burlington wouldn't be wasted, but what would she do all her life if she didn't marry? Many girls, like her teachers, did not. Could she be a teacher herself?

Julia, nearly seventeen, couldn't wait to see William again. He was finishing at the grammar school soon and didn't plan to go to university. He would need to find a job in commerce, perhaps with an uncle, or in government. What would she do all day long? Once back in St Catharines, she would have to consider her options in life. She was yet too young to marry.

Of the three Canadians, Isabella was the most disappointed by her parents' decision to bring her home after only two terms. She had settled in at St Mary's and made close friends in her eleven months away from home. Bella had discovered she had musical ability, and she loved being the only harpist at the school. Early on, Miss Winans recognised the young girl had a good ear and a beautiful, albeit untrained, voice. She encouraged Bella to compose and sing. Bella had got better marks for English composition and comportment over her second term too. And now her parents ordered her to return, just as she was experiencing success!

❦ ❦ ❦

On "Breaking Up Day", the departing pupils lined up in the Circle with their respective chaperones for the ten-minute walk to meet the train. If family members were not available to fetch daughters home, escorts were assigned based on the girls' destinations. Miss Stanley was taking a group to western New York, where she planned to spend the April vacation with her own family at Stanley Corners. Among her travelling party were three new graduates—Anna Bull, Elizabeth Scribner, Julia Tredway—and Julia's younger sister Ellie.

Anna and Ellie were struggling to keep up with Elizabeth and her best friend, Julia Tredway. The two graduates walked together, arm in arm, relishing every minute of their last days as school girls in Burlington. In Elmira, Elizabeth would have to bid farewell to Julia who was going on to her home in Lockport, New York. They had struggled through the hardest lessons together in Senior A. When would they see each other again? The Scribner family was moving to Wisconsin this summer! They promised to write each other every week. Anna would also leave the train in Elmira where her father would conduct her over a tedious route on branch lines northwest to Dansville to vacation at home until she returned to the Hall as an assistant teacher.

❦ ❦ ❦

FRIDAY, 3 APRIL 1857

Miss Stanley conducted the Canadian girls as far as the Canandaigua station. There, Aunt Arabella Burns met her nieces and Lizzie to escort them back across the Niagara River in the cars. All three girls were excited to have another chance to catch a glimpse of the great cataract as the powerful locomotive chugged west across Mr Roebling's bridge. Going west, Isabella Burns should at last be able to see Horseshoe Falls! But would she ever get to go for a ride on the *Maid of the Mist*? Perhaps this summer, if she had to be in Canada. This would be her first plea to her father!

"Julia! It's there! See the mist? It's the falls! Look!" exclaimed Bella, as she pulled her sister by the sleeve. Bella peered out the window as the three passenger cars rumbled across Roebling's magnificent suspension bridge. "Isn't it wonderful?"

Julia looked up from her book, pulling her arm away forcefully. Her sister had been talking about Niagara Falls for the last

186

two days. Julia was clearly not excited about seeing them again. After all, she had gone home last spring for vacation and seen them for the third time. They were better visible from the east because of the curve of the Niagara Gorge, but often they were shrouded in mist. But, of course, it was Bella's first glimpse of one of the Natural Wonders of the New World. As an older sister, she should be excited for her, should she not?

"Yes, Bella, they are wonderful, aren't they?" she said, trying to muster some enthusiasm. "Remember Papa promised he would take us all on the *Maid of the Mist* this summer when it is warm?"

"Oh, I do hope so! You can get drenched under them, Papa said. You must wear oilcloth coats and hats and waterproof boots on the boat or suffer the consequences. He said they are awfully loud."

Lizzie rose from her seat across the aisle and asked, "Did I miss them? Oh, for pity's sake! What was I thinking, sitting on the wrong side?"

"No, Lizzie, look back of us. Can you see the mist still?" asked Bella.

"Just barely. I can't believe I was talking to your aunt at that very moment! She said we shall be in St Catharines in under an hour."

❦ ❦ ❦

Mr Burns and Mr Fuller met the travellers on the station platform. After fond kisses all around, the fathers arranged to have the trunks delivered to their homes when the baggage cars were unloaded. When final good-byes were said, the Burns' driver, Patrick Coffey, helped his passengers and their hand luggage into the carriage. Aunt Arabella was delivered first to the home of her sister, Ann Burns Campbell, with whom she lived. The Campbells lived in Academy Street too, half a block from the Burns.

Patrick brought the carriage to a halt under the *porte-cochère* of the Burns' house and then helped the girls exit the vehicle. Young Mary Carroll, only fifteen years old and new to service with the family, opened the heavy oak door to greet her employer and the two Burns daughters whom she had not yet met.

When Julia and Bella entered the house, Mrs Burns was in the small front parlour waiting for them with little Llewellyn and Elizabeth. The towhead baby boy, dressed in a crisp white cotton dress, babbled and toddled through the room, clutching a rag-doll. Six-year-old Libby was playing with a pair of Frozen Charlotte figures that Emma had bought for her at Fitzgerald's Toy Shop in St Paul Street. She was pretending they were chasing each other down the edge of the carpet.

"Mama! I am so glad to see you!" exclaimed Bella as they embraced.

"Isabella, thank the good Lord you are home safe! Julia, let me look at you! You have both grown so tall!" Their mother held them for a long time, and tears brimmed her eyes. She was still somewhat emotionally labile even eighteen months after childbirth.

Julia kissed her mother's cheek and then picked up Llewellyn. Lewie squealed with delight at his sister's attentions, even though he had no idea who she was. He had been an infant the last time she saw him.

Bella picked up Libby and spun her in the air, causing the little girl to giggle and shriek. Her full linen skirt flew open round her limbs as they went up and down, the girl's boots coming ominously close to a table full of bric-a-brac and an oil lamp.

"Isabella!" shrieked her mother. "You will break something!"

Bella put Libby down and straightened her sister's dress with a half-smile. "Sorry, Mama." Bella sat on the settee and beckoned to Libby to sit on her lap.

Julia grimaced. Despite her mother's emotional welcome, it was a relief to be home again after nearly a year away, thought Julia, bouncing her baby brother on her knee. She wanted to send a message to William and to see him again after so many months. Perhaps Kitty would deliver it for her. His letters had been understandably few, as he was so busy with his studies at the grammar school. They had all been very dry, as they had to pass the careful eye of Mrs La Motte, who read every one before it was delivered to its recipient. Julia guessed she would have to wait until Sunday to see him. Perhaps at St George's, after the service, they would be able to talk to each other.

"Mama, where is Emma? Why isn't she here to welcome us?" asked Bella.

"Emma? She is out for the afternoon. She is giving lessons at the church," replied her mother.

"Lessons? What kind of lessons? To whom? At St George's?"

"No, no! At the Negro church, the British Methodist Episcopal Church, dear, over in Geneva Street. She joined the Refugee Slaves' Friends Society last autumn."

"What is that, Mama?" asked the girl.

"It is an organization created to resettle the American slaves here in St Catharines. Your uncle Elias Adams and Mr Merritt established it years ago, Isabella. Did she not tell you in her letters?"

"Oh, she did tell me all about it, Bella. I guess I didn't think to pass on the news," added Julia.

"Then what is it all about?" pursued Bella.

"Have you not heard about slavery in America after living there for nearly a year, daughter?"

"Mama, there weren't any slaves in Burlington," replied Bella impertinently. "The maids at school were mainly Irish."

"But there were coloured people in the town, and they were free," interjected Julia, noting the tension in her mother's voice. She tried to smooth things over by taking over the conversation. "The first free man we ever saw there was the Rev. Mr Benny Jackson. He's a porter who meets the trains with his cart. Everyone in the town knows him, Mama. We also met James Huggs and his mother who worked at the Beldin House. And we heard about a famous old soldier named Oliver Cromwell who lived in Burlington too. He was in the American Revolutionary War, but he died a couple of years ago. He was one hundred years old and lived on the other side of the High Street. They say he was in General Washington's army from Boston to Yorktown." Julia surprised herself with her knowledge of Mr Cromwell, as American history was not her strong suit. She took a deep breath as she finished her recitation.

"How fascinating, Julia. Emma has become quite interested in helping the American refugees. She and two of her friends meet with groups of women to teach them reading, writing, and sums three afternoons a week. She didn't go during the height of winter, but now that the weather is better, she has taken it up again. She seems to enjoy it immensely," said Mrs Burns.

"There were many girls from the South, though, Mama,

189

whose families owned slaves—girls from very large farms," continued Julia. "They call them plantations in the States. Faraway, in Alabama, Georgia, and Mississippi. They grow tobacco and cotton and corn, even rice on them. But we never talked to those girls about slavery. We were too busy with our studies, and besides, they lived in other rooms."

"And who was in your room with you last term, Julia?" asked Mrs Burns.

"Mama! I am sure we wrote you about our room," answered Julia, surprised at the question. "We had a young teacher in charge of it. She had studied long enough to graduate from St Mary's. Her name is Lizzie Adams, and Emma knew her. Then there were the four girls from Lockport and last winter two new girls from New York State, too. They were quite nice, all of them," said Julia. "We were eleven, plus Miss Adams."

"Yes, of course, dear. I forgot you must have told me all that. I am so busy with the children, you know. Emma was such a help to me, especially in the winter months when I wasn't feeling well. I do wish she were here now to welcome you. When she is out of the house, it is so difficult dealing with the little ones."

Julia didn't know how to respond to this complaint. She didn't like that her mother was ill. Last spring when she was home she thought it was just a temporary weakness after the baby. But now she could see that her mother's problems were more serious and lingering. She wondered if Kitty was enough help. Perhaps they needed a governess, since the monthly nurse was gone.

"Mama, where's Norman?" asked Bella, breaking the awkward silence among them.

"Why, of course, he is still at school," snapped Mrs Burns.

Again, Julia sensed her mother's annoyance. "Well, Bella, how about we go upstairs and unpack?" she suggested, glad that she thought of an excuse to change the subject and leave the room. "I imagine Patrick has got our valises up by now."

"Yes, by all means, Julia," said Bella, as she collected her reticule from the divan. "Mama, we'll be down for tea."

❧ ❧ ❧

They found Kitty at the top of the curved polished mahogany

stairs. She was hurrying down the hallway from the servants' stairs toward the girls' room, following Patrick, who was delivering the last of the girls' hand luggage to their room.

"Kitty!" exclaimed Bella. "I'm so happy to see you again!" The younger girl flung her arms round the ladies' maid and wouldn't let go.

"Bella, what are you doing to Kitty?" asked Julia. "The poor girl!"

As Bella released her prey, Kitty wiped her hands on her apron. "Afternoon, Julia. Afternoon, Bella. Welcome home. How was your journey?"

"Fine, thank you, Kitty. We are so happy to be here. When does Emma come home to-day? I forgot to ask Mother," said Julia.

"She should be back soon. She walks Norman home from school after her lessons."

"She walks all the way from Geneva Street to St George's School and then home?" asked Julia.

"Oh, yes, in good weather, but not alone. She and her lady friends walk together."

"Of course," said Julia. "Well, let's get to it then."

After only a few minutes' work, Bella sat down on the bed. "I'm hungry, Julia. Do we have to do this now?" asked Bella.

"Stop whining, sister! Tea won't be ready till Cook has made it and little Mary has set it out. Be still, and get busy!"

Kitty said, "I'm sure you are tired, Bella. I'm here to help with all this. Never you mind it now."

"Oh, Kitty, you needn't baby her anymore. She is quite capable. At St Mary's Hall, she had to make her own bed and put away her belongings. She even knows how to mend stockings now!" said Julia with a laugh.

Bella huffed and threw herself down on the bed. In two minutes, she was snoring gently. Kitty covered her with a quilt as Julia went on unpacking.

❧ ❧ ❧

As Emma and Norman entered the house, they saw Libby on the stairs taking two steps at a time, a feat she had learnt watching

Norman. Their mother was bent over Lewie, helping him walk up the stairs.

Mary took their wraps and hung them in the closet under the steps.

"Mama," said Emma, "let me carry Lewie upstairs. Does he need to be changed? I'll do it." Emma picked up the toddler and took him to the second floor nursery.

"Oh, thank you, dear heart. What would I do without you? Norman, how was school?" asked Mrs Burns.

"Oh, you know, Mama, recitation after recitation. But I got high marks for arithmetic to-day," answered the boy, puffing out his chest.

"Well, that is wonderful," said his mother. "I am glad you are a good boy at school."

"Yes, Mama, *I* am, but David Smith was *not*. He got into a lot of trouble out of doors before class. He and Edward had a terrible row."

"Oh, my, what did Mr Elliott do about it?"

"Well, he took David by the ear and sat him in the corner on the high stool, Mama. Everyone tried not to laugh. He is always pestering Edward about his marks. This time Edward stood up to him, and David popped him in the nose. Down he went in the mud, and Mr Elliott came at a run. He saw it all, so David will get the rod at home to-night."

"That is awful, Norman. Will you tell Papa about that at tea?"

"Yes, of course, Mama. Are my sisters back?"

"Oh, yes, dear. They're upstairs now."

"Yippee!" exclaimed the boy, as he bounded up the stairs.

❦ ❦ ❦

Sunday morning arrived, and Julia dressed hurriedly, leaving her dark hair loose in spite of Kitty's protestations. Julia rushed downstairs to join the rest of the family for breakfast. Emma was already at table with her parents, Norman, and Libby.

"My, you look well rested this morning, Julia. You positively glow!" said her father when she came into the dining room.

"Why, thank you, Papa," she said, leaning over to give him a peck on the cheek. "Good morning, Mama."

"Good morning, Julia. Where is Isabella?" asked Mrs Burns.

"Kitty was just finishing her hair, Mama, and I didn't want to wait for her. At St Mary's we always had to wait to go together with our dormitory. It's nice to be free from so many rules."

"Free from *some* rules, my daughter, perhaps. But you will need to pin up your hair before we go to church. It's not decent," said her mother with a frown.

"Oh, Mama! Must I? I left it loose all day yesterday in the cars." Julia wondered why Mama hadn't mentioned it when she arrived.

"Well, perhaps that was Aunt's fault, my dear, but you will pin it up as your mother wishes before you enter the Lord's House," said Mr Burns in support of his wife.

"Oh, fine! After breakfast, then. Kitty will have to do it. I shall have to eat quickly. Are we all walking to church together this morning?" Julia asked, deftly changing the subject. She peered out the long window framed by heavy patterned draperies and said, "It looks like such a heavenly day!"

"Yes, we should do that, especially since you've been sitting in a train for three days," said Mr Burns. "I'll let Patrick know we won't be needing the carriage."

"Will you see William to-day, Julia?" asked Emma, out of the blue.

"Well, you know that I shall, Emma. He's always at church on Sunday, is he not?" replied Julia.

"No, I mean, will you be meeting him?"

"Yes, of course, I shall speak to him, Emma. What do you mean?"

"Yes, what do you mean, Emma?" asked Mr Burns. Raising his eyebrows, he looked straight at his eldest child. As much as he loved Emma, he knew she could be critical of the romantic Julia, perhaps even a bit jealous of her sister's close friendship with William.

"I simply mean, will William be allowed to walk her home, Papa?"

"Honestly, Emma, he is our cousin. What in the world are you implying?" asked Julia.

"Nothing, nothing at all. Of course, he is our cousin. And you haven't seen him for nearly a year, and you probably wrote to him every week at school," said Emma petulantly.

"Yes, I did. We are best friends, Emma. What is wrong with that?"

"Daughters, stop this bickering at once!" said Thomas Burns. "Let's eat our breakfast and be on with our day. It seems we need some time in the Lord's house to help us remember how to live together after such a long time apart."

❧ ❧ ❧

St George's Church of England, the Burns' parish, was established as a garrison church for troops stationed in the region in 1792. The stone building was constructed in Academy Street in 1840 after a fire destroyed the original one near St Paul Street. The façade and tower built of Kingston limestone were added as a memorial to Thomas and Mary Merritt, the parents of William Hamilton Merritt, and generously given by William's uncle Nehemiah Merritt.

The Burns family arrived ten minutes early and took their customary seats in the family's box pew across from the Mittlebergers. When Uncle Henry took his place with Eliza and their sons, the Burns family was already kneeling to pray their private devotions before the service began. William peeked round his parents and caught Julia's eye across the aisle. He winked at her; she blushed and turned her face away, luckily much hidden by her bonnet.

After the recessional of choir and minister, the Rev. Mr Atkinson gave the benediction. The congregation rose and began to exit the church through the narthex while the organist continued to play. The Mittleberger and Burns families lingered in the aisle and were among the last to leave. Julia and William walked together down the steps and through the paired red doors. He held her elbow as they descended the last set of steps. William stopped and took both her hands in his. He looked down intently at her face. "Julia, I'm so glad to have you back!"

"Thank you, William. It's grand to be back home again! It really is! Have you been studying diligently since your last letter?" asked the girl with a wry smile. He seemed to be taller than she recalled.

"Well, yes and no. Examinations aren't until next month, but

I've been reading a lot and practicing my surveying round town."

"Have you, indeed?" Julia asked, gazing up into her cousin's blue eyes.

"Well, yes. Since the weather's nicer, I've been outside taking measurements. It's quite fun, actually! I'll have to show you sometime. P'raps we can go out one afternoon and try it."

"I can't imagine how that works, William. Numbers aren't really my strong suit. What have you measured so far?"

"Well, I've surveyed our land and yours and Uncle John's. To make sure the lots are accurate, that's all. We use these chains." He pulled a length of thin chain links out of his pocket. "You see it's standard. Every piece of land is measured in chains."

"I see," said Julia. "And were ..."

"May I walk you home?" He offered his arm.

"Of course," said Julia, as she opened her parasol.

Norman and Libby ran up to the young couple and pulled at them both.

"William! Bet you can't catch us!" dared Norman, as he turned to run the two blocks home.

"Oh, yes, I can!" replied William, as he took off after Norman and Libby.

Julia stood there, abandoned and infuriated. After eleven months' absence, William leaves her to chase her two siblings whom he could have seen every day of the week!

CHAPTER 23

The Fullers

JUNE 1857

Lizzie still didn't fully understand what was so urgent that she had been called home to Canada last spring—something about trouble brewing in America. Lately her parents had been talking about the possibility of a war between the States because of the slavery question. Since she had got home, she had also heard them discuss the serious business and banking problems happening in both Canada and the States. That made her worry a bit, but she didn't know their family's income was assured because of Mrs Fuller's generous inheritance. When Lizzie's maternal grandfather, Samuel Street, died in 1844, he was rumoured to be the wealthiest man in Canada. Because of the inheritance, Mr Fuller never needed to take a salary from either of his parish churches.

Despite her initial fears, Lizzie had been perfectly happy at St Mary's Hall. She enjoyed her nature studies and had learnt to love the girls in her dormitory like sisters. She had become good friends with her classmate Susan Harker and had spent a vacation month with her family. Yes, she missed her own parents and siblings, but after just one term at St Mary's Hall, she had got the

hang of the recitations, the marks and the routine of early mornings, chapel services and early bedtimes. And no little brothers
around to distract her from her studies!

But now that she had been home for two months, she was
getting bored. Did she miss the strict schedule and constant in-
tellectual challenges at St Mary's Hall? What was she going to do
all summer long? Since her return, if the weather was nice, she
took walks in the woods and fields and helped her mother tend
the flowers and shrubs in the front garden. On rainy days, she
would listen to her mother play the piano-forte while she tried
her hand at spinning wool from their sheep. And there were always at least buttons to sew on or stockings to mend with so
large a family. A few times a month she would write to Dick and
Sam who were finished with school and working in Hamilton
and Stratford respectively. They were not good correspondents,
however.

Her youngest brother, Henry Hobart, born while she was in
Burlington last summer, was ten months old, creeping on the
floor and getting into everything now. Thankfully, Mrs Fuller did-
n't ask Lizzie to care for the baby; Lizzie preferred to play with
children who could talk and explore the outdoors with her. Most
mornings she spent some time teaching Val, now six, to read. He
was a quick learner and could spell his whole name: Valancy England Fuller. Together they took little Shelly into the nearby Beech-
woods or to the pond edge to catch frogs.

Even with all those different activities, Lizzie Fuller felt confined. Particularly on the many rainy days lately, she just couldn't
bear sitting inside for so many hours. Every afternoon she would
wait for Mary Margaret and Laura to get home from school so
that she could share in their experiences. She was surprised how
much she missed being a pupil.

Lizzie decided that she would discuss her future with her parents. This summer would be a fine holiday because she could be
out of doors on dry days, but she couldn't go on idle like this, especially when winter came. After all, she was fourteen and a half!
Laura was helping Mary Margaret at the Common School as her
unpaid assistant, preparing to go to the Normal School as soon
as she turned sixteen in January. Lizzie would have to come up
with something to do until she too was old enough to go up to

Toronto. It was a problem she would have to solve. At dinner to-morrow afternoon, Lizzie intended to broach the subject with her parents.

❦ ❦ ❦

One thing that she appreciated more now was being allowed to speak during meals. At first it had been so difficult for her to keep quiet at St Mary's Hall. She understood and accepted the rule because the number of girls all in one room would have created an insupportable din, but once at home, it was a relief to be rid of that unnatural behaviour.

Mrs Fuller called Val and four-year-old Shelton from play to eat dinner in the big farmhouse kitchen where Katie Dean, the maid, was feeding Henry. Mary Margaret, as the head teacher of the Common School, took her dinner at school along with Laura and the pupils who lived too far from home to return for the mid-day meal. Most days only Lizzie and her parents gathered to eat in the dining room.

Covered by a crisp white linen tablecloth, the rectangular mahogany dining table was long enough to seat the entire family. Matching white linen napkins in monogrammed silver napkin rings sat at each of the three places. The china plates and crystal glassware glistened on the tablecloth. Matching serving pieces on the sideboard contained the main course and vegetables. Ellen stood by to serve the three.

When everyone was seated, Mr Fuller said the grace.

"Papa … Mother," began Lizzie. "I've been thinking. Laura's going up to Toronto in January to the Normal. I am going to be so bored without her here. In fact, I'm bored now. What can I do when she is away?"

"Lizzie, my dear, what would you like to do?" asked her father, as he tucked his napkin into the collar of his shirt.

"I don't know. That's the thing."

"Well, there are only a few things you *can* do at your age, Elizabeth," said her mother. "You're just fourteen."

"But I'll be fifteen in February, and after that only one more year till I can go to the Normal."

"Do you want to be a teacher, Lizzie?" asked her father.

199

"Well, what else can I do? I'm too young to be married."

At that remark, her father nearly choked on his first bite of roast pork.

"Would you like to help Mary Margaret when Laura leaves?" her mother asked, looking sidewise at her husband, who coughed to clear his throat.

"I guess so. If she lets me teach about nature, I would love it. I don't want to sit there and listen to recitations all day long. I want to take the children outside to see the world like I do here."

"That sounds like a wonderful idea, my darling girl," said Mr Fuller. "It mayn't help with the superintendent's examinations in the spring though."

"I never did very well with those examinations, Papa. Memorising answers is so boring," said Lizzie.

"Just so, my dear, just so. I understand you love to be outside, but this is the method that Dr Ryerson requires."

"Who is Dr Ryerson?" asked Lizzie.

"Egerton Ryerson is the Superintendent of Education for Canada West, Lizzie. He is the man in charge of all the schools, how they operate, and how they are funded and supplied. He's a converted Methodist. We don't agree on all things—for example selling the Clergy Reserves a few years back—but he has promoted the idea of free schools for all children. We do agree on that score," explained Mr Fuller.

"Well, just the same, I don't fancy standing up in front of the whole township and showing what I don't know!"

"I understand that, dear, but you needn't do that anymore. We're not going to send you back to the Common School at your age."

"What about the new grammar school, Papa?" asked Lizzie.

"Well, the council just passed that last Tuesday, my dear."

"But you are a trustee, Papa, are you not? Can't you make sure I can go?"

"But, my dear, 'twill be mostly boys there, and we haven't a master hired yet."

"Will science be taught?" asked Lizzie.

"I don't know, dear. It's a grammar school. The chief classes are Latin and Greek."

"Oh, pooh, I could do that, I am sure! But I'd rather do science. Why don't you have science?" persisted the girl.

"Oh, Elizabeth Fuller! Will you never be satisfied?" asked her exasperated mother.

"No, I guess I won't be, Mother. I can't imagine my life without knowing about the world outside this house!"

❦ ❦ ❦

MONDAY, 6 JULY 1857

Lizzie walked into the council chamber of the Thorold Town Hall on the arm of her father. Since there was no school building yet, classes for the grammar school were going to be held here.

Rev. Mr Alan Dawson, the newly hired head master, shook hands with Tom Fuller and nodded to Lizzie. She curtseyed to the clergyman.

"Are you ready, Miss Fuller?" Mr Dawson asked. "Be seated here at this desk. I'll just be a moment. Your father may stay in the room while you work." The man disappeared into the hallway.

"Yes, surely," she said. "Papa ..."

"You'll be fine, Lizzie. Go on. Sit down and be comfortable."

Lizzie took off her bonnet, placed it on the chair beside her, and sat down. She arranged her skirt round her and kicked off her shoes and wiggled her toes. Then she took out her pen case, a pencil, and a piece of gum rubber from her reticule. She was ready to write if Mr Dawson required, as long as he supplied the ink.

Mr. Dawson returned to the chamber with a sheet of paper for Lizzie. On the paper was one sentence:

When the snow stopped falling, we went out to the barn where the animals were waiting to be fed.

"Mr Dawson, what do you wish me to do?" she asked.

"Why, parse it, my girl. What else?" he answered.

"Oh, right, of course," said Lizzie with relief. She was suddenly thankful that she had been required to do so much parsing at St Mary's Hall last term. She thought it was quite fun once she got the hang of it, drawing bubbles, small and large, round the clauses and words, identifying the many parts of speech featured in the practise sentences.

She got right to work on the parsing and within five minutes put down her pencil with obvious satisfaction. She checked her work and looked up expectantly at her father and Mr Dawson.

"Already finished, eh?" asked the head master.

"Well, yes, Mr Dawson. We did a lot of that in our grammar class at my other school. Anything else?"

"Turn over the paper, Miss Fuller, and you will see."

Lizzie did as she was told and saw two fractions to be reduced, an addition problem, and a division problem all with fractions. She had spent many weeks doing fractions in arithmetic class a year ago, but during the last winter term she'd had the course in algebra. She hoped she could remember all of the rules for fractions. She sighed and began to work. Halfway through the problems, her pencil point was dull; she took out a folded piece of sandpaper from her pen case and sharpened the pencil point, and then went back to the problems. The room was getting warm now. She wanted to push up her long sleeves but she dared not for decency's sake. She was afraid she would make a silly arithmetic mistake now in the stuffy room.

At length she put down her pencil and checked her figures several times. Satisfied, she looked over at her father with a quizzical expression, shrugged her shoulders, and gave the paper to Mr Dawson.

"Ah, yes, let me examine your work." He studied the parsing carefully, making unusual faces as he tried to read the labels. Turning the paper over, he saw the correct answers and smiled broadly.

"What's next?" asked Lizzie.

"Next? Uh … why … that's it, Miss Fuller. Your father assures me that you have a fair hand and can read fluently. I read the catalogue from St Mary's Hall; you have studied many subjects there. Your father also brought me your marks for the last term, and they are very good. No one gets a ten there, he says. Your knowledge of geography is above average."

"Well, I *have* travelled a fair bit lately," said the girl. Lizzie winked at her father and tried in vain to contain a wry smile. She waited for the verdict, confident now.

Seconds later, Mr Dawson said, "Congratulations, my dear. It's perfect. You are the first female student to enter the Thorold Grammar School."

"Do you hear that, Papa? I can go back to school!" Jubilant, she sprang out of her seat and skipped to her father who sat on the bench against the wall.

"I had no doubts, Lizzie! No doubts at all," said the proud father. "Let's go home to tell Mother."

CHAPTER 24

The McFarlands

SATURDAY, 8 AUGUST 1857, PORT ROBINSON

Margaret Jane awoke to a crash of thunder and heavy rain pounding on the roof. She could smell the wet ground outside through the window left cracked open overnight. It had stormed all night, hot humid air clashing with colder, somewhere over the Niagara Peninsula. She got out of bed and shut the window, dressed quickly in a thin linen frock, and ran down the back stairs. She took a hooded oilskin cloak off the hook in the hallway and pulled on a pair of rubber shoes before making her way to the back house. When she returned, she found her mother and Agnes in the morning room, strangely quiet, finishing their breakfast tea.

"What terrible weather! What's going on?" asked Margaret Jane, as she looked at them both. She poked at the fire in the fireplace. A fresh flame leapt up and briefly warmed her after her quick but damp excursion to the back house.

"Agnes is ready to have the baby, dear. I doubt either Maria or Frances will be in to-day. The lanes are too muddy from so much rain overnight. We daren't send for Midwife in this weather

205

either. She is liable to get her waggon stuck where she lives. John is still out somewhere too. He didn't leave a note again," said her mother.

"I heard him go out sometime during the night. What shall we do then?" asked Margaret Jane.

"We are going to help Agnes as best we can, dear," said Mrs McFarland.

"Well, Agnes, how *are* you?" asked the young girl, peering down intently at her labouring sister-in-law.

"I've been trying to walk through the house as Mother suggested, but I have to stop and sit down when the pains come," said Agnes.

"Are you hungry?" asked Margaret Jane.

"Not really, but I would take another cup of tea when it's ready. And two lumps of sugar, please."

❧ ❧ ❧

As the day wore on, there was still no sign of John, not that a physician was needed for a normal childbirth, but the family was concerned for his safety. The rain came in waves, and the wind blew round the house, at times making a high-pitched whistle. The women moved into the parlour and stayed warm and dry in front of the new enamel stove. Mrs McFarland and Margaret Jane watched over Agnes, cheering her on during contractions.

When dinnertime came, Mrs McFarland fixed enough for everyone to eat, but Agnes still had no appetite. Mr McFarland went to his desk to work on some figures while the expectant father went out to feed and water the animals sheltered in the barn.

Margaret Jane studied Agnes' furrowed brow and distended belly. "How long will this take, Mama?"

Her mother replied, "It could take all day, dear. It's her first child. Often it is a long labour."

"What can I do to help?" asked the girl.

"Not a thing, dear one. Just be good company for Agnes. She is doing all the work. The baby is coming as best it can."

❧ ❧ ❧

It was midnight, and everyone went to bed early to get as much rest as possible before the anticipated delivery. Dunc and Agnes tried to sleep, but the labouring woman was so uncomfortable she got up every fifteen minutes to pace. When she thought she could stand it alone no more, she shooed Dunc out of the bedroom to summon his mother.

Margaret McFarland had given birth herself six times. As a farmer's wife, she had helped some of their ewes give birth too, but she had never attended another woman. She had always had a midwife and her sister-in-law nearby for her own deliveries. Since she had never had problems, she didn't consider herself qualified to direct a birth. When Agnes' first pregnancy had ended early last fall, Margaret and her daughter had stood by helpless. Unfortunately, in this situation Margaret was again the most experienced individual in the house while John was still out somewhere in the township, unaware that his sister-in-law was in labour.

Agnes was in bed, lying on her side, experiencing increasing discomfort. She let out a loud "Ahh!" that was enough to bring Margaret Jane flying out of her bed in the next room. She had been awakened already by Dunc's urgent knocks on her parents' bedroom door and then his footsteps clattering down the stairs.

Margaret Jane knew instantly the sound was from Agnes, and she peeked into the young couple's room through the door Dunc left ajar. "Agnes, what is it?"

"The baby is coming right now, Margaret Jane. I know it! Your mother went downstairs to get more linens. Please help me!"

Margaret Jane stopped in her tracks, trying to think fast. All of the pages of that French medical book ran through her mind at once. It was too late to get it out of John's library now; she would never be able to find the right pages in a hurry. She hoped she could remember the important bits, *les principes*, as the author called them.

"What should I do, Agnes?"

"I think it's time to bring the baby out!" Agnes took a deep breath and with all of her effort pushed one last time.

Margaret Jane reached out, expecting to catch the baby in her hands, but instead found the tiny moist infant lying face down on the bedclothes. In the dim light of the oil lamp on the bedside table she could see it wasn't moving. *Was it breathing?* she wondered. She saw the umbilical cord coiled round its neck.

Margaret Jane slipped her fingers gently under the twisted and slippery bluish cord. Carefully, she brought it over the little matted head. She positioned the baby's head below the shoulders as she had seen in the illustrations, rubbed its back firmly forward several times, and it took one breath and then another, followed by a lusty cry. She patted it on the back several times more, and it turned a nice shade of pink. Margaret Jane gave the newborn just as it was to the exhausted but happy mother. As she did, her own mother arrived with a jug of hot water and linen towels and warmed flannel blankets to put round the baby.

"Agnes, am I too late?" asked the new grandmother.

"Yes, apparently so," said her daughter-in-law with a sigh. "And my dear young sister has taken good care of us both."

"Margaret Jane McFarland! At fourteen, you have become a midwife!"

"Yes, Mama, I know it's what I want to do. I want to help people, especially women and babies. I am sure of it," said the girl.

❦ ❦ ❦

Hours later, John McFarland tramped into the mudroom at the back of the house. He doffed his soaked and now ruined leather driving gloves, hung up his oilskin cloak and hat, and sat on the oak bench to take off his rubber boots. He entered the quiet kitchen, wondering where everyone was.

He doubted the family had gone out to church in this weather. His parents and siblings were nowhere to be seen. With no one to cook for him, he began to open cupboards, looking for something to eat after his long night sitting with an elderly patient suffering from pneumonia. He put on the kettle for tea and greedily chewed on a stale scone he found in the breadbox. He took a juicy peach from the basket on the table.

Mrs McFarland appeared and greeted her tall, blond son. His thick curly hair was damp and uncombed.

"Why John, you look a sight! Where were you stranded all night?"

"Oh, I was stranded all right, with the Williams family over in Fonthill. It was Mr Williams who knocked at the door last night. His old mother was suddenly ill with fever and chest pains. The storm was raging when I was ready to leave them. I had no appetite for driving through it. More storms kept coming. The lightning was intense. Poor Chelly was frightened, although she was safe in their barn. I slept as much as I could there with her to keep her calm, lying on the seat of the buggy. I had one miserable thin blanket for cover. At least we were dry in the barn, but it's still very foggy out there. It was a difficult drive back."

"Oh, that sounds terrible, John. I'm glad you are home safe and sound. I'm sure you are tired and hungry. Now, let me fix you some breakfast. Oh, I almost forgot! We have a new member of the family to-day."

"Agnes? I didn't think she would be confined for at least another fortnight. What happened? Are they all right?" asked the young physician, remembering that Agnes had already lost one tiny baby.

"Oh fine, fine! She had pains all day long after you left yesterday. They began early in the day and continued all through the evening. She went to bed and awakened after midnight sometime. He came while I was downstairs getting linens and hot water."

"It's a boy, then?"

"Yes, a lovely first boy named Frederick Blake. Guess who delivered him?"

"Not Father, surely! Er … Dunc … nay … yourself?"

"No, son, both of them were elsewhere at the time, as was I," replied his mother with a smile. "Your father was fast asleep, in fact!"

"Well, it wasn't Maria. She's not here. Nor Frances. What the devil? You're not telling me it was little Maggie? Ha! I should have guessed from all of her airs wanting to be a physician," he scoffed.

"Why, yes, it was, John. She did a good job of it too. She took the cord from the baby's neck and got him breathing right off. Agnes was lucky to have her there, all of fourteen years old and midwifing!"

"Oh, Mother, she will never leave me alone now. I shall never hear the end of it. What am I to do with her?"

"You might want to talk to her seriously about her studies,

John. She is a bright girl, and she's now found a purpose. She can do more than keep house. I have been selfish and badly misjudged her abilities; she wants to help women and be challenged in life," said Margaret McFarland, weeping tears of pride. It had been a long day already in the McFarland household.

❦ ❦ ❦

A sunbeam shone into Margaret Jane's bedroom window later that morning, waking her from a deep, satisfying sleep. The rainstorms were gone. She rubbed her eyes, stretched her limbs, and pulled the cotton counterpane tighter up to her chin. She was very pleased with herself indeed. Helping Agnes with little Frederick was the best feeling in the world. It made her wonder once again how to get John on her side. He never seemed to have time for her. He thought she was still a child. He called her Maggie, a nickname she abhorred. She decided that to-day she would demand his attention, ask him all the questions she had saved up in her mind, and then convince him she was serious. She wondered if he had returned from his nighttime call yet.

Before Margaret Jane could get out of bed, she heard her brother come upstairs, shut the door to his room, and click the latch. Then she heard her mother in the hallway. When Margaret Jane peeked out, Mrs McFarland told her that John had gone to bed after his long stint doctoring and miserable night's sleep. Margaret Jane was disappointed but reasoned that the timing of her dissertation and plea was important. John needed his sleep, or he might dismiss her out of hand. He found it easy to do so even when he was well rested.

❦ ❦ ❦

Given the disrupted family schedule, supper was later than usual that evening. John came downstairs just as Margaret Jane and her mother were laying the table. Once seated at the round walnut dining table, the McFarlands, save new parents Agnes and Dunc who were upstairs with little Frederick, joined in a thanksgiving before beginning the meal. As head of the household, Duncan McFarland led the heartfelt prayer for the safe delivery of the baby, Agnes' recovery, and John's return after the storm. Then they enjoyed a celebratory meal of cured ham and potatoes from the cellar, fresh green beans from the garden, and the end of last summer's cucumber pickles, followed by a fresh raspberry pie. Conversation centred on not only the new arrival, but the amount and quality of the rain and how long it would take to dry the mud on the various paths on the farm to better tend to the animals. Getting in the grain harvest was going to be difficult unless the weather turned warm and sunny long enough to dry out the fields.

Margaret Jane was unsure this was the best time to bring up the subject of her education, but she was excited, having helped with the birth, and she wanted to restart the conversation about how she could become a physician. The whole family was tired from the activity of the last twenty-four hours. Despite his afternoon in bed, John looked fatigued. *Perhaps he mightn't fight back as he usually does when I try to talk to him about learning medicine,* thought Margaret Jane.

Or, she could be miscalculating his mood and cause a real row if he became wrathy.

She decided to try anyway.

"John, I have a confession to make. In my free time of late, I've been studying your medical books when you are out. I hope you don't mind. I had so many questions, and I still do, but I have learnt so much from them," began Margaret Jane.

"Ah, here we go again," said John, dropping his fork noisily on the plate and running both hands through his hair. He glowered at his father who, showing no reaction to Margaret Jane's revelation, continued to eat.

"Now, John, hear her out," pleaded the mother. "I told you how she worked with Agnes. The baby wasn't breathing, and she did what had to be done. Quickly, I might add. She didn't panic a bit. You have to agree that the babe is in fine shape despite being wee."

"All right. All right. I know what is coming. What do you want me to do, Maggie?"

"First, and this might seem a small thing to you, please call me by my name. Maggie is my baby name. I am Margaret Jane," asserted the young girl. Her eyes flashed indignantly as she pulled her own long unruly curls back and sat up straighter in her chair.

John frowned at her from across the table.

Their father put down his own fork and wiped his mouth on the napkin tucked in his shirt. "Son, we have known for years that Margaret Jane is a clever lass. That is why we sent her down to St Mary's Hall. It is clear now to me that she deserves to continue her studies. She still has another year before she can go to the Normal School in Toronto, for she must be sixteen. Is there a way she could be useful until then, lad?" asked his father.

"Useful how? Useful to me? She is but fourteen!"

"I'll be fifteen next month!" protested Margaret Jane.

"Aye, of course, she is young. What can she do now that would help her learn what she wants to learn?" persisted their father.

"Well, I don't know. Maybe she could go to the Common School again."

"The Common School! I am too old to go to that little schoolhouse, John, and you know it. I was bored there two years ago! Can't I help you somehow?"

"Now really, I doubt people will be impressed by my bringing my baby sister along on a call, do you? What could you do for a family whose father is dying? Can you bleed someone? Will you pick up a leech, girl?"

Margaret Jane wasn't a fan of bleeding or touching a leech. She decided not to answer his challenge and turned instead to her father.

"Oh, Father! I don't want to go to the Common School again. Is that the only possibility?"

"Could she teach at the Common School? Is she qualified?" asked his wife.

"I believe she is qualified, being fourteen, but they have a teacher already," said Duncan.

"They might need an additional teacher. That school is crowded," said Mrs McFarland.

"I don't want to be a teacher! I want to help people—women, children, and babies. How can I learn to do that, John? Tell me!"

John looked at her earnest young face. "I cannot believe this. I've no idea how you should proceed with this insane idea, little sister. But I see that you are determined. Let me think on it and make some inquiries."

Margaret Jane stared at her brother, stunned. *How did it hap-*

pen? Had she just won him over? Did her plan work? Had she worn him down?

Amazed, she got up from her place at the table, threw her arms round his shoulders and hugged him as she had never hugged him before. Their Scottish family was not usually so demonstrative, but she thought this called for an unusual response. He was shocked at her reaction and stiffened under her embrace.

Margaret Jane felt such joy that she couldn't contain herself. She kissed and hugged both her parents too before she began clearing up the table.

🐞 🐞 🐞

DECEMBER, 1857

The last few weeks seemed like a dream to Margaret Jane. She was a pupil again, this time at the new Thorold Grammar School. Her brother John had been key to this wonderful development. One day in October, he was treating Mr Fuller at his home at Beechlands when Mr Fuller told him that Lizzie was a pupil at the school, the only female there, in fact. Margaret Jane had missed the date for the beginning of summer term when Lizzie started, but she passed the entrance examination and was accepted for the autumn term that began on 19 October. The Fullers offered her a room to stay in their house while she was at school so that she wouldn't have to travel the four miles from Port Robinson every morning. On fine days, Lizzie and she rode a horse to school, much faster than walking, or if Mr Fuller were going to town that day, he would take them in his buggy and they would walk back to the rectory together. Margaret Jane went home on Sundays to play with her infant nephew and see her parents.

Life couldn't be better for the fifteen-year-old now. She was living with Lizzie again, and they were both thrilled to be scholars together once more. Lizzie was relieved to have another female in the school with her. After St Mary's Hall, it was a challenge to study in the same room with boys. But both girls were used to their brothers' teasing and let the schoolboys' annoying comments roll off their backs for the most part. Lizzie had some immunity because she was the rector's daughter, and most of the boys were parishioners at St John's. Margaret Jane, on the other hand, was fair game.

One Monday morning the young man seated behind Margaret Jane brought a small vial of water in his pocket. When everyone was settled in their places, the master began his lecture on Cicero. Timothy Moore took out the vial and uncorked it. He looked to his left and right, hoping that no one in the row would notice and give him away. He poured the water into his hand and blew it into Margaret Jane's neck, as he feigned a loud sneeze. It was great theatre.

Shocked with the sudden wetness, she stood from her desk and turned to look at him. She saw the vial still in his right hand and knew immediately what he had done.

Mr Dawson asked what was the matter between them.

"'Tis nought, sir," she said. "Timothy must be catching his death of cold, sir. I *do* hope it doesn't come to pass," she said, as she glared at the boy.

She sat down firmly as if to say she were going nowhere. She took her handkerchief from her reticule and proceeded to wipe the water off her neck and dabbed at her neckline. The boys snickered. The master, certain all was resolved, went on with his lesson.

At the end of the hour, Lizzie and Margaret Jane conferred. They would have to come up with a plan to avenge the attack, though certainly not in a violent way.

❦ ❦ ❦

A few days later, Margaret Jane and Lizzie came up with a plan. The two girls waited patiently until they thought Timothy had forgot all about his prank, treating him the same as the other scholars. One day Lizzie innocently asked the boy when his birthday was, and happily it was coming up soon. On that special day, Margaret Jane brought in a seed cake made just for him, wrapped in brown paper and tied with hemp string. She gave it to him at the end of the school day, wishing him a happy birth-day.

He quickly tore the string and paper off and said, "Why thank you, Margaret Jane. This is so nice of you." Timothy broke into the cake, popped a large piece into his mouth, and began to chew. He made a face and spat it out on his desk. "Ugh! What is this? Why, it's horrid!"

"Oh, my! Is it? I guess I'm not much of a baker, am I?" the girl asked innocently and without apology.

Margaret Jane winked at Lizzie, who knew exactly how much salt they had poured into the batter yesterday.

CHAPTER 25

Toronto

JANUARY 1858

Following the election of the sixth Provincial Parliament in December, the government continued to perambulate. Toronto was designated the meeting site for 1858 and for the 1859 and 1860 sittings, the legislative body agreed to be located once more in Québec City. Desperate for a neutral party to end the sixteen years of bickering about a permanent location, Prime Minister John A. MacDonald and the members asked Queen Victoria to decide the issue once and for all. On New Year's Eve 1857, the monarch chose Ottawa, a logging settlement on the border between Canada East and Canada West. It was an excellent choice, as the town had never hosted Parliament. Ottawa was also farther from the American border than any of the cities vying for the honour and thus less likely to be attacked by any warring neighbours from the south.

The news of Her Majesty's decision reached Canada three weeks later. The Taylors and their fellow government officials celebrated, relieved to know that their days as nomads would be over once the Parliament buildings were constructed in the sleepy backwater town up the Ottawa River. It would take years to build all of the necessary roads, housing, and businesses in the new provincial capital. An economic coup for the residents, the queen's decision fueled investments in real estate there for years.

❦ ❦ ❦

JUNE 1858

Since Harriet returned to Canada nearly two years ago, she had been either at the heights of rapture or the depths of despair. At first, she relished being in charge of her father's large rented house in King Street, close to Parliament. She was no longer confined to the countryside at Bellevue. The city of Toronto was exciting! Fennings flattered her when he tasked her with deciding menus, making lists of groceries with the cook and ordering other supplies for the household. Harriet ensured the maids were performing their duties inside and that Eamon was apprised of the family's transportation needs. But gradually she tired of these responsibilities and wished she were back at St Mary's Hall.

She longed to be a carefree pupil again. She missed the intimacy among her school friends and, incredibly, New Jersey. Though she thought Burlington provincial and unsophisticated, it was quiet and clean, compared to downtown Toronto. Harriet enjoyed exchanging weekly letters with her best friend Julia across Lake Ontario in St Catharines. She could confide her true feelings to her, and Julia, for her part, poured out her own thoughts and worries. Lately, Julia was concerned about her mother who, she suspected, might be having yet another baby. Julia had also giddily confessed her love for her cousin William. The two girls never judged one another.

This past winter, her second running the Taylor household, she had become annoyed by the endless duties thrust upon her. She had little time to pursue her own interests or meet new friends in town. Most of all, she missed having time to devote to her watercolours. On her walks along the promenade, she imagined how she would capture the light on the lake, or the seabirds wheeling over it. She thought often of her favourite teacher at St Mary's Hall, Mr Engstrom, the jolly artist from Norway. He always encouraged her to paint.

After her eighteenth birthday, Harriet began to accompany her father to dinner parties and, during the peak of the winter social season, many of them were at the homes of much older married couples, friends of the older Taylors, Uncle John and Aunt Betsy. Some had bachelor sons with whom Harriet endured dull dinner conversations met with polite smiles. The young lady thought that, so far, all of them left much to be desired as a potential mate.

Harriet was heartened a few months ago when her father met Miss Nanton through a mutual friend. He showed new energy and happiness as he began to spend evenings out of the house courting her. Without an iota of guilt, Harriet was relieved to know that, if they married, and it already looked likely, she would no longer have to be his housekeeper. She could go back to being a carefree young lady again and perhaps be courted herself. Despite Aunt Betsy's best efforts, she had not met any suitable young men that she liked and, unlike Julia, did not wish to marry any of her cousins. She was certain of that!

❦ ❦ ❦

Georgina Rosalie Nanton was the daughter of John, a British government official, and his wife Rosalie, née Laborde. For years, the Laborde family had owned Gomier, a plantation on the Caribbean island of St Vincent, where African slaves tended crops of coffee, bananas, sugar cane and corn, as well as tobacco, indigo, and cotton. The Nantons and their young family were posted to London for a time but in 1825 returned to the island where Georgina was born three years later. They remained there during the tumultuous period leading up to the slaves' full emancipation in 1838.

Mrs Nanton died in 1845, and her widower removed with his children to Toronto; shortly after their arrival, John also succumbed at the relatively young age of fifty-one. Georgina's siblings felt pressured for economic reasons to choose a mate as soon as possible. However, they indulged and supported her, the youngest of the five orphans. She declined her first offer of marriage at age nineteen, preferring to wait until a more appropriate mate appeared, one she loved. Alas, that had not happened in a decade, and now, at twenty-nine, she knew she should accept Fennings' suit if and when it came. She would be glad to become mother to his three children and their own.

Cheerful and kind, dark-haired Georgina was only eleven years older than Harriet, and they got on well, sharing an appreciation of art and Parisian fashion as well as the sophisticated social life in Toronto. Georgina was more like an older sister than a stepmother to Harriet. She had shown immediate affection and understanding for Mary and Georgie too, accepting their attachment to old Miss Fellows. Whenever Georgina visited the Taylor home, she was happy to spoil the two younger children with little gifts she brought. Harriet fervently hoped her father would propose marriage soon, so she could get on with her own life.

❦ ❦ ❦

SEPTEMBER 1858

Fennings and Georgina were married on Wednesday, the eighth of September in an Anglican ceremony at old St Paul's Church, Toronto. The quaint wood frame church in Bloor Street was slated to be moved on rollers to the Potter's Field cemetery; an elegant, larger stone one was under construction for the growing parish off Yonge Street. Georgina asked Harriet to serve as her bridesmaid since both of her sisters, Britannia and Caroline, were married; Harriet was flattered by the request. Aunt Betsy and Uncle John Taylor hosted a sumptuous wedding breakfast at their home in Beverley Street, St George's Square. It was a joyous occasion attended by members of both large families and a few close friends, including Frederick Kingston, a client and friend of the bride's brother Augustus. Mr Kingston, a wine and spirits importer, supplied whisky, wine, and Champagne for the event.

❦ ❦ ❦

Frederick Kingston had left his law practise in London to start the business in Toronto at the suggestion of his elder brother, George Templeman Kingston. George and his family had removed to Canada after their father Henry died in 1851. Following three years as principal at the Nautical College in Québec City,

George was named director of the observatory at the University of Toronto in August 1855. At the same time he became chairman of meteorology, a new field of study at the university. The scientist quickly became engrossed in his teaching responsibilities and serious lobbying to set up weather reporting stations throughout Canada West.

George, his wife Harriette, and their two young children, George and Alice, lived in a modest house on the university grounds. Upon arrival, Frederick found rooms to let with Mrs Monroe, a widow who lived nearby at the corner of Church and Ann Streets, a lively neighbourhood near the Normal School. Despite living quite close, the two brothers did not often see one another; they were both intent on pursuing their careers.

When Frederick needed legal help to set up his business, Mrs Monroe recommended Augustus Nanton who lived close by in Gerrard Street. The two men hit it off immediately, and Augustus quickly found a property to house the new concern. Frederick W. Kingston Wine & Spirits was established in Wellington Street, a location convenient to the wharves of Toronto Bay.

A few months later, Augustus invited Frederick home to dine with him, his wife, the former Mary Louisa Jarvis, and his sister Georgina who lived with the couple. The merchant brought a jug of his port wine, and the foursome enjoyed themselves immensely, discovering many common areas of interest. Thereafter, Frederick had a standing invitation for Sunday dinner at the Nantons', only two blocks from his boarding house.

Georgina came to love and admire Frederick but didn't consider him a suitor. He had left the lawyering he was trained for to live in British North America, opting instead to pursue his father's business, wine-importing. Annual tasting and buying trips took him down to Québec to board steamers back to Liverpool, thence to London and Europe, for months at a time. Georgina was seeking a husband who wouldn't travel without her. She wanted a predictable and safe home life with a husband and children; she did not want to worry about her darling drowning at sea.

With regular and frequent visits to the Nanton household, the bachelor became like another older brother to Georgina. After meeting Fennings at a dinner party, she wasted no time introducing him to Frederick; the two men liked each other straightaway.

They both enjoyed discussing politics with a good cigar and fine brandy.

At the first opportunity, Georgina introduced her good friend Frederick to Fenning's daughter Harriet, hopeful she would consider him a match. Unfortunately, Harriet's first impression was that he was a nice man, but not a potential mate; he was so much older than she. He wasn't very tall, but had an earnest demeanour. Like his brothers, he had a straight nose and small mouth with a rather prominent chin. He kept his beard and sidelocks, as well as his moustache, trimmed to a medium length. His hair, greying at the temples, was parted on the side in a vain attempt to disguise its thinning on top. She was impressed that he was from a good family—one grandfather had been knighted, Georgina said—and his traditional English manners were impeccable. Frederick's most charming asset was his sincere and plentiful attention to her when they were together. His brown eyes always looked directly into hers when he addressed her. She liked that he also appreciated her desire to travel and shared her interests in art, culture, and languages, but the fact remained he was sixteen years her senior.

❦ ❦ ❦

With the next legislative session scheduled to begin in January 1859, Fennings and Georgina decided to leave Toronto immediately for Québec instead of taking a wedding trip. They both had responsibilities: he, his government work; and she, being mistress of their household and stepmother to Harriet, nineteen, Mary Elizabeth, fifteen, and Georgie, nine. The newlyweds planned to lodge in a hotel until they could find a suitable house to rent. Harriet and her siblings were uprooted again.

With all of their belongings packed in crates and trunks, the Taylors took the overnight paddle steamer that stopped at the major north shore ports of Lake Ontario: Port Hope, Cobourg, and Kingston. In Kingston, the ship entered the St Lawrence River and took on more passengers at Ogdensburg, New York and Cornwall before going through the Lachine Canal to Montréal. After a day's rest there and a bit of shopping, the family continued downriver to their new home in Québec City.

CHAPTER 26

The Cycle of Life

FRIDAY, 31 DECEMBER 1858, ST CATHARINES

It was a quiet evening at the Burns house. Hours old, the new-born baby girl lay in the cradle beside her mother's bed. The woman also was sleeping peacefully; the birth of her eighth child had been blessedly easy.

Snow was falling gently outside. In the nursery Emma and Kitty sat side by side on the settee, watching Libby and little Lewie settle in their beds. The gaslight was turned low; Kitty had just banked the fire for the night. The two young women, still fast friends, whispered together.

"Kitty, I am so relieved now that Mama has had the babe. I prayed that 'twould be delivered safely, and God has answered my prayers."

"Indeed, Emma. Let us give thanks." Kitty took Emma's hands in hers.

The two were silent in their devotions for a minute. When they were finished, Emma said, "I wonder how much longer I must remain in my position, Kitty. Will Mama be able to take back the household again? I fear she will not. With every babe she has, she appears older and less willing to take part."

"I daren't guess, Emma. We must wait and see what time brings."

"But I tire of all this! I wanted to become a teacher, and now I remain at home, never going to Toronto to study. In fact, 'tis Julia who might go to Toronto, not I. Why, she doesn't even want to be a teacher! She wants only to be married and have babies. I know it!"

"Aye, perhaps. But she's yet young, and her head is easily turned," said Kitty.

"But Papa seems to let her do whatever she wants. Then it is I who must scurry round the house."

"You have your work at the church, at least."

"Yes, it is the one thing that keeps me sane, the fact that I am helping those women. They are doing well, especially Emelia Russell. I think she would be an excellent teacher to the others if I were to leave."

"Oh, no, Emma! You can't do that. This is also the one thing that gives you pleasure, is it not?"

"But I'm so tired, Kitty. I'm too young to feel so tired."

"Yes, to-night you are tired, and for good reason. It's been an exhausting day. Why don't you go in now? Julia and Bella are already abed. And Happy New Year, my friend."

❦ ❦ ❦

SUNDAY, 1 MAY 1859

Little Florence Britannia Burns was baptized at St George's Church on a rainy spring Sunday after Easter. Following the eleven o'clock service, the family returned home in carriages to enjoy a celebratory dinner together. The Campbells, Aunt Arabella Burns, and the Mittlebergers contributed to the joy in the house, with the women taking turns to hold and admire the darling four-month-old girl who cooed and smiled at them. The child's uncle and godfather, Judge Robert Easton Burns, attended from Toronto; her middle name honoured his recently deceased second wife. He had married the former Britannia Nanton only two years ago. Bella missed seeing her cousin, Edward Burns, Uncle Robert's fourteen-year-old son; he was over in Toronto studying at Upper Canada College.

❧ ❧ ❧

St Catharines
27 May 1859

My dear friend Hattie,
I have just had some rather upsetting news from Laura Fuller up in Thorold. Her father has learnt it through the churchmen's records. It is with deep sadness that I write to let you know of the death of our beloved Bishop Doane on 27 April. He was in his home at Riverside, abed for many days. It may have been a fever that took his dear life just days before his sixtieth birth-day to-day. According to the report, the entire town turned out for the funeral. The procession included the state governor and marched from Riverside to St Mary's Church, where there was an overflowing crowd of clergy and townspeople. Mrs Doane was not in attendance, as she was still in Florence, Italy with her daughter. Laura says she went there for her health. I know you are quite busy since your father married, but I thought you would want to know, and I was not sure if the news had got down to you in Québec. I am well and so is my family, though I become bored with tutoring Libby. Papa would like me to go over to the Normal in January for the new term, but I am not sure it is what I want. Laura is teaching in Thorold again, and Lizzie and Margaret Jane were studying at the Grammar School together, the only girls, until January when Lizzie started at the Normal. I hope to have a letter from you soon.

Your loving friend,
Julia

CHAPTER 27

Romance

SUMMER 1859, TORONTO

Frederick Kingston's decision to remove his company from Toronto had been an easy one to make. Shipping would be cheaper and faster from the St Lawrence River port of Montréal with its recently completed railway lines and a new bridge. Montréal was also more centrally located than Toronto and promised rail access to the markets of the northern New England states and the ice-free winter harbour of Portland, Maine. Montréal was eclipsing Québec City as the major Canadian port of entry and also offered a larger and growing population for his products.

In June, Frederick's first friends in Toronto, Augustus Nanton and his wife Mary, held a dinner party to wish him a fond farewell before the merchant left the city. Many of his customers, mostly barrister friends of Augustus, attended with their wives. Frederick was paired with an attractive young widow for the evening, but conversation between them was awkward. Frederick was preoccupied, and the lady had just recently ended her mourning period. Augustus and Mary exchanged knowing glances. They suspected that Frederick was interested in a different woman, perhaps someone in Montréal.

Prior to leaving Toronto, Frederick sent a letter to Fennings Taylor to let him know he would be in Québec on business for a fortnight and staying at a boarding house in the St Louis quarter. Georgina was thrilled to see her good friend again, and the Taylors held a formal dinner party in his honour. Harriet was included in the intimate group of eight as his table companion. She proved to be a brilliant and charming conversationalist, and they enjoyed each other's company despite the considerable difference in their ages. Frederick was smitten. Later that week, having obtained Fennings' permission, he called on Harriet in the afternoon and asked if he could court her. Frederick was relieved when she enthusiastically agreed; it was the first time he had ever courted a woman. And after that visit, Harriet had thought of nothing else but the dashing wine merchant from Montréal.

Sitting at her mother's *bonheur du jour*, Harriet wrote Frederick twice a day on scented stationery kept in the drawer of the dainty desk. She was disappointed when he didn't maintain the same level of correspondence. In fact, he left on a six-week buying trip in September, paying her only one visit before he steamed out of the harbour. She had to accept the fact that he was a busy man. She received all of his attention when he was with her, but his business responsibilities took precedence when they were apart.

When Frederick returned from Europe at the end of October, he took up residence again at the boarding house and courted Harriet daily for a fortnight straight. The couple spent afternoons together under the watchful eye of Georgina or Harriet's sister Mary. They took walks in the St Louis quarter if the weather were mild, or if not, they played cards together with Mary and Harriet's cousin Maria. The evening before he returned to Montréal, Frederick asked Fennings for Harriet's hand in marriage, and by Christmas they were formally engaged. Frederick gave his fiancée a fourteen-karat rose gold ring topped with seed pearls and a large amethyst.

The couple fixed a wedding date for June when the Parliament session would be over. They were to be married in the modern way, by bond and licence, rather than by publishing the banns for three weeks at the cathedral. Frederick thought this was best given the difference in their ages, his involvement in the wine and spirits business, and the fact that few people knew him well in Québec City. Why open up their match to public scrutiny? There were people who had strong feelings about drink in 1860.

With Frederick in Montréal and Harriet over 150 miles away in Québec City, the engaged couple were able to maintain the customary decorous distance. They even ceased direct letter correspondence for the interval before the wedding. Georgina opened all of his letters and read those that Harriet wrote to him. Harriet was glad of the short engagement; she wanted to be with Frederick all the time.

❦ ❦ ❦

MAY 1860, QUÉBEC CITY

Harriet and Maria Taylor were close friends. Although cousins of different generations and three years apart in age, they had always been childhood playmates. Each time Parliament changed its meeting site, their two families moved with it, since both their fathers, Fennings and his Uncle John, were essential public servants. The girls were constant companions throughout the removals, sharing both happy and sad moments. After Maria met Frederick, she cheered on her cousin's romance, and not so secretly wished the same for herself.

Maria and her parents, Harriet's Great-uncle John and his wife Betsy, lived in the new suburb of *Ste Foye*, not far from Fennings' house near the old St Louis Gate. The house was large enough to accommodate frequent visitors and their own large family. The two young ladies saw each other frequently and enjoyed shopping together in the old town, especially now, for things Harriet needed to start her household.

Harriet was visiting one afternoon when the dressmaker was at the elder Taylors' house for the first fitting of Maria's bridesmaid costume. Maria was standing on a wooden pedestal so the woman could put pins in to mark the hem of the hoop skirt. Harriet, seated on a tufted lady chair, was sipping a cup of tea.

"Father told me this morning that the Prince of Wales is coming to Canada this summer. Did you hear of it, Harriet?" said Maria.

"Yes, of course I did, Maria, back in February, but his provisional calendar was announced to-day in the newspaper. Father showed me it this morning. His progress will be lengthy—from Nova Scotia to Toronto and even down into the States."

Maria, annoyed at her cousin's curt response, frowned. "Father said there'll be plans for balls and celebrations wherever he goes, but he's concerned that there might be trouble from the Orangemen."

"Well, I know nought about that. Politics don't really concern me. Do they you? At any rate, Frederick and I shall be abroad when he is here … I rather wish I could be here though … I'm sure the balls in Toronto will be wonderful. Father says Cousin Esther will probably be on Bertie's dance card in Toronto! My Denison cousins expect to be invited to all of the events because we are UEs through our great-grandfather Lippincott. There may even be a procession or two through the city. No doubt it will be even better fun than the queen's birth-day. Roman candles and all."

Maria cringed. She always cringed when Harriet brought up her Loyalist status; it was the behaviour of hers that most bothered her. She herself was not so designated, as both her parents had arrived in British North America long after the American war was over.

Maria bit her tongue and shrugged off the hurtful remarks, "I imagine so … Father said His Royal Highness will be received here at Parliament House. I hope to be presented to him at some point. Perhaps at the cathedral … He'll be the first member of the royal family to ever sit in the Royal Box there, you know. Father says we shall all accompany him to Montréal in August, where he will officially open the new Victoria Bridge. I allow your father will be going up there with Mary and Georgie with us. Then in September the prince will go to Ottawa to lay the cornerstone of the new Parliament building. I am sure we shall all attend that ceremony too."

"That doesn't sound very exciting. There's nought much up in Ottawa yet, is there? Where will you stay?"

The dressmaker finished her pinning and beckoned Maria to step down so she could adjust the bodice of the dress.

"Oh, I'm sure Father has a plan. Perhaps just to remain in the steamer cabin overnight, since there are only two decent hotels in the town, and the prince will take one of them entirely. We would probably dock right beside the royal ship, don't you think?" asked Maria, needling Harriet in return.

"I have no idea, cousin. Father said no ladies will be presented to him because Prince Albert Edward is only eighteen. Still a minor. He says the queen and Prince Albert are at their wits' end and are sending him away to see the real world. They're concerned their son might develop a poor reputation."

"Well, I should like to have one dance with him at least, at the ball here. It's on the twenty-second of August. I hear that he loves to dance and that he is very good at it," said Maria, grimacing as the dressmaker pulled her corset tighter.

The conversation ended as tensions rose between the two friends. Maria, though stung by Harriet's remarks, remained hopeful that she would be able to participate in some of the royal festivities. Harriet was disappointed she would miss them all and more than a little jealous of her cousin in Toronto who would get to dance with the Prince of Wales.

She reasoned it was essential to have their wedding in June. She and Frederick would be gone for the summer months when the weather in Europe would be optimal and ocean travel more pleasant. Deep down though, she wished she could have postponed their wedding trip to experience some of the excitement the royal visit was sure to bring. But she would never consider asking Frederick to alter their plans; she didn't want him to think that the Prince of Wales was more important to her than her new husband!

❦ ❦ ❦

THURSDAY MORNING, 14 JUNE 1860
RUE ST LOUIS, NEAR THE GATE

Harriet was awake early to-day, despite going to bed late after the final pre-nuptial dinner party. She sat up in bed and reached into her nightstand to fetch a small package wrapped in crisp white tissue paper. Harriet was anxious to give the little box to Maria, who was still sleeping peacefully in the bed.

She tapped Maria gently on the shoulder and whispered, "Wake up! It's Thursday!"

The groggy young woman rolled over and Harriet sighed. "Maria! We have to get up! We have to get dressed for my wedding! It's already seven o'clock."

Maria reacted to this message, sat up and rubbed her eyes. "Oh, I think I celebrated too much last night, Harriet! Must you marry a wine merchant?"

Harriet, satisfied that her cousin was fully awake, handed her the gift. Maria untied the gold ribbon and took off the paper. Inside she found a tiny seed pearl ring and necklace. She put the ring on immediately, finding that it fit her little finger perfectly. "Oh, Harriet, how sweet of you! This darling necklace will look lovely with my frock. I was going to borrow one of Mother's, but this one is even better, a gift from you. Thank you, dear cousin." She teared up as she embraced Harriet.

"You are quite welcome, Maria. You are my dearest cousin and have been my friend for years and years. Thank you for being my bridesmaid."

"I'm going to miss you so when you're living in Montréal."

"And I you, Maria, but surely you can stop with us any time you want to make the journey. The house is small, but we have an extra bedroom."

Harriet rang for their light breakfast to be brought upstairs; there would be an elaborate wedding breakfast after the ceremony this morning. While they waited for the tray, they undertook their morning *toilette* and began to dress.

Georgina knocked and entered the bedroom where the girls had just finished their tea and bread. Georgina, now in her eighth month of pregnancy, had decided to forgo the wedding day festivities. She was uncomfortable enough that she didn't want to appear in public, though happy and proud she had introduced Harriet to her soon-to-be husband.

"Harriet, dear, I have something for you. You know the tradition of the sixpence in the shoe, don't you?"

"Why of course, 'Gina, but I'm afraid I don't have one. Canada doesn't have such a coin anymore."

"Oh, this one is English. It's been handed down in my family for years. My sister Caroline used it when she married Mr Nash. Britannia refused it when she married Judge Burns. She said it was utter nonsense."

Harriet remembered Britannia had died at forty-two after just two years of marriage. She took the sixpence from Georgina's palm and studied it before placing it in one of her wedding boots. "Thank you, 'Gina. I plan to have a long and happy marriage!" Harriet embraced her thirty-one year-old stepmother.

"You're welcome, dear. You know I fervently share your hope. I love you both."

Georgina turned to tighten Maria's corset before she helped her into her dress of striped grey taffeta; its scoop neckline displayed the necklace of seed pearls nicely. The dress featured a hoop skirt with a pink flounce at the hem. Lastly, Georgina arranged Maria's dark hair and pinned on a shoulder-length veil of tulle held in place with a wreath of tiny pink rosebuds. Maria would put on her grey kid gloves before she left for the church and carry a matching nosegay of roses.

🦌 🦌 🦌

THURSDAY, 14 JUNE 1860
CATHEDRAL OF THE HOLY TRINITY, QUÉBEC CITY

The morning sun streamed through the three brilliant and colourful altar windows of the cathedral, flooding its creamy interior walls with the strengthening light of late spring. The pierced barrel vault ceiling, punctuated by intricate diamond shapes, echoed the windows and the curvature of the sanctuary. Elegant Ionic columns, painted in white and gold, stood sentinel among the polished oak box pews, dividing them to form the three aisles of the nave. Pink and white roses filled the air with their delicate scent. In the gallery, an organist played softly. Frederick William Kingston and his friend, groomsman Hervé Bernard, stood in the chancel, waiting with the minister.

Harriet had chosen to be married in Québec City rather than Toronto where the bulk of her mother's Denison family lived. Whenever the Taylors resided in Québec, the Cathedral of the Holy Trinity was their parish church; she felt at home worshipping there. The two military architects of the cathedral, Captain William Hall and Major William Robe, had adapted the design of St Martin in the Fields, in Trafalgar Square, London, to the harsh Canadian climate and available building materials. The edifice was a political statement when it was consecrated in 1804. The British Crown and the Church of England meant to show determination to stay in British North America among the people of Catholic Québec, a territory acquired from France in the Treaty of Paris.

The bride and her father arrived in a leased wedding carriage, pulled by a single grey mare for good luck. It stopped in front of the cathedral steps, and a footman helped Fennings out of the carriage. The footman then assisted Harriet and her sole bridesmaid, Maria, who ensured the bride's delicate wedding clothes weren't damaged as she left the vehicle. Harriet took her father's arm and they ascended the steps to the centre doorway of the cathedral with Maria behind them, holding up both train and veil. When the threesome entered the church, the sonorous eight-change bells pealed high in the tower, telling all within earshot that a wedding was taking place.

The petite twenty-year-old bride was radiant in the ivory taffeta gown with a high neck and long full sleeves trimmed with lengthwise strips of Brussels lace. Its wide hoop skirt featured a scalloped overlay also embellished with lace. Georgina was flattered that Harriet wanted to wear the same dress she herself had worn barely two years ago. Wearing a white wedding dress was a newer tradition popularised by the young Queen Victoria for her marriage in 1840. Only the very well-off could afford to own such a garment and wear it once. Georgina had kept it, thinking that Harriet might soon need it. She had hoped hoop skirts would still be in style when the time came, and they were.

Harriet's long, wavy hair was arranged to show off Georgina's tulle illusion veil, its edges embroidered with roses by nuns in Belgium. The chapel-length veil was held in place with a circlet of lilacs snipped that morning from Fennings' garden. It was accented with fragrant orange blossoms. Harriet's uncle George Taylor Denison and his wife Mary Ann had brought the fragile flowers in the cars, packed in straw and ice. The blossoms came from the conservatory of Judge Harrison, the Denisons' neighbour in Dover Court Road on Toronto's west side, with his best wishes.

Harriet carried a bouquet of sweet-smelling white roses tied with a pink silk ribbon that reached to her hem. She wore a new pair of heeled ivory dress boots with Georgina's sixpence sliding under her foot, a constant reminder of her well wishes. However by the beginning of the ceremony, she was acutely aware that her toes were uncomfortable. Perhaps she should have chosen a pair of soft kid slippers instead. At any rate, she wished she had taken more time to break in the boots as Georgina had recommended. Harriet hadn't wanted to chance spoiling them. As a result, she was now suffering.

❦ ❦ ❦

Young George Taylor, brother of the bride, and his cousin, Fred Selletto Taylor, ushered the fifty or so guests to their seats in the front-most box pews. The guests greeted each other quietly as they took their seats and knelt to pray. Some were colleagues of the Taylors at the Parliament. Most were family members from Harriet's side: Denisons, Taylors and Georgina's Nantons from Toronto. Notably absent were any Kingstons. Frederick's elderly mother did not cross the Atlantic from London to witness her son's marriage. No one knew where his brother William Kingston was at the moment. A writer of adventure books for boys, he travelled often with his family to gather ideas. Professor George T. Kingston was occupied with his duties at the observatory in Toronto and declined to travel so far for a wedding. His three other brothers were likewise involved with careers and families in England.

However, Harriet's beloved Uncle Robert Denison *had* come all the way from Toronto and surprised her with plans to stay for the week-long festivities. Harriet hadn't seen him since the Taylors left the city almost two years ago. Robert's wife, Emily, elected to stay home on the Denison farm with their two-year-old, Robert Francis; she was expecting a baby in a few months too.

❦ ❦ ❦

Fennings and Harriet entered the vestibule of the cathedral. Maria arranged Harriet's veil over her train and took her place for the march up the aisle. When the Reverend Mr Jacob Ellegood nodded, the organist began the processional, and Maria, escorted by her brother Fred, led the way to the chancel. Once there, Harriet removed her white silk gloves and conferred them and her bouquet to Maria. The ceremony was brief and dignified with a homily on marriage delivered by Mr Ellegood. After the wedding vows were exchanged, Hervé gave the plain gold band to the clergyman; Mr Ellegood blessed it. Then Frederick solemnly placed it on Harriet's third finger saying, "With this ring, I thee wed in the Name of the Father, of the Son and of the Holy Ghost. Amen".

The bride and groom faced the altar again, and Mr Ellegood led the company in the Lord's Prayer. After several more prayers, the minister intoned, "Those whom God hath joined together let no man put asunder."

Frederick firmly squeezed Harriet's hand as the clergyman, now smiling broadly, pronounced them man and wife. Not only was Mr Ellegood the assistant curate of the recently rebuilt Christ's Church Cathedral where Frederick worshipped in Montréal, he was also married to Harriet's aunt Harriett Taylor, her father's sister. Uncle Jacob was honoured to perform the ceremony for his niece at the beautiful Anglican cathedral in Québec City.

The couple knelt for his final blessing. Harriet tried to stifle sobs of happiness and relief as she rose and turned to face the congregation. She offered her left arm to Frederick and walked sedately down the aisle beside her bridegroom, looking straight ahead, trying to ignore the happy smiles of their guests, as was the English custom.

The minister and witnesses signed the church register in the vestry as the church bells announced the news to the neighbourhood. Fennings signed in a large proud hand as father of the bride. Hand in hand, the bridal couple descended the four low steps out of the building to the garden where they greeted their friends and relatives in a receiving line. Through a shower of rice, Frederick helped his new wife into the bridal carriage waiting behind the cathedral in the old *Place d'Armes*. A surprise from Fennings, the beautiful white open carriage was decorated with spring flowers and pulled by four white horses, again for good luck. The coachman drove them through the narrow *Rue des Jardins* to the *Rue St Louis*, where children cheered them and ran beside the vehicle all the way to the city gate. Once again, people came out to greet the wedding party on their way up *Rue de Sal-*

aberry. Minutes later the newlyweds arrived at the elder Taylors'
house, where cooks had laboured for days on the dishes to be
served to the wedding guests, accompanied by many bottles of
Champagne provided by the bridegroom.

CHAPTER 28

Mr and Mrs Kingston

SATURDAY, 23 JUNE 1860, QUÉBEC CITY

Frederick and Harriet spent their wedding night, and several days after with her father's family, attending dinner parties with the relatives visiting from Toronto. On their ninth day of marriage, the newlyweds left the Port of Québec City aboard the *North Briton*, a clipper ship fitted with modern coal-powered auxiliary steam. On board were 129 passengers, and the several first-class passengers enjoyed meals together at tables set in the wide passageway between the two rows of cabins. Harriet, on her first sea voyage, was impressed by the comfort of the bed and the accommodations overall. The cabins even had wallpaper!

Harriet spent the long days at sea either sketching or reading the guidebook Frederick had given her, *Environs de Paris*, by Adolphe Joanne. She ticked off the monuments she wanted to see there and dreamed about visiting the city for the first time. Ten days later, the ship completed its three thousand-mile voyage and arrived in Liverpool. Harriet was grateful that there had been only three rough days of sailing, and she had not suffered greatly from *mal de mer*. After a good night's rest in the Adelphi Hotel to recover from the feeling of rolling on the sea, Frederick surprised his new wife with his plan to visit some of her family's ancestral towns before they went on to London.

The newlyweds began by taking a short railway ride on the historic inter-city line from Liverpool to Manchester, the first such service in the world when it opened in 1830. With prior clandestine help from Aunt Betsy, Frederick arranged to stop at the home of her cousin, Edward Denison. Mr Denison lived in the Manchester neighbourhood of Rusholme, namesake of the estate in Toronto built by Harriet's uncle, George Taylor Denison, II. Two days later she and Frederick travelled to the medieval city of York and established themselves in a venerable inn located just outside the city walls at Marygate. They explored narrow streets, churches, and markets in the old town, and every evening the old innkeeper impressed Harriet with tales of Vikings terrorising the countryside one thousand years ago.

On a cloudy, cool day they boarded a packed *diligence* to take them southeast to the East Riding of Yorkshire. There, Harriet's second great-grandfather, George Denison, had sailed from the little river port of Hull, becoming the first Denison in Canada in 1796. The Kingstons went on to the village of Hedon in Humberside, a few miles past the port, where they stopped for a few days at an inn. On Sunday, Harriet felt surrounded by the spirits of her ancestors as they worshipped at the twelfth century parish church of St Augustine of Hippo with its beautiful stone tower. After the service, they spread a blanket under a splendid oak tree and passed an hour or two eating a picnic whilst discussing what they wanted to do when they finally reached London.

Another all-day train ride brought the couple to Cambridge. Harriet and her husband wandered the charming town and university buildings where three of Frederick's five brothers had been students. Harriet thought it was a beautiful place to study, and she wondered why Frederick had not been sent up there too. He had studied at home with tutors before matriculating at King's College in London. She dared not ask why he stayed in London. Perhaps there was a financial reason or some resentments existed among the brothers about their parents' expectations? Had he simply preferred to study the law at Lincoln's Inn?

It was too soon in Harriet's marriage to broach these delicate subjects and possibly open old wounds. She would no doubt learn more as time went by. She hoped it was just a matter of distance and obligations, not want of affection, that kept the siblings from seeing each other.

❦ ❦ ❦

MONDAY, 16 JULY 1860, LONDON

The couple's several rail excursions throughout the English countryside had been much more enjoyable than those Harriet remembered in North America. On either side of the rail bed, colourful summer wildflowers such as primroses bloomed, and cornflowers and daisies swayed among the lush green grass. The cars had more comfortable seats. The trains were more often on time, adhering closely to published schedules in the railway guide, and there were fewer interruptions along the lines. In some places there were several tracks laid in the same direction so one's train did not have to wait on sidings for others to pass. She marvelled at the engineering feats of man.

At the Eastern Counties Railway Terminus in Bishopsgate, a district of east London, Frederick and Harriet collected their hand luggage. He instructed a porter to send their trunks and *portmanteaux* to the hotel. Frederick hired a Hansom cab to drive them through the four miles of congested streets to Regent's Park. Harriet had never seen a conveyance like it. It was designed to be maneuverable between other vehicles and used only one horse. The driver sat above and behind a compartment just big enough for two passengers, and he spoke to them through a trap door in the ceiling. She was shocked when Frederick said the driver would not let them out until he was paid. The man could lock the doors of the cab from above with a long rod.

"Number 56 York Terrace, if you please, my good man," said Frederick.

Frederick intended to spend a month in London before proceeding to the Continent and had arranged to take a flat in Watson's Hotel in York Terrace overlooking the south entrance to Regent's Park. The hotel occupied a section of one of the palatial terraces originally conceived by John Nash, the famed Crown Architect who planned the development of that part of west London in 1811.

Harriet stared out the window for the entire hour of their journey as the cab rumbled over the cobblestone streets. She marvelled at the size, style and condition of the various buildings she saw. Some were newer, made of local brick, three and four storeys high, and some seemed to be old shanties. Crowds of people were everywhere. The acrid smell of coal smoke was pervasive; sometimes the smoke was so thick her eyes watered. London, the largest city in the world according to Frederick, was like Toronto, but on a scale she found hard to believe.

After taking Old Street Road and the City Road through districts which, Harriet thought, were quite jumbled and ugly, they passed the welcome green patches of Euston and Park Squares full of mature shade trees and inviting paths. Harriet thought perhaps they might promenade there one afternoon.

As the driver neared the St Marylebone Church, Frederick knocked on the trap door. He ordered the man to turn right into York Gate and stop in front of number eight. The cab turned left at the end of a massive stucco building that took up an entire block, coming to a halt in front of a portico flanked by two Ionic columns. The portico had side walls to keep one protected from London's frequent rain.

Harriet's first thought was that there was no front garden. One walked right from the street into the house. *How odd!*

Frederick leaned over his wife's lap and pointed out the window. "This is where we lived for many years, my dear, after we returned from Portugal. Until Father died."

Harriet was surprised at Frederick's wistful tone; she had never known him to be sad in the short time they had known each other. She didn't know what to reply. He must still be grieving the loss of his family home. Since she had moved so often in her life, she couldn't relate to his attachment. It was just a building. But what a building!

The two identical Regency style buildings facing each other at York Gate featured impressive Ionic façades. A four-storey pavilion was at either end, like bookends; between them were three smaller residences with three window bays each. Because there was no door on the street side, one had to enter these houses from the lane behind. When the residences were built in the 1820s, the exterior walls were made of white stucco; but now nearly forty years later, they were stained with soot from the smoke of wood and coal fires all over the city, resulting in a greyish cast. At one end of the block stood the parish church, St Marylebone, where the Kingston children born in London were baptized. At the north end, through the iron gate, the York Gate, was the beautiful 400-acre Regent's Park, now a mass of green in summer.

Frederick said, "My dear, I know you're tired from travelling right now, but I should like to pay a visit one day to our old neighbours here at number nine, the Westbys. The Kingston brood were friends with the Westby children for years. In fact, I had a terrible affection for Caroline, but it went unrequited! On the other hand, young Horatia suffered the same affliction for me, and I spurned her brutally." Frederick laughed at the memory of his adolescent infatuation. Harriet was relieved that he had shrugged off his momentary melancholy.

He knocked on the trapdoor again. "Drive on," said Frederick, and the cab turned around and out of the lane.

Once through the York Gate, Harriet saw the little stone York bridge and many tall trees on the far side of it. *There must be a garden to paint somewhere in there*, she thought.

❦ ❦ ❦

TUESDAY, 17 JULY 1860, WATSON'S HOTEL

The morning sky was cloudy and grey, threatening rain. After break-fasting at the hotel, Frederick hired a carriage, despite the weather, to ride along the terraces facing the Outer Circle of Regent's Park. He wanted Harriet to get an impression of the neighbourhood. She was struck by the beauty of the collection of "palaces" along the road. Despite their appearing to be unique dwellings, each one was divided into several houses as those at York Gate were. She had never seen so many large buildings together. London had banned the use of wood in construction after the disastrous conflagration in 1666 that destroyed most of the original medieval city. The majority of Toronto's old structures remained wood frame despite changes in the building codes after the 1849 fire that damaged the market district and the first St

James Cathedral. Québec City's residences, by comparison, were unassuming and quaint, many made of native stone. Harriet couldn't decide which city was her favourite; they each had their charm. But she hadn't yet seen Paris!

For their second excursion, Frederick hired a carriage to take them by the lovely Park Crescent down Portland Street to Cavendish Square. Harriet admired the elegant houses facing the square and imagined them living in one. The sky cleared, Frederick dismissed the driver, and they walked back to York Terrace through Harley Street with its yellow brick-front terraced houses. Frederick pointed out where his parents, Henry and Fanny, had first lived and where Emily, William, and Laura, their three eldest children, were born. Little Emily had succumbed as an infant, a first tender heartache for the parents.

On Sunday, Frederick proudly escorted his young wife to St Marylebone Church in the New Road. Since Frederick and the rest of the Kingstons had been gone from the parish for nearly ten years, he knew only a handful of worshipers. He recognised Mr Nicholas Westby and the Honourable Mrs Westby straightaway though; the kindly old couple introduced them around and insisted the newlyweds join them forthwith for dinner at their home in York Gate.

❦ ❦ ❦

TUESDAY, 24 JULY 1860

Harriet was nervous about meeting her mother-in-law to-day. She had planned her outfit down to the last detail. Harriet was going to wear a new dress saved from her *trousseau* for this special occasion. Her other dresses were now in need of some care after being worn for over a month. To-day she put on the deep purple and grey plaid taffeta one with a hoop skirt trimmed with twin rows of wide matching purple ribbon going down to the hem. Between each row were bows of the same colour, fashioned into butterfly shapes. The bodice was narrow, and the sleeves, adorned similarly with the purple ribbon, were of billowing white lace that ended at her wrists. She had to take care lest the lace become soiled on the steamboat ride down the Thames from the Westminster wharf. She wanted to make a good impression.

Frederick had tried to reassure her that his mother was a warm and friendly person, but Mrs Kingston had sent Harriet only one brief, formal letter during their engagement. Harriet wasn't sure how she should greet her. A curtsy or take her hand? The lady was born in the last century, for heaven's sake!

At age seventy, Mrs Kingston had declined to sail across the Atlantic to British North America for her son's wedding despite her daughter Laura's offer to accompany her. Laura wanted to see Canada after reading Frederick's letters. She hadn't been on a sea-going ship since the family returned to London from the British Factory in Oporto when she was sixteen. But most people would agree that a wedding was not important enough to risk one's life travelling to and from America! Harriet wasn't offended; she understood well, having just made the arduous voyage for the first time herself. She didn't look forward to the return trip to Canada although their sail over had been uneventful.

❦ ❦ ❦

BLACKHEATH, GREENWICH

The hired carriage rolled into the paved stone courtyard through the open gate of the yellow brick wall that surrounded the house at Stainton Place. The driver was familiar with Mrs Kingston's house and stopped in front of the oaken front door. At one end of the yellow stucco dwelling was an interesting four-storey turret, and there were several brick chimneys emerging from the roof. The house was large, with four bays of windows across the front and dormers punctuating the third floor roofline.

Bess Cribb, the Kingstons' long-serving parlour maid, opened the front door wide when Frederick knocked. Her mistress had told her to expect them to-day.

"Bess! So glad to be here again! Is *Mater* waiting for us?" he asked. He motioned for Harriet to enter first, and she picked up her hoop at an angle to pass through the old door. The house design pre-dated hoops.

"Yes, Mr Kingston, Mistress is in the sitting room. She's anxious to see you."

"Is anyone else here?" he asked, as the driver set their several bags down in the foyer.

"No, but Miss Laura is in her bedroom having a lie-down, Mr Kingston. We were unsure when you would arrive."

Frederick dismissed the driver and then turned back to the two women. "Darling, this is Bess. Bess, my wife, Mrs Kingston."

"How do you do, Mrs Kingston?" said the maid to Harriet, bobbing to her, her white cap fluttering up and down on the top of her head.

"Er ... pleased to meet you, Bess." Harriet looked straight into the woman's soft brown eyes and smiled. She was finally getting used to being called by her married name.

"Leave your bags here with me. I'll take your bonnet and gloves too, ma'am. Now that you're home, you won't need them. Keep your shawl though, lest you are chilly."

"Thank you very much." Harriet unpinned the amethyst brooch holding the two purple ribbons together under her chin. She took off her spoon bonnet and fastened the pin again on the ribbons before handing it all to the maid. *Home, hmm. That's nice to hear,* she thought.

Frederick took Harriet by the hand up a gleaming white staircase with gold and white wallpaper covering the walls. His mother had not changed her decorating taste despite her move to the country. Large paintings of ancestors were hung high, one of whom was Mrs Kingston's father, Sir Giles Rooke, born in 1743 and knighted for having successfully prosecuted two men who opposed the Crown.

Shortly after the death of Frederick's father in 1851, his widow removed from York Gate to Greenwich, the harbour town across the winding Thames downriver from London. Fanny Kingston took up residence there with Frederick's three sisters, Laura, Harriet, and Caroline, all unmarried at the time. There followed the scattering of her sons. William, the oldest, found a quiet place nearby in Stainton Road to write and the following year married Agnes, the sister of Kingston business partner, Charles Kinloch. Edward and Charles Kingston were still studying at Cambridge when their father died and lived there until they finished their degrees. Frederick leased a flat for himself and his youngest brother Francis at number 13, Serle Street near Lincoln's Inn; it was a convenient location for his own work as a barrister, and for Francis, a clerk at the Kingston office in Milk Street.

The house at Blackheath was designed to maximise natural light. The ground floor breakfast room was on the east side of the house to profit from any morning sun. A combination drawing room, study, and library occupied the southeast corner, but the space was rarely used since there were no men living in the house. The parlour on the south side was well illuminated at mid-day for entertaining visitors. The north side dining room was dim but convenient to the steps leading to the basement kitchen. There were some drawbacks to living in this smaller, less formal house though; the back steps were narrower and steeper and the staff missed having a dumbwaiter to carry the heavy trays of food upstairs as they had in York Gate. They appreciated how much cooler the little stone summer kitchen was to work in, but it meant a trek across the garden to serve the food. The advantages of this newer house were numerous though: gas light, modern plumbing, and a water closet on every floor.

❦ ❦ ❦

When she heard footsteps, Mrs Kingston put away her needlework and stepped into the passage to meet her guests.

"My darling boy! You're finally home! It's been nearly a year since I saw you last. I've missed you," his mother said. The tiny lady reached out both arms to embrace her son. Her thinning grey locks were carefully arranged over cushions to give the impression of having more hair. She wore three gold rings with gemstones, but they swung loosely on her slender fingers. Her rose silk dress was trimmed with white lace, and an Italian mosaic locket hung round her neck on a gold chain.

"*Mater*! It's delightful to be back. I always miss London, despite its dirt and noise. York Gate was a welcome sight again, but Greenwich is that much quieter. It is a haven from the City."

"Right you are, my son. We still like it very much over here. Ah, this is your lovely bride. Harriet, be welcome, my dear," said Mrs Kingston, extending a pale hand.

"Pleased to meet you, Mrs Kingston," said Harriet, taking her mother-in-law's hand briefly but firmly in her own. She made a half curtsy. Mrs Kingston gave her hand a gentle squeeze and a pat before letting it go. Harriet was surprised but relieved that the lady was so friendly to a complete stranger such as herself.

The couple followed her down the passage into the dimly lit sitting room. In the corner was a round table, covered with a white linen tablecloth and gleaming china and silverware, set for four.

"We shall have tea presently," said Mrs Kingston, ringing for the maid. "I'm sure Bess has told Cook already to keep the pot aboil. Please make yourself at home, Harriet. Frederick, dear, will you please turn up the gas?"

Harriet looked around and felt at ease. The furnishings and decorations were not as grand and formal as she expected, having seen York Gate and the hotel. She sat in an upholstered chair next to the window, Mrs Kingston beside her on a settee with Frederick. Harriet was still unsure how she would get on with her aged mother-in-law, but so far she seemed cordial.

Laura Kingston appeared in the doorway before a conversation could begin. She was a few inches taller than her mother, and her cheeks had more colour. At forty-five, her hair was salt and pepper, parted in the middle with long curls framing her face. She was clad in a simple yellow and blue striped summer dress with sleeves covering her elbows, perhaps with several petticoats underneath but clearly no hoop.

"Freddie! I'm so happy to see you. And good afternoon, Harriet, my dear new sister. Welcome to Blackheath." She walked over to Harriet, took her hand and gave it an affectionate squeeze, just like her mother had done. "How was your journey?" she asked, looking at them both with her deep-set dark eyes and a wide smile.

"It's been wonderful so far, Laura. We've seen a lot of England. We've visited all of Harriet's family towns," answered her younger brother.

"Well, not quite all, Frederick, dear. Father comes from Hackney. We haven't been there yet, have we?" chimed in Harriet.

"We were close to it the day we arrived when we got to the end of the line in Bishopsgate. Your father said his mother came from Shoreditch. That's really the same area; they changed the name. P'raps we can take a day to go look around over there again if you wish," said the new husband, anxious to please his wife.

❦ ❦ ❦

After four days exploring Greenwich and trying to find something to talk about with Mrs Kingston at Blackheath every evening, Harriet was ready to go back to Regent's Park. Laura happily agreed to return to the hotel with them for a few days' holiday in the city she dearly missed. Harriet appreciated Laura's genuine friendliness; she was reminded of Georgina and how she had been a welcome light in her motherless life. Harriet was happy for some female company after so many weeks spent travelling with her husband. She was used to having Maria and Georgina nearby and missed them.

Before they left the right bank of the Thames, their sister, Harriet Kingston Kinloch, invited them all for a meal after church on Sunday, as was their custom. Harriet Kinloch was near the end of her third pregnancy now and tired easily. Caroline Kingston had moved in six months ago to help her sister with the two little girls; Agnes and Frances, were just one and two years old. Auntie Callie earned her keep running after the tots and doing as many other household chores as she could.

The four Kingstons made the ten-mile trip by carriage to Wandsworth where the Kinloch family lived in a modest brick Georgian-style house in Melrose Road. After a delicious dinner of roast joint, potatoes, and summer vegetables, followed by a pudding, Harriet Kinloch presented her new sister-in-law with her tweed riding habit. It no longer fit after nearly three continuous years of childbearing, and she had no time to ride for pleasure. Harriet Kingston thanked her sincerely for the thoughtful gift. Harriet herself had last ridden a horse two years ago when the Taylors lived at Bellevue in Toronto, and she hadn't packed riding clothes for her wedding trip.

The day was full of smiles and laughter; the newest Harriet Kingston felt welcome in the large family and valued as another sister. The Kinlochs bade their guests farewell at the dock after an afternoon stroll together with the children. Laura crossed the Thames with the newlyweds, and her mother returned alone to Blackheath.

❦ ❦ ❦

MONDAY, 30 JULY 1860, YORK TERRACE

The next morning, Frederick, Harriet, and Laura took a carriage to visit the British Museum, a vast Neo-classical building in the Bloomsbury section. There Harriet dared to touch the Rosetta Stone, key to ancient languages, that French Emperor Napoleon I had brought back from Egypt. The three visitors also admired the controversial marble statuary taken earlier in the century from the Parthenon in Athens by Britain's Lord Elgin. Harriet's favourite exhibition was the collection of exotic artefacts brought back from the South Seas by Captain James Cook. She'd love to see those islands in person, but it meant a long and hazardous sea voyage. She admired the courage of seafarers and was shocked to learn that the captain hadn't returned from his third voyage of discovery.

The three spent most evenings together playing cards and draughts after supper, save one elegant dinner party with the Westbys, a grand re-union with three of the Kingston brothers: Frederick, Charles, and Francis. The highlight of Laura's London holiday was going to Westminster Abbey again, thanks to Harriet's insistence. Laura had only been in the old church twice in her life; it was too far away to attend regularly from Regent's Park, and out of the question after removing to Greenwich. The idea of parish churches was to serve a small congregation who could walk to them on the Sabbath. Since it was most likely a once-in-a-lifetime event for Harriet, Frederick relented and had them all driven down to Westminster on Sunday morning where they were surrounded by beautiful architecture and music.

On Monday Laura returned to Blackheath. Harriet wished she could know her married sister-in-law as well as she now knew Laura. She had some female questions about marriage she couldn't ask old Mrs Kingston—as friendly as she seemed—or, of course, Laura who was a spinster. Georgina had explained the basics before the wedding day, but Harriet had some new concerns. She wished Georgina were here now.

❦ ❦ ❦

On their last Sunday in England, Frederick and Harriet went into the City of London to worship at St Paul's, the cathedral designed by Sir Christopher Wren. After the service, they climbed up to the dome and laughed as they tested the famous whispering gallery along with other tourists. They dined in the nearby Cathedral Hotel before taking a cab back to St Marylebone for one more tea with the gracious Westby family. Because of the crowds of Londoners usually in Regent's Park on Sunday afternoons, the Westbys recommended avoiding it, as most residents did. Heeding their advice, the Kingstons walked back to Watson's along York Terrace West, enjoying the sunset after an altogether pleasant day.

After four weeks touring London, it was time to pack the trunks and be off to the Continent.

Harriet had enjoyed meeting members of her new Kingston family and their friends. Every day was an adventure. London was immense and exciting. Harriet wondered if Paris could hold a candle to London. Could she ever go back to the sleepy province of Québec?

CHAPTER 29

On the Continent

TUESDAY, 14 AUGUST 1860, DOVER, ENGLAND

The boat train arrived in time to board the luxury packet ship, *Prince Frederick William* for its eleven o'clock sailing. Harriet joked about its being Frederick's own vessel, since he and the German prince shared the same name. Though the weather was good when they set off, the crossing was rough. A late afternoon thunderstorm drifted over the English Channel. The winds rocked the boat, and lightning and thunder frightened the passengers who were unaccustomed to being on the water in such a tempest. Harriet didn't feel well at all when the storm hit and the waves were crashing over the bow. She was glad it was a short distance—only about twenty miles—and it took just a hair over two hours despite the weather.

After enduring an hour with the customs inspector looking through their trunks to find something to tax, Frederick found a room for them in a hotel near the depot. It was a wise choice instead of continuing on to Paris by overnight mail train. Harriet didn't feel much like eating after the turbulent boat ride, but her mate ate heartily: his usual glass of sherry to start, a bowl of cream of fresh asparagus soup, *sole à la Meunière* with potatoes and mixed vegetables, accompanied by a crisp Chablis. He followed with a *salade composée*, an array of cheeses ending with a serving of apple tart with port. The wine merchant lingered over his three-hour meal while Harriet sipped consommé and nibbled at the crusty bread. She drank some bottled flat mineral water, avoiding the *limonade gazeuse* that the *garçon* suggested to all his summer customers. She went to bed early, and her husband joined other male guests downstairs in the smoking room to enjoy a Cuban cigar and his favourite brandy.

Harriet felt better in the morning after a good night's sleep. Following *petit déjeuner*, they repacked for the day's journey and caught the morning train to Paris. The little engine chugged through the French countryside, stopping at each village along the way until they got to Lille to change lines. There they had a plain but filling meal at the station buffet before continuing their journey.

Frederick ensured their baggage was transferred before the couple boarded a longer set of cars going south to the French capital. Hours later, Harriet finally finished the 800-page guidebook for Paris; she was elated to be seeing the City of Light after reading about it for so long. She clutched his hand tightly as the train pulled into the *Embarcadère du Nord*; she was finally in Paris and with a husband she adored, two dreams come true.

As their carriage passed through *quartier* after *quartier*, Harriet was dismayed to see so much disruption. Frederick explained that many districts of Paris were under construction because of the massive redevelopment scheme of Emperor Napoléon III and his engineer Baron Haussmann. Hundreds of houses and tenements were being rased in order to build wide avenues. The plan to replace narrow medieval streets that were easily barricaded by dissidents would also bring light and air into congested neighbourhoods where contagion spread quickly. Ditches were being dug in the streets to lay the first sewer pipes and gas lines. Gas streetlamps would permit residents to walk safely outside at night and escape the summer heat of their stifling flats.

Months ago, Frederick had written to reserve a quiet courtyard room for them in *Hôtel Meurice* across from the Tuileries Palace and near the Louvre in the historic first *arrondissement*. The lovely hotel was located among the arcades of *Rue de Rivoli*, just a short walk from *La Madeleine*. The church, inspired by Roman temples, dominated the top of the *Rue Royale*, a street that boasted jewellers and fancy shops and ended in the once bloody *Place de la Concorde*.

Their hotel room was hot even with all of its tall windows opening out to the balconies; there was no cross-ventilation. Harriet was fanning herself furiously with a battered fan left behind in the rail car. Frederick considered asking for a different room, but decided they would only be there for a few days before going on to Switzerland. He knew Paris was always hot in the summer; that is why the rooms were *bon marché*! They planned to return to the city when it would be cooler.

❦ ❦ ❦

The next day, during an afternoon promenade, they passed *Maison Duvelleroy*, the famous Parisian fan maker's shop in the *Rue de la Paix* near the Place Vendôme. Harriet couldn't resist the temptation of the beautiful and unusual ladies' fans in the windows, true works of art. As an artist herself, she admired the colours, textures, and intricate designs. She insisted on going in, and Frederick indulged her. One agonising hour later, Harriet decided on two: one of carved ivory decorated with white ostrich feathers and another of polished tortoise shell with a painted landscape scene. They would be perfect to combat the Paris heat and go with the new dresses she had just ordered in the *Rue de Luxembourg*. Frederick was sure she would be the most stylish lady in Montréal.

On Sunday, Frederick and Harriet attended the eleven o'clock service at St George's Anglican Church in the *Rue Marbeuf* in the *huitième arrondissement* near the old hippodrome. Afterward they easily found a restaurant serving on Sunday, for Paris lacked the same strict laws about the Sabbath as London. Everything was open in Paris on Sundays, perhaps a holdover from the anti-clerical sentiment of the 1789 revolution. There they ordered a three-course luncheon instead of a mid-day dinner. The Parisian custom was to dine late! After their meal, the newlyweds strolled through the Louvre with hundreds of other art lovers.

For their last afternoon in the capital, Frederick hired a *fiacre*, and they attended the horse races at the hippodrome in the *Bois de Boulogne*, the large new park on the western outskirts of Paris. As there were no stands yet, the well-dressed ladies and gentlemen meandered about during the intervals between races, chatting with friends. It was Harriet's first horse race and she enjoyed cheering on the riders as they galloped round the oval. Harriet, with beginner's luck, chose several winners, and they took a few extra *francs* back to the hotel that evening.

❦ ❦ ❦

Before they departed the *Meurice*, Frederick reserved a flat there for the month after their return from Switzerland. Harriet would need final fittings for her new clothes, and they undoubtedly would have to buy another trunk for their additional garments and souvenirs. There was plenty more to do in Paris; they had only got a glimpse of *Notre-Dame*, and Harriet wanted to see the newly renovated *Sainte-Chapelle*. They also hadn't had time to visit the palace of *Versailles*, a short train ride away but far enough out of Paris to warrant an overnight stay. Paris was wonderful, but they didn't want to be there any longer in the heat of summer; the wealthiest Parisians were all out in the countryside. Switzerland would have much more pleasant weather.

Frederick and Harriet boarded the first morning train bound for Dijon, a tedious, eight-hour journey. Harriet sketched some buildings that featured the Burgundian city's colourful terracotta roofs: green, yellow, and black tiles arranged in striking geometric patterns. They spent the night in a musty hostelry near the *Porte Guillaume*, where they tried to understand the regional accent of the innkeeper and vice-versa. The next day, after a brief stop in the wine-growing region of Mâcon, the train brought them to Lyon, an ancient Roman hillside town built at the confluence of the Rhône and the Saône Rivers. Frederick and Harriet were lucky to find a room there, as visitors had already begun to stream into the city for the inauguration of the splendid new *Palais de la Bourse* on Saturday, the twenty-fifth. The emperor himself and his trend-setting wife, Empress Eugénie, would be there to open the building that housed a museum of art and industry.

❦ ❦ ❦

At last the final leg of the trip was upon them. The railway line from Lyon to *Genève* was completed just two years ago in the wake of Lyon's last severe inundation. This journey would be slower because of the gradual climb into the mountains, but at the end of the day, both Kingstons would have their first glimpse of the Alps. Harriet was exuberant; she had never seen such huge, snowy mountains, except in her beloved geographies. Frederick loved seeing the joy on his young wife's face as she experienced new vistas.

The locomotive spewed smoke as it struggled up the tracks to the enchanting little city by the lake. The weather was stormy; it rained all afternoon, and Harriet couldn't see very far out of the windows. To make matters worse, she had a persistent vague stomach upset. She thought perhaps yesterday in Lyon she had eaten something that had gone off. *The escargots?* she wondered. *Or too much wine?* The cars' straining and jolting over the tracks didn't help. In any case, she was sure she would feel better after they arrived at their destination.

❦ ❦ ❦

THURSDAY, 23 AUGUST 1860, *GENÈVE*
The maid had just finished putting away all of the Kingstons' clothing in the two armoires when Frederick gasped.

"Darling, you'll never guess what happened after we left Paris!" He set aside the newspaper, *Le Figaro* from Paris.

"What is it, Frederick? Something shocking?"

"Well, yes, it *is* shocking, my dear. *Notre-Dame* was robbed! The criminals entered through a small window and took gold chalices, vases, and crosses from the presses where they were stored. They removed the jewels from them, put them in a net and tossed it into the Seine to be retrieved later. The police recovered as much."

"Oh, my, have they found the culprits?"

"No, of course, not yet. It's only been a day. This is the afternoon paper that came with us on the train, with the barest of details. It happened early Wednesday morning when we were already in Dijon."

"That *is* shocking, dearest. I hope they are soon caught," said Harriet. "Shall we go out for a walk before dinner? I badly need some air."

"Yes, darling. Let's do. The sun will be going down behind the mountain soon and it will be chilly. Take your shawl and wear your best bonnet. I want to show the *Genovois* the prettiest Canadian woman they've ever seen." He kissed Harriet tenderly on the forehead.

❦ ❦ ❦

Harriet and Frederick exited the *Hôtel Métropole* arm in arm. In the distance was *Mont Blanc*.

"It looks just like the lithograph in my book!" exclaimed Harriet. She was in awe of the massive mountain's magical appearance in the late afternoon sunshine.

"Alpenglow," said Frederick.

"What's that?"

"The way the sun lights the mountain at this time of day, when it is low in the sky."

"It's stunning," said Harriet.

The lovers strolled along the quay in front of the *Jardin Anglais* where twenty pleasure boats bobbed, waiting for their owners. They watched a steamboat dock after its journey round the sparkling mountain lake; it discharged sixty passengers who disappeared into the town.

❦ ❦ ❦

FRIDAY, 24 AUGUST 1860

After Harriet and Frederick break-fasted in their room, they dressed to go shopping. Frederick planned to buy his new wife a *Gübelin* wrist watch. It was a rather new company in the town, but in London he had heard of their excellent reputation. Harriet had never owned a wrist watch, and when she saw the one her husband selected for her, she thought it was the most exquisite thing she had ever seen. It had a slim rectangular face of white gold trimmed with tiny diamonds and a double black cord to hold it in place on her slender wrist. The jeweller showed her how to set the time and how to wind it by pulling out the tiny stem. He cautioned her not to overwind it and not to wet it. The man slid it over her hand and closed the clasp with a snap.

Harriet beamed. She wanted to throw her arms round Frederick's shoulders and hug him tightly, but she knew it would be considered improper behaviour in public. She thanked him profusely instead and squeezed his hand. She could embrace him later in the privacy of their bedchamber.

Their last stop was the confectioner's shop where they bought several pieces of chocolate. The shopkeeper put them into a little black box tied with a gold-coloured bow. Frederick tucked it into a pocket of his coat, and they walked back to their hotel, ready for the mid-day meal. Harriet was looking forward to enjoying those chocolates.

❦ ❦ ❦

SATURDAY, 25 AUGUST 1860

In the morning, the Kingstons walked from the hotel to the *Jardin Anglais* and boarded the steamer to take them up the lake. It would be an all-day excursion with luncheon taken on the boat. Frederick wanted to see Evian, a spa town that was becoming a holiday destination because of its mineral water sources. They would be back at the hotel in time for dinner.

Harriet delighted in the majesty of the snow-capped mountains surrounding the lake. The blue sky was filled with puffy white clouds, and the sun sparkled on the azure water dotted with sailboats running before the wind. She understood why August was the high season in Switzerland; the weather was perfect. The steamboat hugged the coastline and called at several small towns on the south shore before arriving at Evian. Harriet and Frederick spent the hour wandering about the town, stopping to sample the vaunted elixir of Evian, and visiting *Notre-Dame de l'Assomption*, known for its beautiful fifteenth century carvings.

On the way back to *Genève*, Frederick offered Harriet the last piece of chocolate. He took the morsel out of his pocket and unwrapped the tissue paper. It was very soft now in the heat of mid-day. Harriet was wearing white gloves, so he fed her the gooey chocolate treat. It had a marvellous hazelnut filling.

"*Merci, chéri!* That was delicious," said Harriet.

"*Je vous en prie, ma précieuse!*"

Frederick left for the washroom to rinse off his chocolate-covered fingers, and Harriet felt her stomach turn. She realised that she was going to be sick. She didn't know what to do, where to go, but she knew she had to relieve this feeling straightaway. She left her seat and sprinted over to the railing of the boat, pushing by other passengers who gave her strange looks. She held back her ringlets and trailing bonnet ribbons before all of her tasty meal from two hours ago and the last bit of that wonderful Swiss chocolate fell into the flowing waters of *Lac Léman*.

When Frederick returned from the washroom, he wondered where Harriet had gone. Her reticule was there on the bench. He looked to his left and recognised his poor wife, retching over the side. He fairly ran to her and put his arm round her convulsing shoulders. "My dear Harriet, whatever happened?"

"I don't know. It just came over me so suddenly," she said, tearing up. "I couldn't stop."

He took out his handkerchief and wiped her mouth tenderly.

"And it was the last piece of our delicious chocolate!" she moaned.

❦ ❦ ❦

SUNDAY, 26 AUGUST 1860

The Kingstons joined the other Episcopalians visiting *Genève* who were walking from all directions to Holy Trinity Church, the English church in *Rue du Mont Blanc*. The eleven o'clock service was familiar, and Frederick said a prayer for his wife to be well after yesterday's debacle on the steamboat. He was becoming concerned with her frequent complaints of stomach upset. He had never known her to speak of such ailments in the short time they were married or in her letters to him.

After church they returned to the hotel and sat down to a *table d'hôte* consisting of four courses. The meal began with a cream of fresh wild mushroom soup followed by salmon; beef and fowl with vegetables; a salad; and five puddings to choose from, including fresh cherries, sponge cakes with stewed fruit, fruit creams, and a plum pudding with brandy. Harriet ate heartily, and Frederick believed his intercession had been heard by the good Lord.

❦ ❦ ❦

The next day Frederick had planned a morning walk out to the confluence of the Arve River with the Rhône, about a mile outside of town. Harriet was still abed and feeling queasy. Frederick was perturbed. He thought she had probably overeaten yesterday after her stomach upset. He was beginning to question the wisdom of the long trip away from Canada. Perhaps it was just too much for his young bride.

At last Harriet rose, washed, and dressed, donning the white lightweight woolen dress Laura lent her, with just one petticoat for decency—slightly shorter than the length she usually wore with a hoop, and therefore easier to tramp in. She took no coffee but ate a bite or two of plain bread. It was now two o'clock, a late start for any kind of outdoor activity in the mountains. As they left the hotel, she tied the gay blue and white gingham ribbons on her Leghorn, an Italian straw bonnet they had bought in Paris. They set off on the path to the river according to directions given them by the concierge. After about thirty minutes' wandering along the undulating course of the Rhône, they came to the point where the Arve joined it downstream of the lake. They sat on a large rock to rest, and Frederick took his wife's hand in his.

"My dear, I confess I'm ignorant of what to do. I fear you're not well."

"Oh, Frederick, yes. I *have* been feeling off lately. I know not what it is. P'raps just all the different foods ... or the wines. It seems my digestion is easily upset."

In the distance, a bolt of lightning illuminated the darkening sky. Five seconds later there was an ominous rumble of thunder. There was no shelter to be had. Frederick took Harriet by the hand and pulled her to her feet.

"Darling, we must fly. It's not safe to be out here in the open. Can you run?"

"I'm sure I can," said she. She was wearing the new ankle-

261

length walking boots made for her in London. She couldn't remember the last time she had run like that. It must have been at
Bellevue with her cousins years ago. Young ladies normally had
no reason to run.

Five minutes later they were being pelted by fat raindrops, and
when they got back to the hotel, they were both soaked to the
bone. Frederick called for a hot bath for each of them and sent
their wet boots out to be dried and waxed. They spent the rest of
the afternoon by the fire, reading. After dinner they sat in the
lounge, comparing stories with the other guests while the rain
and thunder continued outside unabated until midnight.

❦ ❦ ❦

Anxious to see some high alpine scenery, Frederick had asked
the hotel to engage a guide to take them out Tuesday for a *randonnée*. Jean-François Diderot met them at the hotel after breakfast and explained that he would take them twelve miles on the
railway to a village called Chancy. Before they left the hotel, he
checked to see that they had sturdy boots, appropriate hats and
rain garments, and determined if they were fit enough to walk
the distance.

At the railway they joined another group of English travellers
from the *Hôtel des Bergues*, accompanied by Michel, the brother
of *Monsieur* Diderot. The two operated a thriving guide business
for the new English tourism trade. Both had years of experience
mountaineering. To-day's group were novices, all of them, so the
walk was to be only about five miles and not too steep or high.
Frederick took a *baton* for himself and one for his wife from
among those Michel offered.

Neither Harriet nor Frederick had ever walked into such
mountains before. Frederick had trudged up *Mont Royal* in Montréal soon after he arrived there, but that was years ago now, and
the hill was less than one thousand feet in elevation. Last evening
they had heard about people going all the way to the top of *Mont
Blanc* at over fifteen thousand feet and having difficulty breathing. The Kingstons would be satisfied just to see beautiful views
and some new kinds of flowers and small animals or birds.

Once in Chancy, the group left the railway and ambled

through a meadow, where a herd of brown and white cows grazed peacefully on the thick grass dotted with pink clover and daisies. In the distance they could see the foothills of the Alps, low dark green mountains, with grey clouds above, concealing the sun. White-capped mountains, dominated by *Mont Blanc*, stood sentinel behind the *Préalpes*. The group was happy that the air was fresh and cool for their walk, as the day before had been unusually hot, resulting in thunderstorms.

Finally, they reached their picnic destination, a large pond, where the visitors immediately frightened off a pair of egrets feeding in the reeds. Some mergansers swam lazily beyond them and paid them no mind. Michel and Jean-François each took a blanket out of their rucksacks to spread under a tree. Everyone found a spot to sit and began to eat, their appetites stimulated by the cool air and exercise. Each guide had a light meal and a skin of wine for himself. Frederick and Harriet had bought a canteen and a rucksack on their first day in Switzerland, and in it they carried their own nourishing *collation* of bread, ham, cheese, and plums from the hotel.

Harriet washed down her dark bread and local cheese with some spring water from the canteen. She offered a small, juicy red plum to her husband, who ate it in one bite before offering her one in return. Some of the party shared chocolate and small pastries. While others went off hunting for birds or mushrooms, Harriet took out her sketch pad and pencil from the rucksack and went through the meadow examining the few wildflowers left there.

When it was time to start back to Chancy, Frederick offered his hand and helped Harriet to her feet.

"Feeling all right, dear?"

"Oh, yes. I was hungry, but now I feel like falling asleep."

"Well, we shall be back in our chamber soon enough. One foot in front of the other now."

Harriet and Frederick followed the guides back to the railway stop. The trail was gentle as it sloped down to the river. The sun came out brightly from behind some clouds, and its August warmth beat down on the group. Harriet took out her handkerchief to dab the moisture above her lip and on her brow. She was feeling very warm indeed.

Then everything went black.

"My dear! Harriet! My love!" Frederick was calling to her, patting her hand as she regained consciousness. She looked up into his face, and the sun's rays were all round it, like a halo. Next to him was a man she recognised but didn't recall his name. He was putting a cold cloth on her forehead, and it was getting her hair wet. She brushed it off her face and tried to sit, pulling her Leghorn back into place.

"Frederick? Who is that?" asked Harriet.

A woman pushed Jean-François out of the way. "Miss, stay down. Rest a bit. You have perhaps over-exerted?" said the woman with an accent from the west of England.

"Madam, this is my wife. Are you perhaps a nurse?"

"My word, no, I am not a nurse," she said indignantly. "But I *have* had seven children, and I know a lady with child when I see one," she whispered.

"With child?" asked Frederick, incredulous at the thought.

"Yes, how long have you been married?"

"You are impertinent in the extreme, Madame!"

"Ten weeks last Thursday," answered Harriet drowsily.

"Aha, plenty of time then!" said the woman, Mrs Greene.

❦ ❦ ❦

Harriet and Frederick walked arm in arm back from the railway to the hotel, both grinning. They had no idea if Mrs Greene were correct or not, but it was surely a possibility she was with child. Could that not explain why she felt so ill? And so tired every afternoon?

That evening they celebrated the thought with a bottle of Champagne at dinner, and no one else at the table knew why.

CHAPTER 30

Turning Point

WEDNESDAY, 29 AUGUST 1860

It was Harriet's twenty-first birth-day, and once more she felt queasy in the morning. To-day Frederick had planned to take her to the Botanic Garden and the *Jardin Alpin*. He had a gift for her to open first that would be useful after their visits to the gardens. The ceremony would take place as soon as she felt like getting out of bed. He was hoping to see her smile when she saw his modest offering.

"My dear Harriet, I hope you will like what I have for you. I bought it in Paris."

"Paris? Why, we were there ages ago, dear one! You were thinking ahead, weren't you? But birth-days aren't so important, are they?"

"Oh, this one is, twenty-one! It happens only once. Now you are of majority. I am no longer married to a minor!" He laughed.

"Well, let me have it then! I shall prove I can still act the child." She ripped off the string holding the stiff brown paper together, expertly tied by the Parisian shop girl. Inside the carton were a box of watercolours, brushes, and a packet of paper.

265

"I hope it includes all the essentials. The shop girl assured me it did. Perhaps you can paint what you sketched yesterday."

His wife put her arms round his neck and kissed him thrice on the lips. "Oh, thank you, thank you, thank you, my darling husband! I can't wait to paint some of the beautiful scenes here. You are so thoughtful."

❦ ❦ ❦

After a leisurely luncheon, they spent the afternoon strolling about the gardens, admiring the different species, some unknown to the Canadians. Harriet was anxious to return to the hotel to capture her memory of the flowers on paper with her new paints. She spent an hour on one painting, trying to recreate the light and shadows, before she had to stop to dress for dinner.

Frederick and Harriet dined alone in a cosy restaurant in the *Rue du Mont Blanc*. She enjoyed her favourite meal of freshly gathered mushrooms made into a cream soup followed by tender veal, vegetables, and a strawberry cream at the end. Frederick insisted on a different wine with each course. Then he ordered a bottle of Champagne to finish and raised his glass to toast the health of his new wife.

Hours later, Harriet awoke and violently relieved herself of an overfull stomach. She washed her face and brushed her teeth again, before she quietly returned to bed so as not to disturb her husband. She lay awake wondering if she were going to feel this way to-morrow. She really shouldn't eat such rich foods so late in the evening. *It was much better to have the largest meal at midday*, she thought. She prayed to God to relieve her of the nausea.

In the morning, Frederick allowed her to sleep while he dressed and went downstairs for some breakfast. Harriet slept until ten while he read the London papers. He had so many questions about women and wished that woman Mrs Greene were staying in their hotel. She might know the answers, even though she was disagreeable. He regretted he had been unable to discuss such things with his sister's husband, but that would have been awkward and mildly improper.

Harriet spent the day in bed, propped up on pillows, without the energy to read, let alone open her new paint box. She dozed

266

off and on, periodically racing to the water closet when she felt sick. Frederick called for some broth and tried to feed her while it was still warm. She gobbled down a piece of fresh brown bread with butter, but that quickly resulted in another attack of nausea.

❦ ❦ ❦

"Darling, I think we should call for a physician. It's been two days now since you have eaten. You've no energy at all. You can barely walk. My sweet girl, I insist."

At this point, Harriet indeed had no will to oppose her husband's suggestion. The physician was French-speaking and arrived carrying a black leather bag. After a brief interview and even briefer physical examination, he told her that she was merely suffering from a chronic case of indigestion. He opened his bag and removed a tortoise shell case containing a double-edged lancet and a small jar of dark green leeches from which he took one. After the doctor scratched her skin with the lancet, the beast attached itself and fed for an hour, visibly enlarging. Harriet couldn't bear to look and turned her head away. It was a peculiar sensation—the slimy thing sitting on her, sucking out her life-blood. It didn't hurt at all. After it had its fill, the leech fell off, leaving three curious red marks from its teeth. The physician placed it back with the others, bandaged her wound, and prepared to take his leave.

"Madame, I trust you will feel better in the morning. I shall return on Monday afternoon, sir, and daily thereafter until she is well. Try to eat and drink something mild in the meantime. I shall leave instructions with the cook downstairs." The doctor bowed to Frederick and left the hotel room.

Frederick wondered if he should have asked the doctor if Harriet could be with child. *Had Harriet thought to ask him?*

❦ ❦ ❦

SUNDAY, 2 SEPTEMBER 1860
Harriet was unrelieved of her nausea, despite yesterday's visit from *Monsieur le Docteur Le Brun*. Frederick was beside himself. He disliked the idea of leeching his wife; she was clearly weaker

267

to-day and still unable to eat. Needless to say, they missed church that morning.

"Darling, I want an English doctor for you. I'm going downstairs to see if one lives in the town," said Frederick.

When he returned from his errand, having sent a message to the only English physician in *Genève*, he found his wife in her long night dress, on her hands and knees, trying to crawl to the water closet. After that she was sick almost continuously for the next fourteen hours. Harriet, nearly as pale as the sheets of the bed, began to cry and beg for water. Water was also rejected. Frederick was becoming frantic himself, but he didn't want to see that French doctor again.

Harriet finally slept, having nothing left in her stomach to remove. In the morning the sky opened, and it poured rain. There was still no response from the English doctor. Frederick had an idea, however.

"Darling, I recall Mrs Greene and her group were staying at the *Hôtel des Bergues*. I am going to see if she remains there. She seemed very knowledgeable. Perhaps she has some ideas for us."

Harriet nodded and closed her eyes, thankful that her dear husband was taking charge.

❦ ❦ ❦

Frederick could have sent a message to Mrs Greene, but unwilling to leave anything to chance, he instead ran through the torrent down the *Rue du Mont Blanc*. He crossed the stone bridge over the outflow of the Rhône at the lake's edge and reached the *Quai des Bergues* where the four-storey hotel named for it stood. Frederick went to the reception desk and asked if Mrs Greene were still there. Indeed, she was, and owing to the weather, she hadn't left for the day.

Mrs Greene, a plump lady clad in a black and yellow plaid dress, allowed Frederick to hold her umbrella over the two of them as they dodged the puddles in the street.

Once in the bedchamber, Mrs Greene took one look at Harriet and reached for her wrist to feel her pulse.

"Are you a physician, Mrs Greene?" asked Frederick.

"I am most decidedly not, but my late husband was. I used

to go out with him on calls. He taught me a few things. This young lady needs to drink something, anything she can keep down. She is fading. Her pulse is weak. Call for some fresh mint tea immediately and some ginger biscuits. Failing that, some salty ones. I shall order the maid to make her a sponge bath and I shall do it myself."

Frederick did as he was told. His wife felt better after the bed bath taken while he was banished from the room. Soon after, Mrs Greene had Harriet nibbling a ginger biscuit and sipping the tea. Harriet was very grateful to the stranger-lady. Imagine if she hadn't been on that *randonnée* with them to Chancy?

❦ ❦ ❦

Monday afternoon *Monsieur le Docteur Le Brun* returned to check on his patient, but Frederick paid him at the door, telling him his services were no longer required. The doctor turned abruptly and stomped down the stairs. Although Harriet was feeling slightly better now thanks to Mrs Greene's morning ministrations, Frederick had decided they should go back to Paris as soon as possible. He wanted her to see a better doctor, and there were plenty in Paris. He went to the ticket agency and spent the rest of the evening packing the trunks with the maid while Harriet remained in bed. They would leave in the morning with one sack of ginger biscuits and another of spearmint leaves, thanks to Mrs Greene.

❦ ❦ ❦

WEDNESDAY, 5 SEPTEMBER 1860, PARIS

After a miserably hot, all-day journey on the slow mail train from *Genève,* the Kingstons arrived at the *Embarcadère de Lyon.* They were relieved to find available a large, airy room at the *Hôtel Meurice* again and cancelled their October reservation for a flat; Frederick guessed they would only stay about a week before going back to London. He made an appointment straightaway in the suburb of St Cloud with *Monsieur le Docteur Clermont,* whom the manager of the hotel recommended as being the best for "woman problems".

During the interview, Harriet, unfamiliar with French medical terms, was at a loss as to how to explain her symptoms, save *la nausée*, but she finally determined he was asking her when she had last been "unwell". Actually, she had not been unwell since she was married. *Oh, my! Georgina had said something about that being important to observe*, thought Harriet. After an intimate examination of her abdomen, the physician told her in no uncertain terms that she should abandon her corsets and that she was most definitely *enceinte*. He advised her on what to eat in order to avoid being sick and told her that her child would arrive sometime in the spring. But spring sounded far, far away if she must continue to feel this way.

Harriet loosened her corset, giving her some relief, and hoped she was over the worst. Then she had an upsetting thought. *All of her new Parisian dresses would have to be altered or set aside for months! Oh, what a waste!*

While she remained in the hotel the following day lest her nausea worsened, Frederick went round to the dressmaker's and tailor's shops. Their orders were not yet completed, so he paid to have the clothing sent on to London where they would bide their time until Harriet felt ready for a sea voyage. Now that these priorities were addressed, he permitted his wife to set the pace for the rest of their stay.

Harriet tried for three days to eat the food *Monsieur le Docteur Clermont* recommended. She felt a bit stronger each day, but was still nauseated in the morning and couldn't think of eating until noon. She surrendered to sleep every afternoon. On the fourth day though, she resisted the urge to nap and persuaded Frederick to take her to *la Sainte-Chapelle* on *Ile de la Cité*. The exquisite thirteenth century chapel built for Louis IX had been emptied after the French Revolution and converted to secular offices. In an extensive years-long restoration, its beautiful narrow stained glass windows had been replaced, and Harriet wanted to see the afternoon sun streaming through them. The visit was a complete success. The interior was breath-taking with its ceiling of blue and gilt. Harriet was in awe of the windows' red and blue hues and wanted to capture the rose window with her watercolours. She took out her sketch pad and quickly drew the design, noting the colours in the margin.

They exited the church and made their way across the cobblestones to the nearest bridge, the *Pont Neuf*, to return to the hotel. As they were crossing it, Harriet was stricken. She covered her mouth and looked desperately at Frederick as if asking what she should do. She gripped the wall of the old bridge and contemplated the Seine. She tried to hold back, but could not.

Though Frederick would have preferred a carriage, he hailed a passing omnibus and helped her aboard. Once in bed at the hotel, she slept through the dinner hour and then tried to eat what *Monsieur le Docteur Clermont* ordered. The next day, determined to see more of the city, Harriet again insisted on going out. They walked down the *Champs Elysées* to the *Arc de Triomphe* in the glorious September weather; they climbed the stairs to the top of the arch to look down on all of the people, happy children, carriages, dogs, and buildings along the wide avenue. There was one more thing she wanted to do before they left the City of Light—to visit the *Bois de Boulogne* to go horseback riding. Frederick put his foot down. Now that she was in the family way, he had to protect her from herself. They had their first row; Harriet locked herself in the water closet and whimpered for an hour.

They made up by agreeing to attend a performance of *Tartuffe* by Molière at the nearby *Comédie Française*. Harriet was placated.

CHAPTER 31

Royal Visit

TUESDAY, 18 SEPTEMBER 1860
THOROLD TOWNSHIP, CANADA WEST

The hired coach pulled by four strong horses left the lane at "Beechlands" and started down the Thorold Stone Road toward Queenston. It followed similar coaches and carriages all going in the same direction.

"Papa, how much longer till we are there?" asked Henry Fuller. The youngest in the family was now four years old and sat on Laura's lap, looking out the window of the coach.

"Henry, we've just left the house," pronounced his mother.

"There, there, Henry. 'Tis a good question. 'Twill be a long ride, so I hope you'll sing with your sister." Tom Fuller looked at Laura and winked. His musical daughter usually had a song or rhyme ready to amuse the tot. She seemed to have a rapport with the little one.

The Fullers were going to witness the dedication of the new obelisk at Queenston Heights. The memorial to Tom's godfather, Major General Sir Isaac Brock, was being erected near the site

273

where the soldier fell in battle on 13 October 1812. To-day was a very special occasion throughout the entire Niagara Peninsula. The Prince of Wales, Prince Albert Edward, in the middle of his grand tour of North America, was stopping briefly to dedicate the four-foot tall stone monument marking the spot where it was thought Brock had died. Major Thomas Richard Fuller, Tom's father, had served under Brock and had become his good friend, resulting in Brock's being godfather to the infant Tom. After Brock's death, Major Fuller retired from the 41st Regiment in ill health and died in 1813 at Adolphustown, a Loyalist settlement on the North Channel upstream from Kingston. He left his widow, Mary England Fuller, and their three-year-old son, Tom.

Mary Margaret, Laura, and their mother were attired in new summer dresses, for the September sun was still warm. The younger boys were duly scrubbed and unhappily dressed in their Sunday best. Not all of the Fuller children were present for this special outing. The twins, Dick and Sam, age twenty-two, were employed; Dick worked for the Great Western Railway in Hamilton now, the prince's next stop, and Sam was up in Stratford starting a hardware business. Willy was in Toronto at Upper Canada College doing the summer term.

Yesterday, Lizzie went with Margaret Jane and her parents to spend the night at the old McFarland homestead on the Niagara River. She hoped to meet her family at the event if they could find each other in the crowd. Dunc McFarland, Agnes, their little son, Frederick, and year-old Aggie had also left yesterday to stop a few days with Agnes' Blake family in Niagara, a shorter drive for them to Queenston Heights for the eleven o'clock event. The senior Duncan McFarland, attired in a new blue uniform with gold epaulettes, was among the honoured veterans of the War of 1812 gathering to salute the Prince of Wales.

❦ ❦ ❦

It had not taken as long as expected to bring the prince from his lodgings at Clifton where he was staying in the former home of local businessman Samuel Zimmerman, a famous victim of the Desjardins Canal railway accident. The young man and his travelling party arrived at the heights thirty minutes early, throwing all of the organising committee's plans into chaos. Instead of having two hours to reminisce, the old soldiers from Toronto and Niagara ended up with only one, but they had already made good use of the hour to renew acquaintances. Prince Albert Edward took his place on the platform where some of the ladies were already seated, ready to review the splendid, uniformed militia.

It was a scramble to form the various participants into a procession. Once assembled, the Highland and Volunteer Rifle Companies from Toronto, led on horseback by Lieutenant Colonel Richard Lippincott Denison, Harriet Taylor's uncle, paraded through arches built in the prince's honour to a waiting platform. The Toronto men positioned themselves on one side of it. On the other were the St Catharines Rifles, directed by Mrs Fuller's brother, Colonel Thomas Clarke Street, committee member and proud contributor toward the new monument. Down the middle of the carriageway strode over one hundred veterans, arranged oldest to youngest; Duncan McFarland, age fifty-eight, was nigh the last in the group.

After the old soldiers were aligned, they saluted the prince with their raised swords. Prince Albert Edward delivered a speech prepared in advance by his aides in response to a solemn address from Sir John Beverley Robinson. Following the speeches, Sir John presented Tom Fuller to the prince, and the two Canadians accompanied His Highness to the top of the hill where the original Brock monument stood. The heir to the British throne climbed the tower, surveying the landscape and the Niagara River below before he raised the Union Jack, officially completing the tower's repair. The group then descended to where the new obelisk waited. The prince smiled broadly as he spread some mortar on the pedestal and watched the obelisk be placed into its final position. The Reverend Mr Thomas Fuller then offered a prayer in his godfather's memory and for all those others who fell in the battle.

Immediately after, the prince and his entourage sought his carriage to take them to the steamer *Zimmerman*, waiting in the Niagara River. After a brief sail downriver to the town of Niagara, the prince accepted gifts of local fruits, listened to speeches, and admired the gaily decorated arch built at the wharf. The royal entourage then took the steamer to St Catharines via Port Dalhousie, where again there were plentiful decorations, speeches and throngs of well-wishers in the centre of town. Finally, the prince's party embarked from St Catharines railway station in a special train to Hamilton, where there would be yet more ceremonies, speeches, and another ball given in his honour.

CHAPTER 32

Homecoming

From the stern of the steamer, Harriet smiled at the antics of the dolphins playing in the ship's wake and the seals sunning themselves on the shore. She gasped at the breaching minke whales and the pod of glistening white beluga whales, that glided silently along the surface before disappearing to hunt prey on the river bottom. Seagulls also followed the ship, a welcome sight after days at sea. The young woman pulled her dark purple cloak closer round her in the wind as she watched the mouth of the Saguenay River and the pioneer fur trading and whaling village of Tadoussac fade into the horizon.

Within hours they would be docking in Québec City after their four-month long wedding trip to Europe. It was the experience she had dreamt about as a young girl, though sadly cut short by her falling pregnant and being ill. Only once they returned to London was she able to eat normally. They had spent almost a month there allowing her to recuperate.

Frederick had originally planned to end their grand tour with

277

a wine-tasting and buying trip to Porto; he wanted to show Harriet where he was born. His bride had looked forward to sailing down to sunny, exotic Portugal; but after she became ill, Frederick insisted they return to London. He asked Charles Kinloch to do his buying for the new season and wrote a letter to the Factory delegating the selections to his brother-in-law, stating parameters and shipping instructions for his order. For the first time, he would import wines without having taken so much as one sip of the product.

Harriet's health was now his priority.

Once back in London at Watson's Hotel, they received sad news: Mr Nicholas Westby had died on 24 August, the day they arrived in *Genève*. They went out to the High Street and bought Harriet a ready-made mourning costume, for she had no suitable garment for calling. At the first opportunity, Frederick and Harriet paid a visit to the widow, the Honourable Mrs Emma Westby and her family, Harriet's first such official duty as Mrs Kingston. They did not, however, announce that Harriet was expecting a child.

A new life begun, and the loss of another, in the space of a few weeks, thought Harriet. She said a silent prayer for the Westbys and for herself.

On the bright side, she had visited her English ancestral villages and got to know some of Frederick's large family: his mother, three sisters, nieces, and two of his five brothers— Charles and Francis—plus a few of Frederick's barrister friends and their wives during their stay. She had seen exotic animals in the London zoo and explored its beautiful Botanic Garden, not to mention the charms of Paris and *Genève*.

Now their honeymoon was coming to an end. Frederick needed to return to his business responsibilities in Montréal. Harriet was joyfully feeling better and able to eat, even on the rolling steamer coming back. She hadn't yet seen the house that was to become her home, and she was anxious to establish her household before their baby arrived in just a few months. She had much to do and showed Frederick her lists, updated daily. He would smile and kiss her squarely on the mouth, beaming with love for his much-younger mate. He had lived the bachelor's life long enough to know how precious was the love of an intelligent and caring woman.

🦌 🦌 🦌

Upon landing in Québec City, the newlyweds stopped for a week with the Taylors. Georgina was thrilled to hear that Harriet was expecting. Her father was shocked at first but then elated that he would soon become a grandfather; he himself had just become a father again last summer. Harriet yearned to linger with them after being away for so many months. Beyond seeing her father and Georgina again, she wanted to spoil their baby daughter. Her stepsister Florence was born soon after she and Frederick had left for Europe. The happy, healthy infant was now four months old, babbling, smiling, and kicking. Harriet had had only a few chances to practise with Frederick's little nieces over in Surrey last summer. She wanted to spend time with her sister Mary, who had left her studies at the Ursuline Academy and was at home. Brother Georgie was studying with a tutor to prepare him for grammar school. Like Harriet and Mary, he wasn't keen on academics yet and, at age twelve, had no professional ambitions.

Then there was Maria. Harriet had to spend some time with her cousin, telling her all about her experiences in England, France, and Switzerland. Maria was sure to be ready to share her own stories of the Prince of Wales' visit and the ball she attended in August. There was much to talk about!

Harriet was torn. She wished very much to set up housekeeping in Montréal, but she also wanted to ask Frederick to extend their stay. The young wife was just about to bring up the subject when Frederick made the decision for her. *Fait accompli*! The businessman sent a telegram to his business in Montréal to let them know that he would be back at the end of the week. Harriet was crestfallen but made plans with Georgina for them to return to spend the Christmas holidays together. Of course, she would have to have Frederick's approval.

CHAPTER 33

A Letter from Montréal

THURSDAY, 22 NOVEMBER 1860, ST CATHARINES
Julia tore open the envelope with the familiar handwriting. It was postmarked Montréal. It had been months since she had heard from Hattie Taylor Kingston. Julia hadn't been invited to the wedding in June, but she could not have interrupted her studies at the Normal to go to Québec in any case.

Montréal
15 novembre 1860

My dearest friend Julia,
First off, I hope that you, William, and your family are well. I am ashamed to admit I last wrote you several months ago from Harwich on the English coast. So much has happened since then, as you can well imagine. We spent some weeks in England, first in the countryside, before we stopped for a month at a hotel in London's Regent's Park. I met Frederick's mother and sisters and I especially got on with Laura, who was an excellent guide to the city. I did not get to meet

their brother Edward, a priest in Dorset, but Charles and
Francis who work for the family company in London are quite
agreeable. Frederick and I spent a week shopping in Paris be-
fore going on to Genève where events took a turn. My dear
friend, I am expecting a child in the spring! But I confess I
was so ill in Switzerland that I was not sure I would continue
living. I was sick every day for weeks and only through the in-
tervention of God himself did I overcome my illness. I remem-
ber well the problems your mother had and how you worried
over her. I pray that all goes well for me at the end of this or-
deal. At any rate, Frederick and I are now settled in our petite
maison *and awaiting the babe. The winter has begun, and*
we have several inches of snow outside the door. The house is
snug and warm, and Frederick cares for me well. His business
is not far away and I see him for dinner every day.

Please write me soon.

Affectionately,
Hattie

Julia skimmed the letter and let out a shriek upon reading of
Hattie's pregnancy and rushed upstairs to share the good news
with Bella.

❦ ❦ ❦

Now that Hattie was in the family way, Julia was even more
anxious to be married herself. Though he had never said the
words, she was sure that William loved her. He was twenty-one
and had finished his studies at St Catharines Grammar School.
He was gainfully employed, working in the office of the city treasurer. Julia was sure he could support a family now. She was teaching at the St George's District School, but would be glad to give
it up, even after completing an arduous teacher training course
in Toronto. They saw each other at church and family gatherings
every week. Julia wanted to tell him she loved him, but she worried that he might rebuff her because they were first cousins. She
hoped the long Christmas holidays might offer an opportunity
for them to express their feelings.

CHAPTER 34

A Long Winter

SATURDAY, 22 DECEMBER 1860, QUÉBEC CITY

Three days before Christmas, Harriet and Frederick travelled on the Grand Trunk Railway to *Pointe Lévis* across the river from Québec City. Before boarding in Montréal, they learned the ferries wouldn't be running that day, and the annual ice bridge had yet to form. When the train reached its destination, the couple disembarked and were immediately besieged by *canotiers* vying to take them across the tidal St Lawrence River in their *canots d'hiver*. Frederick began bargaining with a gruff old man called Jean Tremblay. Frederick wanted Tremblay to take them and all their baggage across at once in his dugout canoe. The man, dressed in a lightweight wool jacket tied with an arrow-patterned red sash, pulled his red wool cap down around his ears and refused, saying it was impossible; he had room for many more passengers than two. He would bring over their trunks in his next crossing, but for this trip, it was only to be people. Frederick was annoyed. He strode away to find another canoe to take the baggage so that it would arrive at the same time they did. He did not want Harriet to be detained in this weather.

While all of these negotiations went on, Harriet and the other women waited inside Tremblay's shanty, out of the cold wind, huddled over a small cast iron stove. The temperature outside was near zero. She was glad to have worn her beaver *pardessus* and hat with a thick wool scarf pulled across her face. She pushed her gloved hands farther into a rabbit fur muff and wiggled her fingers to keep the circulation going. Frederick, the collar turned up on his thickest cape, was also wearing a beaver hat and soft deerskin gloves backed with bear fur; he stamped his feet to keep warm. It was half past three, and the sun was beginning to set; he was worried they would have to cross in the dark if they didn't get started soon.

Twenty minutes later, the trunks and valises were brought down to the ice and snow-covered shoreline, and Frederick consigned another crew to take the baggage across. Tremblay tried to renege on his agreement to transport the Kingstons, wanting to keep the additional business for himself. The *canotier* told them to go instead with his brother-in-law Pierre Chabot, whose canoe was about to arrive from Québec. Frederick stood his ground. Passengers were already being packed like sardines into the canoe that was pulled up over the thick ice along the river's edge. The specially-designed thirty-foot long vessel, carved out of a single pine tree trunk, had rounded sides, a flat bottom, and upturned ends like sleigh runners.

Tremblay counted his passengers so far: *un … deux … trois* and ended abruptly at *treize*. He turned to Frederick and said, "*Non*, you come wit' me, *M'sieur*. I cannot leave with t'irteen. *Le mauvais sort!*"

Relieved, Frederick helped Harriet climb into the vessel. They sat on small platforms, and Frederick covered them both with one of Tremblay's sealskins. The bristly grey fur felt heavy on their limbs, but they were very warm. Harriet had never ridden in a *canot d'hiver*. Whenever the Taylor family had wintered in Québec, they had just remained in the city, content to wait for warm temperatures and spring rains to melt the ice.

Frederick tried to assure Harriet the ride across would be safe. Nevertheless, she prayed as they sat, waiting to begin the crossing.

The fifteen passengers watched as Tremblay and his crew of five rubbed bear grease on their hip-length leather boots held up by shoulder straps. Frederick wondered why they hadn't done this while they waited for the baggage to come down from the train.

Then he smelled the crew's breath and realised they must have been sharing a flask of *caribou* behind the shanty. He said a silent prayer for a safe crossing.

The tide was running out, and the current was swift. Tremblay and the crew ran as fast they could, pushing the canoe over the thick band of shoreline ice. The canoe glided over it on its flat bottom. After crossing several yards of weaker ice, the men jumped one by one into the canoe, just as it slid into the moving water. Harriet moaned and leaned closer to Frederick. Old Tremblay steered from the stern while two men on each side paddled to drive them forward. A man in the bow served as pilot, pointing out the best route through the floating ice while correcting their course to account for the current. Tremblay sang a familiar *canotier* tune into the cold air as the men paddled in unison. The pilot saw a long stretch of solid ice ahead and he cried *"Trottine!"* Up and over the ice they went. All four paddlers put a leg out to propel the canoe across the bumpy surface.

As the canoe again dropped into the frigid water, the crew resumed paddling. In the middle of the river where the current was strongest, all six men fought to keep them on course to their intended landing spot. Floating ice was already piling up, creating walls three feet high; the *canotiers* pushed them away with their long paddles. The canoe rocked back and forth as it contacted the ice, creating eerie sounds. Just as they neared the *Québec* shore, the bow became wedged between floating blocks and the canoe started to head downstream. Tremblay yelled a command as the pilot tried in vain to dislodge the bow. An older crew member, balancing precariously, shoved a block hard with his paddle. When a chunk broke away, he faltered, dropping into the fast-moving water. Harriet screamed. The man behind her extended his paddle to Louis Gagnon, pulling the poor fellow, now soaked to his hips, back into the canoe. Gagnon, still gripping his paddle with one gloved hand, lurched heavily toward some passengers before retaking his position. Like his friend Tremblay, Gagnon had been doing this job every winter since he was twelve years old. Tremblay and the other *canotiers* earned a handsome fee for their skill. They were across the half-mile distance after an hour of strenuous, dangerous work.

In Québec City at the idled Grand Trunk Railway ferry wharf, Frederick hired a driver with a sleigh and horses. This time he bundled Harriet under a shiny black bearskin for the ride through town. Harriet was looking healthier to-day, as the cold air had chapped her cheeks, though her husband was still very protective of her after she had been ill for so many weeks in Europe.

In the twilight, the horses trudged up the long and winding *Côte de la Montagne* to the *Porte St Louis*. Harriet smelled pungent wood smoke discharging from every chimney as the sleigh jostled them along the familiar, narrow cobbled streets. The driver knew where the Taylors lived, as he often drove Fennings round the city. Fennings had no hired man here and no horses; he occasionally borrowed his Uncle John's vehicles to drive for pleasure. His generous uncle frequently took him to work at the new Parliament building inside the city's old wall, along with his own two sons who now worked as clerks for the Parliament. Even though Québec City was compact, it was difficult and even unsafe to walk so far. The streets were often icy or muddy, and the old plank walks were in many places rotting and falling apart.

Fennings' house was near the old city gate where *Rue St Louis* became the *Grande Allée*. The *Grande Allée* was fast becoming a popular residential district where there was open land to develop. Designed with six bays and an off-set hallway, the house had enough space to accommodate guests and his whole family at its present size. The three-storey house was built of local grey stone cut into rectangular blocks and its roof was in typical Québecois style, steeply-pitched, and intended to shed months of winter snow. Like many other dwellings, it featured a roof ladder to aid in putting out chimney fires, a constant threat from the numerous fireplaces and stoves needed to keep the house warm year-round.

❦ ❦ ❦

Georgina met her guests at the front door and embraced both of them affectionately. "How was your journey to-day, dears?" she asked.

"Exhausting, 'Gina. We had a long stopover in Richmond Junction, and then we had to take the *canot* over, you know," said Harriet. "It was a harrowing experience I don't ever want to repeat. One old man conducting us nearly drowned in the river when an ice block tipped him! We are lucky we got through at all so late in the day, he said. I am ready for a hot bath and a comfortable bed after spending the whole day in the cars. I found the seat not very agreeable to me in my condition."

"You need to get warm now, dear one. Come into the parlour and sit in front of the stove. Take off those cold boots," said her stepmother.

Harriet doffed her boots and donned a pair of warm fur slippers waiting at the front door. She enjoyed some sandwiches with a steaming cup of tea from Georgina's monogrammed silver teapot while her father and Frederick talked business and politics together in the drawing room over a brandy. Frederick had already sent them a case of wines for Christmas.

"Where are Mary and Georgie?" asked Harriet. "I expected to see them at the door."

"They're at Uncle's. Betsy invited them to stay there just so we could have a little time together in the quiet," said Georgina. "Wasn't that thoughtful? She knew you'd be tired after travelling all day. They'll be home to-morrow."

"And Florence? I was hoping to see my little sister this evening. I need to practise with babies! The doctor still tells me I should have mine in the spring."

"So you said in your letter. That's a lovely time to have a child, just when the weather turns warmer, and you can be outside again. I shall ask Nurse to bring Florence down before supper."

❦ ❦ ❦

Frederick and Harriet settled into the guestroom on the second floor. After a soaking bath, Harriet put on a woolen nightdress, knelt, and gave thanks to God for their safe arrival, before she climbed gratefully into the featherbed, stretched out, and fell asleep in no time flat. Frederick joined her after a cigar and more brandy with her father downstairs.

In the morning from the bedroom window, Harriet admired

the fine view of the town spread out below, the St Lawrence River, its south shore in the distance and the chunks of ice floating in between. The afternoon newspaper reported what the family already knew: the ferry was closed for the season and the citizens would have to wait for the ice bridge to solidify in order to reach the other side of the river by sleigh or on foot. The adventurous and those with a schedule to keep could take the *canots* across. Frederick had fully expected this and planned his business schedule accordingly, leaving trusted managers in Montréal to handle his affairs. He guessed it would only be a fortnight before they could cross the river again by sleigh for their return trip home.

❦ ❦ ❦

TUESDAY, 15 JANUARY 1861

At last the long Christmas holidays were over, and the new year was welcomed in. The latest deep snow sparkled like diamonds in the winter sunlight under a cold, clear blue sky. The temperature had been frigid long enough now so that at last the ice bridge held, despite the nightly efforts of the *canotiers* to break it up to preserve their business. Fennings borrowed Uncle John's sleigh to deliver his daughter and her husband to the right bank of the St Lawrence to catch their train back to Montréal. Harriet lingered and kissed her father good-bye one more time, his bushy whiskers tickling her face.

Fennings said to Frederick, "Take care of my daughter, son. She's very precious to me."

"And to me also, sir," replied the son-in-law, knowing full well that Fennings, widowed at thirty-four, was concerned about his daughter's impending childbirth. Harriet blew him another kiss and waved to him through the window as the locomotive pulled away.

❦ ❦ ❦

SATURDAY, 13 APRIL 1861, ST ANTOINE'S WARD, MONTRÉAL

Harriet was uncomfortable and tired of being pregnant. Her baby was supposed to be born in the spring. It had now been spring for almost a month. The midwife had come to see her again on Saturday and told her the babe would arrive soon. Harriet thought it should have happened by now. She felt as if she had been with child forever!

She awoke with the first pains at a quarter past midnight. She was able to doze again, but got up every hour and a half to walk until they subsided. Frederick woke with her each time and watched helplessly as she moaned through her discomfort. This pattern continued until morning.

At eight o'clock, Aunt Betsy came into their bedroom with a pot of tea and some toast for the anxious parents-to-be. Frederick had told her about their interrupted night of sleep. Aunt Betsy had graciously agreed to come from Québec City to await the birth of the Kingston baby and to help Harriet with the newborn's care. She had been with them now for a month.

"Harriet, you need to get up and move about, dear. I found it always helped me to move about," said the mother of ten.

"But I have, Aunt, all night long. Now I just want to curl up and sleep. I'm so tired, and my back hurts so."

"No, my dear. Let's get you up and feed you first. I'll help you put on your dressing gown."

Harriet sat gingerly on the chair beside the fireplace where Frederick had just added a few logs. She leaned back and sighed. Aunt Betsy handed her the cup of tea.

"It's got two lumps of sugar for energy and some milk," said the older woman.

Aunt Betsy helped Harriet walk every hour. They paced all over the second floor of the house.

Frederick did not consider going to work. Although his place of business was just a few blocks away, there was no need for him to go out and leave his labouring wife to-day. Business concerns would wait.

Harriet refused any food. She drank another cup of well-sugared tea. At half past four in the afternoon, the young woman requested a hot bath in hopes of being able to relax, or even sleep a bit. Meg heated the water and helped her mistress into the copper hip tub. The warm water felt good on her exhausted, swollen body. When the next pains came, she sank farther down into the bath and tried to breathe calmly. At intervals, Meg poured on fresh hot water from the stove.

At six o'clock, Frederick and Aunt Betsy asked the maid how Harriet fared. Meg said she had been in the tub for over an hour and kept asking her to add hot water. Aunt Betsy was concerned now; it had been eighteen hours of pains and no baby had come. Long labours for first babies were not unusual, but at Betsy's insistence, Frederick sent Eliza the cook out to fetch the midwife. Harriet declared that she would be fine. She had faith that God would keep her safe. Aunt Betsy thought otherwise.

Before the midwife arrived, Meg got Harriet out of the tub, wrapped her in warm towels, and helped her into a fresh night dress. The midwife examined the labouring woman. She determined the baby was large, and it was not moving into position, as it should. She had Harriet assume a posture that sometimes helped mothers shift the baby's position.

After another hour, Frederick became alarmed that the midwife had nothing else to offer to speed the process. It was getting dark now, and he sent Eliza with a message for the doctor in Bonaventure Street. Eliza and Dr Scott were back in thirty minutes. He ordered the midwife aside and took command of the situation. After examining Harriet himself, the man determined that the child's head was too big for Harriet's pelvis. She was losing strength, and although now having contractions every three minutes, the baby was not making adequate progress. Harriet began to moan and cry; she was in agony! She just wanted it to be over.

The doctor took Frederick and Aunt Betsy out of the bedroom and into the hallway. He was blunt; he explained the situation and his plan. If the child could not be born, Harriet might die. If the child were sacrificed, Harriet would most likely live. Frederick was quick to decide he wanted his wife to be saved, and Aunt Betsy agreed. There would be other children but not without his beloved Harriet. Dr Scott returned to the bedside and prepared to administer chloroform through a cone that the midwife would place over Harriet's nose and mouth. Minutes later, Harriet lost consciousness, and the physician readied a scalpel, sutures, and a pair of long, oval forceps.

❦ ❦ ❦

SUNDAY, 14 APRIL 1861

After a sleepless night in the second bedroom, Frederick entered the room where his young wife lay nestled in the bedclothes. She looked like an angel after all she had been through. She was still beautiful to him, even with her tangled hair and swollen face. Unfortunately, despite the best efforts of a physician and midwife, their first child had been stillborn after a prolonged labour. They named the baby Henry Frederick after his grandfather and father. Frederick was relieved that his cherished Harriet had survived the ordeal, but there was a hole in his heart for the little son they had lost.

❧ ❧ ❧

Montréal
13 May 1861

Dear Julia,

I wish I had happier news to tell you. Our son was born 13 April, but he was so big I nearly died with the hours of pains. Finally the doctor relieved me, but the child did not survive. I could not look upon it. Frederick is heartbroken to lose our little boy, named for his father and himself. He mopes round the house and drags himself to the business when I plead for him to go. I cannot bear to see him so. Aunt Betsy refuses to leave my side, but I just want to be alone. Please tell me that I shall feel like myself once again. I fear that I shall remain in this melancholy, despite the happy promise of spring.

Affectionately,
Hattie

20 May 1861
Dearest Hattie,

I just received your letter in the morning post and tears flowed from my eyes. Despite the blurred lines, I have reread your letter many times with no new perspective other than what Bishop Doane would counsel. Go to the Lord with your cares and heavy burdens. He will comfort you in your time of need.

I do have some good news to share and perhaps this will lighten your mind to know that William has confessed his love to me and I to him. We have yet to tell our parents, but I think we shall be married soon. As soon as we are engaged, I shall gladly take leave of teaching!

Your friend always,
Julia

CHAPTER 35

Life in St Catharines

JUNE 1861

It was obvious that Emma had been taking extra care with her appearance for the last month. Julia and Bella had both noticed that she had asked Kitty to arrange her light brown hair in a more fashionable style instead of the plainer one that she usually chose because it was quick to do. Emma was blossoming. Both sisters were happy to see it but wondered what had caused the change.

They decided to ask her when she got home from her volunteer work that afternoon. The two were sitting on the verandah watching for Emma's approach, when Bella gasped.

"Bella, what is it?" asked Julia.

"Do you see what I see?" Bella pointed down Academy Street.

"Oh, my goodness, it's Emma and Pierce Anderson, from church!"

"It most certainly is. And they look cosy, do they not?"

"I wonder how long this has been going on and if Mama and Papa know," said Julia.

"Well, let's do ask them!" Bella rose from the wicker chair, and, before Julia could restrain her, raced down the front walk, leaving Julia behind, arms akimbo, mouth open in disbelief.

"Bella! Wait! Stop!" shouted Julia.

Julia respected Emma's privacy about this now obvious budding relationship, knowing her own feelings about William and their own possible march toward marriage.

Emma, at twenty-two, had never had a beau. It was difficult in St Catharines to find a man from a good family, of one's own station and religion, and with an acceptable income. Many girls ended up like Julia, enamoured with a cousin with whom they had grown up. At least a cousin was coming from a known family.

Emma was enjoying her conversation with Pierce so much that she hadn't spied the ambush before they arrived at the front gate. She was turning to say good-bye to him when she saw Bella running toward them.

"Why, Pierce! It's so lovely to see you to-day!" said Bella, face flushed from the sudden exercise.

"Likewise. How are you to-day, Miss Burns?" asked the young man, as if breathless young girls accosted him *every* day of the week. Pierce Anderson was unremarkable in appearance. He was of medium height, with rather sad-looking brown eyes and wavy medium brown hair. He was dressed like the conservative bank clerk he was, on his way home from work on a warm summer afternoon. However, in order to escort his new friend home, he had gone out of his way. He had walked a distance from the bank in St Paul Street north to the coloured section of town, where Emma was teaching women to read and write at the British Methodist Episcopal Church.

Emma scowled at her younger sister, who was still interrupting conversations no matter where she was. *It is a childhood habit that has never been corrected by our parents*, she thought.

"Very well, thank you, Pierce," replied the still impulsive eighteen-year-old.

"*Mr Anderson* was walking me home from the church," said Emma crossly.

"I can see that, Emma. What a beautiful afternoon for a walk! Would you care to come in for tea, Pierce?"

"Isabella! How impertinent you are! Perhaps Mr Anderson has to be home for tea. His mother and sisters await him, I'm sure."

"And Wilson, remember Wilson, Emma," corrected Bella. Wilson was a schoolmate of their brother Lewie.

"Oh, Wilson will be there certainly," said Pierce with a good-natured laugh. "My little brother never misses a meal."

"Well, p'raps another time, Pierce?" teased Bella.

"Isabella, I wish you would stop!" said Emma, on the verge of tears. "I wish you would stop … immediately!" she growled under her breath, jaw clenched.

"Bella! Mama wants you straightaway!" called Julia to the rescue, seeing that the situation was becoming intolerable to Emma.

"Well, Pierce, I hope you have a lovely evening! I have to say good-bye now. I'm wanted inside," said Bella, by way of excusing herself with a curtsy.

"And you as well, Miss Burns," said Pierce, with a smart bow and a tip of his hat.

Bella strode triumphantly back to the house where Julia awaited her, furious, on the verandah.

"I can't believe you did that to Emma, Bella. I heard every word, and you should be ashamed of yourself. I don't even want to see you right now. Go inside, and pray God to change your behaviour."

"What on earth do you mean, Julia? I just greeted the man and invited him to tea!"

"You know it was not your place to do so. When will you ever grow up? Now go away. Leave Emma alone!"

❦ ❦ ❦

SEPTEMBER 1861

Emma and Pierce had spent nearly every afternoon together for the last month. He had been to tea with the Burns family each Sunday afternoon, and it was obvious that Emma was very much in love with the shy young man. He was the sole supporter of his family, his mother having been widowed before she emigrated from Ireland to escape poverty and hunger there. Instead of pursuing his education at the grammar school, at age sixteen Pierce had taken a clerk position at the Niagara District Bank. He was an earnest, hard-working young man, but the strain of providing for his mother and siblings showed on his face even at twenty-six. He was rarely seen smiling, although when approached by any one of the Burns girls, his small, deep-set eyes lit up, especially for Emma.

For Emma's part, she was hopeful that Pierce would propose marriage. At this point in her life she had no illusions about her prospects. His family consisted of three younger sisters and Wilson. The girls, Margaret, Elicia, and Jane, were as yet unmarried. It was possible that he would not see fit to add another mouth to feed until the sisters married. Emma knew well that, once married, babies came regularly, and that would be an additional economic burden for a bank clerk's salary. Perhaps it was too much to hope!

Pierce, having finished his last sip of tea one Sunday afternoon, asked Emma and Bella, lately required to chaperone the couple, to take a walk with him. They excused themselves from the Burns' dining room, and Emma asked Mary to fetch the girls' bonnets and shawls. Bella took hers and followed them outside, keeping a discreet distance behind, shuffling through the new fallen leaves. She disliked this new role Papa had assigned her, but he had insisted for propriety's sake once he realised the serious nature of the young people's relationship.

As they passed St George's Church, Pierce broached the subject he had been dreading for weeks. "Emma, my dear, I need to tell you something," he began, still walking.

Emma stopped short, and so did Bella, now leaning against a tree looking away but also trying to hear the conversation.

"What, Pierce? It seemed to me that something was bothering you to-day," she said. *You were even more quiet than usual*, she thought.

He dared to take her hand in his. Emma's heart jumped at his touch.

"Well, you'll find out soon anyway ... I've given my notice, yesterday in fact."

"Your notice! My word! What've you done?" she asked, fearing the answer to her question and pulling back her hand.

"I have given my notice to the bank ... so that I can join the New York Cavalry in October."

"The New York Cavalry! Oh, my word, no! What are you saying? You're going away from me? From your family? From St

Catharines? Oh, Pierce! I can't believe it!" she began to sniffle and looked for a handkerchief. He thoughtfully provided his own.

"There, there, Emma!" He tried to comfort her, touching her face tenderly to move an errant strand of hair. "This war betwixt the States won't last long, I'm sure! The North will win the next big battle, and I'll come home again."

"How can you say that? How can you be sure? Why are you putting yourself in danger like this? We aren't Americans! It's not our fight, Pierce!"

"I've been watching what you do with your fugitive slaves, such good work, teaching the women to read and write, Emma. But what am I doing? I handle money all day long, inside a dark building, day in and day out, six days a week. I can make a difference! I can go fight the Rebels who want to keep people like our new neighbours captive!"

"But you could be killed! Wounded! Imprisoned! That is just not the same, Pierce. Oh no, it's just not the same. How can you do this to your family? Your father is gone! What will your sisters and brother do without you? What does your mother say?" She wanted to say, "And what will I do?"

"Mama is not in favour, of course, but my pay will go a long way to help all of them. I'll make four hundred twenty dollars, Emma! That is so much more than what I earn at the bank."

"If you survive, that is! Oh, Pierce, I cannot stop you from going. We are not betrothed. You are my good friend, and I shall miss you and pray for you. But I shall never understand why you choose to do this."

"I'm so sorry to ruin a Sunday walk with you, Emma. I had to tell you soon. I didn't know if one day would be better than another. So, there it is," he reached for her hand again, but she pulled away and turned her back to him.

"When do you leave?" asked Emma, fighting back the tears.

"In a fortnight, dear Emma."

❦ ❦ ❦

THURSDAY, 26 DECEMBER 1861, BOXING DAY

Henry and Eliza Mittleberger, along with their two sons, gave their wraps to Mary at the door and picked up the packages they had brought for the Burns family. Before Mary had a chance to announce their arrival, Bella flew by them with barely a nod and darted into the parlour.

Her mother, Henrietta, seated at the fireside, was reading *Great Expectations*, a gift from her daughters. The now traditional Christmas tree sat decorated, atop a gate-leg table; beneath it, Libby played dolls on the floor with Florrie. Julia was watching them intently until she heard the heavy door knocker. She stood in anticipation, but was met instead by her sister.

"Mama! Julia! Have you heard the news?" asked the tearful Bella.

"News? What news?" said her mother, putting her book down on a nearby table.

"Oh, my, it's Prince Albert. He's died!"

"Oh, no! The poor queen! Can you imagine? So young. No husband and nine children!" said her mother.

"How do you know this, Bella? What happened?" asked Julia.

"I was reading the newspaper with Papa. The report said 'twas gastric fever. He'd been ill for several weeks and died on the fourteenth of December. I can't believe it. They were so happy. What ever will she do?"

At that moment the visitors entered the room. William took Julia by the hand and looked down into her eyes. "Happy Christmas, Julia!"

Startled by his cheerful greeting, she looked at him, then at his parents and brother Charles.

William whispered in her ear, "We have also come to speak to your father."

❦ ❦ ❦

After Thomas Burns, William, and his father joined the group in the parlour, the two families made small talk as they enjoyed cakes and drank tea. The youngest Burns children opened the myriad of little packages their two cousins had carried across the snowy path cut between their houses. In turn, Henrietta presented gifts to her brother and Eliza. That afternoon, William, whose eyes were usually merry, especially at Christmastime, looked instead serious. After two excruciating hours, Julia watched the Mittlebergers leave together, still not knowing what had been discussed behind closed doors in her father's study.

Mr Burns was visibly perturbed as he closed the front door. He was aware of the longstanding affection that Julia and William Mittleberger felt for each other, but he had no idea the young couple was contemplating marriage. His lovely dark-haired daughter, Julia, had spent a year at the Normal School in Toronto, but apparently during that time away, she had only pined more for her cousin. Julia was still young, just twenty-one, and well-educated, having spent five terms at St Mary's Hall and now holding a teaching licence. Surely eligible young men in the county would seek after Julia if they knew she were of marriageable age.

St Catharines was a small town compared to Toronto, and his daughters' prospects for an ideal match were limited to professional men who worked for government or businesses. William certainly belonged to that worthy group and he was kind and attentive, but marrying a first cousin was a last resort in most families.

❦ ❦ ❦

Thomas closed the door of his study and bade Julia sit on the settee. She looked up at him expectantly. He sat beside her and took her hand in his. He kissed it gently.

"Daughter, as you may have guessed, William has asked my permission for you to marry." He paused, considering what else to say. "He's a fine young man with a bright future here in the city government, but you're both close in age and close in kinship. That is of great concern to me. Your uncle Henry has given his blessing, as he believes William loves you genuinely. He's even offered some land to build a house for you. I've requested of him some time to consider his proposal. I've asked to delay any decision until after June."

"June? Papa, that's six months away! Why do you need so long to decide? Why do you need any time at all? We love each other. We have always loved each other!"

"The greater question is that you are first cousins, my dear

299

Julia. Are you certain there is no one else in this town who could be a husband to you? Someone from the parish? I would like you to be introduced to some other young men before I give my consent. I shall begin making inquiries to-morrow."

Julia began to cry. She stood and wanted to stamp her feet like Bella would have. "This is so unfair! There is no one else in this town that I could ever love. And William feels the same way."

"Julia, I have made my opinion known. You will do as you are told," said her father.

❦ ❦ ❦

Julia couldn't bear seeing William at church week after week. They avoided talking to each other on arrival and exit. They managed weak smiles and averted their gaze when they attended any gathering. Emma felt sympathy for her sister and William. She had the opposite problem, missing Pierce and only receiving sporadic letters from him in the States.

Every Sunday afternoon that winter, Thomas Burns invited one of his law clerks home to dinner to meet his three marriageable daughters: Emma, Julia, and Bella. When none of them seemed eager to establish a relationship, he invited the Benson sons to dine with the family. Conversations were always halting; Emma was in love with Pierce and Julia was intransigent. Bella was clearly still too young, impetuous and self-centred, to entertain any conversations with businessmen or attorneys.

Thomas was beginning to despair. He had run out of ideas.

One evening in April, Emma knocked at the door of his study. "Papa, may I speak candidly with you?"

"Of course, my dear Emma. What is the matter?"

"'Tis Julia, Papa. She cries herself to sleep every night."

"I see. And why do you think that is?"

"William, Papa. She loves him so. They've always been the best of friends. Julia and William grew up together. They're meant to be together, I think. I wish you would reconsider your position on their marriage."

❦ ❦ ❦

1050 Dorchester
Montréal
1 October 1862

Dearest Julia,

We received your wedding announcement yesterday, and I write to wish you and William well in your marriage. Such wonderful news! I am sure it was a beautiful occasion with all of your sisters and brothers in attendance. I wish I could know William. He must be absolutely charming. It is unfortunate that we live so far away from each other, my friend. I miss our old talks at St Mary's Hall. Oh! To be in Burlington again and carefree!

Frederick and I have some news too: we are expecting a child after Christmas. This time I was less sick, but my clothing hangs on me. I confess that I am still fearful, but God has blessed us, and I must believe He will keep me and the baby safe. I am praying every day that I can do this successfully. I ask your prayers.

It has been a beautiful autumn here with brilliant colours but no snow yet. Please write soon with your news, dear friend. I am sure you are happy beyond words.

Affectionately,
Hattie

❦ ❦ ❦

JULY 1863

Henrietta and Emma Burns were sitting in the cool shade of the leafy oak trees in Julia's back garden, watching the antics of the black squirrels. They had walked less than two blocks to the house where Julia and William had set up housekeeping after their wedding last September. William had bought the house, although his father had offered the young couple a building lot carved out of his fifteen acres of orchards and gardens. William and Julia had no desire for so much land, and they were happy in the Duke Street house where they had a bit more privacy. William was Clerk of the Division Court now; it was a ten-minute walk to work, and he came home for dinner every day at one o'-

clock. He considered it a pleasant ritual established by his father and one he wished to continue in his own household.

Julia was holding her six-week-old baby boy George on her shoulder. It was a warm day even for July in Canada West. She fanned herself and the sleeping baby between sips of an iced glass of raspberry vinegar.

Bella came running into the garden, panting.

"Bella, dear, what is it?" asked Henrietta.

"Mama, it's a message for Emma. Mrs Anderson sent it over. Here, Sister," she held out a folded paper to Emma.

Emma hadn't had a letter from Pierce in over seven weeks now. Her heart was in her throat as she took the note from Bella's hand. Reading it once, she reread it and read it a third time. Then she stood and tore it into tiny pieces, letting them fall to the ground.

"My life is over," said the young woman, as she walked out of the garden gate.

❦ ❦ ❦

Corporal Pierce Anderson had indeed lost his life in the battle of Beverly's Ford, Virginia, far from his home in St Catharines. He died of infection after a minor flesh wound, but lacking enough medical supplies and clean water, the young man succumbed a week later of fever. He was buried in Virginia in a marked grave with eleven others who perished in the battle or shortly thereafter. He was the only Canadian in the company. His commander wrote his mother that he had served the Union Army with honour and distinction.

❦ ❦ ❦

JANUARY 1864

The following months were difficult for the Burns family. Since the tragic death of Pierce, Emma had given up tutoring at the British Methodist Episcopal Church in Geneva Street. She required alterations to her wardrobe, as she had lost interest in eating, just picking at her food. The sorrowful young woman resisted Bella's attempts to get her out of the house to shop in St Paul

Street. Emma dragged herself to church on Sundays; secretly, she blamed God for taking her beloved from her. She was angry. Listless and short-tempered, she looked older than her twenty-five years.

The joy surrounding the birth of the first Burns grandson was overshadowed by the sadness of their eldest daughter. Little George Burns Mittleberger, born at the end of May, was cooing and sitting up now. He was healthy and eating well, despite being exceedingly small when he was born. It was all a mother could ask. Julia was pre-occupied with his care, expanding her motherly duties to fill each day.

The house was quieter now that Lewie was at St George's School in Church Street all day, and Norman was away at Upper Canada College in Toronto. Bella visited Julia often to take a break from dealing with her duties at home as well as Emma's grief. Her father had decided Bella would instruct the precocious Florrie in reading and writing. A reluctant teacher, she valued some time away from her pupil, a quick learner who challenged Bella at every turn. Florrie could already count to one hundred and write her name and a few short words on her slate. She wanted to read books, but since there were few to be had for a girl of five, Bella helped her write her own stories with illustrations in pencil. Bella much preferred teaching Libby, no longer at school at thirteen, to sing and play the new piano-forte the two girls had persuaded their father to buy. Last summer, Mrs Burns allowed the instrument to be installed in the parlour, whose pocket doors could be shut.

Bella thought often of Miss Winans, her harp teacher at St Mary's Hall. It was Miss Winans who had ignited her study and appreciation of music so many years ago. She wondered what had ever become of her sweet, indulgent teacher. Would Papa be willing to buy her a harp too? Hopefully she would still remember the basics of how to play if that day ever came.

❦ ❦ ❦

"Mama, my throat hurts," complained Florrie Burns.

The tot had slept late that morning. After waking in the nursery shared with Lewie, she stumbled through the hallway to her mother's bedroom. Her father was already at work in his law office.

"What is it, my love?" asked Henrietta Burns.

"I don't feel well a tall!"

"Come here, Florrie," said her mother. "Let me feel your head."

Florrie leaned into her mother's ample bosom, and Henrietta felt her forehead. She looked lovingly into the cherubic face of her youngest child. Since her last pregnancy, her mood had stabilised, and in the ensuing years, she had regained much of her former energy and compassion.

"Oh, Florrie, you are indeed hot, dear, and your face is red. You must go back to bed straightaway. I shall send for the doctor."

"Mama! I don't want to see the doctor. He'll hurt me! He scratched my arm so hard the last time! He made me bleed! I don't like him a tall!" cried the child, remembering her smallpox vaccination.

"Now, now, Florrie. Don't fuss so. Let's take you back to bed. I don't think Dr Jukes will hurt you this time. He will make you feel better. On your way now," said Henrietta, taking her small daughter's hand in hers.

❦ ❦ ❦

There was no telling whether the doctor would be out on another house call at this time of day. Patrick took the horse and sleigh down and fetched him from his home in St Paul Street.

"Open your mouth, Florence. I want to look in it," ordered Dr Augustus Jukes sternly.

"Owww, my throat hurts," whined Florrie, once she was seated in the windowsill where there was better light.

"I know, my dear. But I need to see what your throat looks like. Show me your tongue."

The tiny girl obeyed, revealing a white-coated tongue covered with small red dots.

"I need to look at her chest and back, Mrs Burns. Will you please remove her shift?"

After he finished his examination, he was certain of his diagnosis: scarlatina, a contagious childhood disease that was making the rounds of the town. She had the fever, swollen neck glands, sore throat, coated strawberry tongue, and red rash covering her face and neck. Soon it would spread to her chest and back and itch like all get out. *Poor thing,* he thought. *I hope she survives it. So many children do not. It spreads through an entire family so rapidly.*

"Send your man with this note to the chemist, either Mr Mills or Boyle in St Paul Street. He will make a poultice to alleviate the itching that will come over her soon. You can put some oatmeal in her bath too. The chemist will also prepare something to help with any nausea she may have. Don't force her to eat if she vomits. Keep her separate from the others, Mrs Burns, and let me know if any of the others fall ill."

"Of course, Doctor. Thank you for coming."

"You're very welcome, Mrs Burns. I'm sorry she is so ill. Keep her quiet in bed with the draperies closed. She might be sensitive to the light. Let her rest, and feed her lightly if she's hungry. Broth and the like."

"I shall do all that you say. Let me see you out, Dr Jukes."

❦ ❦ ❦

Florrie suffered with the itching and discomfort of scarlet fever for a fortnight. She seemed to be getting better, when one night she awoke and went to her mother's bedside, complaining that her hips hurt. The discomfort seemed to move from joint to joint over the next few days. She developed a fever again and cried out from the pain in her chest when she breathed. Despite being only five years old, she had no energy and was unable to get out of bed by herself to use the chamber pot.

❦ ❦ ❦

Julia and her infant stayed prudently away from the household while Florrie was ill. She would never take such a chance with her first-born. William would have never forgiven her after they had worried so over little George. She sent cheery notes to Florrie on a daily basis and drew funny pictures to amuse the girl. Julia would have to wait until the crisis was over before they could risk a visit to her parents' home.

Florrie's terrible illness served to bring Emma back from her sadness; it provided her an opportunity to help heal her little sister. She and Bella took turns with their mother caring for the child, Emma taking the overnight hours so that Mrs Burns could sleep. Emma remembered nights spent with Nurse McIntire at St Mary's Hall when she tenderly cared for her while ill with a bout of *cholera morbus*. Emma thought the young Irish woman always looked smart wearing a long white apron over her crisp blue and white gingham dress.

After Florrie rallied, Emma briefly considered becoming a nurse herself at the new hospital being planned in St Catharines, but she knew her parents would never approve. Well-bred young ladies, daughters of barristers, were not meant for that kind of hard work. She would have to find something else to do with her life.

CHAPTER 36

At Last a Student

WEDNESDAY, 5 OCTOBER 1864, GENEVA, NEW YORK

Once again, the enrolment of the first year class of the Medical Department of Hobart Free College was less than the year prior, likely a consequence of the ongoing War of the Rebellion and the effect of a competing medical school in Buffalo. The men had heard there would be a woman joining them, and they were curious as to what she would be like. On the first morning of lectures, they mingled in the gas-lit lecture hall and watched as a petite, red-haired woman demurely descended the steps, looking straight ahead. She took a seat in the empty first row directly in front of the professor's dais, doffed her bonnet, and put it on the floor beneath her. She took off her gloves and stuffed them into her reticule. She waited.

Mr Bliss, the anatomy assistant, arranged the students alphabetically across the first row so that absences could be easily noted. Margaret Jane remained in her seat and was soon flanked by Peter Keiser and Lorenzo Phinney. The assistant then issued each student a long, white canvas apron. It barely covered Margaret Jane's full skirt, although she had put on only one flannel skirt underneath for modesty's sake. After the instructional session was over, the students politely introduced themselves to her, but Margaret Jane walked alone as she followed them out of the building.

The assistant led them across the street to the gross anatomy building, a small structure dubbed the "dead house". It was warm inside and reeked of putrefaction, despite the windows' being left open for ventilation on this early fall day. Many of the neophytes had to turn away at the sight of the three male corpses lying supine on long tables. Trays of medical instruments sat beside them, ready for use.

Margaret Jane, overcome by the unexpected odour and the sights, darted outside and found a bush behind which she promptly vomited. She had seen dead and dying people before with John, but not in such an impersonal setting. She wiped her mouth on the scratchy hem of the apron, wishing she had a tooth brush handy. A few deep breaths later, she returned to the laboratory, composed.

"The Lady Bird is back! Feeling better now, dearie?" jeered Mr Matthews, one of the youngest future physicians. His friend, Mr Williams, leaned into him and joined in a hearty guffaw.

Peter Keiser gave Margaret Jane a sympathetic look. She held her head high, grimaced, and said nothing. *Best not to start anything with this lot,* she thought.

The anatomy assistant pretended not to hear or see anything as he drew lots to divide the student doctors into three groups. Margaret Jane was relieved not to be assigned with the two immature youngsters. Her partners in the laboratory, aside from Peter, were already engaged to be married and showed her the respect they would have given their fiancées. Peter was the first in the group to dare befriend Margaret Jane McFarland.

❦ ❦ ❦

That first evening, seated at a small desk in her rented room, she rewrote her class notes and read the first hundred pages of the anatomy textbook with relish, trying to memorise all she could. As she turned out the gaslight and closed her eyes, she at last remembered that to-day was Lizzie Fuller's wedding in Toronto.

❦ ❦ ❦

WEDNESDAY, 2 NOVEMBER 1864

The young woman struggled on tiptoe to see the paper posted on the wall beside the lecture hall door; she was much shorter than the men crowding in front of her. Everyone was trying to see the marks for the first comprehensive examinations. Groans and sighs of disappointment along with chuckles of satisfaction were heard.

Then one student let out a shout, "Why, that little Canuck witch!"

Margaret Jane McFarland's name was at the top of the list, first in her class overall. Anatomy, Chemistry, Materia Medica, Pharmacy, Physiology, and Pathology. Six different professors had recognised her excellence.

Peter defended her. "Hey, there, Matthews! Miss McFarland earned her marks honestly. I know it. I've been studying with her regularly. I demand you apologise now, or we shall meet outside."

Lew Watson, another anatomy partner and the oldest man in the class at twenty-eight, moved to stand beside Peter to emphasise his support. Daniel Hennessey, the fourth member of her anatomy group, took a position, blocking Matthews' escape via the front door. William Beach, the only married man in the class, faced him, followed by the remaining students. Young Matthews saw they meant business. He turned to Margaret Jane, chastened. "Miss McFarland, I admit fervour. Please excuse my outburst. I congratulate you on your industry."

❦ ❦ ❦

The next morning in the Materia Medica lecture room, Margaret Jane reached her assigned seat in the third row centre. On it she found a cadaver's male part. Her face turned bright red as she considered her response to this latest affront. Apparently Matthews' apology yesterday was hollow. Determined to show their disdain for her once again, the two perpetrators in the room were unable to contain their glee and gave themselves away.

The anatomy professor, Dr Hiram Eastman, demanded to know the nature of the commotion in his classroom. Margaret Jane glared at the two eighteen-year-olds, not knowing what to do or say. Lorenzo Phinney calmly picked up the organ and asked if one of them were missing something. The rest of the men, now her allies, erupted in laughter.

Dr Eastman was not amused, as his lesson on the sanctity of the human body, albeit that of executed unclaimed murderers, had obviously been lost on the young culprits. He sent them both to the dean's office, and their seats remained empty for the rest of term.

❦ ❦ ❦

WEDNESDAY, 21 DECEMBER 1864

It had been another taxing day for Margaret Jane. After a quick breakfast alone in the third floor room she rented from the Fitch family, she attended three hours of lecture on chemistry, including demonstrations. She took copious notes to study later as Dr Hadley and his assistant performed the experiments in front of the class. The young medical student ate her dinner at one o'clock with the Fitches before three more hours of lecture, this time on physiology and pathology. After supper there had been the usual evening demonstration of gross anatomy and dissection in the awful, foul-smelling "dead-house". She wouldn't have had any appetite all day had it been scheduled earlier.

Margaret Jane trudged back to the house through a foot of fresh snow with more falling. In the chilly third-floor room, she started a fire in the little airtight stove with some kindling and a few lumps of coal brought upstairs by young Johnny Fitch. Huddled in front of the stove, she spent an hour reviewing her notes from Dr Nivison's physiology lecture. It would be so much more efficient and enjoyable to study late at night together with her colleagues, but the men lived in different boarding houses scattered all over Geneva and the lake effect snow was piling up in the town, making movement difficult.

Though once determined to read from her chemistry textbook, Margaret Jane fell into bed, exhausted, in the now warmed third floor room. Only the camaraderie and support of her close friends—Peter, Daniel, and Lew—made it all bearable: the weather, the hours of study, the dissections, and the separation from her family. She was looking forward to Friday when she would go home to Port Robinson for Christmas week.

❦ ❦ ❦

TUESDAY, 3 JANUARY 1865

Margaret Jane knocked on the door of the dean's office in the Middle Building. She wondered why she had been called there on her first day back in Geneva.

Dr John Towler bade her enter the room; she was surprised to see Professor Eastman there too. She gave them each a brief curtsy and then sat in the chair Dr Towler indicated in front of his desk.

"Good morning, Miss McFarland. I welcome you back to the College. I want to begin by saying you have done excellent work for this past term. Dr Eastman and I both congratulate you. However, we've encountered a problem placing you for practical experience. None of the physicians in western New York have agreed to take you on for training. Even here in Geneva, the ladies we asked seem to prefer a gentleman doctor. 'Tis a new experience for them. I know you can appreciate the difficulty we face."

Margaret Jane looked down at her folded hands in her lap, trying to think what to say.

"But sir, Dr Blackwell goes before me. How did *she* achieve any direct experience?"

"Fifteen years ago, Miss McFarland, she faced difficulties here too. She spent some months working at Blockley, in Philadelphia."

"Philadelphia? But what am I to do, sir? I'd rather not go to Philadelphia."

"I've an idea, and I hope you will agree."

"And what is that, Dr Towler?"

❦ ❦ ❦

FEBRUARY 1865, PORT ROBINSON

Margaret Jane returned to Canada as soon as she completed

311

her first sixteen weeks of medical school in January; there would be no more classes in Geneva until October. When Dr Towler was unable to find a placement for her near Geneva, he wrote her brother. John agreed to take her on again, apparently having found her helpful when she went with him on calls. Margaret Jane was disappointed; she wanted to see and learn something different and challenging. A larger problem was her mother's expectation that she be there to help her. Once home, Margaret Jane immediately had to establish that she was returning primarily to continue her medical training, but as a member of the household, Margaret Jane felt a responsibility to help the family in some way. Maria and Frances, the two house servants, were fully occupied with the housekeeping and cooking. Agnes was busy with her four children, including little Gertie, and she was expecting another baby in the spring.

At length the three McFarland women agreed Margaret Jane would begin every day with some housework and get Freddie off to the Common School. John proposed to have her see patients with him in his office in the afternoons and accompany him on any night calls.

❦ ❦ ❦

After just three weeks of the established routine, Margaret Jane was frustrated. It seemed she was spending more time caring for her nephews and niece than she was working with John. She welcomed mornings when she woke early and could read his books alone in her room. He had recently got a new one, *Gray's Anatomy*, filled with excellent illustrations of every part of the body. Except in the evenings after the children were in bed, she had no time to herself. If she went out on a call with John, their sleep was interrupted, and they would both be cross the next day. Margaret Jane knew that when the growing season arrived, she would have to keep up an even more demanding schedule of garden work in addition to being with the children and keeping her hours with John in his consulting room. Then when Agnes gave birth, there would be even more responsibility thrust upon her.

❦ ❦ ❦

1 *March 1865*
Port Robinson, Canada West

Dear Dr Blackwell,

I hope this letter finds you and your colleagues well. I write to-day to ask your help in providing me with practical experience in medicine. I have completed the first sixteen-week course of lectures in the medical department at Hobart Free College, Geneva, under the direction of Dr Towler, earning excellent marks. Unable to find a position for me in the environs, Dr Towler arranged for me to work again with my brother, Dr John Cameron McFarland, M.D., here in Port Robinson. I am grateful to my brother, but I have already worked beside him for more than three years whilst at grammar school and thereafter. I would like to have experience in New York City. I sincerely hope that you will accept me to work with you and your staff for a period of not more than six months. My second course of lectures in Geneva begins 1 October. Of course I seek no compensation other than gaining knowledge and having the privilege of working with you at the infirmary.

Thank you for your kind consideration. I genuinely hope I can be of use to you and the patients of your clinic.

Very sincerely yours,
Margaret Jane McFarland

❧ ❧ ❧

MONDAY, 17 APRIL 1865

The air was cold, despite the brilliant sunshine that made the snow sparkle like diamonds. Yesterday's spring storm had dropped another foot of heavy, wet snow over the Niagara Peninsula. Margaret Jane came back into the house from harnessing the big horse to the sled, helped her niece Aggie bundle up in her hooded cloak and gaiters, and took her outside. Aggie took her place on the seat, shoved her little hands into the rabbit fur muff as Margaret Jane covered her limbs with a piece of buffalo hide.

The coarse, curly brown hairs kept the little girl well insulated on these excursions. Then, feet wide apart for balance, Margaret Jane stood in front of the tyke and got the horse going with a loud click of her tongue. The horse trudged through the snow, dragging Margaret Jane and the five-year-old down South Street to the Port Robinson General Store. Margaret Jane was anxious to see what was in the post to-day. She hadn't checked since Wednesday.

Andrew Murray was finishing up with a customer when Margaret Jane and Aggie walked into the dark, cramped little store. It held every possible dry good needed to live in a village like Port Robinson. Aggie immediately went to look at the tempting colourful candies behind the glass-front counter.

"Good morning, Miss McFarland. What can I do for you today? 'Morning, little Aggie."

"Good morning, Mr Murray," Margaret Jane greeted. "Well, first off, please, we are here for a half-pound of coffee beans, a packet of tea, a sack of sugar, and a tin of baking soda, but *I* am looking for a letter to myself, Mr Murray. From the States."

"The States, eh? Well, there is *news* from the States. I've just read in the Toronto newspaper that Mr Lincoln was shot and has died."

"Shot! The president? Oh, my! How terrible! What happened?"

"Don't know much beyond that, Miss. I expect the police are looking into it down there in Washington where it happened."

"In Washington, eh? What will happen to their government now?"

"No idea, Miss. I do no' know how all that works down there."

"In any case, is there a letter for me, Mr Murray?"

"Let me see ..." He shuffled through a stack and looked in the family's box above his head. "Here you go, and a few others for your brother and father."

Margaret Jane accepted the bundle and found the one letter addressed to her. She tore it open and read it quickly. It was short and to the point. She took her charge by the hand and ran out the door into the sunshine. Aggie wailed about getting a candy, but they were away before Mr Murray had their purchases collected.

❦ ❦ ❦

MONDAY, 1 MAY 1865, NEW YORK CITY

As the train sped along at over thirty miles an hour, Margaret Jane McFarland admired the varying shades of light green displayed by tender new leaves fluttering on the trees that lined either side of the railway tracks. She was travelling east this time on the New York Central Rail Road, in part following the course of the old Erie Canal. It was a route different from the one she had used years ago to reach New Jersey from her home. Past Syracuse and Utica, the cars went on to Albany, the state capital. She crossed the Hudson River to Greenbush, site of her grandfather's imprisonment in 1813, and boarded the Hudson River Rail Road, owned by magnate Cornelius Vanderbilt. The tracks traced the picturesque Hudson, at times coming closer than a mile. The locomotives could go faster now, and after just a two-day trip, she disembarked the car in the largest city on the continent. The train came right down the middle of Eleventh Avenue, scattering horses and people in its path, and stopped at the uptown station.

Following directions in Dr Blackwell's letter, she rode a horse car from Thirty-Second Street over to Broadway and took another south to Fourteenth Street. The car stopped to discharge its passengers in front of the huge six-storey Fifth Avenue Hotel. Margaret Jane gasped; it was the tallest building she had ever seen. Across the street she glimpsed Madison Square Park with its two beautiful fountains. Trees offered shade to well-dressed people promenading its walkways on a beautiful spring day. *Some of them no doubt live in those elegant brownstone houses facing the park*, she mused.

A third car brought Margaret Jane along Eighth Street to 126 Second Avenue. She got out with her two valises and paid the driver. Then she turned and climbed the eight steep steps to enter the clinic for indigent women and children established by the Blackwell sisters and their partner, Dr Maria Zakrzewska.

A young raven-haired woman with small dark eyes greeted her and bade her sit in the waiting area on one of the tapestry-covered settees. Fifteen minutes later, tiny Dr Elizabeth Blackwell came out of the examining room with her last patient of the day.

The formerly blonde, now greying, middle-aged doctor had deep-set blue eyes, though one was a prosthetic made of glass. The left eye had been removed after an infection years ago in Paris. She wore a waist and skirt of plain charcoal cotton goods and over them, a white doctorial sack that buttoned in front.

Dr Blackwell shook Margaret Jane's hand, smiled, and said, "Miss McFarland, I'm happy to have you with us for these few months. You've come highly recommended by your professors. Our infirmary is small, but we stay very busy in the clinic. We have thousands of visits every year now. We welcome your help."

"Doctor Blackwell, I'm very grateful that you're allowing me to work here. I intend to be helpful in any way possible. I only wish I could stay to study with you."

"You might know we have applied to open a medical school, along with our usual nurse training."

"Yes, I heard that. It's so exciting! Those ladies will be very lucky to learn from you."

The doctor showed Margaret Jane into the examining room and closed the door behind her. After an hour's discourse on her basic hygiene principles for the infirmary and clinic, Dr Blackwell said, "Miss Barry will help you take your valises upstairs and show you your bed. You will accompany the resident physician on ward rounds. They're on the second floor. She'll show you the delivery room and nursery as well as the operating room on the third floor."

"Right now? This afternoon?" Margaret Jane had eaten her dinner hours ago up in Greenbush and was already hungry again. She wished she had been less anxious to reach the infirmary.

"Oh, yes, Miss. Straightaway. Tea is at seven. I will see you then."

❦ ❦ ❦

Margaret Jane soon adjusted to the Spartan accommodations of the New York Infirmary, reminiscent of her school days at St Mary's Hall. She shared the garret with three other interns and took her meals with them and the Blackwell sisters in the basement.

After seven days of long hours seeing patients in the clinic with Dr Elizabeth, Margaret Jane was given some free time. She decided to explore the first neighbourhood where the infirmary was started in the old Roosevelt house at 64 Bleecker Street, near Seventh Street. She quickly determined this part of New York with its tenements was crowded, dirty, and smelly. No wonder Dr Blackwell insisted on teaching clients good hygiene. People were teeming everywhere. Some soldiers, returning from the recently ended War Between the States, were still in uniform. Others were immigrants from Europe who had just arrived in the steamers sitting at the docks of both rivers flanking the island of Manhattan.

Later that day, she walked down to the oldest part of the city, where businessmen rushed to and fro. Shops, restaurants, taverns, boarding houses, and hotels stood on each block. Young boys hawked newspapers on every corner. Headlines still screamed about the paddlewheel steamboat SS *Sultana* that exploded ten days ago on the Mississippi River, killing more than a thousand returning Union prisoners of war. According to one journal, the new president, Andrew Johnson, after being Mr Lincoln's vice-president for a mere three weeks, was taking the reins of government seriously now despite some initial missteps. Johnson was trained as a tailor, and otherwise not formally schooled. Wags hoped he would call up his executive experience as governor of Tennessee and be an effective president. The country was facing many challenges after losing President Lincoln to an assassin's bullet. Americans were still reeling from the shock.

❦ ❦ ❦

FRIDAY, 29 SEPTEMBER 1865, GENEVA, NEW YORK

Margaret Jane was anxious to begin her second and last term as a medical student. After five months' work in New York with the dedicated and inspiring women doctors, she was even more committed to becoming a physician, no matter the obstacles she encountered. Of course, she was grateful to her brother, who allowed her to observe and assist him all those years; she had learned much from John and his rural practise. It was this experience that had ensured her acceptance to the Medical Department at Hobart. She had helped women in labour, watched old

317

people die, as well as learned how to set broken limbs and bind all kinds of traumatic wounds that farmers and their families suffered. However, he had always refused to let his sister treat his patients directly. For example, John had never permitted her to suture, though she had seen him do it many times. Once when one of their piglets gashed itself, he let her do the honours with catgut. She was impressed by how much pressure was required to push the needle through its skin, and she was proud and happy to see the squirming little animal heal so quickly.

Margaret Jane had learned even more during her summer in New York City, diagnosing illnesses with Dr Elizabeth Blackwell, assisting Dr Emily Blackwell in surgery, and following the resident physician on her rounds. She had seen new and important practises in medicine there, such as washing patients, signing prescriptions, and keeping thorough records. In the tenements, she had witnessed the ravages of smallpox, cholera, and phthysis among the immigrant population. After much deliberation, Margaret Jane chose cholera as the subject of her required thesis because her older sisters had died from it as young children. She would have to be even more disciplined this autumn, so as to have enough time to research and write at night. She had kept copious clinical notes whilst in New York City and would incorporate her experiences in the paper.

She finished putting away her things in the familiar little room on the third floor of the Fitch home and stirred up the fire in the airtight. Hobart students had already begun lectures, but the medical students had three more days of free time before their term started. Margaret Jane and her good friend Peter made plans to spend as much of it together as possible before the first day of lectures. They took picnics to the countryside and walked the bluff overlooking Geneva's shining Seneca Lake, discussing their summer exploits and sharing their dreams for the future.

❧ ❧ ❧

TUESDAY, 3 OCTOBER 1865

Using a cane and walking with a limp, John Alonzo Northup arrived late and took his seat beside Margaret Jane in the lecture hall. The soft-spoken Union army veteran greeted her and nodded to Peter sitting next to her. Northup put his cane on the floor in front of them as a second new member of the class of 1866, Horace Montreville Moody, took his place beside him.

The lecture began with Dr Frederick Hyde's rapid-fire delivery of his important principles of surgery. Margaret Jane's pen sped across the page, dipping periodically in her ink bottle. The two men couldn't keep up with Dr Hyde or match her practised scribbling. When Dr Hyde dismissed the class, they introduced themselves and asked to copy her notes straightaway while the information was fresh in everyone's mind. Peter joined the trio, and together they walked outside into the crisp fall air and sunshine. As they made their way to the library, Horace told how he had interrupted his medical studies in Ann Arbor, Michigan to enlist in the Union army. He was assigned to serve as an assistant surgeon with the rank of lieutenant. John, a former sergeant, became a hospital steward after being wounded. The two met when they both served at the Union army hospital set up on the grounds of the United States Naval Academy in Annapolis. After he was mustered out, John took Horace's advice and studied in Michigan for a year, but he missed his family in New York, and determined to study there instead. Both friends were then accepted at Hobart, and were now studying together.

In the weeks following, the four students got to know each other well. Margaret Jane often recalled her struggle to get an education after she left St Mary's Hall and her fulfilling but exhausting months working in New York City. She and Peter listened as Horace and John recounted their painful war experiences. Horace admitted his fears when required to perform as an assistant surgeon after only one year of medical study. John told them how he came to value the nursing skills of women on and off the battlefield. He was honest about how frightened of amputation he was when he took a ball to the calf at Gettysburg on 2 July 1863. He was lucky; there were two well-trained nurses there who kept his wound from being infected. It was the horrific battlefield deaths, injuries and hasty surgeries he witnessed that made him decide to become a physician.

❧ ❧ ❧

TUESDAY, 23 JANUARY 1866, GENEVA, NEW YORK

After eight months of sixteen-hour days poring over books and studying cadavers, helping her brother care for their neighbours in Port Robinson and the surrounding townships, plus her affirming experiences in New York City, Margaret Jane McFarland proudly took her medical diploma in a dignified ceremony in the Presbyterian church. The only woman in her class of twelve, she claimed the highest honours after oral examinations by the faculty and witnessed by the curators of the college. At the graduation ceremony, the president of the college, the Reverend Dr Abner Jackson, M.D., congratulated her for her accomplishments, and recognising her skill as a diagnostician, handed her a roll of parchment tied with blue ribbon. It was beautifully hand-written instead of engraved in Latin, with the title *Domina* Margaret Jane McFarland. After his remarks, Dr McFarland delivered her thesis on cholera in children. Her classmates applauded led by her three good friends: now Doctors Keiser, Moody, and Northup.

Only one person from her family attended the rite. When John wrote that he was coming, she was not just surprised, but honoured. It showed he unequivocally accepted her choice of vocation, despite the strong resistance he had once offered. He had at first belittled the robust education offered at St Mary's Hall, suggesting it put ideas in her head. Now the two siblings were colleagues; they discussed issues as equals. They shared the same knowledge and desire to help people who needed care. In their months of work together she had proven herself. Her fellow medical graduates sang her praises to John that day, and he was proud of his little sister, Maggie.

Margaret Jane McFarland, M.D., returned to Canada with a new identity. At the tender age of twenty-three, she was a "woman doctor" in the United States, but as a foreign medical graduate, as well as a woman, she could not be licenced as a physician in Canada. Instead, she was going home to be her brother's assistant again, until attitudes and regulations changed.

CHAPTER 37

A Mission in Toronto

SATURDAY, 1 DECEMBER 1866

"Margaret Jane?"

"Yes, sir."

"It is I, Willy Fuller. I am here to fetch you home."

Margaret Jane failed to recognise Willy Fuller. He was now twenty-one, and a handsome, dark-haired young man with green eyes stood before her, top hat in hand. His side whiskers were long in the current style, and he wore a well-tailored suit and vest under a woolen coat trimmed with a beaver collar and cuffs.

"Willy! Oh, my. It can't be. It's been so many years! You were just a lad the last time I saw you in Thorold."

"Well, yes, Margaret Jane. I was away at school for a good many years here in Toronto. One changes after so much schooling, am I correct?" He picked up her suitcase. "Is this your only grip?"

"No, I have a larger one in the baggage car. It's tagged and should be delivered later to the rectory."

"Very well, then. Shall we be off? I left the buggy just there in Front Street. Mind your step," he said, as they left the shelter of the grand new station.

321

From the Great Western Railway station, it was a short ride up Yonge Street to Queen. There Willy followed the horse-drawn streetcar route and drove by elegant Osgoode Hall, the pillared home of the Law Society. Willy pointed out the 150-foot spire of St George-the-Martyr Church before they passed St Patrick's Market. The horse knew to turn right into Renfrew Street and then left into a lane leading to the rectory. They stopped at the front door that faced the north wall of St George-the-Martyr Church, a mere fifty feet away.

Willy tied the horse and buggy to the hitching post and helped Margaret Jane down. The young man led her up the front steps of the brick house and opened the front door. As she passed by him, her hoop skirt fit easily through the wide doorway. *Since the house was finished recently, it must have been designed with hoop skirt fashions in mind!* she thought.

When he heard the horse whinny outside, ten-year-old Henry came bounding down the front stairs into the vestibule, calling for his mother. He was excited to have a visitor. As the youngest in the household, he was accustomed to the constant adult company of his sister Laura, brothers and parents, and the boy always welcomed a new face. He was the pet of the lady members of the congregation.

"Margaret Jane!" he exclaimed, as he impulsively put his arms round the young woman's waist.

"Henry, is that you? You're such a grown-up boy now," said Margaret Jane. He was only five when they removed from Thorold to Toronto, and Margaret Jane hadn't seen him since. He was quite tall for his age and had long dark curls and blue eyes. *Definitely a charming Irishman like his papa,* she thought.

Willy said gruffly, "Henry, mind your manners! You know better than that!"

Henry let go of Margaret Jane and solemnly bowed at the waist. Margaret Jane curtseyed in return, stifling a laugh. She felt more a sister to the lad than a visitor.

Mrs Fuller appeared and embraced Margaret Jane warmly. She had welcomed her as a fourth daughter when she lived with the Fullers at Beechlands during her grammar school years with Lizzie. Mrs Fuller led her upstairs to the guestroom, and they chatted like old friends. She was very much interested in how

Margaret Jane was working with her brother's medical practise and asked her several questions related to her own health. Margaret Jane, feeling awkward, demurred.

A few minutes later, Laura wandered into the room and took Margaret Jane by the hand. "It's so wonderful to see you again, Margaret Jane. Lizzie has told me all sorts of stories about you and your experiences," said Laura.

"Has she? I hope they were good ones! Laurie, you haven't changed at all. Look at you. How do you like teaching right next door to your home?"

"Oh, it was definitely a change from having a classroom of fifty children at the Common School in Thorold. However, I am no longer next door. I enjoyed St George's for the first year, but then I took a position at Mrs Forster's School as music instructor. Unfortunately, she's just closed it, and I'm at home now and giving piano lessons to children. But a group of clergy plans to begin an Episcopal school for girls at her house at Pinehurst, to be very much like St Mary's Hall. I'm hopeful to teach there when it opens."

"I pray it comes to pass for you, Laurie. Lizzie hadn't told me that bit of news. I think she is pre-occupied right now. Do you agree?"

"Yes, I quite agree!" said Laura.

❦ ❦ ❦

SUNDAY, 2 DECEMBER 1866

Margaret Jane awoke naturally before nine o'clock that morning. She dressed in her best Sunday clothes with the help of the Fullers' ladies' maid who worked a half-day on Sundays. She donned a new woolen frock, ordered especially for this important visit to Toronto. It was a print, in white and Waterloo Blue, with a deep yoke and long sleeves that buttoned over her wrists and featured a moderately wide hoop skirt trimmed with a black band encircling the hem.

Downstairs in the dining room, she enjoyed a full Sunday breakfast with Mrs Fuller, Laura, and three of the four Fuller sons still living at home: Willy, Val, and Henry. Shelly, fourteen, was next door at the church with his father, both having break-fasted earlier, preparing for the Sunday services. Margaret Jane felt a bit embarrassed by her not attending her hosts' church, but the Fullers knew very well, after all these years of friendship, that her family and she were Presbyterians. According to the conversation at breakfast, to-day was the first Sunday in Advent. She remembered how Advent was observed by the pupils at St Mary's Hall in anticipation of Christmas. It would have been a nostalgic experience for her to attend the Anglican service, but her Presbyterianism was stronger now. She had attended services regularly at Geneva, drawing needed strength for her studies. Since her return to Port Robinson, she had gone to the little Presbyterian church there whenever she was free. Her church attendance came second, after the needs of patients.

After the meal, Margaret Jane put on her fitted grey wool coat trimmed in red fox fur, grey kid gloves, and her warmest bonnet, of sheared beaver, to counter the freezing December temperature. She wore her most comfortable walking boots, and in a little tapestry bag were her good black kid slippers to wear indoors. For extra warmth, she had brought her velvet muff, but she stuffed it in the bag to use later.

Yesterday at tea, she had reluctantly accepted Mr Fuller's kind offer to be driven to the Knox Presbyterian Church in Queen Street West this morning. She was already grateful for the Fullers' offer of a room at the rectory while she was in the city, but she didn't want to wear out her welcome. The independent young physician from Port Robinson would have gladly paid a sixpence for an omnibus ride to-day, something not available in her village. But it was Sunday, and the Lord's Day rules forbade public transportation. In summer or autumn, she would have been willing to walk—Lizzie lived only a mile or so from the church—but Toronto's dirty streets would have ruined her new dress. And the risk of her slipping on ice and falling on the plank sidewalks was real to-day, not to mention encountering unsavoury characters recovering from a Saturday night overindulgence. Navigating a city like Toronto unchaperoned was unwise for a young lady.

Margaret Jane would be dining to-day with Lizzie and her husband James McMurray. When pressed, she agreed to have the Fullers' carriage and driver wait at the church to take her on to Lizzie's home. She appreciated the Fullers' love and hospitality. They were a second family to her.

After the service ended, the driver took her west again into Queen Street, dodging puddles in the rutted street as best he could. Margaret Jane recognised yesterday's landmarks of Osgoode Hall and St Patrick's Market before the carriage turned south into John Street toward the freezing lake. At Front Street, the driver made a right turn and then quickly another, stopping in front of Lizzie's modest brick, semi-detached house. Number twenty Windsor Street, a three-bay, side hall design, was on a large corner lot with a mews behind it. The young couple lived in one of the first residential sections built in old York near the original Parliament buildings overlooking Toronto Bay.

As she had arrived well before the appointed meal time, there would be plenty of opportunity to catch up with her old school friend. They corresponded regularly, but it had been six months since she had last seen Lizzie and James, when they crossed the lake to visit his family in Niagara and Mary Margaret's in Chippewa. Lizzie was now expecting their first child, and Margaret Jane was anxious to see her friend in her present delicate condition. Lizzie was always such an active girl, and Margaret Jane found it hard to imagine how she would cope with her confinement.

Margaret Jane knocked on the front door after thanking and dismissing the coachman. Presently, Catherine Vance, one of Lizzie's three servants, opened the door, took her calling card, and invited the guest into the vestibule. Cat laid the card on a silver salver and took it to her mistress. A minute later the maid returned to the vestibule, took Margaret Jane's wrap, and showed her to the parlour, where James and Lizzie were waiting. Lizzie read the visiting card aloud this time, "Margaret Jane McFarland, M.D., Port Robinson".

"How formal you are, Doctor McFarland!" said Lizzie, as she stood to greet her dear friend, holding out both arms. They embraced, and then Margaret Jane stood back to look at Lizzie in her maternity dress. "You look wonderful, Lizzie! So healthy and happy!"

"I haven't been able to get her to rest much, Margaret Jane. Don't you think she needs to rest?" asked James, voicing the concern of a first-time father.

"Oh, I think she'll rest when she needs to, James. Right now, she should be full of energy, getting things ready for the baby."

"I am. I've collected all the things in the nursery in case Baby comes sooner than we expect. What do you think, Margaret Jane?" asked the tall mother-to-be, as she twirled around in her lightly fitted, plaid woolen dress. "I tell you, I haven't been cold these last three months!"

"That will happen. You're slim and trim as ever, my friend. Please do show me the nursery before dinner, though," Margaret Jane insisted. "When James' friend arrives, I doubt we'll be allowed to talk about babies."

"His name is Warren," reminded James with a wink. "I'll see you for dinner, ladies. I have some work to do before he arrives. You two enjoy yourselves."

"Of course, you're right. We shall have to talk about other things when we're with the menfolk! Follow me this way upstairs," said Lizzie.

❦ ❦ ❦

Promptly at one o'clock, Cat Vance answered another knock at the front door. The gentleman took out a card from its engraved silver case and placed it on the tray Cat offered. The maid hung the caller's hat and coat on the carved oak hall stand before escorting him into the parlour.

"Mr Rock, please be seated. Mr McMurray is in his study. I shall tell him you are here. The ladies are still upstairs," she said.

❦ ❦ ❦

"I hope you like him, Margaret Jane!" whispered Lizzie, as she closed the nursery door. She led the way, carefully descending the steep and narrow front stairs.

The two friends entered the parlour, and both gentlemen stood up. Warren bowed.

James made the introductions and offered each a sherry. Margaret Jane took the delicate crystal glass from him and sat on the settee beside Lizzie.

Warren started the conversation. "James tells me you came in the Fullers' carriage here this afternoon. I hope you'll let me drive you back in my buggy. It's not much to look at, but it will be getting dark when we leave."

"That's very kind of you, Mr Rock. I do appreciate the offer, but I'm not afraid to walk back to the rectory. I'm sure it's less than a mile."

"James, tell her she must go home with Warren," said Lizzie to her husband. "It's not safe for her to walk alone that distance. It's not Thorold Township. It just isn't done. And 'twill be too cold and dark. After all, it's December. You'd ruin your beautiful clothes, dear one. You can be *too* brave," remarked Lizzie, who recognised her friend's *naïveté*, as well as her new investment in fashion.

"Yes, we insist. Warren is perfectly respectable, Margaret Jane," agreed James with a grin.

"Do say yes, Miss McFarland," said Warren, flashing earnest blue eyes.

"Oh, my. I didn't think Toronto was so dangerous, but you are right. It is cold to-day, and the sky looks like it might snow," said Margaret Jane.

"Well, then, that is settled. My mind is relieved," said Warren. "Tell me about your work."

"I was going to ask you the same thing, Mr Rock."

"Please, call me Warren. We are friends of friends, after all."

"Yes, you are," said James with a smile.

They both started to talk at the same time. Margaret Jane blushed, and Warren said, "Go ahead, you first."

"Oh, my life is not very interesting. I work with my brother John in Port Robinson. We are physicians together. We go out to visit patients any time of day. Some are young, some old. Some dying, some having babies. Every day is different."

"I so admire physicians. You are obviously brave, to do all those treatments ... I guess by comparison, my life is boring. Papers. Always papers and the occasional day in court."

"Well, we both have students with us now, though," said James. "That adds a new dimension to our work. Training the next barristers."

"That's true. It's both a burden and an asset, as my Mr Adams has been quite helpful of late, copying work and delivering it to clients around the city. Who's apprenticed to you, James?" asked Warren.

"Charles Corbould. Fine chap. He'll make a good barrister one day, but he's just starting out. He's barely twenty."

"Ah, yes. That is young. He must have money! I was still teaching at that age," said Warren.

"Teaching? Where?" asked Margaret Jane.

"In Pelham."

"Pelham! I grew up in Port Robinson."

"Yes, I know. Elizabeth told me."

"Of course, she would have! How did you like teaching then?"

"Well, I'm a barrister now, aren't I?" Warren said with a grin. "Truly, I wasn't good at it. I was only there to save money for the fees at the Law Society."

"Oh, my, Mr Rock, I did the same thing! I took Mary Margaret's position, Lizzie's sister, at the Common School when she married. I taught there in Thorold for a few years, but I always knew I didn't want to be a teacher. Some days I had too many children in the building. Other days the place was half empty, especially if the weather was fine and the boys were needed in the fields. It was so frustrating. I had the feeling that most of the children didn't want to be there either."

"Yes, I remember days like that too. Schooling was very much optional in Pelham. One d—"

"So when did you come up to Toronto, Warren?" Lizzie interrupted.

"Toronto? Oh, I guess it was in fifty-six, nearly ten years ago now. I had to attend classes and lectures at Osgoode."

"Osgoode Hall? The Law Society?" Margaret Jane asked. "Willy pointed that out to me yesterday on the way from the station. What a lovely big building it is! Did you board there too?"

"Why, yes, while I was studying in town. Then I found the Burrell family had some rooms to let. It was a much more comfortable arrangement for me." He paused, wondering how to ask Margaret Jane the burning question in his mind. He decided to blurt it out plainly.

"How did you come to be a physician, Margaret Jane? You are a *rara avis*."

"Ah, a Latin scholar! That is truly a long and dull story that I am sure you wouldn't want to hear, Mr Rock," said Margaret Jane.

"Warren," he corrected. "I won't fall asleep listening, I promise."

"Well, Warren, I'll try to keep it short in any case. As a child I loved to read, but I got rather bored my last years at the Common School. My parents sent me away to study in New Jersey with Lizzie, where we made some wonderful friends. Unfortunately, I was there less than a year, but that is when I started to think about learning medicine. When my family called me back to help at home, I started reading my brother's medical books, quite on the sly, you see. Then Lizzie and I got to go to the grammar school, thanks to Mr Fuller. After that, I persuaded my brother to let me go out on calls with him in the evenings and sometimes during the day when I could get away from the house. At first, he wasn't happy about it, but I guess I helped him enough with the families that he eventually relented and decided to support me. In fact, it was John who talked to Mr Fuller about my going to the new grammar school in Thorold. Lizzie and I were there together for its first year." She took a breath from her recitation.

"My word, you were *both* pioneers there," said Warren. "I imagine the boys made life difficult for you?"

Lizzie answered, "Oh, yes, they most certainly did. They didn't like it much if we made better marks than they!"

"As we often did!" said Margaret Jane, with a wink.

"So that gets you through grammar school, I imagine, but how in the world did you get a medical education? Ladies aren't allowed at the colleges here."

"Oh, I know that only too well. I asked them all first because I wanted to stay in Canada West. But again, Mr Fuller helped me. He knew Dr Jackson, the president of the college where I went. With his intervention, I was accepted at Geneva, where they've already graduated two other women."

"Geneva Medical College. That's in New York State," added Lizzie.

"Why, yes, I've heard of it. Were there other lady students there with you?" asked Warren.

"Oh, my word, no. I was the only one in my class. The first lady to graduate from there was an Englishwoman, Elizabeth Blackwell. She's presently in New York City. She established her own infirmary for women there with her sister, who is also a physician. I was fortunate to have worked with her there for a few months."

"But what chance have you to be able to practise here on your own? It's not New York City," Warren observed.

"Well, the reason for my visit to Toronto is to pursue a licence. I have an appointment to-morrow with Dr John Dickson, the president of the General Council on Medical Education. He is here for meetings with candidates. I plan to plead my case. My brother just received his licence from that body; it's new, just created last spring. I thought I would start the process. I don't have high hopes, but I have to try."

❦ ❦ ❦

After a delicious four-course dinner, neither Warren nor Margaret Jane wanted the afternoon to end, but she saw Lizzie was tired and needed to lie down and rest. James called for Warren's buggy to be brought out from the mews. The couple thanked their host and hostess and left together, bundled up against the cold.

As the door closed, Lizzie and James joined hands and kissed over her large belly, confident that their matchmaking was an early success.

❦ ❦ ❦

THURSDAY, 17 JANUARY 1867, PORT ROBINSON

Margaret Jane was at the post-office in the back of the general store, tapping her foot with impatience as she watched the postmaster go through the pile of letters. It had started to snow heavily, and she wanted to get back to the house before the snow got too deep.

What is wrong with him? Margaret Jane wondered, exasperated. Andrew Murray was having difficulty reading the names on the letters, moving them farther and then closer to his nose and squinting. Perhaps he needed spectacles now. She wanted to offer to review the letters herself; she would find hers easily—if it were there to-day. She had checked every day since she had returned from Toronto and been disappointed that the news she so wanted never came.

At long last, Mr Murray took a letter out of the unsorted stack and handed it to her: "Miss M J McFarland. Here you are, Margaret Jane. I hope the message is a good one."

Margaret Jane hesitated. She wanted to open it straightaway but dared not show her emotions if she were disappointed. After all, she was a physician now, but everyone in the village knew her from childhood. She had been trying hard to develop a public persona as a professional woman. She decided to wait until she got home. The title of "Miss" on the paper did not give her a good feeling, however.

❦ ❦ ❦

Margaret Jane walked into the house, took off her boots, and found John at the desk in his office reading the latest issue of the *Lancet*.

"John, it's come." She sat on the settee and took the letter out of the pocket of her snow-covered coat.

"Maggie, mind your coat! Go hang it up, you're dropping snow all over the carpet!" He was short-tempered and calling her by her baby name again, treating her like a child.

Why is he in a bad mood? He had got his medical licence, after all! Margaret Jane thought. It was she who was waiting to learn her fate. Realising she was in the wrong though, she stood and took her coat out to hang on its peg. When she returned, she opened the seal and handed it to her brother. "You read it. Be kind when you tell me it's denied."

He took the paper and read it to himself. He frowned, and she knew immediately what it said.

"I'm sorry, Maggie. It seems graduating first in your class and endorsements from three physicians for your work after Ridgeway aren't enough for the Council. Let alone the pioneering women physicians from New York City."

"I knew it!" said his sister. She ignored his use of her hated baby name. This time, it seemed endearing. "What can I do?"

"*We* will continue as we have been, Sister. You are a fine physician. You needn't have a licence from the General Council on Medical Education to help your neighbours in their hour of need," said John.

❦ ❦ ❦

At sixty-four, Duncan McFarland had a stellar reputation in Canada West. He was not only a patriot but also a Reformer for responsible government. He had served his country on multiple occasions: as a militia commander in the 1837 rebellion, commander of the local corps that policed the canal workers; and Commissioner of the Queen's Bench. As an elected member of Parliament, he had even moved his wife and daughter out of Port Robinson for the sessions in Montréal and Toronto, leaving his farm to his sons' oversight.

Why should I not use my name and considerable influence to procure a medical licence for my daughter? he wondered.

Margaret Jane was adamantly against this, however. She wanted to be recognised for her own knowledge and accomplishments. After all, it was she who had cared for the village residents while John was away with the Port Robinson volunteers last summer during the Fenian troubles. Certainly, John had done the heavy work of amputations and bandaging of battle wounds, but she had handled all of the routine needs of the population during those four awful days in June. Wives worried about their men, waited for their return, not knowing whether they were alive or dead, wounded seriously or not. If wounded, would they be able to continue farming? What would become of the families if the father were killed by the American raiders?

It had been a terrible experience for the whole of Niagara. Some of the captured raiders were prosecuted in a special court of Assizes in Toronto, but many were released and sent back over the border to perhaps launch another attack. The Fenians were nothing if not determined and impassioned for their cause of freedom for Ireland. But why did they have to pursue their fight in peaceful Niagara?

CHAPTER 38

Joy, Loss, and Frustration

FRIDAY, 4 SEPTEMBER 1868, TORONTO

"Mother had nine children, Laurie! I don't know how she coped, being with child so often. I am worried I can't do what she did," said Lizzie Fuller McMurray.

"Don't fret so. You've just given birth. You can't expect to feel yourself yet," assured her sister.

"I know I felt better than this last time, Sister!" moaned Lizzie, as she took baby William to her tender breast.

"Well, it's only been a week. Give your body a chance to recover. I'm here to tend to little Leonard. You concentrate on Willy. I shall take care of the household. Mother told me exactly what to do. Luckily I'm not teaching yet!"

"I am indeed lucky to have you with me, dear sister. Thank you. Mother was wonderful to come for the last month, but you know, it's Mother. Everything had to be her way. How are the plans coming along for moving to the Bishop's Palace?"

Laurie let the harsh comment about their mother pass without response. She had always had the better relationship with their female parent. Her younger sister was still Papa's little girl.

Lizzie and Mrs Fuller were of opposite personalities.

"Very well. Mr Langtry says it will be ready for the pupils. They will begin to arrive in just a few days," replied Laura.

"I am so glad Bishop Strachan knew the school was named for him before he died. Papa revered him so much. He reminded me of Bishop Doane in the way he promoted education throughout his life."

"Yes, he certainly did. Their legacies will live on at both schools."

Lizzie's maid appeared at the doorway of her bedchamber. "Begging your pardon, ma'am," murmured Annella. "The post."

"Thank you, Annie," Lizzie said, taking the letters from the girl.

Lizzie shuffled through the stack with one hand as she held the nursing baby with the other. There were several from friends in the neighbourhood, presumably offering congratulations on the birth of her second son, and many from her father's parish. She found the one she wanted to read first.

"Laurie, if you please. It's from Margaret Jane. See what she writes! I haven't heard from her in months! She has been such a bad correspondent since she and Warren got married."

Laurie took the letter and opened it; she read it aloud before she handed it back to Lizzie.

"It's short and to the point, as usual. She says she had a baby girl on the twenty-eighth last. That's the day after William was born! Her name is Ethel Sara. They also removed before the baby arrived, and she gives her new address. They are doing well in London, but she won't be doctoring again for quite a while."

"Oh, that is splendid! A little girl. I have so wanted to know! I'll write her back as soon as little Willy here has had his fill!"

❦ ❦ ❦

FRIDAY, 11 SEPTEMBER 1868, ST CATHARINES

The verandah of the William Mittleberger house in Duke Street was hung with black crape fabric, and inside, the draperies were drawn over the front windows; it was quiet as a cemetery. The two little boys, George and Clark, normally allowed to play on the carpeted stairs with their toy soldiers and drums, were banished to the nursery on the second floor.

In the middle of the parlour, a tiny white casket was set on the gate-leg table, also draped in black. Inside lay the sweet remains of Beatrice Mittleberger, eight months old. The little daughter of William and Julia had fought courageously for her life against the wracking spasms of whooping cough, giving in at last to eternal repose. After sixteen days gasping for air and being unable to keep enough food down, the infant had died of hunger and dehydration.

Both parents, exhausted and pale, stayed upstairs in their bedroom for most of the morning, dreading what the day would bring. It should have been a happy day, the occasion of their sixth wedding anniversary.

Katie had brought them breakfast at eight, but Julia ate nothing, while William took only tea and toast, leaving the boiled egg untouched in its shiny brown shell. Emma and Bella, emotionally drained from being with their sister and her family till late the previous evening, arrived at nine to mind their young nephews in the nursery. At two o'clock they would all have to steel themselves to go downstairs and greet their family and neighbours, leaving the children to the servants. The parents would bravely accept the inevitable expressions of sympathy.

Little Beatrice, William and Julia's first daughter after two sons, had been the light of their lives. She was a daily joy, offering relief from the energy of her boisterous brothers who kept Julia on edge with their antics. Julia was particularly shaken, as she had been hopeful that Bea would pull through. The child seemed to rally five days ago and then went rapidly downhill, losing her fight with the scourge of childhood, pertussis, on the ninth of September.

❦ ❦ ❦

JULY 1870, LONDON, ONTARIO

Margaret Jane was furious. She couldn't wait until Warren came home for dinner to-day. In the morning post, she had just received a response to her appeal to the General Council in Toronto. How could they require something like this, at this time of her life? Just to get a piece of paper? She had been practising as a midwife for the last three years, in spite of having studied medicine and having practical experience with John all those years in Thorold Township.

It was so unjust. She wanted to help all of her neighbours, not just women in childbirth. Had she wasted her life so far getting an education? Tiny Port Robinson Common School? St Mary's Hall? Thorold Grammar School? Geneva Medical College? The months spent in New York City?

Should she have invoked her father's name in her last request? He had offered. Should she have asked Harriet's uncles Colonel George and Robert Denison to write her a recommendation? After all, they had billeted with the McFarlands during the Fenian troubles in '66. Surely they knew she was working as a physician the whole time, taking over for both Colonel King and her brother while they were away doctoring the troops at Lime Ridge and Ridgeway. Then poor Col. King was shot in the ankle and endured the brutal amputation of his leg in Buffalo. He was still struggling to recover and practise, John said.

Tears streaming down her face, she pulled little Ethel up onto her lap and rocked her, smoothing her daughter's unruly ginger curls. She so wanted this recognition and to open her own medical practise, but she would not leave her husband and daughter for a year to sit in a lecture hall at the Toronto School of Medicine.

1050 Dorchester Street
Montréal
19 Septembre 1870

Ma chère amie, *Julia,*

My dear friend, how I miss you so! How I miss our frequent letters. I know you are occupied with your family, but I yearn to hear from you, dear friend. Oh! to be with you again and see your happy face, dancing eyes and lovely dark curls!

Once again, fate has dealt us a terrible blow. The summer illnesses attacked all of our children relentlessly, and took our darling Harriet Theresa one month ago to-day. She was only sixteen months old and such a cunning thing.

Frederick adored her. Mary Frances is inconsolable at losing her little sister. It is my first experience losing a child whom I had grown to love. I know you went through it too, losing little Bea.

I confess I have had a difficult time going to God with this, Julia. How ever did you cope?

Your friend always,
Hattie

39 Duke Street
St Catharines, Ontario
25 September 1870

Dear Hattie,

I apologise for being such a poor correspondent. I know I haven't written for many months. We too suffered heartache this summer. Our little William went to the Lord in July after the summer illness passed through the city. He was born only last winter and was just able to crawl upon the carpet a bit before he took ill. He was a charming little fellow and made his brothers laugh. I know it's hard to accept. God's will be done. What else are we to do?

I promise to write you more often, I promise, but now I am close to tears thinking of our losses. To be a mother is to suffer, is it not?

Yours truly,
Julia

CHAPTER 39

Laura

MAY 1873, TORONTO

The city's blanket of snow had finally melted even in the shadiest spots. The last ice storm was a fortnight ago, and the early bulbs were beginning to bud in the Fullers' garden at the rectory. The prevailing northwesterly winds thankfully kept the city smoke moving south out over the lake. To-day was a welcome cloudless day when blue sky and sunshine were abundant. Laura Fuller put on her bonnet and cloak to leave the school building, glad to be able to walk home from the Queen Street omnibus stop without wearing her galoshes. Puddles were drying up in the sudden warmth too.

After eleven years, Toronto felt like her home now. When her father was appointed rector of St George-the-Martyr in 1861, the Fullers removed to the city across the lake. It was a slow, rough, late-season crossing because they had waited until after Mary Margaret wed in November. Tom Fuller performed the ceremony, marrying his eldest daughter to the Rev. Donald Ian Forbes McLeod, an Anglican minister born in Scotland. They lived in Chippewa, where Donald was rector of Holy Trinity Church. The Fuller twins, Dick and Sam, were also married now and pursuing careers elsewhere in Ontario.

Laura had taught at the Bishop Strachan School since the day it opened at Pinehurst on 12 September 1867. It was established with the same intent as St Mary's Hall: to be an academic boarding and day school for girls. Begun by a council of clergymen who wanted a rigorous education for their own daughters, it included a strong foundation in church teachings. Its namesake, Bishop John Strachan, had supervised the proliferation of English churches throughout Ontario during his tenure. Before he was ordained, he had taught some of the local clergy, including Laura's father, at schools in old York, Kingston, and Cornwall, and they honoured him by naming the new institution for him.

In the past six years, the school had moved twice due to ever-increasing enrolment. The current location was the late Sir James Buchanan Macaulay's former home, Wykeham Lodge, at the intersection of Yonge and College Streets; after its renovation into classrooms and living quarters, the old house was called Wykeham Hall. The property adjacent to the University of Toronto was an original park grant awarded to Macaulay when the town of York was settled in 1793. Pupils and their chaperones loved to wander through the still forested land between the two institutions.

❦ ❦ ❦

Laura was constantly bemused by her pupils at the school; they reminded her so much of the girls she had met at St Mary's Hall. Boarding school girls were boarding school girls, she guessed: fun-loving together, but often sad to be sent away from their families.

In spite of having qualified to teach all subjects at the Toronto Normal School, Laura had reverted to her first love, the piano. She supervised the training of over forty girls at the school, many of whom studied the instrument only because it was required and still a societal expectation of well-bred young ladies. Laura realised that few of her pupils were as gifted as their teacher, and this grieved her very much. However, when a girl exhibited graceful technique and a feeling for the music, Laura showered that pupil with praise and encouragement. It was more difficult to do the same with the ones who showed little talent or interest, and she knew it was those girls who needed even more encouraging words. Alas, she was only human. She prayed daily for strength, compassion, and energy in this regard.

One Friday afternoon, Laura entered her parents' home and picked up the post from the walnut hall stand. She found a letter addressed to her in an unfamiliar masculine hand. "T. M. Benson!" she murmured. "What does *he* have to say?"

She wasted no time opening it.

🐝 🐝 🐝

Terralta
Port Hope, Ontario
28 April 1873

My dear Miss Fuller,

Please forgive the sudden, and perhaps surprising, nature of this missive. I have just undertaken to reread and discard letters of sympathy and condolence I received upon the death of my beloved wife over two years ago. In so doing, I came upon a most sweet and sympathetic letter from you. I am asking you quite bluntly if you would consider my suit. I realise that we live quite a distance apart, but if you would accept my first attentions in the form of letters, I would be grateful. When my work brings me to Toronto in the near future, I would be very happy to call on you and your parents. I remember very well meeting you at your brother's wedding to my sister here years ago and also at my own wedding to Mary Edith in Toronto. I was most favourably impressed when we met, and I remember how often she wrote you after our marriage. She called you "my dearest friend Laura" and insisted on seeing you whenever she visited her family in Toronto. My dear Miss Fuller, if you would accept the genuine sentiments in this letter and promise to respond, I would be eternally indebted to you.

Most sincerely yours,
Thomas Moore Benson, Esquire

🐝 🐝 🐝

Laura nearly swooned. She read the letter again and then bounded upstairs to find her mother in her sitting room.

"Mother, have you seen the post to-day?"

"Why, no, my dear. I've been here mending since dinner. What's the matter?" asked Cynthia Fuller.

"It's a letter from T. M. Benson in Port Hope. You remember my friend at the Normal married him? Mary Edith McCaul?"

"Well, of course, dear, he's Dick's brother-in-law. Don't I recall that Mary Edith died in childbirth?"

"Yes, sadly. It was two years ago December, Mother. I wanted to go to her funeral, but the weather was abominable. Their little newborn baby girl died too. It was horrible. T.M. still lives at Terralta."

"Yes, it's his mother's house. Alicia Lowe Benson was widowed in the Desjardins Canal disaster. She is still a widow, isn't she?"

"Yes, I believe she is."

"Well, what does he say, dear?"

"Mother, he wants to court me. Just like that! He said he read my sympathy note again and remembered Mary Edith and I were such good friends. I loved her like another sister. And, of course, we are nearly family, since Dick is married to his sister Emma. He wants to call on you and Papa."

"Laura, dear, what are you thinking?"

"I am going to consider him, Mother. I am thirty-one! I am sure he is a good man. A barrister. Why not?"

❧ ❧ ❧

JUNE 1873

Laura was in a tizzy. She had tried on three different frocks and was unhappy with them all. Her mother tried to calm her, saying that all of them were appropriate and becoming, but Laura lacked confidence. She was unused to the distractions of men and fashion, and it was so hot to-day. She did not want to wear something that would add to her discomfort. She wished Lizzie were there to advise her. Although Lizzie was not much interested in fashion either, she did seem to put herself together well enough these days, despite having four children.

T.M. was to arrive in thirty minutes. What was she to do?

"Laura, you look beautiful in all of them," her mother insisted. "You have no reason to doubt yourself. Your lovely green eyes go well with any of these colours. Choose one, dear, and let's get on with it. We still have to manage your hair."

"Mother, you choose then. I just cannot cope with this now. What if he doesn't like me when he sees me? It's been five years since we met, and that was only briefly at Dick's wedding."

"Laura, you have not seen *him* either. Suppose you cannot bear him?"

"Oh, I don't think that's possible, Mother!"

🐦 🐦 🐦

Thomas Moore Benson had been in the study with Mr Fuller for more than forty-five minutes. Laura was beside herself with worry, wringing her hands. What in the world could the men be talking about for so long? She and her mother were waiting in the parlour, seated on a new medallion back walnut sofa delivered last week from a furniture maker in Yonge Street. Mrs Fuller would call Jane to bring the tea as soon as the men emerged.

At last they appeared in the doorway, laughing. Then, assuming a more serious tone, Mr Fuller gestured to T.M. to approach his wife.

"Honoured to see you again, Mrs Fuller," he said with a bow.

"And I am pleased to welcome you to our home, Mr Benson," said Cynthia Fuller.

Tom Fuller then took his daughter by the hand. "T.M., this is our Laura."

"Pleased to see you again also, Miss Fuller," said the man.

"And I, Mr Benson," murmured the young woman, her head bowed as she dipped a curtsy. Her long hair was arranged with curls piled high atop her head in the latest style for spring seen in *Godey's* magazine. Cynthia had selected a navy blue silk dress with camel colour trimming for her daughter to wear for this special occasion.

When all four were seated, Cynthia rang for the tea, and within ten minutes, Laura was pouring from the porcelain teapot while Jane passed thin bread and butter slices along with fresh Victoria and oatmeal cakes baked that morning.

Mr Fuller began by clearing his throat, followed by a long sip of tea. He placed the cup back on the saucer and addressed his daughter. "Laura, as you know, T.M. is a successful barrister with a promising future in Port Hope." Tom Fuller paused. "He is presently living at Terralta with his brother and mother, along with his two little girls. They have a nurse for the children, but he would like you to consider him as a prospective husband, and I have agreed. If you so desire, my dear," he added.

Laura blushed and looked down at her folded hands, considering what to say in response. "Papa, we have been corresponding for two months now, and I would like to continue getting to know T.M. But I rather think I would like to spend some time in Port Hope, with his family, to see if it is a situation I would like."

"Oh, I do agree, Miss Fuller," said T.M. "That's a splendid idea. When would you like to come? It's quite pleasant there now, overlooking the lake. There's always a breeze through the house and it's much cooler in Port Hope than here in the city."

"Papa?"

"My word, Laurie, of course, you may go. You should meet your little step-daughters, by all means!"

Cynthia arched her eyebrows, "Tom, they're not even betrothed. Aren't you putting the cart before the horse?"

"Oh, my, yes, of course, my dear. I just meant that the sooner Laurie meets the little girls, the better for all concerned," said Tom Fuller.

"Then it's settled. You tell me the dates, and I shall make the arrangements with *Mater*," said T.M. "I shall also delegate my present work to my apprentice. That's my brother Frederick. I shall postpone taking on anything new while you are stopping with us. Would a month be enough time, Miss Fuller?"

"A month? I imagine that would be fine. School doesn't start again until September," replied Laura.

"Capital!" said her father. "To-morrow I shall buy your train ticket."

❦ ❦ ❦

The next afternoon, Laura and her mother went to the dressmaker's shop to have eight new dresses made for her holiday in Port Hope. They had a grand time looking at patterns and fabrics

344

together. Laura was overwhelmed by the choices of trimmings; she was accustomed to wearing the subdued colours and designs expected of a teacher: grey and shades of blue or brown, sometimes dark green. None of them did justice to her English rose complexion or dark locks. Her order, however, included daytime and visiting dresses in pale green, violet, blue, peach, rose, and a cream-coloured one striped in dark purple. Her favourite design was of ecru silk trimmed in bright blue ribbons. Her most daring choice was for evening in yellow satin; it would show her narrow shoulders to good advantage. She hoped there would be an occasion to wear it to a party in Port Hope.

After the seamstress, they took swatches to the milliner and ordered three new bonnets to go with the dresses on order. Lastly, Laura bought a new parasol that would be useful on strolls around the town; her old one was showing signs of wear. Laura Fuller would pack her trunk again as she had years before to go to St Mary's Hall, but this time her wardrobe was ample and sophisticated. She could also wear the jewellery discouraged there. Her mother lent her some of her own collection for her holiday: a diamond necklace and matching bracelet; three pairs of earrings; and two brooches from Italy, one cameo and one of gold.

❦ ❦ ❦

On the first of July, the Grand Trunk Railway inaugurated its new Union Station south of Front Street in Toronto, near the lake shore. It was an opulent Italianate design by Thomas Seaton Scott and the largest station in Canada. Four days later, Laura embraced her father and mother at the station as she left Toronto unaccompanied for the first time in her life. The sixty-mile trip east wouldn't take long in the cars, about two and a half hours, including the necessary stops to take on travellers at towns like Oshawa and Bowmanville.

Laura arrived in Port Hope in the early afternoon. T.M. met her at the little stone station in a gig just big enough for two. He pointed out the sights as they drove around the town: St John the Evangelist Church in Pine Street, the Town Hall in Queen Street, the Music Hall in Walton Street, and the Trinity College School.

Laura was surprised to learn it was the same school started in the home of Rev. Mr William Arthur Johnson in Weston, outside the city limits of Toronto. Port Hope had successfully lobbied to have it moved to the town in 1868.

The horse pulled the passengers up a long hill and came to a three-storey brick house overlooking Lake Ontario. This was Terralta, the Benson family home built by T.M.'s father Thomas. It indeed had a breath-taking view of the lake from the high land, as its name implied.

T.M. helped Laura out of the carriage, and they left the horse with the hired man who would now take the waggon down to the station to fetch her trunk. Together they entered through the front door of the house and found Mrs Benson in the drawing room, ready to meet the woman who might become her son's second wife.

Mrs Benson, a petite grey-haired lady of sixty-seven, did not rise from her chair when the couple entered the room. Instead, she held out her hand and let her son bring it to his lips.

"*Mater*, may I present Miss Laura Abigail Fuller," he said, stepping behind Laura.

"I am happy to see you again, Miss Fuller. Please sit down beside me," the woman said, indicating a chair to her right. "It is so good of you to stop with us, and for such a nice long time too. I look forward to getting to know you. We shall have tea coming in just a few moments," she said, as she rang for the servant.

"Thank you for the invitation, Mrs Benson. I am also anxious to know you and the children. Where are they?"

"The girls are upstairs with their nurse. They will have their supper with Mary, and then we shall see them before we dine, after their baths. How was your journey to-day?"

"It was quite pleasant. Thank you, Mrs Benson."

After an awkward pause, T.M. picked up the conversation. "Miss Fuller, perhaps you'll entertain us while you're here with your music? We have a piano-forte in the parlour. Your father told me you are very accomplished."

"He is biased, of course! But I would like that very much. 'Tis my habit to play every evening at home."

When the tea arrived, there were cucumber sandwiches and fresh strawberries from the Bensons' garden behind the house. The conversation dropped again, and Mrs Benson asked a pointed question. "Are you very fond of children, Miss Fuller?"

Laura swallowed her bite of sandwich and replied, "Well, I don't suppose I ever thought about it, Mrs Benson. I'm a trained teacher … of course … I went to the Normal. But music is my real love. Of course, I come from a large family as well. Nine of us children. The three oldest are married now. Dick … of course, you know him!" Laura blushed, realising again that Dick was Mrs Benson's son-in-law, married to her daughter Emma. She continued, "Sam, his twin, and my older sister Mary Margaret have children, but we don't see much of them, as they both live away from Toronto. My younger sister Elizabeth and her husband James have four children now, and so I have a baby niece and three nephews. I see them often, as they live quite near the rectory. Little Elizabeth is quite cunning, like her mother. And of our four little brothers, just one is married. Valancy and his wife, Louisa, are in the city. They just had a little girl in May. Henry is the only one at home now. He's sixteen and still at the College. So, yes, I've been among children all my life. I'm sure it's different if you're a mother though, isn't it?"

"Oh, yes, indeed. Being a mother changes everything. You see life through that particular lens until the end of your days," said Alicia Benson.

❦ ❦ ❦

Terralta
Port Hope

7 July 1873

Dearest Mother and Papa,

I apologise for not writing yesterday, but we have been occupied every minute with the girls. It is so endearing to have them shower me with kisses. They climb into my lap whenever I sit down. Ethel is 6, and Emily is 4, both dear ones with dark curls and hazel eyes like their father. I shall be so lucky if they love me like a mother someday.

Terralta is a beautiful place. The house overlooks the lake that to-day is shining in the sunlight, glistening like a jewel. T.M. says it is only about twenty years old and was built for his parents just before his father was killed. It does need some updating, and he has already made some plans. He said he will show them to me while I am here.

Yesterday we took a ride with the children through the countryside outside of Port Hope and had a picnic. We laid a blanket on the grass and unpacked a hamper with ham, cold potatoes, and strawberries with fresh bread from the oven. The girls ran to their hearts' content and rolled on the grass until they could run and giggle no more. Little Emily fell asleep in my arms on the way home in the carriage. I am sure their nurse will scold me for allowing them to romp so. Their pretty dresses were grass-stained. I guess I am going to be an indulgent stepmother to them! Lizzie will be surprised to hear this. Did I ever tell you how she rolled down the hill at the Laurel Hill Cemetery in Philadelphia? I was so annoyed with her that day.

I shall close for now and put this out for the post. I am glad Port Hope is such a short journey from Toronto. We shall be able to visit you often.

Your loving daughter,
Laura

CHAPTER 40

Something in the Post

JULY 1874, ST CATHARINES

"Here you are, Miss," said Margaret Crittens. The younger of the Burns' two live-in servants delivered the afternoon post to Bella, sitting at her harp in the darkened parlour. The heavy draperies of her parents' house in St Catharines were drawn to keep out the summer heat of the late afternoon sun beating down on the west side of the house.

"Thank you, Margaret," said Bella, taking the bundle. She opened the draperies, blinking as her eyes adjusted to the sunlight, and began to shuffle through the letters.

Most of her father's business mail was delivered to his law office in St Paul Street, but there was often correspondence for the several members of the family still living in the large house in what was now called Church Street. Norman, who returned from the Royal Army three years ago after serving in Bombay, worked as a secretary in St Catharines. Lewie and Florrie, still pupils in local schools, lived with their parents, along with Emma and Bella, both now in their thirties. Last October, Libby married her beau Dr Frank Warren in a ceremony attended by family members at St George's Church. The

349

couple were living in Whitby on the north shore of Lake Ontario.

Among the letters were two envelopes postmarked from Burlington, New Jersey, one addressed to Emma, and one to Bella. Bella opened hers. She took out a card and read the following printed message:

> *The desire has been expressed, in various quarters, for a Re-union of the Graduates of St Mary's Hall.*
>
> *A very favourable time for such a gathering would be Bishop Doane's next Birth-day, May 27, 1875.*
>
> *It will be gratifying to hear from you on the subject, and to receive suggestions as to the best ways of making the occasion one of pleasure to the Alumnæ, and of advantage to their Alma Mater.*
>
> *Please address Miss Stanley or Mrs Lewis, at the Hall. Burlington N.J., June 25, 1874*

Bella gave a shriek of joy and ran out of the parlour to the bottom of the front steps, calling, "Emma! Emma! Come down at once!"

Emma was at her desk composing a letter to the Toronto *Globe* about the continuing social problem of intemperance. Since she was seventeen, she had been encouraged to embrace any number of causes as a community member. Now she felt the most serious one in need of her attention was drink.

She had witnessed in the town of St Catharines too many examples of men who, due to alcoholism, abandoned their families. The many "navvies", or canal workers, were often seen on payday leaving taverns after squandering their money on drink. It sickened Emma to know that their wives and children would suffer as a result of their behaviour.

This was the aim of the letter she was writing to-day, to ask relief for the women and children. After so many years of campaigning, she was seeing scant results.

Bella called again. "Emma, come downstairs!"

The earnest letter writer closed her ink bottle and set down her pen, rose from her chair, and leaned over the railing at the top of the stairs. "Bella, what in the world is so important that you interrupt my thoughts?"

"Come down and see for yourself, Sister!" replied Bella.
"All right, I am coming."

❦ ❦ ❦

After reading the card, Emma and Bella discussed what to do.
Did they want to travel five hundred miles, all the way to New
Jersey, just to honour Bishop Doane's memory? Did Emma care
enough to spend the time and money to see the campus where
she had spent but a scant year of her life? It was nearly twenty
years ago now since she had left. She was sure the school would
be much changed in that time. What was the point?

"Oh, Bella, I don't know. I was only there—what? Two terms
and a few weeks? And I haven't kept in touch with anyone there
since Lizzie Adams died. Do *you* want to go?"

"Well, I was there about the same length of time as you, of
course. I wonder if Julia would be interested in going. Funny, she
didn't get a card," mused Bella.

"Oh, the postman probably delivered it right to her. He
knows who she is and where she lives. She has her hands full
with the children, wouldn't you agree? Would William permit
her to go all the way to New Jersey for such an occasion?"

"Oh, I should think he would approve if she wished it. He
adores her so. But you are correct, little Arthur will still be too
young to leave. 'Twould take at least a week altogether taking the
fastest route. And I doubt she would abandon her boys to the
care of young Katie Sexton," added Bella.

"I agree. I still believe she needs more competent live-in help,
but she is adamant about staying in their present little house.
There is no room for more servants. At least she has Cook and
Mary Rose coming in now. They are both reliable," said Emma,
as she went about rearranging the tintypes on the table, a habit
of hers.

"I wonder if the Fuller girls are going? Lizzie's been married
forever. In her last letter, Lizzie said Laura was to marry T.M. Benson in Toronto in June. I haven't heard from her in a while. I
guess she is occupied with the children," said Bella.

"Yes, of course. And Harriet, Julia's friend. They might still
correspond."

"Oh, they do. She remains in Montréal. Hattie has a couple of children too. They must be getting on now. She married young. Then dear Margaret Jane. She always owes me a letter, but I am sure she is busy too," added Bella.

"Let's walk over to see Julia, Bella. We can sort it out together."

❦ ❦ ❦

Julia, now thirty-four, her chestnut curls streaked prematurely with grey, enjoyed marriage and motherhood. Her three little boys somehow filled all of her time. Baby Arthur was a bit colicky at the beginning, but now they were settled into a good routine. William's hours were predictable at the town hall, and he was an attentive husband and father. Both parents still grieved for little Bea and the little boys they had lost, but Julia took solace in running her household, and William doted on his sons. The busier she was, the less time she had to remember the pain of losing her only daughter and two young sons.

Katie Sexton answered the door and showed Emma and Bella into the parlour. Julia came down a few minutes later, carrying little Arthur on her hip. The two aunts took turns making a fuss over him before Julia gave him to Katie, who put him up to nap.

"Julia, have you read your post to-day?" asked Bella.

"Well, no. I haven't had a minute yet. It's on the hall table. And Katie will serve the tea for us. She'll bring it in as soon as she is finished with Arthur. What's in the post?"

"St Mary's Hall wrote to suggest there be a re-union of old girls in Burlington. Next May, in fact," explained Emma.

"Really? Wouldn't that be interesting! To see our school sisters again! Imagine … Is Mrs La Motte still alive? And Miss Stanley?" said Julia.

"In fact, Miss Stanley is invoked in the invitation, Julia, and a Mrs Lewis, but not Mrs La Motte. I allow she would be over sixty now," calculated Bella.

"Oh, my, it's such a long trip, and I've done it already several times. Emma, do you care to go?"

""Twould be an adventure, but I have little interest in a place where I spent only a year's time." She paused. "I would like to see Miss Stanley again, if anyone. She was so kind to me when she conducted me to Canandaigua when Mama was ill. We wrote each other for years, only lately less frequently. I'm glad to hear she's still at the Hall," said Emma.

"I shall discuss it with William to-night, but I imagine 'twould be too upsetting to leave the boys for that length of time, do you not, sisters?"

"We rather thought you would say that, Julia!" said Bella with a laugh and a wink.

❦ ❦ ❦

St Catharines, Ontario
5 August 1874

Dear Lizzie,

I am writing you this short note with a singular purpose. I am sure you have been very busy, my dear friend, but I wanted to apprise you of the fact that St Mary's Hall has written us suggesting a re-union May 27 next. I wonder if you and Laura would consider going? Perhaps you have not heard about it if your current whereabouts are unknown to the school. Therefore, I am letting you know that Emma and I are determined. Yes, all the way to New Jersey again! I hope you can get away to join us. Dear Miss Stanley is still there!

Julia will write to Hattie. I hope I am still your dearest old friend from St Mary's Hall.

Fondly,
Bella

CHAPTER 41

Re-union

WEDNESDAY, 26 MAY 1875, BURLINGTON, NEW JERSEY

Through a light mist enveloping the city, Emma glimpsed the steeple of St Mary's Church from the window of the afternoon train from New York City. "Bella, I can't believe we're arriving in the rain just like I did so many times with Julia! I hope the weather changes for to-morrow's events. I don't fancy walking all the way to St Mary's Church with umbrellas and galoshes, do you?"

"No, of course not, and I don't suppose we could hire a hack to take us there, like we did in New York City, could we? We would be looking down at our dear sisters trudging along!" laughed Bella. "With any luck 'twill clear off. It's been an awful trip if you consider the weather with all this rain. But, even so, it was wonderful to see New York City for the first time. It's so like Toronto, full of all different kinds of people."

"Yes, it's a big port like Toronto, but I think there are also many problems to be solved in both cities. I saw crowds of poor women and little ragged children in the streets. So many of them looked exhausted and hungry. I wonder where they live and how their fathers provide for them."

"Emma, you always dwell on the sad and serious side of life. I rather enjoyed the shops and restaurants we visited! The ladies were so smart-looking and well-dressed. I felt very much the country mouse!"

"That is where we differ, dear sister. See how you focus on appearances! Life *is* serious to me, but it seems you are only looking for fun."

"Life is too short, Emma. We won't any of us live forever. Try to enjoy yourself with our old friends here, won't you?"

"I wonder if I shall know anyone to-morrow. I come for your sake. I was here only for those two winter terms. I don't even count that vacation month or the three weeks of lessons before Papa called me back."

"You'll never forgive him for that, will you, Sister? It seems you've counted the days! I was here for only two terms too! I spent the September vacation month just once like you did, but for me, they were all glorious times away from home. I got to know the girls from Lockport and Lizzie Fuller in those months. And of course, Margaret Jane and Hattie were here for their last summer term with me too."

"Ah yes, Harriet. I can't believe she and Julia have maintained their friendship all these years in spite of not actually seeing one another. You received a letter from her before we left, didn't you?"

"Yes, Julia told her I would bring it along with the others."

The train came to a halt at the modern wooden station located near the intersection of High and Broad Streets in the centre of town. It was built in the 1860s conveniently near the old Beldin House, now renamed the City Hotel. The two women collected their things and prepared to disembark. They had accepted an offer to stay in Burlington with Dr Franklin Gauntt whose two stepdaughters, Louisa and Fanny, attended the school with Bella for her summer term. Bella hoped that she would recognise her schoolmates after so many years away. Other St Mary's Hall families in town, such as the Woolmans and the Silpaths, had also offered lodging to returning graduates and were at the station to collect their guests. Miss Stanley and her committee had carefully arranged the event down to the last detail.

🍂 🍂 🍂

The perpetually optimistic Bella was right, and fair St Mary's Hall weather prevailed. After several days of rain, the sun came out on the bishop's birth-day, Thursday, the twenty-seventh of May. The first order of the day was a family service of Morning Prayer at half past eight in the Chapel of the Holy Innocents. Emma and Bella rose early to enjoy a plentiful breakfast in their lodgings with Mrs Gauntt and Mrs Gauntt's married daughter Fanny Moffett DuPay. Fanny, who graduated from the Hall in 1861, was a pupil at the time of the bishop's death. She described the grief that she and the other pupils had suffered when he died. The whole school had gone into deep mourning.

The three young women quickly lost track of time with all their talking. When Fanny looked at the clock in horror, they abruptly thanked Mrs Gauntt for breakfast and left the table to find their wraps. They had to walk briskly from the Gauntts' house in East Broad Street to make up for lost time. As they reached Talbot Street, Bella asked Fanny if she knew Miss Ada Winans' whereabouts.

Fanny's face clouded, and she stopped walking. "Oh my, you don't know? It's a scandal! Don't ask Miss Stanley about it, by all means. After she graduated in fifty-three, Miss Winans left Burlington to study opera in Italy. That's when she met Prince Troubetskoy in Florence. He was a Russian diplomat, and his family was close to the tsar. He told her he was divorced, but apparently he wasn't. He deceived her in every way! She came back to teach here … much chastened I imagine. That's when you knew her. But after *my* graduation, she went back to New York City to live with her cousins. Then she returned to Italy and to him, apparently. She had three sons with the man! Just like that! Miss Stanley was heartbroken when she heard because she always thought Miss Winans was a true talent, and she loved her like a daughter. The last we heard he had divorced his wife in Russia and married Ada. They live with their sons in the north of Italy somewhere."

"Oh, dear, that *is* a scandal. I can't imagine it. The poor thing. I do recall she had a sweet soprano voice," said Bella. "And she undertook to teach me the harp. I am deeply indebted to her for that."

Emma remembered the teacher well from her last term at school. She frowned. "Miss Winans was certainly always daring, wasn't she? I suppose that's a lesson to us all, Bella."

Bella received Emma's message loud and clear and felt insulted. She quickened her pace and left Emma and Fanny behind as she made her way alone down Talbot Street.

❦ ❦ ❦

One hundred eighty ladies of various ages returned that morning to the venerable school on the Delaware River to celebrate the birth-day of its founder. The heavy perfume of purple lilacs and red rose bushes greeted the eager visitors in the school gardens, where blooming tulips and irises also boasted their various colours. Emma, Bella, and Fanny followed the crowd of "old girls" entering the Main House from the Circle. Waiting in the front east parlour was Miss Nancy M. Stanley, the one person still at St Mary's Hall whom Emma remembered fondly. She was yet slim, but now quite grey-haired, and Emma guessed she was about sixty years old.

"Miss Stanley? It is I, Emma Burns, your former pupil and correspondent!" said Emma, by way of introduction. She bobbed and offered her gloved hand.

"Emma Burns! My word! I saw that you were coming, my dear! How lovely to see you again. I was so happy to know that you could attend." Miss Stanley squeezed Emma's hand affectionately. "And here's Isabella too. So nice to see you again, my dears. Welcome back to the Hall."

"Thank you, Miss Stanley," said Bella, as she too offered her own hand and curtseyed.

Emma took a red covered book from her reticule. "Miss Stanley, I have brought back Eliza Adams' copy of *Uncle Tom's Cabin*. All of our family has read it and I cherish it, but I think she would like it to remain here in the library for other girls to read. I have inscribed it in her memory."

"Emma, that is a lovely gesture. I know you were good friends with Eliza. Her death was such a tragedy. Thank you for your thoughtfulness ... Well, dears, I would love to visit here longer with you, but I believe the bell for chapel will be ringing shortly.

Shall I show you the way? We can drop the book off in the library on our way to the chapel. The interior is much changed since you were here. When did you leave school, Isabella? I well know when Emma left, as we shared her last train trip north," she said.

"I left after the winter term of fifty-six with my sister Julia and Lizzie Fuller," replied Bella. "It's been eighteen years!"

With that, the bell tolled, and the alumnæ in the parlour began to move toward the familiar sound. Miss Stanley led the still chattering ladies through the hallways to the library of the new building, where she placed the volume on a dropleaf table. The group gained entrance through the south doors of the chapel, found a rear pew empty, and knelt to say a prayer of thanksgiving before the service started.

❦ ❦ ❦

The summer term inmates faced each other in the choir pews while staff and alumnæ filled the nave of the familiar little chapel with its white walls and dark ceiling. The women crowded into the pews, compressing their skirts. Thank goodness hoops had gone out of style, but bustles made sitting difficult for other reasons. The former pupils soon discovered the right angles of the narrow pew benches built for schoolgirls were even more uncomfortable for older women. Their knees complained about the hard floor on which they were expected to kneel.

Immediately after the service, the alumnæ gathered in the airy first floor School Room of the new dormitory building connected to the chapel. There, the women reverently crowned the oval portrait of Bishop Doane with a wreath of fresh pansies, his favourite flower, grown in the school greenhouse for the occasion. As soon as the little ceremony ended, sounds of laughter, surprise, and disbelief could be heard all over the school as the former pupils recognised old friends and explored familiar spaces as well as the magnificent new ones.

The four-storey building had been completed six years before. The new School Room was filled with pupil desks, and the supervising teacher's desk sat atop a dais at the entrance to the room. Tall windows lined the east and west walls that admitted early morning and late afternoon light. A wide turned staircase at the south end led upstairs to two floors of dormitories. The dormitories were of a traditional open plan without any privacy walls. The residents were already used to this design in their previous spaces and paid no mind. There were large windows and modern gaslights in these areas too. Centre columns, whose capitals were decorated in carved plaster, supported the high ceilings along the length of each floor. The present occupants most appreciated the modern gravity water source fed from a cistern on the roof; it supplied a large bathing room on the third floor. At least here there was some accommodation for privacy with about a dozen tubs enclosed by partitions. It was quite an improvement of the hygiene arrangements that the oldest alumnæ remembered.

The fourth-floor garret—gained by a steep, narrow, and winding stairwell—was also undivided and had an unfinished sloped ceiling and large dormer windows. Tall triple windows on either end of the rectangular space allowed for some welcome cross-ventilation whenever the wind came off the river in the summer. The chambermaids and scullery maids shared these living quarters.

Nowhere was out of bounds to the "old girls" that day. The connected basements of both new and old buildings created a musty maze of underground space to explore. In the cellar of the new building was a commodious eating room and a modern kitchen. Plenty of light poured in from the above ground windows that provided a view of the still well-tended gardens behind the bishop's house. A link hallway led from the new basement to the Nursery structure. At the south end of the Nursery building was the old icehouse with its eight-inch thick oak door to keep the temperature and the food inside cold. It was accessible to the new kitchen through the basement hallway. Continuing through the dimly lit area to the chapel annex and the Main House, the visitors reached the original kitchen and familiar dining area.

The first floor of the three-storey east annex was still used for classrooms with staff rooms on the second and dormitories on the third. An additional building attached to the east annex of the Main House was now where old Mrs Lippincott's house had once stood. Opened in December of 1857, it contained a spacious art room on the first floor with large windows overlooking the river. The second floor provided living quarters for the present Rector, the Rev. Mr Elvin K. Smith and his family. The third floor was a large open dormitory with modern bathrooms nearby.

"Emma, this is so different. I hardly recognise the place! Look! I wish we had had this art room for painting. The north light is wonderful with these big windows overlooking the river," exclaimed Bella. "When I left school in fifty-seven, this was in the midst of construction."

At precisely half past ten, the ladies gathered in the Circle and, as during their school days, paired off arm-in-arm to begin the ten-minute walk to St Mary's Church. Emma and Bella joined the group walking down the Green Bank. They passed the Shippen House and "Stone Cottage" again, the charming stucco dwelling of the long since deceased, but still well-remembered Presbyterian minister, the Rev. Mr Cortlandt Van Rensselaer. Then they turned right into Wood Street; along the familiar route, they admired the new houses and well-groomed gardens of the London neighbourhood, as well as the ones once occupied by teachers such as Camille Baquet and Anders Engstrom. When the former pupils of Bishop Doane entered the leafy churchyard, they stopped briefly at his flower-adorned tomb behind the church to offer a quick prayer for his peaceful repose. The ladies were reminded that the school's beloved founder had died in 1859 after suffering an infection, one month before the energetic teacher would have celebrated his sixtieth birth-day. Mrs Doane had succumbed sometime after in Florence, Italy, where she had gone for her health the year before with her daughter Sarah.

Nearby was the recently erected marble coped tomb of Mr Engstrom, the beloved and popular art teacher who had died the previous spring. Bella stopped to say a special prayer of thanksgiving for the life and talent of the dear Norwegian, who had taught girls at St Mary's Hall for over thirty-five years.

The alumnæ filled the nave of the neo-Gothic church while the regular congregants sat in the transept and the galleries, a welcome departure from the custom of their school days. This time, as visitors, they could see the host of ministers, the pulpit, the altar, and the school choir sitting in the chancel. The "old girls" admired the brilliant colours in the windows and the dark woodwork used throughout. Above the altar, like a chandelier, hung the "skeleton skirt", as the girls used to call it, a mitre shape of open iron work covered in gilt.

The processional included clerics from several eastern states and those who stayed after the Annual Diocesan Convention held on Tuesday and Wednesday. The recently consecrated Bishop of New Jersey, the Right Reverend John Scarborough, took his place on the bishop's throne in the chancel. It was a magnificent piece of wood carving with a canopy topped with a globe and cross. A gilt cross was affixed to its side for all to see. In his remarks, the rector of St Mary's Church Rev. George Morgan Hill welcomed his honoured guests, including the new bishop, whose cathedral was now in the capital city of Trenton, and Bishop Doane's younger son the Right Reverend William Croswell Doane, Bishop of Albany. Other celebrants included the Rev. Dr D. Caldwell Millett, rector of St Mary's Hall in the 1850s; the Rev. Dr Francis J. Clerc, current rector of Burlington College; the Rev. Dr Thomas Gallaudet of New York City; the Rev. J. Nicholas Stansbury, rector of Christ Church, Newark; and clergy from the Diocese of New Jersey, including the Rev. Drs. Walker and Hyde, and the Rev. Messrs. Parkman, Perkins, Pettit, and Fiske.

After the service of Holy Communion concluded, the ladies scattered for the two hours of free time before dinner was served at the Hall. Some set off for High Street to see the shops; others returned straightaway to the campus to continue their reminiscences. Many returned by a different route to promenade down Wood Street, admiring its several historic houses. One was famous now because General Ulysses S. Grant and his family had lived in it during part of the American War Between the States.

Three hundred people attended the dinner that afternoon, including former and current pupils, faculty, trustees, and friends of the school, who enjoyed the meal outside in the beautiful weather. Mr J. C. Garthwaite, lifelong friend of Bishop Doane and the eldest living trustee, delivered a speech followed by several others. When the company broke up, the alumnæ were free again to visit or return to their lodgings to rest until tea at six o'clock. Bishop Scarborough, assisted by Mr Hills, conducted a service of Evening Prayer for the alumnæ at St Mary's Church, a calm and familiar end to a day filled with happy memories and activity.

❦ ❦ ❦

The next day, Emma and Bella break-fasted early again at the Gauntts'. Dr Gauntt told them how the enrollment at the school had lately shrunk because of the bout of typhoid fever that had gripped the city November last. Burlington's government had taken steps to improve the water quality, but it would take some time for St Mary's Hall to recover its reputation due to the number of girls taken ill. Emma and Bella were disturbed to hear this, but after visiting New York City, they weren't surprised. Many cities needed to modernise their infrastructure due to growing populations.

They made the short walk back to St Mary's Hall with Fanny Gauntt. At half past nine, all 180 former students sat at familiar old desks in the new School Room. There was much chatter, and Principal Smith called the meeting to order with an authority that silenced the excited voices. Bishop Scarborough offered an opening prayer followed by a brief address made sweeter with vestiges of his Irish accent. Then Miss Stanley, dressed in a dark green striped waist and full plaid skirt, took charge. She began by reading a telegraph reply from Miss Mary Rodney who had left her post at St Mary's Hall in Burlington to become the first headmistress of a new school, St Helen's Hall, in Portland, Oregon:

"The Graduates in Oregon greet their Alma Mater and Sisters."

After that the true business of the day began. The committee that organised the re-union had drawn up a constitution for an association. The document was distributed among the alumnæ present and they ratified it, proclaiming the name "The Society of Graduates of St Mary's Hall". It outlined the aim of the organisation, its structure, and its functions. Following that, the body elected Miss Caroline Louisa Mitchell, class of 1845, as the society's first president. Mrs Phoebe Babbitt Vermilye, the first-ever graduate of St Mary's Hall, class of 1844, became vice president; Miss Mary Taylor, class of 1863, treasurer; and Miss Ella Kirkbride, class of 1865, secretary. Miss Harriet T. McPherson, class of 1858 and teacher, became the first registrar of graduates. Other alumnæ volunteered to serve on an executive committee, including Bishop William C. Doane's wife Kate, née Condit, class of 1852.

After the elections were concluded, all of the graduates proudly signed the constitution to become bona fide members of the new association. Emma and Bella, as former students, became associate members of the Society of Graduates when they too signed the articles. One of the articles provided for an annual business meeting with social re-unions held every five years beginning in 1880.

Following the signing, Miss Stanley spoke from her heart about the dear memories she had of all "her girls". She mentioned the conversations she cherished with senior girls on the last Sunday before each graduation, and reminisced about how the Senior A girls worked so hard to create the traditional cross of lacquered ivy that they delivered each Christmas Day to Bishop Doane to decorate his study. Then she addressed the serious need for graduates and former pupils to love their school and to provide for it in perpetuity. Emma and Bella remembered Dr Gauntt's remarks at breakfast and realised that there must be a great financial need to support St Mary's Hall at the moment. Miss Stanley went on to suggest that a scholarship in Bishop Doane's memory be created and when she finished making her case, the entire company applauded, much to her embarrassment. Bishop Doane had never condoned such behaviour! How much St Mary's Hall had changed since his passing.

With the important business accomplished, the alumnæ fell back into conversations with dear friends before the bell rang at noon to bid them to a short service of Morning Prayer. On leaving the chapel, Emma and Bella stopped to admire the beautiful stained-glass window over the remodeled south doorway, a memorial to Bishop Doane designed by Owen Doremus.

The highlight of the day was a musical performance at four o'clock. Two students, each at a grand piano-forte in the School Room, played a piece called *The Reunion*, a grand march for two pianos composed by Mr George Hewitt, long-time professor of music at St Mary's Hall, to honour the alumnæ. Then a chorus sang a sweet poem set to music by Mr Hewitt, "What is That, Mother?", written by Bishop Doane. The Hewitts were an accomplished, artistic family and well-respected in Burlington. Mr Hewitt's daughter, Eliza, had been a music teacher at the Hall since the 1850s, and the family still lived nearby. His son George had trained with John Notman, the architect of Riverside and the Chapel of the Holy Innocents, and he was now in partnership with architect Frank Furness of Philadelphia.

Before they left, the alumnæ went to the principal's office to update their addresses, and Miss Mitchell gave each lady a copy of her poem, "Heart's Ease", a Romantic pæan to the founder of St Mary's Hall, Bishop George Washington Doane.

Heart's Ease
For Remembrance
Reunion of St Mary's Graduates
May 27, 1875

The birthday of the Right Reverend
George Washington Doane, D.D., LL.D
Founder of St Mary's Hall

Dear Alma Mater! I would lay
My garland at thy feet,
While many loving hearts, to-day,
Thy Name with blessings greet.
'Tis but a garland from the wild.
Fresh blossoms, fair and bright,
That little children, tired with play
Caress with pure delight.

Here's Flowering Almond, like the Rod
Of Aaron, God's High Priest;
And Pyrus, with its scarlet hood,
All glowing for the Feast.
And snow-white Spirea, "Peter's tears,"
That, like an angel bright,
Keeps watch anear the shrin-ed dead,
Through all the solemn night.

Narcissus bears his crown of gold
Set on a star-like shield;

And violets purple in the light
Like amethysts afield.
Deep lessons sing they to my soul,
Of all the sunshine fair,
They 'neath the storm and winter skies
Taught flower-hearts to wear.

Once more I turn my garland o'er,
While roses bloom and shed
Sweet perfume like anointing oil,
Poured on a kingly head.
And lilies, bending heads of prayer,
'Mid shrouding leaves of love,
With incense breath, they call our thoughts
From Earth to God above.

And last, 'mid garland treasures see,
Fairest and proudest flower,
Brave Heart's Ease, with her purple robe,
And more than royal dower.
'Tis with her legend I would bind
These garland buds in one,
And count "remembrance" chiefest boon
That life from time hath won.

Remembrance! ah this day recalls
Him, Bishop, Father, Priest,
Great Founder of St Mary's Hall —
All his, this Birthday Feast.
Ah! Heart's Ease, thou hast tears for dew,
With mem'ries fond and deep;
Yet, while we mourn, God guards our dead —
In peace, the righteous sleep.
C.L.M.

FOR MISS STANLEY
Burlington, May 1875

❦ ❦ ❦

Emma and Bella were exhausted from all of the conversations, and their feet hurt from exploring up and down the staircases. As they prepared to return to the Gauntts', they sought Miss Stanley to say good-bye. They found her in the east parlour with Bishop Scarborough.

"Emma, dear, allow me to introduce you and Bella," said Miss Stanley.

"And who are these two beauties, Miss Stanley?" asked the cleric.

Both women curtseyed and extended their hands, which the bishop took in his own and squeezed, his eyes bright with love for all of his St Mary's Hall daughters, young and old. "How do you do, ladies? I hope you've enjoyed your stay here in Burlington. How do you find our school now?"

Bella was first to respond. "The new buildings are marvelous, Bishop. I wish I were a pupil here again! I would love to use the new art room in particular," she said.

Emma chimed in, "I loved strolling through the garden paths again. I was only here for two winter terms. I was always gone by April. I remember well the beautiful changing leaves and the autumn blooms during the October vacation month I spent here, though. There are so many different flowers in bloom now in May. The riot of colours in the garden is lovely. And the ginkgo tree is thriving!"

"I recall someone put flowers on our breakfast plates every morning. I never knew who that was," Bella added.

"Yes, indeed, Bishop Doane always rose early to pick flowers for his pupils: to start the day off with a bit of colour and fragrance. He cherished all of his daughters, as the polished corners of the Temple," said Miss Stanley, with a wistful smile.

CHAPTER 42

Letters to Our Sisters at St Mary's Hall

1 May 1875

Dearest St Mary's Hall Sisters,

I was so happy to hear that Miss Stanley and her committee put this lovely occasion together, but I am sad that I cannot be with you all to relive the wonderful memories of the time we spent together at our beloved alma mater. I learned so much about living together and sharing while I was a pupil there. Emma and Isabella will be with you to venerate our founder, dear Bishop Doane, and show our pride in the school that offered us such a rich and varied education.

I have been married for nearly thirteen years to my cousin William, whom I have known since we were children, of course. William is the town treasurer and clerk here

*in St Catharines. We have three sons: George, 12, Clark,
10, little Arthur, born last year, and a babe due any day
now. Of course, we have known heartache too, like so many
other families, in the loss of three of our children: Beatrice
in 1868, William Jr. in 1870, and Henry in 1872. But I
believe in God's goodness to us. His will be done.*

*After my five terms at St Mary's Hall, I came home to
St Catharines with Bella for good. I tutored our little sister
Libby for two years before Papa sent me for a nine-month
term at the Normal School. They taught me the newest
methods of instruction there, but I was so lonely up in
Toronto (and living with a very odd family) that Papa let
me come home. I don't know what I would have done if he
had insisted on my staying on in the city for practise. I
taught instead at the nearby St George's Ward School. After
William and I decided to marry, I had just four months to
prepare my trousseau, and because I was engaged, I had to
resign my post at the school. So I had plenty of time to work
on my hope chest linens. It was a lot of effort, but I have
used every bit that I knitted, embroidered, or tatted, useful
skills honed at the Hall in our precious free time!*

*I dearly hope you enjoy your sojourn in Burlington. I
think of you all often and wish you a grand time exploring
dear old St Mary's Hall. Perhaps I shall be able to attend
another re-union when the children are older.*

I am Very Truly and Fondly Yours,
Julia Maria Burns
(Mrs William Adams Mittleberger)
St Catharines, Ontario

❦ ❦ ❦

6 May 1875, Hamilton, Ontario

My dear friends,
   *Firstly, I want to thank Bella Burns for letting us know
about the re-union. I so wish I could be with you for this
wonderful celebration of Bishop Doane and our alma mater,
but I have many family obligations at the moment.*

James and I have been married since '64 and at present have three sons: Leonard, 8; William 6; Louis 5; and a dear little daughter, Elizabeth, who is 2. James is a barrister, but he and my brother Val just went into business together to build the new Toronto Railway Station. They also own a warehouse together in the city.

In March last, Papa, already the Archdeacon of Niagara, was elected the first Lord Bishop of Niagara when the Diocese of Toronto was divided. He was consecrated five days ago on first May in a lovely ceremony that the whole family attended at St Thomas' Church here in Hamilton. My family and I were very honoured to attend the solemn, moving service. Nearly all of my brothers and sisters were there with their families too. We took up four pews! Laura did not attend, but I shall let her tell you why!

In the end I loved my three terms at St Mary's Hall and wish I could have stayed longer with the friends I made there, friends I still have! St Mary's changed my opinion of schooling. I so wanted to continue learning when I got home. Thankfully, the choices for girls' education in Canada were increasing by 1857. At that time, Papa agreed to be a trustee of our town's first grammar school. Somehow he persuaded the other three trustees to allow girls into the school. I attended (the focus on Latin was a bit boring after the variety of courses provided at the Hall!) for three years. Then just before my seventeenth birthday, I was accepted to the Normal School in Toronto. The course there was a very long, trying year for me because of the way I was being trained to teach, but I got a first-class certificate with grade B! I taught at a Common School in Toronto, lodging the first year with a family who had pupils there, before my parents removed to Toronto.

Little did I know that I met my future husband when I was fifteen. His father, an old school friend of Papa's, was rector of St Mark's Church in Niagara. He eventually took Papa's post as the Archdeacon there. So, of course, the families met often, and we knew each other well. In fact, Papa McMurray just preached the sermon at the consecration. James and I have a lovely home in Toronto, and we are *blessed with four healthy children. I teach my little ones every day, so I have my own little school at home! The boys love being out of doors as much as I do! They can all climb the trees in the garden now. Elizabeth tries her best to follow them.*

Please embrace each other for me, and know that I shall be thinking of you on those days in Burlington when you meet again. I shall also say some prayers for my old friend, dear Bishop Doane. I remember our talks fondly.

Many thanks to Emma and Bella for carrying this letter for you all to read.

Sincerely yours,
"Lizzie"
Elizabeth Street Fuller
(Mrs James Saurin McMurray)
St Patrick's Ward, Toronto

❧ ❧ ❧

1 May 1875, Terralta

Dear St Mary's friends,
Many thanks to Emma and Bella Burns for carrying my letter to New Jersey.

I regret not being able to join you in celebration, but I have a good reason. I married Thomas Moore Benson on 25 June 1874 and am expecting our first child soon. T.M. was first married to my friend, Mary Edith McCaul, who sadly died in childbirth with her third daughter. I am now stepmother to their two sweet daughters, and I love them like my own.

Of course, I spent only one term at St Mary's, not really enough time to develop the long-lasting friendships that Lizzie has. I remember fondly the shoe storms on Saturdays and all the pianos being played in nearly every room at practise time! I didn't mind staying in Canada once I learnt my mother was having another baby. The little boy was born in July 1856 and was called Henry Hobart after the late Bishop John Henry Hobart, one of the founders of the General Theological Seminary in New York City and also what later be-

came Hobart College in Geneva, New York. Little Henry was
the first baby baptized in the new St John the Evangelist
Church in our native Thorold. Of course, Henry is 18 now!
Before he was born, Papa had just been given an honorary
doctorate from the College. He wanted to return that honour
by naming the baby after the churchman he so admired.

Once back in Thorold, I was much improved in health
(the chlorosis problem) and I went back to our old Common
School to help our sister Mary Margaret that summer.
When I turned 16, I went to Toronto to attend the Normal
School, where I spent a year studying and practising teaching at the Model School. I came back home to Thorold to
teach when Mary Margaret moved to the new school in
Thorold. Of course, Mary Margaret had to leave her post
when she married the Rev. Donald MacLeod in November
1861. Now Mary Margaret and Donald have four children
and live in Chippewa near the Falls. He is rector of Holy
Trinity Church there.

After Mary Margaret married, Papa was appointed Rector of St George-the-Martyr, and he removed the family to
Toronto. I began teaching again, first at the parish school
and then at a small girls' school. I was a member of the
original faculty at the Bishop Strachan School for Girls in
Toronto, founded in 1867, a reasonable double for St
Mary's Hall in its mission to educate young women of the
English church.

T.M. (our Father-Bishop is still called Tom!) is a barrister. (He has cousins down in St Catharines who know
the Burns family. Small world!) We have just finished renovating his parents' beautiful old home here in Port Hope.
It has an expansive view of Lake Ontario, and the town is
now just a short train ride from Toronto. We see our Toronto
family often.

I wish all of you a joyous re-union in Burlington and
send my prayers for pleasant St Mary's Hall weather for all
of the festivities!

Yours sincerely,
Laura Abigail Fuller
(Mrs Thomas M. Benson)

❦ ❦ ❦

5 Mai 1875

Mes chères amies,

 Thank you to Bella Burns for carrying this letter to you all the way to Burlington, and to Julia who let me know about the re-union. I thank Miss Stanley and her committee for organising the festivities. I would have made the journey to Burlington, but alas, I have a baby daughter, Aimée, who is eighteen months old. She is a dear little thing that I cannot bear to leave for even a minute. Frederick and I also have two sons, Freddie, 12, and Charles, 8, and a daughter, Mary Frances, who is 10 now, and all attend school here in Montréal. Truly the most important thing in life is family.

 After I left St Mary's Hall, I returned to Toronto and ran Father's household until he married a charming woman named Georgina Nanton. They quickly had six more children. So I have now a huge family of six brothers and two sisters altogether. Their children and ours are quite close in age and are good friends and play-mates when they visit. Father is still engaged in government as Deputy Clerk to the Canadian Senate and has written biographies of famous Canadians in his book Portraits of British Americans. *He and his family live in Ottawa, where the Parliament sits permanently now since Confederation in 1867. It is not too long a trip on the train, so we see them regularly.*

 As for me, I met Frederick in Toronto just before Father remarried and removed our family back to Québec-Ville in 1858 (yes, again!). In fact, it was my stepmother, Georgina, who introduced us, and Frederick swept me off my feet! We were married in Québec-Ville at the beautiful Cathedral of the Holy Trinity on 14 June 1860. Dear Frederick is almost my father's age—17 years older than I—52 now. He is an excellent husband, father, and provider for us. Frederick is a wine merchant here in Montréal Ouest, but he travels to Europe every autumn. Of course, I worry over his safety crossing the sea, but we are blessed with a comfortable life.

My sister Mary married John Mortimer Courtney, and they live up in Ottawa near Father and have a little son, Reginald. My brother Georgie is yet unmarried and lives with us right now. He is 26 and works for Frederick. Our two domestics at the moment, Eliza and Margaret, are sisters from Ireland. They remind me so much of the sweet young women who served us at St Mary's Hall twenty years ago ... dear little Lucinda who kept the fires up for us all winter.

I still adore living in Québec province. Of course, you remember I always loved speaking French with M. Baquet and how he teased me about my accent!

I hope this letter finds you all well at St Mary's Hall. I send you my best wishes for a delightful visit to our alma mater.

Please greet Miss Stanley for me. She was so kind whenever I experienced failure and disappointment. I thank God that I was fortunate enough to attend our famous school and make life-long friends, even if I was not a top student! I think of dear Mr Engstrom whenever I take out my watercolours. I would have loved to see him again.

Amicably,
Harriet Esther Taylor
(Mrs Frederick W. Kingston)
1050 Dorchester Street
St Antoine Ward
Montréal-Ouest, Québec

❦ ❦ ❦

3 May 1875
Beloved sisters,

First of all, thank you to Lizzie Fuller McMurray for letting me know about the invitation back to Burlington, and to Bella for delivering this letter. I am afraid I did not ever transmit my various whereabouts to St Mary's. If it hadn't been for my continued friendship with Lizzie and Bella, I would not have known about the wonderful opportunity presented.

Unfortunately, I cannot be with you at the Hall to cele-

brate the great man who believed so strongly in the impor-
tance of educating women to be leaders in their families,
churches, and communities. I benefitted so much from the
discipline and rigorous education there, though it was less
than a year's duration. Bishop Doane believed that girls
could learn as much as boys and created a place where they
could do so.

I thought long and hard about making the journey to
the States once more. Alas, I have a great many responsibilities here at home. After leaving St Mary's, I spent the first
year in Port Robinson helping my family. You might remember that at school I wanted to be a physician. The singular
experience of assisting in the delivery of my nephew made
that desire even stronger; however, in 1857, there were no
medical schools for women in Canada as there were down
in Philadelphia, and of course I was much too young at the
time to study medicine anyway. But after my fifteenth birth-
day, I attended a new grammar school with Lizzie Fuller. I
thank the Lord for Mr Fuller, who assured that girls were
welcome there! The Fullers were also kind enough to lodge
me, and that cemented my unending love for their big, wonderful family. After three years' study at the grammar
school, I went back to Port Robinson and convinced my
brother John to allow me to work with him in his medical
practise. I loved helping him and our neighbours at all hours
of the day and night. I did this for nearly two years as a sort
of apprenticeship.

I became head teacher of the new Thorold Common
School when Lizzie's sister Mary Margaret married in 1861,
and the rest of the Fullers removed to Toronto. However, I
soon realised I didn't really like teaching children! I was
able to save a bit of my salary, and Father and John helped
me pay the $3,000 fees for my medical education. Again,
with the kind recommendation of Mr Fuller, I was accepted
to the Geneva Medical College (associated with Hobart Free
College) in New York State. There I followed in the footsteps
of Elizabeth Blackwell, who was the first woman to obtain
an American degree in medicine in 1849. I worked very
hard for those two years, and I even got to serve with Dr

Blackwell in New York City for a few months. After graduation, I returned to Port Robinson, permitted only to assist John in his practise because women were not allowed to be licenced physicians.

Lizzie and James introduced me to my husband Warren! We married in 1867 and settled in London, Ontario. Warren has been wonderful about supporting my efforts to be a physician, even though he is busy with his legal and political work (Reform Party, of course!) I was able to do some midwifery with my brother's endorsement until my first child came along. Our little Ethel arrived in 1868, and then our son Huron (yes, named for the lake and the Indians!) was born four years later. He's two now and running all around, as you can imagine.

In March last, Jennie Kidd Trout was licenced as a physician by the General Council on Medical Education and Registration in Canada, and I have every hope that I shall be soon as well. I have just applied for the fourth time with the encouragement of a physician-friend who allows me to work with him here. I graduated from medical school in 1866, nine years ago! I remain hopeful that I shall be licenced this time. So, as you can see, I achieved my dream, though it took years of hard work and so much waiting! Education and opportunities for women in Canada are improving slowly. I hope it is better in the States; it always has been faster to change! I sincerely hope that you all enjoy yourselves when you meet at St Mary's Hall. The good friends I made in my short time at our dear alma mater will always be irreplaceable and precious to me!

With unending sisterly love,
Margaret Jane (McFarland) Rock, M.D.

Epilogue

The mostly happy outcome of my story is a product of my imagination, but also based on facts. The Canadian census records found on *Ancestry.com* reveal that all the girls from Canada West, save dear Emma, were eventually married and had families. The professions of their fathers and husbands were as depicted; unfortunately, I had to imagine any higher education and career paths for the women. The census did not always document female occupations unless it was that of teacher, domestic servant, keeping house, or having a trade such as seamstress or milliner.

Emma Helena Rykert Burns was named for a little Rykert cousin who had died the summer before Emma was born in 1839. Emma lived at her parents' home in St Catharines until at least 1894 when her mother died in her late seventies; her father, Thomas, died in 1881. In the 1901 Census, Emma was living with her sister Julia, William, and their family in St Catharines. The character and fate of Pierce Anderson is entirely fictitious but based on a family constellation that existed in St Catharines and the well-known phenomenon of mercenary service by Canadians during the American Civil War. I was not able to find out if Emma had a vocation or cause, but I like to think that she made a difference somehow during her lifetime. She died in 1912 at seventy-two.

Julia Maria Burns Mittleberger gave birth to at least seven children, but only four sons survived, and one, Clark, apparently suffered from chronic heart disease. Julia died in 1916, age seventy-five, leaving her husband a widower for five years in St Catharines.

Isabella Ann Burns was single until her forties, when she married her first cousin, widower Edward Burns, whose father Robert was a judge and godfather to some of his brother's children. Edward and Isabella had no children of their own. He was an attorney, and they lived in the small town of Elora, Ontario, northwest of Toronto, with his daughter, also Isabella, from his first marriage. Poor Isabella died at sixteen, one year after contracting tuberculosis (phthysis). Was it a coincidence that he named his daughter after a cousin, or were they close friends as I imagined William and Julia were? In the 1901 census Bella's youngest sister Florence lived with them. Florrie died unmarried in Elora of mitral valve heart disease at forty-eight, hence my assumption that she had had scarlet fever leading to rheumatic heart disease. Bella's husband Edward died in 1907, and she lived to age eighty, dying in 1923 of stomach cancer.

Laura Abigail Fuller Benson's eldest child was Clara Benson, who became the first woman to obtain a Ph.D. in science from the University of Toronto. She taught there for many years. Laura died in Port Hope, Ontario in 1923 at eighty-one, outliving her husband Thomas Moore Benson, a judge, by seven years.

According to census records, Elizabeth Street Fuller McMurray lived in Toronto her entire married life and was the last of the seven St Mary's Hall friends to succumb in 1929. Dying at eighty-six, she lived the longest and was widowed for nearly thirty-five years. In 1901 she still had six children and a nephew living with her after her husband James died. Perhaps she lived so long because of her multi-generational household. Or was it because she might have loved being active and outside in the fresh air? Completely unrelated but interesting is the fact that her son Leonard survived the *Lusitania* sinking and one other shipwreck!

Harriet Esther Taylor Kingston moved to Ottawa with Frederick after the 1891 census, presumably to be near family members. Her sister Mary also lived there along with her husband and son. Harriet's famous biographer-father died in Hampton, Virginia in 1882 where reportedly he had gone for his health. Harriet died in 1911 at seventy-one, seven years a widow.

Margaret Jane McFarland Rock became my favourite but most frustrating "character" because for many months I could find nothing that confirmed her existence after the Canadian census of 1861. Neither could I determine if she had died or been married. My imagination ran wild. I wanted her to be my professional trail-blazer woman who fought hard to be a physician. Perhaps she left Canada to study, but I found no evidence of her in the United States or England. During a research trip to Ontario, I finally had to accept that she had indeed married and became a mother. Sarah, librarian at the Niagara-on-the-Lake library, introduced me to David F. Hemmings' book *The House of McFarland*. There in black and white were the names of Margaret Jane's husband and two children. My heart sank!

Armed with this new information, I researched her again on *Ancestry.com*. Months prior I remembered seeing and being confused by a photograph of a tombstone for a Margaret MacFarlane Rock in London, Ontario, no exact birth date, but the birth year was approximately correct when matched with the 1861 Census. I also found Margaret McFarland, her mother, was buried in the same cemetery in 1889, and apparently not in the McFarland plot with her husband Duncan. Margaret Jane (her middle name was omitted from the monument) was interred there with her husband Warren Rock. Warren died when she was about forty, after only fifteen years of marriage, leaving her to raise two teenage children. Their son Huron was sent to Upper Canada College in Toronto, but according to immigration records, daughter Ethel did not attend school beyond age twelve. So much for educating girls!

According to an obituary provided to me by an *Ancestry.com* contact and Elliott descendant, Margaret Rock traveled to Pasadena, California to attend her son Huron's marriage in 1896. She became ill and died there at fifty-four, presumably of heart disease, barely three weeks after the wedding. Her illness required Huron and his bride to return early from their honeymoon. Her remains were sent to London, Ontario. Is it possible Huron did not know how to spell her maiden name, or did the carver make a mistake? Did Huron know that the original spelling, according to one apocryphal story, was changed to McFarland during the War of 1812 to gain an alphabetical advantage (d before e) in line for food or pay distribution? It is thought a fire destroyed the Presbyterian church records in Port Robinson; after a three-year search, I still had not found Margaret Jane's exact birthdate. I assigned her that of my Canadian grandmother, 4 September, and then discovered that her sister-in-law Agnes was born on that date.

By the April 1891 census, the widowed Margaret Jane Rock was mother to her two children and two young McFarland girls. Margaret Jane had taken in her two nieces, ages twelve and ten, John Cameron McFarland's daughters, one of whom had the nickname Maggie. He and his wife died within five years of each other, leaving three minor children out of seven. Their son Duncan Cameron went to live with his Uncle Duncan Elliot McFarland and Aunt Agnes in Port Colborne where Dunc had become a customs agent at the southern terminus of the Welland Canal. Help from extended family was indispensable in those days of high maternal mortality, communicable diseases and untreatable illnesses. There were plenty of orphaned children who needed a home.

According to a London, Ontario city directory, after Warren died, the real Margaret Jane may have supported the family by selling dry goods and had definitely *not* become a physician as I dreamed for her, but perhaps she was a brave and successful businesswoman. In 1889 she was able to take Ethel and Huron with her as far as Liverpool, England, according to passenger records. Unknown is the purpose of their journey. Did they go to Scotland to find their McFarlane roots in Paisley, Renfrewshire?

Truly all of these women were as "the Polished Corners of the Temple", caring for themselves, family, and others throughout their lives. The mission of George Washington Doane was fulfilled then as it is now.

Acknowledgments

There are many people to thank, and the first are my father John C. Borden, Jr. and my late mother Elizabeth Fitch Codding Borden, who made it possible for me to attend St Mary's Hall (now Doane Academy) for ten years. Our family has deep ties to the school. My mother and her mother, Maude Cleveland Fitch Codding, both graduated from St Mary's Hall, and my brother John was in the third graduating class of the first iteration of boys-only Doane Academy (1966–74). My younger brother Doug also attended the school for a time. We even have a photograph of my father in short pants at age five with fellow pupils digging a garden on the grounds of St Mary's Hall in the spring of 1932 when it was supposedly a "girls only" school. In addition to educating me at St Mary's Hall, Mom and Dad were responsible for planting the research seed when they sent my brothers and me to "look it up" in the family *Encyclopaedia Britannica* when we had a question at dinner. Now people just Google answers at the table with their smart phones. My parents' pride in the Borden family's genealogy also fueled my interest in what went before.

Then, I must recognize the enthusiasm and support of the aforementioned Alice (Lollie) Berger Rogers, who was at my side when I "met" the Burns, Fuller, McFarland, and Taylor girls in the 1855 student register. After every work session, she urged me to find out as much as possible about our early graduates and their usually more famous fathers. Lollie and Michele Colavito transcribed the "Vicksburg Letters" written by pupils Emma and Annie Shannon of Mississippi. Their letters contained invaluable details about life at St Mary's Hall in late 1857. Thank you, Lollie and Michele!

In the fall of 2015, I was sitting in the office of Doane Academy's then new headmaster, George Sanderson, when I took a deep breath and committed to writing this book. I thank him now for supporting the idea and for allowing me continued access to the school archives.

I am greatly indebted to School Historian and Director of Communications Jack H. Newman for his help over many years. Jack shares my curiosity about the history of the school and was always accessible by email when I had questions during the writing of this book. He wrote *St. Mary's Hall and Doane Academy* in 2012, which I consulted often for inspiration. His work and mine also could not have happened without the late Mrs. Susan Low, former history teacher at St. Mary's Hall-Doane Academy, who ensured the school's historical records were retained.

I am very grateful to the trustees of St. Mary's Hall-Doane Academy who guided the school through tough times in 1999 and hired John F. McGee in 2000. Mr McGee, headmaster from 2000–2015, was a visionary without whose energy and commitment Doane Academy—Bishop Doane's legacy—would not be the success it is today. Among those trustees was Alice Collins Fisk, St. Mary's Hall, class of '61, who became an important leadership donor and my good friend and driving partner to many meetings. Doane Academy's trajectory changed because of her generosity and that of Henry and Lee Rowan. Many thanks are due to Christina Cecchi '85 and Kathleen Lisehora Keays '88 for their continuous encouragement and enthusiasm for this project. I also want to acknowledge the talented Chuck Magee for his ongoing restoration of the school—especially the Chapel of the Holy Innocents—and for creating the Eliza Greene Doane Archives, a space John McGee made available to store records and realia in Odenheimer Hall, site of many hours of research. Thank you, all!

Several other people had a hand, however unseen, in my creation of historical fiction. Kay Phelon Allen, a good friend and a writer herself from St. Mary's Hall, class of 1939, inspired me to get on with it when it was just a germ in my mind! Thanks go to the Reverend J. Connor Haynes, rector of St. Mary's Church, Burlington, who answered questions about the history of his parish in the 1850s. Thank you also to my daughter, Anneliese Heckert Burch, D.O., who reviewed the medical scenes. In Philadelphia, Stewart Low, class of 1978, who works at Independence Historical Park, corrected the location of the Liberty Bell in 1856 when the book was near final edit. In Marble, Colorado, Charlotte Graham Whitney, a chronicler of local lore, and her husband Doug encouraged me to keep writing when I had research notes surrounding me and the dishes were piling up. In turn, they introduced me to Alyssa Ohnmacht, owner of Light of the Moon, Inc., who designed this beautiful volume. Talented editor Kayla Henley deserves high praise and gratitude for valuable suggestions and patient corrections. I appreciate very much and thank Sasha Williams for the charming line drawings that decorate each chapter. Also in Carbondale, Colorado, the monthly Writers' Group offered this neophyte pointers on modern styles of creative writing. Thanks are also due to my several alpha and beta readers, including Kay Phelon Allen '39, Bonnie Dix Cavanaugh '67, Christina Cecchi '85, Patty Frederick, Martha Conway Gabriel '63, Sue Ludtke, Mary Ellen Popkin '79, Peggy Fenimore Morris '57, Betty Rahn, and Diane Wolny.

Finally, and most importantly, I want to thank my husband Clark W. Heckert for the love, indulgence, patience, and support he has given me through more than three years of late dinners and hyper-focused discussions, not to mention driving through Toronto for a Sunday morning "jump-out squad" tour to find and photograph sites featured in this story. I love you!

Glossary

Alma mater – Latin, nurturing mother; former school, or hymn

Andante Favori – a piece of music written by Beethoven

Arve – a tributary of the Rhône River

Au Clair de la Lune – a famous, favorite French folk song

Basque – a fitted jacket or bodice extending over the waist to the hips, worn with a skirt

Baton – a walking stick

Bois de Boulogne – a large park on the west side of Paris

Bonheur du jour – a small desk, literally "happiness of the day"

Bon marché – cheap

Canots d'hiver – winter canoes

Canotier – the man who paddles the canoe

Caribou – a traditional drink made of red wine

Champs Elysées – the avenue in Paris between the Arc de Triomphe and the Place de la Concorde; French for Elysian Fields, mythological Greek paradise for dead heroes

Cholera morbus – Latin, ordinary gastroenteritis, not the same as epidemic Asian cholera

Collation – a snack

Comédie-Française – Parisian theater established in 1680 by King Louis XIV's decree

Diligence – a long distance carriage or stagecoach

Doctorial sack – a long jacket worn in the clinical setting by physicians

Domina – Latin honorific given to Dr Elizabeth Blackwell on her medical diploma

Embarcadère – early term for train stations in Paris

Enceinte – pregnant

Escargots – snails

Escritoire – secretary desk with drawers

Etudes – musical studies for practise

Exactement – exactly

Fait accompli – something already decided

Fiacre – horse-drawn four-wheeled carriage for hire in Paris

Francs – French monetary denomination

Garçon – term no longer used, waiter

Genève – Geneva, Switzerland

Genovois – citizens of Geneva

Godey's Ladies Book and Magazine – a Philadelphia publication with fashions, craft patterns, household hints, and short stories.

Grande Allée – a famous street in Quebec City

Gübelin – a Swiss watchmaker

Herr Doktor – honorific for a German doctor, Mister Doctor

Hôtel des Bergues – Hotel of the Bergues

Hôtel Métropole – Hotel Metropolitan

Hôtel Meurice – 19th century hotel still in the Rue de Rivoli

Huitième Arrondissement – (8e) the eighth of twenty-one divisions of Paris

Ile de la Cité – One of two islands in the River Seine, the original settlement of Paris

Jardin Alpin – Alpine Garden

Jardin Anglais – English Garden

Je vous en prie, ma précieuse – You are welcome, my precious one

Lac Léman – Lake Geneva

La nausée – nausea

L'Arc de Triomphe – a triumphal arch ordered by Napoléon to commemorate his victory in the battle of Austerlitz

La Conciergerie – the prison where Marie Antoinette was imprisoned

La Madeleine – church at the end of the Rue Royale

La Sainte-Chapelle – church on the Ile de la Cité

Le Figaro – Parisian newspaper

Le mauvais sort – bad luck

Les Environs de Paris – The Surrounding Area of Paris, a tour guide published in 1856

Les principes – the principles

Limonade gazeuse – carbonated lemonade

Loyalists – UEs, United Empire Loyalists, designated for loyalty to the Crown

Ma chère amie – my dear friend

Maid of the Mist – the tour boat that used to pass under the Niagara Falls

Mal de mer – seasickness

Mater – Latin, mother

Mazurka – a lively Polish dance in triple time

Mea culpa – Latin, I am guilty

Merci, chéri – thank you, dear

Messrs – a title to refer to more than one man

Mes chères amies – my dear friends

❦ *Alma Mater*

Moi aussi – me too

Monsieur le Docteur le Brun – Mister Doctor Brown

Mont Blanc – White Mountain, the tallest mountain in Europe at 15,777 feet

Mont Royal – Mount Royal, a hill for which Montréal was named

Naïveté – the state of being innocent or unworldly

Notre-Dame – Gothic cathedral of Paris on Ile de la Cité

Notre-Dame de l'Assomption – church in Evian

Orangemen – a Protestant fraternal religious society in Canada

Palais de la Bourse – Commercial building in Lyon

Pardessus – heavy overcoat

Parfait – perfect

Petit déjeuner – breakfast

Petite maison – little house

Phthysis – tuberculosis or consumption

Piazza – the open hallway attached to the back of St Mary's Hall

Place d'Armes – Square of Arms in Québec City behind Holy Trinity Cathedral

Place de la Concorde – Peace Square, one site of guillotines during the French Revolution

Préalpes – foothills

Pointe Lévis – a village across from Québec City

Pont Neuf – once the new bridge, now the oldest in Paris

Porte-cochère – the open, covered area of a house where carriages load passengers

Porte Guillaume – William Gate in Dijon, France

Portmanteau – a model of suitcase in leather or canvas

Quartiers – neighbourhoods

Québec – Quebec Province

Québecois – Adjective referring to Quebec or a man who lives there

Randonnée – a hike

Rara avis – Latin, rare bird

Reticule – a woman's small hand bag, typically with drawstring and beadwork. Also anything that can carry necessities while travelling

Rue Côte de la Montagne – a street in Québec City winding up from the Lower Town

Rue du Mont Blanc – Street of the White Mountain

Rue de Rivoli – Rivoli Street in Paris, a fashionable shopping district across from the Louvre

Rue des Jardins – Gardens Street

Sainte-Foye – a suburb of Québec City

Salade composée – mixed salad

Sole à la Meunière – a preparation of Dover sole made with lemon and parsley in a butter sauce

Table d'hôte – host's table, a set menu for lodgers

That our Daughters may be as the Polished Corners of the Temple – In 1837 Bishop Doane invoked Psalm 144 verse 12 in the school's original prospectus and the catalogues that followed; the school's mission was to educate girls who would establish Christian homes and families, thereby growing the Episcopal Church in the young nation.

Toilette – the process of grooming and dressing oneself

Trottine – a command from the canotier to get out of the canoe and run on the ice

Trousseau – a bride's collection of new clothes to begin marriage

Va-t'en – Go away!

Velours royale – a type of velvet fabric introduced in the 1850s

Versailles – the palace where Louis XIV held court

Vogue – style

Verstehen Sie – German, Do you understand?

Waist – shortened term for shirtwaist or woman's blouse

Pamela Borden Heckert was born in Mount Holly, New Jersey and raised in Beverly, New Jersey. She was a student at St. Mary's Hall, Burlington, New Jersey for ten years, graduating in 1967. After a career as a registered nurse in Wilmington, Delaware, she obtained a certificate to teach French and enjoyed teaching adults and children for ten years. Pam's greatest honor was becoming a trustee of St. Mary's Hall, which was renamed Doane Academy in 2008 during her fourteen-year tenure.

Pam enjoys reading historical novels and researching genealogy. While volunteering in the Doane Academy archives, she got the idea for her debut novel *Alma Mater* when she found the characters' names clustered in the archival records of students who attended the school.

Pam has been married to Clark W. Heckert for over forty-five years. Together they have four children and one grandchild. They live in the Rocky Mountains of Colorado.

Made in USA - Kendallville, IN
1209732_9781090341778
12.09.2020 0926